The Sequel to *The Hollow of His Hand*

The Sun Shall Not Smite You

Pamela Goodrode Symonds

PublishAmerica
Baltimore

First printing

All characters in this book are fictitious, and any resemblance to real persons, living or dead, is coincidental.

PublishAmerica has allowed this work to remain exactly as the author intended, verbatim, without editorial input.

ISBN: 978-1-61582-965-1 (softcover)
ISBN: 978-1-4489-9734-3 (hardcover)
PUBLISHED BY PUBLISHAMERICA, LLLP
www.publishamerica.com
Baltimore

Printed in the United States of America

This book is dedicated to

My husband Phillip and
My son Jason.
Thank you for all your
Love,
Support and
Encouragement.

The Sun Shall
Not Smite You

Pamela Symonds   3-'10

Dr. Keller & Staff

May you always be assured
of God's love and protection.

Thanks for taking such
good care of me!

for His glory,
Pam

Psalm 121:6

Chapter One
July 1971

Connie grabbed the telephone on its second ring.

"Yes," she answered when she recognized the female voice. "He's here. TOM!!" she yelled down the hall. "It's Carol Anne."

Connie sat the receiver next to its large black counterpart on the small telephone desk and returned to the bathroom where she wrinkled her nose at the girl in the mirror. Straight blonde hair hung from its center part, draping the girl's round face. She ran a comb through it one more time, feeling its softness, before picking up the purple mascara she so carefully applied to long lashes that surrounded her soft gray eyes.

"You should have blue eyes, like Carol Anne," she told her reflection. "Then you'd be beautiful."

"Connie," her brother called from the hallway.

"What?" She yelled back.

"You gonna be home for a while, I need a favor?"

"A favor?" she replied, her tone falsely sweet. "What could your detestable little sister possibly do for you?"

"Carol Anne's car is broke down and I have to go get her."

"And you want me to fix it?"

"Jimmie's coming over," Tom continued, ignoring her remark. "I need you to stay here and tell him where I'm at."

The girl's eyes widened and her cheeks flushed red. "Jimmie who?"

Tom appeared in the door behind her. "Don't give me that, the only Jimmie we know. My best friend, home from the service before he's shipped to Nam."

"Oh, that Jimmie," Connie replied, picking up her comb and poising it above her head. "When did he get home?"

"Couple days ago. Look, you gonna be here or not?"

"I'll stay," she reluctantly agreed. "But you owe me."

"Yeah, yeah, yeah. I'll call if I run into problems."

Connie watched her brother's retreating form in the mirror and a smile spread across her face.

Jimmie. She saw his sandy brown hair, his charming smile and broad shoulders. She saw him on the football field, diving from the high dive, hitting a home run. Jimmie, with girls all around him, never noticing his best friend's little sister. But she noticed and she had loved him ever since he strode up to their house and introduced himself as the new kid next door. She immediately invited him to her 7th birthday party, but Tom interrupted and said they were too old to join a baby party. Then they ran down the driveway, eager to be about 10 year-old boy business.

Jimmie hadn't bothered with her then; or for the next eight years and after graduation he joined the service for three years while Tom went off to college. Everyone in town expressed their surprise when they heard Jimmie re-enlisted and now headed for Viet Nam. Except Connie, she expressed nothing, sharing her secret love with no one except her worn old Teddy Bear.

"But tonight, tonight," Connie told the mirror. "Jimmie's mine, and he will notice me!" The moment she heard the front door close she ran to her room and pulled a pair of white cut-off hip-huggers from her drawer. She slipped out of her t-shirt and bra and dug underneath her folded shirts for just the right top—a yellow and white stripped halter top. Tying it in back she turned and looked over her shoulder into the mirror, admiring her golden tan against the light clothing. Connie stretched out her toes toward sandals then changed her mind. Barefoot, she padded downstairs and into the living room where she placed a surfing album on the record player. It was Jimmie's favorite. She knew all Jimmie's likes and dislikes. Favorite color, yellow. Favorite group, Beach Boys. Favorite drink, Coke.

Favorite fruit, Raspberries. Favorite car, '57 T-bird, she had one upstairs in her room, a model of course. Favorite cigarette, Kools, she'd tried smoking one once but found the whole process disgusting.

A knock on the door startled her and she looked out the front window. Jimmie's dad's car sat in their drive way. Connie's heart revved up and her mouth went dry. She debated between answering the door and hiding behind the couch. The choice was made for her when the door opened and Jimmie peeked inside.

"Tom," he called. "Mr. Cooper? Anybody home?"

Connie forced herself to yell back. "Who is it?"

"It's Jimmie. That you Mrs. Cooper?"

Connie grabbed a pillow from the couch and drilled it into her unsuspecting visitor's face.

"Do I look like Mrs. Cooper?" She said.

They stood in the kitchen, each holding a cold bottle of Coke, the sound of drums and waves pulsated from the living room.

"So ole Tom's still going with Carol Anne? They gonna get hitched?" Jimmie leaned his six-foot frame against the counter, he wore cutoff jeans and a white tank top. He could hardly believe the creature who stood before him. Tom's little sister had certainly changed in three years.

"Next year when Tom finishes with college. Why'd you re-enlist, Jimmie?"

He shrugged his broad shoulders. "Seemed like the right thing to do. I mean this country's a mess. What with the protests and riots. I've been to other countries and seen how bad they are, communism and dictatorships. We don't appreciate what we have here. The kids, kids I grew up with, something happened to them, they went nuts. I guess it's my way of saying I still believe in America and who we are." He noted the young girl's serious look. "Besides, they offered money," he said with a grin.

She shook her head, "Just admit it, you were probably drunk when you signed the paper or looking for a way to avoid some romantic involvement."

He laughed. "You never did like me, did you?"

"Like you?" she echoed. "How could I? You and that bratty brother of mine were always mean to me—teasing me, breaking my dolls."

"Only because you followed us everywhere."

"No, no, no," she shook her silky mane. "Mom made me. 'Go with your brother,' she'd say."

"Yeah, I remember," he looked beyond her, back into his childhood. How nice if all he had to worry about was a girl looking over his shoulder. A sudden bolt of fear shot up his spine as the day of his departure to Viet Nam loomed before him. He shook it off and drew a bead on the present. "Where are your folks?"

"Tiger Stadium. The Ellisons have season tickets, this week-end they invited mom and dad."

"And left poor Tommy to babysit again?"

She swayed up to him. "But Tom's not here and I no longer need a baby-sitter." She stood so close he smelled coconut suntan lotion. Her soft gray eyes were the color of a kitten she'd had long ago.

"So I see," he replied, his voice rising huskily from deep within his chest. "How old are you, girl?"

"Just turned 18, sorry you missed my party, but then it's not the first one you've missed, is it?" She inched closer and he could feel her breath on his chest.

"You've grown quite nicely."

"Didn't think I would, did you? You thought I'd always be a stringy haired little kid, born to ruin your fun."

"Just goes to show how wrong a man can be." He tried to keep his arms from lifting toward her, tried to visualize her with ponytails and a dirty face but his actions were not under his control.

She smiled and raised an eyebrow as he felt her take a step backward. The phone rang as his face lowered to hers.

"Probably Tom," she said turning. She walked slowly across the room and Jimmie grinned to himself as her game dawned on him. So she really hadn't grown up after all. She was still a little girl, playing little girl games.

"Yes, brother," she spoke into the phone. "I gave him a coke and put on some surfing music. How long do I have to babysit?" She looked at Jimmie, a smile teased her lips. "That long, huh? Well, I'll see if I can dig out some of your old toys and keep him occupied. If that fails, I guess there's always Sesame Street," she paused for a moment, listening. "Oh, yes, how could I have forgotten about that?" Connie hung up. "Guess Carol Anne's transmission is shot. Poor Tom. He says I could be nice and feed you. I think we have some left over chili."

"Ugh," Jimmie made a face. "I hate chili."

"Really? Who would have known?"

Jimmie watched the girl for a moment and decided he'd be wise not to stay here alone with her.

"How about a burger—my treat?"

Chapter Two
January 1, 1996

Windy Jordan's alarm clock drilled her out of a sound sleep. She quickly shut off the noise and reached for the lamp. When its soft glow penetrated the small makeshift bedroom she occupied in her friends living room, her brown eyes focused on a poster she had stuck to the wall the night before.

UNLESS A DAY IS BEGUN WITH GOD
THAT DAY IS IN VAIN.
ANY SCHEDULE KEPT, IS LOST.
ANY TASK ACCOMPLISHED, IS INCOMPLETE.
ANY RELATIONSHIP BORN, IS DESTINED TO DIE.

Windy smiled as she reached for her Bible which lay beside the lamp. "No more Vain Days for me," she informed her black tomcat, Sachel Page, who lay at the foot of her bed.

"January First," she whispered ten minutes later, returning the Bible to the stand. "A brand new year." She quickly slipped her small frame from the bed and shrugged into her robe. In the kitchen she poured herself a glass of milk and popped a pastry into the toaster. On the small kitchen table she found Jenny McCourt's car keys and a note.

Thanks for calling last night; we would have worried when we drove past the car, minus one tire. Take my car to work; I don't plan on being up before noon anyway. When you get home, we'll call the garage to see who's open.

Windy picked up the pencil and jotted down a reply.

Got it all covered, thanks anyway. I'll bring home food for tonight.

Scott Bradley, Jenny's friend, had to leave tomorrow and they'd planned a quiet, 'family' get together, Scott Bradley, Jenny, Windy and their downstairs landlady, Cora Davis. Windy wondered if Scott Bradley looked forward to his dorm in Florida after having spent two weeks in a cold little motel room.

After a quick shower she ran a comb through her brown hair, marveling at its length. She reached her hand behind her back and grasped the ends of the silky strands. Windy finished her morning ritual, then pulled a knit hat over the blow dried hair. With boots and coat on, Windy quietly let herself out of the apartment and tip-toed down the stairway. Once outside she stopped in the cold morning air and breathed deeply. Tiny snowflakes dropped all around her. She only worked a few blocks away at King's Grocery and her New Year's resolutions included getting more exercise, real exercise, not the bending and stooping she did at the store. She arrived as the manager opened the back door. Don Clark's large, black hand held the door as she scooted into the warmth.

"Did you walk this morning?" he asked, his voice as smooth as his flawless dark skin. When she nodded he continued. "Why didn't you call? I'd have stopped by."

"I know you would, but I wanted to walk. It's really not too cold, if you move fast enough."

Her boss shook his head and laughed, "I suppose you're gonna say something about resolutions and weight loss?"

"Good idea, why didn't I think of that?"

The two quickly set about their tasks as the rest of the morning employees arrived. Shortly after seven a.m. Windy opened a box of shampoo and began pricing the bottles.

"Excuse me. Where can I find the razor blades?" A familiar voice asked. Windy looked up into the clear gray eyes of City Police Officer Rick Notts. His leather jacket creaked when he moved, sounding like a saddle. Windy wondered if this man had ever ridden a horse. Would he have been a sheriff if he'd been born a hundred years earlier?

"Shift over?" She asked. Standing, she noticed he stood just a couple inches taller than her.

"Finally. It's been a while since I last worked midnights, what a reminder." He held his hat in his hands and Windy watched him turn it over and over. She liked his hands. Even in his nervousness his hands held steady.

"Lots of 'party' traffic?"

"Too much. There were a couple accidents, one fatality."

Windy frowned. "I'm sorry. That must be awfully hard to deal with. I don't think I could."

Rick nodded. "It's a part of the job I dread. Listen, I'm going to get a little sleep and I'll be back at noon. We'll have that tire fixed and go get your car."

"You're sure it's not too much trouble? I can always call my roommate."

"No trouble at all, I'd be disappointed if you didn't let me help."

"Then run along and get some sleep, you deserve it."

"Yes, Ma'am."

Windy watched the young man's retreating back; he stopped and waved before disappearing around the corner.

Rick Notts jumped into his old black pick-up and started the engine. He touched his left pants pocket feeling the familiar object. Almost three years ago Rick had picked up that broken pencil belonging to a young woman whose picture he stared at. A woman who that night laid in a hospital, a victim of her drunken husband's anger. Those next years Rick had followed Windy's life, a silent admirer. He read in the paper of her marriage to the prominent Dr. Michaels, the physician who treated her during her hospital visit. And just this past fall Rick had seen the doctor in the company of a beautiful, young nurse. Curious, he ran Windy's name in the computer and found her license once again held her maiden name along with an old familiar address. For months Rick wondered how to go about introducing himself to Windy Jordan, not that they hadn't met, he'd bought razor blades from her a couple times. But for all he knew about her, she knew nothing of him, until last night. All the worrying he'd done, all the plotting and scheming went for naught when on his way to work he encountered the very object of his thoughts stranded on a quiet piece of highway with a flat tire.

Rick drove to Joe Kozininski's house, just on the city limits. Joe, now his partner, had trained Rick when he joined the force over three years ago. Their first night out they had come across a car sitting on a jack, its flat tire still on the wheel. Rick changed the tire for the young woman driver while his partner ran the passed-out husband's name. He discovered a bench warrant for the man and Eddie Ray Bilmon became Rick's first arrest. Six months later Rick had stood in Eddie's apartment, looking at a picture of Eddie and his abused wife.

"Strange how things work out," Rick pondered as he drove into Joe's driveway and turned off his truck. "As if there's some unseen time clock and no matter what we do, things happen when they're supposed to, not necessarily when we want them to."

Rick found a key on his ring and quietly let himself into Joe's house, so as not to disturb the sleeping man. After three years, Rick remained the newest man on the force and therefore the only rookie, receiving hours the senior men refused, such as midnights on New Year's Eve.

But Rick needn't have been so quiet. Joe peeked around the corner from the kitchen.

"What cha doin', boy?" he asked the startled young man.

"Thought I'd sleep on your couch for a couple hours. I'm picking up a friend at noon and didn't want to go all the way home." All the way home was, in fact, only ten miles out of town where Rick owned a small farm house and a few acres of land. "How come you're up so early?"

"Ice fishing. Want to come?"

Rick shook his head. Hunting and fishing had never interested him and the idea of standing on a frozen lake in the middle of winter seemed slightly insane.

"No thanks," Rick wondered if Joe had been listening.

"What are you doing at noon?"

"Just helping out a friend." He took his coat off and tossed it on a chair, covering up a stack of newspapers.

"Didn't know you had any friends," his partner teased.

"Guess it's time I made some then."

"Any one I know?"

"I doubt it." Rick had shared his dreams with Joe; going to college and his desire to work for the State Police, Joe had been there when Rick made an offer on his house. But Windy Jordan remained one dream he hadn't shared with anyone. No one knew about the broken pencil, not even his parents.

Rick moved a couple shirts off Joe's couch and found a dirty plate under one of them. "You need a maid, Joe."

"You know how I am about getting too fancy. If my house didn't look lived in, I wouldn't be comfortable. Why don't you sleep in your room?"

Rick smiled at his friend's reference. Twice, in the last three years, he'd stayed the night at Joe's so they could go trout fishing in the early hours of the morning.

"Sounds great," he accepted. "Good luck fishing."

Rick found the second bedroom and pulled the covers back, wondering if the blue sheets had ever been changed. He slipped out of his uniform and into the bed.

"You've got to sleep, guy. You can't let the excitement of knowing you're actually going to pick up Windy Jordan and drive her somewhere in your vehicle keep you awake. You can't dwell on the fact that after three years the object of your dreams will be sitting in the very same truck as you. Because if you think about this, you won't sleep and you'll look like crap when you pick her up and she'll notice how ugly you are and never talk to you again."

With those reassuring thoughts, Rick pulled the covers over his head and closed his eyes.

"Hey, Rick, I thought you had to be somewhere at noon?" Joe's voice filtered through Rick's hazy thoughts.

Noon.

"Hope it's not far away, or you'll never make it."

Noon.

NOON!!

Rick jumped from the bed and grabbed the alarm clock off the headboard. "The alarm didn't go off," he accused.

Joe took the offender from the younger man.

"The alarm didn't get set," he corrected.

"Ah, no. NO. What time is it?"

"Quarter to."

Rick grabbed his pants and pulled them on. "I can make it," he assured himself.

"You wearing your uniform?"

"It's all I have. I didn't plan on doing anything when I came in."

"I got a shirt and jeans you can wear, you're not that much smaller than me." Joe opened a closet. "Most of these are a bit tight, help yourself."

Rick grabbed the first shirt he saw then hesitated. He looked it over to be sure it contained no holes or stains, then he lifted it to his nose, surprised that it smelled clean. "Hey, Joe, you got some gum? I didn't bring a toothbrush either."

"There's a new one in the medicine cabinet. Help yourself."

Rick quickly brushed his teeth and splashed water on his face. He hit the door running with minutes to spare.

Chapter Three

Windy stood by the front door of King's Grocery, debating whether to walk home or call Jenny. Sun shone on the glistening white snow and the bank clock across the street registered the temperature at 27 degrees.

"I may as well walk," she murmured, pulling on her gloves. She searched the street one more time, hoping to see the officer's black pick-up. After all, Cora's tire still lay in the truck bed. Even if she and Jenny found a used tire, they would need the rim.

Windy stepped out into the sunlight just as the truck pulled into the parking lot.

"I am so sorry," Rick apologized as Windy climbed into the cab. "I forgot to set the alarm and my partner woke me when he returned from fishing. Good thing, too."

"You live with your partner?" Windy asked, securing her seatbelt.

"No, I live a little ways out of town and didn't want to drive out there and back." Rick explained as he pulled away.

"Oh," she nodded, her eyes drawn to his hands that gripped the steering wheel. They were strong hands, not soft, but not rough either. A real man's hands, she thought, smiling. After a moment she continued. "Thanks again for helping me."

"Sure, glad to. I did some checking last night and found which stations are open today. There's one fellow who does work for the department, he'll fix us right up."

Again Windy nodded unsure what to say.

They drove a few blocks in silence before she spoke.

"You of all people should warn me about accepting rides with strangers."

"What strangers have you been riding with lately?" He looked at her but she couldn't meet his gaze.

"You."

"Me? I'm not a stranger. Look how long you've been selling me razor blades; that must account for something."

She looked at him unconvinced.

"Well, we've shared pizza," he continued, she smiled slightly, surprised he remembered the time she saw him in the Pizza Shop. They had smiled at each other over melted cheese. "And even a volleyball court." Now she laughed.

"I thought that was you."

"See, how could you think it was me, if I'm just a stranger?"

"Why were you at Wil's?" She asked the question that had puzzled her for years.

"Paying my house payment. Why were you there?"

"Playing volleyball."

"Ahh, would the rest of your team have agreed to that statement?"

Stephan's angry face loomed before Windy. Stephan Michaels, great doctor, good volleyball player and ex-husband. Windy again saw the ball as it left her hand and connected with Stephan's face.

"No," she whispered and looked away. *What are you doing, Windy? She asked herself. Why are you here, in this man's truck, bantering with him like a schoolgirl? Haven't you had enough of male jerks? Do you have to set yourself up for humiliation with the first guy who drives into your life?*

"I'm sorry Windy. I didn't mean to bring that up. But no man should yell at his wife like that. I would have expected the doctor to treat you better, knowing what he did."

Windy turned and glared at the young man. "Knowing what he did? What's that suppose to mean?"

"Well, from when you were in the hospital."

"You know he treated me, you know he married me."

"Yeah," Rick answered tentatively.

19

"Then you must have known he divorced me too, since you knew to take me to Cora's house last night."

Rick's ears reddened, but his face paled.

"Just what do you know about me and how do you know?" She demanded.

Rick guided the truck into an auto repair shop and stopped under a "Jack's Garage" sign.

"I guess I owe you an explanation."

"I guess you do," Windy agreed.

He hesitated. "Let me take care of the tire, and I'll explain on the way out to get Mrs. Davis' car."

"How do you know it's Cora's car and not mine?"

Rick wanted to kick himself. He couldn't believe how badly he's messed things up in a few short minutes. What would he do now? Plead his love for a woman who considered him a stranger, or worse yet a snoop? He'd promised himself to take things slowly, not scare her away. And now look what he'd done.

Jack checked the tire and gave Rick the verdict.

"I can patch it and it'll do for a spare."

"Got any good used ones this size?"

"Yeah, I can fix you up."

"A good deal? It's for a friend."

Jack looked toward Rick's truck and smiled. "A great deal," he said, quoting a price.

A short time later Rick threw two inflated tires into his truck bed, then fed the pop machine some change. He climbed into his seat and handed Windy a cherry cola.

She studied the can for a moment. "How do you know I drink this kind?"

Rick took a deep breath, letting it out as he buckled his seat belt. He pulled onto the road before answering.

"I told you last night, I have a good memory. I once bought a 2 liter in your store and you said I made a good choice, so I took a chance."

"You do have a good memory."

"In my line of work, I have to."

The cab fell silent as Rick wondered what else to say, wondered what she expected to hear. She spoke first. "You were going to explain."

"Yeah." He searched for a way to start. "Yeah. Well, like I mentioned last night—I changed your tire, and arrested your husband on my first night of duty. The next spring Joe and I answered an ambulance call, you were enroute to Community General. Mrs. Davis fed us tea and muffins."

"You know Cora?"

"We met her that night," he answered with enthusiasm. "Isn't she a treasure? I haven't tasted muffins that good since my Grandmothers." He chanced a glance at Windy who just stared at him. "Anyway, she was still a bit jittery and asked us to check the apartment..."

"You were in my apartment?"

"Mrs. Davis gave Joe the key, she was scared. Anyway, I saw your picture and Joe recognized..."

"You were looking at my pictures?"

"Just the one on the table. Windy, I'm a police officer; there are aspects of my job that place me in unusual situations." He stopped, deciding not to make matters any worse.

"So Joe, he's your partner?" She asked. Rick nodded. "He recognized Eddie. Then what?"

"Do you really want to know?"

"Yes, I do."

"Later that night I called the hospital to see how you were and Bernie, Nurse Laswell..."

"You know her, too?"

"Everyone knows Bernie. She said Doc Michaels was taking care of you. By then I'd been here long enough to know he's a good doctor and I felt relieved. About a month later, Mrs. Davis called again. Joe and I returned but no one answered your door, though Mrs. Davis assured us you were there. She was worried because you didn't answer, but said she'd heard you walking around and she thought you were okay, probably wouldn't talk to us." He looked at his passenger, who had looked away.

"We kept an eye out for Eddie but he seemed to have disappeared. A short time later I saw you at the store. I recognized you from your picture and your name tag. That fall I noticed your name in the paper under marriage licenses. I saw you at the Pizza Shop and at Wil's. Then you turned up at the grocery store again and I wondered why so I ran your name in the computer." *Ooops.*

"You checked up on me, like a criminal?"

"It's not like that. I'm a cop, Windy, I keep my eyes and ears open, hazards of the profession, I guess." He glanced at her again. She continued to look out of the window, her pop can remained unopened.

"How do you know Wil?" She asked.

"Joe and I went fishing on his property. I saw a house for sale belonging to him. I made an offer; he said God told him to accept it, so he did." Rick saw a slight smile grace her lips. A moment later the stranded car came into view on the opposite side of the road. He drove past, turned around and parked behind it. After removing his seat belt Rick shifted his position to be able to look at his passenger.

"My name is Rick Douglas Notts, I'm 24 and single, a high school graduate with a couple college classes to my credit. My parents are Doug and Valerie Notts, my sisters are Tami and Tari, we're all adopted. My badge number is 0134, I live at 41072 Cat Creek Road. I attend Valley State, working toward a degree in law enforcement and hope to some day join the State Police. I'm not a stranger, not a psycho stalker. I'm just a guy who's found you in his life."

Windy Jordan sniffed slightly and before he could utter another word she opened the door and slid from the truck. He watched her a moment, picked up the set of keys she'd left on the seat and opened his door.

Well, Rick, he thought. *Three years of waiting and wanting blown in less than one short hour.*

Windy walked to Cora's car. She noted her footprints in the snow all around the car and remembered the wonderful conversation she'd had with her Lord just last night.

I still want no one but You, God. Help me keep my focus on You alone. Thank You for sending this young man to help me last night and today. But Lord, I don't understand why. Who is he and why is he here now? How did I enter his life without him entering mine? I don't mean to be rude to him. I just want to be weary of strangers doing favors, like doctors and policemen. I don't want any man in my life. Men hurt. I know now why you brought Scott Bradley here so I could be done with him and his memories. So I'd put my trust in You alone.

Behind her she could hear Officer Notts jacking up the car. *Okay, Lord, what now? I have to thank him for helping me. How do I do that?* She suddenly thought of tonight's get together and quickly chastised herself for not concentrating. *Sorry, Lord.*

He said his parents are Doug and Valerie, just like the couple I met last night at Mary's. Wouldn't that be a coincidence? She again thought of tonight. *Your mind's wondering ole girl. Does he know You, Lord? If his parents come to church, will he?* Jenny's face appeared before her and she reminded herself to stop at the store and get the food for tonight.

Maybe I should invite him to church or to our house tonight to meet Scott and Jenny. No, that's too personal he might take it the wrong way.

INVITE HIM TONIGHT.

No.

INVITE HIM.

No, Lord, I don't want him to come between You and I.

HE WON'T.

Chapter Four

"You invited who?" Jenny McCourt stood in the kitchen, a bag of shredded mozzarella cheese in her hand. Her blonde hair lay softly about her shoulders and her blue eyes sparkled under just enough make-up.

"Rick Notts, he's a policeman." Windy folded the empty grocery bag and placed it under the sink. "He brought me home last night and helped me today." She took the cheese from Jenny's hand, sealed the bag and placed it in the fridge. "You don't mind, do you?"

"Of course not. I'm just surprised. Who is he, Win, where did he come from?"

Windy laughed. "It's a long story, believe me." The laugh faded. "Jenny, I think you'll understand. I...I believe God told me to invite him."

"God told you to?"

Windy nodded. "Sound far-fetched?"

"Not necessarily. Tell me about it." Jenny sat down at the small table her full attention on her friend.

Windy joined her, eyes looking into the previous night. "Last night, after the tire went flat, I sat in the car waiting for you or someone to come by. I heard a portion of scripture on the radio, something about God measuring the waters in the hollow of His hand."

Jenny nodded. "Isaiah," she thought for a moment, "Chapter 40, I think."

"You know it?" Windy asked surprised.

Again Jenny nodded.

"Did it change your life, too?"

Jenny shrugged. "I don't think so."

Windy marveled at how calmly her friend acknowledged that amazing scripture. "I suddenly understood. God is so great, beyond our comprehension. I knew I wanted only to serve Him and be His child. I want only Him and no one else. I told Him I want no one to come between us. That's when this policeman, Rick, showed up." She paused a moment, letting Jenny follow the train of events. "Today he surprised me. Jenny, he knew so much about me, it was strange and I, well, I treated him quite badly and he was just trying to help. When we reached the car I remembered my talk with God last night and He told me to invite Rick tonight. Kind of an apology I guess. Either that or the devil is in this—trying to pull me away from the Lord after my decision last night."

Jenny stared at her friend. "Is he a Christian?"

"I don't know, I don't think so."

"Could he pull you away from God?"

"Not a chance."

Windy heard the footsteps on the landing and opened the door before Scott could knock. "Welcome, come in."

"Cora sent me up to see what's taking you girls so long."

"I'm putting the last of the cheese on now," Jenny said. "You two go ahead, I'll be right down."

Scott stepped over to his girl and kissed the back of her blonde head. "We'll be waiting." He took the two bottles of cherry cola Windy held out to him. Balancing a pie in one hand she opened the door with the other.

After depositing the food in Cora's kitchen Scott took Windy's hand and led her out into the cold evening. They stood on the front porch.

"I wanted a chance to say good-bye," he said, slipping an arm around her. Windy moved into his embrace, savoring the warmth and security. She closed her eyes and leaned her head against his chest. Neither one needed words as they said their silent good-bye.

"I fall asleep when I pray," she whispered.

"Why is that?"

"Because I'm safe and comfortable and relaxed, just like I am now. Your hugs are like a prayer."

"Are you going to fall asleep?"

"I may," her breath came deep and evenly. "I'd love to curl up in a nice, soft prayer where I feel loved and protected and just fall asleep—as though I haven't a care in the world."

"So let me get this straight," Rick sat in Cora's living room, a glass of cherry cola on the table beside him. "Windy went to Costa Rica to work at a missions' camp because Jenny couldn't go and Scott, who grew up with Jenny, worked there but Windy didn't know you two were friends. Thanks," Rick accepted a plate from Windy who smiled and nodded. "And two weeks ago Scott came here looking for you," he nodded at Jenny, "and found you." He looked at Windy. "But you knew him by Brad, and he knew you by Elaine? Naw," Rick shook his head. "I've heard some stories before, but never anything this bizarre."

"I have." Windy challenged him. "This afternoon, in your truck."

Rick laughed and conceded the point.

The four young people sat in Cora's living room eating homemade pizza. Cora sat in her rocker, picking the mushrooms off her slice and popping them into her mouth. She gazed at the group and thought what nice looking kids they were; Jenny with her long blonde hair and warm hazel eyes. Her cute little nose turned up just perfectly. Windy's wavy brown hair crowned an oval face slightly spattered with freckles. When she smiled you could barely see her soft brown eyes.

Scott's short hair was just a shade darker than Jenny's, his eyes a brilliant blue. Cora thought of the beautiful children they would some day have. But Rick, the newcomer to the group puzzled Cora. He wore his sandy brown hair short and the mustache added a couple years to his young face. His gray eyes held Cora's attention; she knew she'd seen those eyes before.

Well, of course you have, you silly old woman, she berated herself. You just remember him from the times he came here on duty.

"Who did you say your parents are?" Cora asked before she could check herself.

"Doug and Valerie Notts. Dad's a high school teacher and Mom's…a mom; she does everything."

"I don't believe I know them. But you sure remind me of some one."

"Well, I look nothing like my parents, I'm adopted as are my two sisters. Tami and Tari, they're Korean."

"Now why did your folks adopt one baby from here and two from Korea?"

"After '73 it became almost impossible to find babies in the states."

"Why?"

Windy and Jenny exchanged looks. "Roe versus Wade, Cora." Jenny explained.

"Who?"

"That's the court case that legalized abortion in the United States."

"Oh my," the little lady shook her head. "Oh, that's so very wrong." Cora knew the facts, but she had such trouble believing that sort of thing actually happened.

"Were all three of you adopted as babies?" Windy asked and Cora threw her a look of gratitude.

"I was, but not the girls. Tami was four, Tari about a year and a half. They're natural sisters."

"How do you feel about being adopted," Jenny asked. "Or does it bother you to talk about it?"

"Not at all. It's just one aspect of my life."

"Do you have many questions?" Jenny asked. "I wonder, because Windy and I work at a CPC and we often suggest adoption, but I've never really researched the facts."

"My parents wanted me; they raised me and gave me my identity. They're great; loving and helpful, not overbearing. Dad always suggests, never dictates; he doesn't have to, I have no reason to question his authority."

"What about the woman who gave birth to you?"

"I was born shortly before Roe versus Wade; still she could have had an illegal abortion. But she carried me, probably carried the shame and guilt, too. She allowed me to live, to be adopted. She blessed three people with her unselfish act. I have the highest regards for her."

"What about abortion, where do you stand?"

"I believe it's wrong, but I can't tell you why. I don't know any facts one way or the other. When you realize you could have been a prime candidate for something like that, it certainly looks less appealing."

"May I quote you to my next client?"

"You may. Where is this place, this CFC?"

Everyone laughed, especially Windy. "I keep trying to tell people, letters make things too complicated," she said.

"Crisis Pregnancy Center, CPC, ours is named Caring Pregnancy Center." Jenny explained. "We want the girls to know pregnancy doesn't have to be a crisis."

"And you both work there? How did you manage that without my knowing?" Windy cast him a secretive smile. "I suspect there are many things I don't know about you—like why in the world do you insist on pineapple being cooked on your pizza and then take it off before eating it?"

Windy and Scott exchanged glances.

"I guess Officer Notts, there are some things you'll never know about me."

Chapter Five

The evening progressed slowly and with much enjoyment. To entertain Cora, the foursome sat in the middle of her living room floor and played a popular word guessing game, changing partners every few turns. Windy and Jenny knew each other too well to play partners and Windy and Scott had their Costa Rican adventure to draw on. Rick seemed left out until they paired him with Windy. They took the lead early in the second game and won in record time.

As the clock ticked away their time together, the atmosphere grew quiet and more serious. Windy put the game away and began picking up dishes. Rick followed her into the kitchen carrying what he could. He turned on the hot water and opened the door under the sink.

"What are you looking for?" Windy asked.

"Dish soap."

"You're not washing dishes, you're our guest." She saw his frown. "Don't tell me you're a neat nick and you're going to have nightmares about dirty dishes!"

Rick laughed. "Not at all. I like clean, but there are more important things in life to worry about besides dirty dishes. I just thought it wouldn't hurt to spend a few minutes in here, you know, for Scott and Jenny."

Windy thought on that for a moment, then nodded her head. "You may be right." She put the plug in the sink and found the dish soap. Handing Rick a clean cloth she said, "You wash? I'll rinse."

He accepted and plunged the glasses into the hot water. "Thanks for inviting me. I really enjoyed myself."

"I'm glad you came." She watched how he washed the glasses, noting his thoroughness. She stood next to him, feeling his presence. She took a deep silent breath concentrating on his cologne. She liked it, he smelled outdoorsy, like grass or hay.

"It's been quite a while since I spent an evening with people my age. Joe's a great guy and I enjoy his company, but tonight I actually had fun."

"What do you usually do in your spare time?" Her elbow touched his as she reached for a soapy glass.

Rick shrugged. "Try to invent original excuses not to go ice fishing. I'm just not a sportsman." Their hands touched as he offered her another glass. "I do have a small menagerie of farm animals."

"Really, what kind?" Windy placed the glasses in the drainer and began rinsing the plates, her eyes drawn to his hands; she liked them, just plain liked them.

"A dog, goat, couple chickens and a cat."

"No pigs or cows?"

"No, I couldn't eat anything I'd raised."

Windy smiled. "I'm with you. Do you garden?"

"A little."

If I lean my head over, Windy thought, *it would rest on his shoulder just perfectly and I wouldn't have to stand on my tip-toes to hug him like I do Scott Bradley.* She quickly shifted her weight away from him.

Scott walked into the kitchen and lifted the Kleenex box. He smiled at Windy.

"Is it time?" She asked.

He drew a deep breath and nodded. She wiped her hands on a dish towel then handed it to Rick. "C'mon," she whispered, following Scott back into the living room where she sat on the floor beside Cora's chair. Rick sat in the chair opposite her, watching intently.

Scott stood next to Jenny who still sat on the couch. He dropped to one knee and took her hand.

"Jennifer Jane McCourt," he began in a soft voice.

A smile slowly crept across Jenny's reddening face.

"I want to tell you in front of these, our friends and witnesses, that I love you as much or more than life itself. I know we've spent years waiting on God, allowing His will in our lives. I have waited with a longing in my heart that refused to be stilled. I have thought of this moment for so long and I now believe His plan for us is taking shape." He held her hand to his lips and lightly kissed it. "Jenny, will you make me the happiest man in the world? Will you marry me?"

Cora was already on her third tissue and searching frantically for more. Windy drew a couple out for herself, then handed the box to the older lady.

Jenny took a deep breath. "Scott Matthew Bradley, I have loved you forever and will love you as long as I have breath. I have prayed for you everyday, asking God to show me favor by allowing us to share our lives. I am honored that you love me in return. Yes, Scott, I will marry you."

She leaned into his arms and he stood, pulling her up with him. They kissed as though no one else existed.

Windy and Cora blew their noses and Rick wanted to disappear and rejoice at the same time.

Shortly before eleven, Windy noted Cora's droopy eyes; she hated to break up the evening, but knew she must.

"I have to work in the morning folks. Scott, what time does your plane leave?" Scott and Jenny still sat on the couch, their heads together.

"8:42, and I don't want to talk about it."

"You have no choice," she informed him. "I happen to know you don't want to miss your flight because you want to see you parents and tell them the good news."

"You're too smart for me." He stood, helping Jenny up. "I still have your car keys; I'll just take the car tonight and pick you up in the morning."

"I'll be sure to wake Jenny before I leave," Windy reassured him. "She's liable to oversleep, you know."

"Very likely," Jenny agreed, handing Scott his coat. She slipped hers on also. "I'll walk you out."

Windy retrieved Rick's coat from Cora's hall closet. She kissed the little lady on the forehead as Rick expressed his gratitude for her hospitality.

"You will come back?" Cora asked him.

"I would like to."

"Anytime," she yawned. "Oh, excuse me, it is past my bedtime."

"I'll turn the lights off and lock the door." Windy guided Cora toward her room, switching off lights as she returned. She pulled the door closed and checked to make certain it locked.

Rick stood awkwardly in the entry. Outside in the driveway, Windy saw Jenny and Scott huddled next to her car.

"It'll be a long winter for Jenny," she said.

"It'll pass before she knows it."

"My, you're quite the optimist."

"I just know the rewards of waiting. Patience has always been one of my virtues."

"Well, it's an admirable one." Windy held out her hand. "Thanks again for coming. I'm glad you had a good time." She wanted to apologize for her rudeness earlier in the day but found it difficult until she remembered once wondering why Stephan couldn't just admit he'd been wrong. "I'm sorry I treated you badly today. I was on the defensive and I don't know why. Forgive me?"

He smiled and reached for her hand. "I took you off guard. I'm the one who should be apologizing."

"You? After all the help you've been? No, I'm the one who's…oh my," she laughed. "This will never do, I say we start fresh."

"Sounds good to me. Hey, we never finished the dishes."

"Too late now, the door's locked."

They stood in the silence for a moment, Windy acutely aware that Rick still held her hand. Every nerve in her body seemed centered in her right hand, sensitive to the firm softness of his skin.

"I had a great time and I hope you'll allow me the pleasure of returning the invitation some day." Rick said.

She hesitated and a chill crept down her spine causing her to shiver.

"It's cold out here, you should go on up." He squeezed her hand gently before releasing it. "Bye, Windy, I'll see you."

Scott and Jenny called to Rick as he headed for his truck. He greeted them, wishing Scott a safe trip. He drove away without waiting for his truck to warm up and Windy tip-toed upstairs so she wouldn't disturb Cora.

Pulling on her night shirt she heard the door close.

"Windy?" Jenny called softly. Windy stepped into the kitchen and Jenny hugged her, crying, too happy for words.

Rick followed his headlights down the familiar road past Wil's house. The lights were all off as Rick knew they would be. In his mind he relived every part of the evening, especially the closeness of Windy as they washed dishes and said goodnight.

He puzzled over the whole atmosphere at Cora's home. Rick didn't drink, not that he thought it wrong, he just didn't enjoy it. Still most people his age indulged at least a little. To suggest a party without alcohol seemed a bit foreign. Rick sensed something different about these young people. Something impressive. And he'd experienced it before.

As he turned into his driveway and shut of the lights he realized who else had impressed him in this way; Wil and his family, the family who asked God if they should sell their property to him. Did Scott and Jenny, Windy and Cora go to God for such advice, too?

Shrugging, Rick stepped out of his car and walked up to the house. Hopefully, some day he would know the answer.

Chapter Six

Now accustomed to working by herself at the PREGNANCY office, Windy looked forward to her one day a week. January remained slow, with the girls from the college just coming back from break. Toward the end of the month Windy went in but had no appointments. She decided to spend the time reading and studying since she found the material at the office fascinating, though too often horrifying.

Shortly after arriving at the office Windy pulled out the previous year's files and dialed Diana Westfield's number. Her estimated due date read mid October and Windy wanted to know how she fared, if Mark had accepted the baby, if she'd had a boy or girl. The line rang and a recording stated the number had been disconnected.

Windy considered calling Nurse Laswell at the hospital but embarrassment kept her from it. As she dialed the number for directory assistance the front door opened and Windy replaced the phone. Mary peeked into the room.

"Busy?" She asked.

"Not at all. Come on in. You're not in school today"

Pulling her coat off, Mary slipped it over the chair and sat across from Windy. "No, I'm not feeling well, so they called in a sub. I thought the office might be deserted, so I came down to take a test."

"Well, I'm here, but I have no appointments, so I can do it for you. What time is she coming in?"

"Who?"

"The girl who needs the test."

Mary smiled. "She's here."

"Oh," Windy looked toward the hallway. "Is she coming in?"

Mary laughed. "Windy, she's in."

"Oh," Windy hesitated for a moment trying to understand Mary's reasoning, if the girl were in the house where was she? A thought occurred to her. "I see; you sent her into the bathroom to get a sample?"

Again Mary laughed and looked Windy in the eye. "No Windy, she's in the house but not in the bathroom. She's a previous client, she carried to term and Hannah isn't even a year old. That's why I hoped to slip in undetected."

Windy dropped the pen she'd been holding, her mouth almost joined it on the desk.

"You?" She asked.

Mary blushed. "Me. Although I really don't think I'm pregnant, but I want to rule that out before I call the doctor. So, if you'll excuse me, I'll be right back."

Mary quietly left the room, leaving Windy to ponder. True, Hannah wouldn't be a year old until April, and if Mary were pregnant she'd wind up with two babies in diapers for a while. Windy tried to imagine being blessed with just one baby, but two?

A few minutes later Mary returned. "Just as I thought," she said, "negative. But now I can make an appointment to see Dr. Sells."

Windy frowned her disappointment. "I'm sorry."

"So am I, in a way. I'm not ready for another yet, but Andrew and I decided if God determined we were ready, we'd trust His judgment over ours." Mary put her coat back on. "Are you doing anything for lunch?"

Windy thought for a moment, trying to remember which shift Stephan worked today and when he'd expect her home. She laughed and shook her head surprised that such a thought would occur after four months. "No, I'm not doing anything. How about pizza? My treat."

Mary considered the invitation. "I'm not sure about the pizza, how about soup at Peppers Café?"

"Sure, still my treat though. Meet you there about 11:30?"

Mary nodded her agreement.

Windy watched her friend leave, thinking of the jealousy she felt when Mary first announced she and Andrew were expecting Hannah. Now Windy breathed a sigh of relief, knowing if she herself had conceived she'd still be in a marriage that should never have taken place. Jenny's questions about God's will in that union came back to Windy and now she understood.

"No, Jenny," she spoke to herself. "Neither Stephan nor I ever sought God's will. And although I wish I could become pregnant, I'm glad I didn't."

As soon as Windy arrived home she ventured into the basement, quickly locating the boxes containing her few possessions. She couldn't remember which box held all the baby clothes she'd made when she and Stephan were hopeful. Opening each of the four boxes she quickly examined their contents then rechecked them. Stephan had labeled each box according to where the contents had been in his house; they read 'dresser' 'closet', 'master bedroom' and 'pink bedroom'.

"There were enough baby clothes and blankets to fill one of these boxes." Windy mused to herself. "So there must be another one here somewhere." She searched the basement to no avail. Deciding Jenny may have let her put it in the bedroom closet, Windy climbed the two flights of stairs, but found nothing. She looked through her small dresser, already knowing it contained none of the things she sought. In frustration she went downstairs to Cora's, thinking a box may have been stored in her apartment.

"What do you need them for?" Cora asked.

"Oh, I don't need them; I just suddenly remembered about them and wondered where they were."

Again she rechecked the basement then gave up.

The next Sunday Windy sat next to Cora in their usual pew, left hand side, second from the front. She liked being this close, she felt as though the pastor spoke directly to her when she didn't have to look past so many heads. Today Wil Packard walked to the front of the small church with Margie, this month's song leader. Windy liked to hear Wil speak, he didn't preach to the people, he talked to them.

Last October, Pastor Burke announced to his congregation that he found it necessary to relocate to a warmer climate because of his wife's health. Cora had said everyone knew that must happen sooner or later. They would be sorry to see the family leave, but loved Marilyn Burke and wanted to see her well again. In less than a month Pastor Burke answered a call to a church in Arizona. Since then visiting preachers had 'filled the pulpit' and when no one was available Wil could always be counted on. Jenny talked about an interim, a temporary pastor, but he never materialized. Wil and Andrew both were on what Mary called a pulpit committee, a group of five people who looked over pastor's resumes sent to them by the state office. It all sounded pretty complicated to Windy.

Margie led the congregation through a chorus and Wil prayed, asking God to bless their worship this morning.

"Well, we got two important announcements," he continued. "First off, we been talkin to a nice young man who's graduatin seminary this May. He'd like to visit as soon as he can. The pulpit committee would like to invite him. Now, we know he's young and this would be his first church. We been use to the wonderful leadin of Pastor Burke for almost ten years, but this here is a young congregation, why nearly half our people is still in their 20's and that's unusual these days. A young pastor might be a good idea here. Us older folks have a lot of love for young people, I think we'd be good for this fella. So Brother Shane says he'd like to come up durin his spring break from our university in Indiana. He can stay in the parsonage that week, so we'll need a few of you ladies to spruce it up a bit."

A hand shot up and Wil acknowledged it.

"Just how old is this young man?" Windy couldn't see who asked the question.

"He's 26, not married, comes from Stevensville, says he misses the lake. We wrote up a little information sheet, ya'll can pick up one in the back before ya leave. Now," he went on before anyone else could ask another question. "Second announcement; next Saturday, bout two o'clock, me and Missy want to invite everyone over to go slidin on that big hill back a our place. We'll have a pot of sloppy joes, brownies and hot chocolate. Everyone comin should bring a snack or juice or somethin."

Wil sat down and Margie stood, calling out a hymn number. Windy remembered the fun she and Eddie used to have when they went sliding. The kids all thought it was great that 'old' people could still do that sort of thing.

The hour went quickly as usual, and soon Windy, Cora and Jenny were settling into Jenny's car.

"Oh, I forgot to tell you," said Cora. "We have company for dinner today." The girls seldom used their own kitchen since Cora always cooked for them. And as long as she allowed them to help and clean up, they didn't protest.

"Really? Who's coming?" Windy asked.

"Rick."

"Oh, that's nice. What's the occasion?"

"There is none, he just stopped by the other day to check on me, he's such a nice young man, you know. So I invited him to dinner."

Knowing that Rick had checked on Cora didn't surprise Windy.

"Yes, I agree, he is nice. Does he work today?"

"At three, I believe, so the roast is already in the oven." Windy turned to smile at Jenny. Cora knew how to cook a roast and the girls knew how to enjoy it.

As soon as they walked in the door, Cora's phone rang.

"Windy would you get that," Cora asked. "I need to change my dress." Windy did as asked and Rick answered her hello.

"Windy, this may be a little presumptuous, but I wonder if I could bring Joe with me to dinner. He's a lonely ole bachelor too and I know he'd enjoy a Cora cooked meal."

Windy opened the oven, pulled the rack forward and peered into the pan. She laughed. "Please, bring him. We'll be eating roast beef sandwiches all week if you don't."

Chapter Seven

Windy scraped the remains of a plate into Sachels food dish. He stood by her feet, rubbing her legs and purring.

"You should meet Arnold," Rick said, reaching into the hot dish water for another glass.

"Who's Arnold?" Windy asked.

"My cat."

"You named your cat Arnold?"

"Why not, you named yours Sachel." He placed the glass into the other sink.

"Well, my cat's black. Is yours pink?"

"No, of course not. Who ever heard of a pink cat?"

"Well, Arnold the pig was pink."

"What pig?" he asked, lifting his attention to Windy. She wrinkled her nose at him and smiled. *Man she's beautiful*, he thought.

"Arnold Ziffel. You know from Hootersville."

"Hooterwho?" He pictured the blonde woman with the New York hair do and evening gown standing beside her husband who held a pitchfork.

"Don't tell me you never watched Green Acres when you were a kid? You know, Oliver and Lisa and the train, let's see what was the train's name?"

"My, you have an active imagination. What do you do in your spare time? Concoct these stories?" He loved teasing her, her reactions were so genuine.

"It was a TV show from the 60's, my mom used to watch reruns all the time."

"What does a TV show have to do with my cat?"

"His name is Arnold."

"I know that, I'm the one who named him."

She gritted her teeth and hissed at him. "You're impossible!"

"I'm impossible? You're the one talking about trains with names and pink cats!" He reached back into the wash water, captured some suds and flicked them at her. They landed squarely on her nose.

"Ahhhh!" She yelled. "No fair." She found a green bean and aimed for his nose, but he ducked as he scooped up another load of suds. She quickly spooned up some leftover mashed potatoes and held the spoon in firing position.

"You want war?" She laughed.

Rick couldn't think of anything more exciting than a harmless food fight with this lovely creature.

"This is Cora's kitchen, remember."

"I'll clean it up, with your help of course."

"Don't forget, I spent time in the Army, I majored in food fights."

"I believe I could hold my own."

"I believe," came a firm voice from the doorway. "You children volunteered to clean the kitchen, not mess it up." Joe stood with a fake scowl on his face.

"Boy, leave it to the 'old guy' to spoil a good time." Rick grinned at his partner. "Or did you just want in on the action?"

Having turned to face Joe, Windy's spoon now aimed at Rick's partner. In a moment of boldness she released the one finger that held her mushy missile. As soon as the mashed potatoes connected with Joe's cheek she realized what she'd done.

"Oh my," she whispered, unable to take her eyes from the face across the small room. Rick howled with delight. For what seemed an eternity to the girl, Joe stared at her. Then he spoke.

"Well, little one, I've been assaulted with bullets, knives, mud, water, dogs and a gerbil, but I must say this is a first for mashed potatoes." He reached down and picked up a napkin from the table and slowly wiped the offending glob from his face.

"I'm sorry, Joe. I shouldn't have done that."

"Ah, but you did. And although I accept your apology for now, I warn you that I will be waiting for just the right opportunity for retribution."

The following Saturday the girls bundled up Cora and took her with them to Wil's sliding party.

"You don't have to slide down the hill," Jenny assured her. "You don't even have to come outside and watch if you don't want to. I'm sure Missy would welcome your help in the kitchen."

But when they arrived they found Missy clad in a well-worn snowsuit. So, despite her quiet protests, Cora joined the group trudging through the snow.

"I don't know how you girls talked me into this," she scolded. "Imagine an old woman playing children's games."

Still she cheered from the bottom of the hill as each person tumbled down sometimes with a sled or inner tube, sometimes without. Before long Missy noted the older woman shivering and suggested they take the children back and check on their lunch.

The group began to thin out as many of the participants slowly dragged their sleds in the direction of Wil's house.

"Aren't you tired yet, Wil?" Windy asked.

"As a matter of fact, I am," he answered. "But I can't give up yet. I invited my neighbor and he said he might come after work. I've invited him to church a couple times but he resists. If he comes today it'll be that openin I been waitin for."

"Who's your neighbor?" Windy asked, hoping she already knew the answer.

"Nice young fella, policeman name o' Rick Notts."

Just then a shout greeted the two and Windy saw a figure walking through the woods carrying a large inner tube. Her heart jumped when she recognized him.

"C'mon boy!" Wil yelled. "The snow's packed to a glare."

"Windy," Rick said as he joined them. "I hoped to see you here. You look frozen, how long have you been at this?"

"Oh, over an hour. You've got a lot of catching up to do."

"Ready when you are," he challenged.

They headed up the hill to join the other die-hard sliders which included Jenny who called out a welcome to Rick as she flew past.

When Wil saw his neighbor welcomed into the group of younger people he wearily trudged back to his home, knowing his wife would greet him with a hot cup of cocoa and a sweet kiss.

The group now consisted of Andrew, Mary, Jenny, Rick, Windy and a young couple new to the church, Kim and Gordon.

"Let's pile-up on Rick's tube, it's the biggest." Andrew suggested. "Rick you first, Gordon, then me, Mary and the rest of you ladies."

Being the last one on, Windy was designated to push. The crew barely moved until they reached the first bump where they picked up speed and soared down the hill. Windy and Kim bounced off before reaching the bottom and Windy landed in a small bush scratching her already red cheeks.

"Are you okay, Kim?" She called. The girl nodded her breathless reply and they watched the others continue their descent.

When the tube finally stopped they slowly unpiled until only Rick remained. Windy squinted to see if he was alright but Andrew reached out a hand and helped Rick up.

"That was great!" Andrew yelled. "Let's do it again."

"Count me out," Mary replied.

"Me too," Rick rubbed the seat of his pants. "I'm surprised there's any material left here."

"Well, I'll take bottom then," Andrew volunteered.

"Oh, no. I came here for fun, not abuse; I can get that at work." Rick started up again, hauling his tube.

"C'mon Windy, how about something a little tamer?"

She followed him up, offering to help pull the tube but he declined with a smile. At the top he found an abandoned plastic sled, sat down toward the back of it and patted the area in front of him. "Just us two," he promised. She sat down and helped pull his legs next to hers inside the sled. Then he grabbed the rope with both hands, enveloping her in his arms. She leaned back slightly and closed her eyes. This is how it had been with Eddie; warm, exciting, full of life.

"Ready?" Rick asked. She nodded and he pushed off.

They whizzed along the packed-down track, taking an eternity of seconds to reach the bottom where they slid to an uneventful stop.

"Again?" Rick asked as they stood up. Windy nodded.

"But let me pull the sled this time."

"Not a chance. This is men's work."

"Men's work?" she repeated. "You think I'm not capable of pulling a plastic sled?"

"Very capable and on many occasions you may have to, but not while I'm here to do it for you."

Windy smiled. Who was this guy anyway? Eddie would have let her help, they would have pulled the sled together. Stephan would have insisted she use her time more wisely. But Rick just wanted to do this for her. Or so he said.

They climbed aboard their sled and again descended the hill. Mary intercepted them at the bottom.

"Molly said the food's ready. Her mom sent her to get us."

"You ready to give up?" Rick asked his new partner.

"I am hungry," Windy replied.

"Guess we better go then."

They fell in at the end of the slow moving line that wound its way back to Wil's house.

Rick hesitated to help himself to a second sloppy joe. Wil had not told him to bring something and he felt awkward. The older man noticed Rick's empty plate.

"Have another sandwich, Rick, there's more than plenty."

"Oh, I'm not that hun..." he decided on honesty. "You didn't tell me everyone was to bring something."

"First-timers ain't. Next time you come you'll have to pay your way."

Rick smiled his agreement as he placed another hamburger bun on his plate and lifted the lid on the pan. He refrained from another handful of chips, choosing instead a portion of desert.

Taking his place on the living room floor next to Windy he pointed at the glob on his plate. "What is this?"

"I don't know, but it sure is good, isn't it? Connie brought it."

Rick sighed and shook his head. "Who's Connie?"

Windy nodded toward the blonde lady sitting next to Mary on the couch, Hannah perched upon her lap.

"Connie's the one who loves babies. All babies, even ones with stinky diapers and gooey faces."

Rick watched the woman for a moment, noting the way she looked at the baby she held. He could hear her soft baby-talk and see the sparkle in her gray eyes.

"She doesn't look old enough to be Mary's mother."

"She's not. She isn't married, I don't know if she ever was. I don't think she has any children."

As if in reply the blonde woman glanced at the couple sitting on the floor. She smiled and Rick smiled back, nodding his head slightly.

"Did you kids have a good time?" she asked.

Windy nodded. "You should have joined us."

Rick expected an excuse from the woman.

"Next time. I was a little…late in coming today."

Rick pointed to his desert. "This is great!! How did you know I love raspberries?" He immediately regretted his familiarity with this unknown woman and started to apologize. But her genuine smile stopped him.

"Just had a hunch," she replied.

Chapter Eight

Monday morning Windy lifted the box from the stack in the storeroom and slowly made her way down the dog food isle. She didn't normally work in this area but Kyle called in sick and Don asked her to work both sections. She readily agreed welcoming the change. The lifting hadn't been much heavier until she got to the larger cans of dog food but now she could feel the difference and puffed her way down the isle. Nearing the appropriate shelf, Windy quietly grunted her relief. As she leaned forward to set the box down a muscle in her low back cramped. Her left hand slid from under the box and she felt it dropping. A second later she felt a stab of pain in her right index finger.

"I intend to take you over for x-rays," Don repeated. "You're covered on the store's insurance, and from the size and color of that finger, I'm certain you've broken it."

"Well, let's just put a splint on it, we have some in the medicine section."

Don shook his head and held Windy's coat out for her to slip her arms into. He stood ready in his coat, car keys dangling from his fingers.

During the short drive to the hospital Windy told Don about the great time she'd had sliding at Wil's two days before. She knew she was chattering, but couldn't help it; the anticipation of possibly seeing Stephan made her nervous. She wasn't fearful or excited, just didn't want to see him. Once inside the emergency room, Don found her a seat and went to register her. Windy tried to refrain from looking around but when a familiar face stepped into the large open waiting room she couldn't keep from smiling.

"Diana?" She called to the slender woman carrying a bundle of blankets, a diaper bag slung over one shoulder, a purse over the other. Windy jumped to her feet and followed the familiar face as it turned a corner. "Diana?" she called again.

Diana stood in front of an elevator, nervously watching the floor indicator. Her glance at Windy caused the girl to realize a conversation wasn't what Diana waited for. She decided on a quick look at the baby and a hasty retreat.

"I'm sure you're in a hurry," Windy started. "So I won't keep you. Just like a look at your baby."

Diana pasted on a smile. "Oh, hello, Windy isn't it?"

Windy felt the chill. "I'm sorry to bother you." She turned to go.

"Oh my, you may look at my baby. I wouldn't want to deprive you. After all, you were instrumental in her birth."

She slowly pulled back the pink blanket to reveal a soft round face under a shock of black hair.

"Girl?" she asked. Diana nodded. "What does Mark think about her?"

Windy remembered meeting Diana last summer at the Pregnancy office where the woman insisted an abortion was the only way to keep her boyfriend.

"He hasn't seen her." Diana offered no explanation.

Windy nodded and continued to cover the awkwardness she felt. "What's her name?" Using her uninjured left hand she pulled at the blanket to get a better view and noticed the covering; pink material with soft blue and lavender bunnies. The binding was hand sewn with little, even stitches.

When Diana didn't answer, Windy looked up and the other woman looked away.

"Stephanie," she replied. "Stephanie Diane...." Windy noticed the large gaudy green ring on Diana's finger; the same ring that once "graced" her own hand. "Michaels." Diana finished.

Suddenly the elevator door opened and Dr. Stephan Michaels stepped out. He looked at Windy, surprised, but quickly regained his composure and slipped his arm around Diana.

"Hello, Win-dee," he greeted her. "To what do we owe this pleasure?"

Windy stared at him for a moment as the truth sank in. She lifted her swollen hand and calmly replied, "A broken finger."

The doctor in her ex-husband took over and he reached out to examine the injury. Just as naturally she pulled her hand away.

"Is some one looking at it?" He asked.

"They will."

The three stood in an awkward silence. Windy wanted to run but she couldn't move. The baby whimpered.

Diana gently rocked her still sleeping daughter and Dr. Michaels spoke again.

"Win-dee, I believe you've already met my wife, Diana. And this is our daughter, Stephanie." His voice contained little emotion. No taunting, no remorse. Just facts.

"Yes," Windy nodded. "I…I know Diana. And…and the baby is…she's, well, she's beautiful. Congratulations…on…on everything."

An anger welled up in the young woman. Anger at Stephan for so easily pushing her aside and replacing her. Anger at her own body for denying her the privilege of motherhood. Anger at the unknown Mark who allowed another man to care for his child. Anger at Diana for giving Stephan what she could not. As the anger brewed she felt the tears rising and resolved not to give in to them.

"I'm glad you were able to use the baby things I made." She stared at Stephan daring him to deny her.

"Yes, I knew you wouldn't mind. After all you have no need for them."

Windy stared at the heartless man for a moment then turned to his wife.

"Diana, I'm truly happy for you, and proud of you for the courage you showed in carrying your baby. Had I had the opportunity, I would have gladly given you the things I made. Will you accept them now with my best wishes?"

Diana raised her eyebrow but remained silent.

"Stephan, may I see you for just a moment, alone?"

"Anything you have to say to me can be said in front of my wife."

"No, it can't." With her rising blood pressure, her finger now throbbed until she felt the pain pushing into her head. She looked directly into his eyes, determined not to be pushed aside again.

"Very well," he conceded, nodding to an open door behind the nurses' station. She moved in the direction he indicated and when they were safely behind the door she looked at him again.

"You had no right keeping those baby things. I made them. They were mine." She kept her voice level, her eyes unwavering.

"I disagree. I believe I purchased the material with which they were made, directly or indirectly."

Windy swallowed and licked her dry lips. "Some of it, yes, but not all. Whoever bought the stuff is not the issue, it's that you kept them and didn't bother to ask me if you could give them to Diana."

"I believe ownership to belong to the purchaser. And as I stated earlier, you have no need for them."

"I could use your logic then and demand I be paid for the time I spent making them."

"Oh, Win-dee," he laughed. "You were paid, far above your worth. You lived in the grandest house in this city and were provided for by a rich, old fool, until he awoke, that is."

"I won't argue with you, not when your ears are closed to the truth." But what is the truth? She asked herself. Stephan had everything he wanted now; a fertile wife, one baby with the prospect of more. But why would Stephan give his precious name to Diana's child when he would never have considered giving it to one of the abandoned babies left in the hospital nursery? And why not? Diana was obviously a woman born into a better class of people than the mothers of crack babies. But what about Stephanie's father, Mark? As Windy recalled from her first conversation with Diana the young man was doing his internship at this very hospital. Stephan could have easily checked into his background. Besides this was a girl baby in question here, not the child responsible for carrying on the revered Michaels name.

Stephan might have everything he wanted, but did he have what counted most? Windy thought of a verse she'd heard, but didn't remember all the words, something about gaining the world, but losing your soul. Was that in store for Dr. Michaels? She looked at the man who stood before her. This was the man she had lived with, shared an intimate relationship with, she shuddered involuntarily. Had she really given herself to him, this stranger, this older, graying doctor? That part of her life seemed more a foggy dream than reality.

Her mind raced around and for a moment she pictured him in his bedroom, undressing, about to slip into bed beside her. But the picture quickly erased as the very thought became repulsive to her.

Then she saw the man before her for who he was; a 'self-sufficient' man, alone in all his glory and wealth, a man with a soul that desperately needed a Savior.

"Stephan, whatever you think of me, doesn't really matter. If I wronged you as you believe I have, then I am sorry and I ask your forgiveness. And in return, I forgive you of any hurt you have caused me…"

"Any hurt I caused you?" His lip curled up as he looked at her in obvious disgust. "I paid your bills, I housed, clothed and fed you. I offered you a place among a society in which you didn't belong. And now you forgive me? How dare you even consider that I need forgiveness." His tone became low and angry. "But, can I forgive you for the way you weaseled into my life, promising what you knew you couldn't give? Yes, I am man enough to forgive and I have had no trouble forgetting. Excuse me now, Win-dee, I much prefer the company of my wife and child."

With those words he turned and left a speechless Windy to silently watch his retreating figure. Windy stood motionless for a time, gathering her thoughts as she resisted the feeling of complete helplessness. Again she marveled at the very idea of Dr. Michaels having been her husband. She would have stood there, staring, had a nurse not looked in the open the door.

"Are you Ms. Jordan?"

"Miss," she corrected from habit.

"Well, you're being paged."

Pushing through the fog of her amazement Windy could hear her name being called over the PA, telling her she was wanted in the Emergency room. For a moment she didn't know why and she stared at the nurse hoping to find some clue.

"They're ready to see you now," the nurse said. "For your hand I assume."

"My, hand?" Windy repeated gazing at one hand, then the other. "Oh yes, probably."

Chapter Nine

"Windy, can I ask you a question?" Don's voice pushed through the emptiness of her thoughts and she willed herself to look at him, to nod in consent.

"It's personal," he stated giving her a chance to change her mind.

She smiled. "Ask away, Don." After what she had just gone through with Stephan and Diana what could Don possibly ask that would bother her?

"You've been divorced," he started.

"Twice," she interrupted in a rare admission.

He looked surprised. "Twice? Oh, yeah, that's right. Guess I'd kind of forgotten."

Windy shrugged. "Wish I could forget."

He nodded but kept silent, evidently losing his nerve.

"What did you want to ask?"

"Well, how bad is it? I mean really. Is it as bad as some make it out to be? People get divorced everyday, but they live through it, get over it."

Windy hesitated for a moment, drawing on her knowledge of her boss. He wore a wedding ring and she'd seen pictures of a woman and children on his cluttered desk. Was he now considering divorce? Would his marriage hinge on what she had to say.

"No, Don, it's worse. Anyone who's been through a divorce can tell you, but they often don't want to talk about it."

"Why not?"

"It's not something to be proud of."

"Why did you get divorced? You've been through it twice, it must have been something you wanted. Unless of course," his voice lowered, "you weren't the one to file."

Windy geared herself up to speak of facts and leave the emotion out of this conversation. She knew for now, that was the only way she could have it.

"I married young, right out of high school. A year later I had a miscarriage and my husband started drinking," Windy silently asked the Lord for forgiveness of the change in timing of those last two events. "He became physically abusive which eventually landed me in the hospital where I met a concerned," she almost choked on that word, "doctor who..." she stumbled, "helped me obtain a divorce. We married and" She wanted to be truthful but not mean, "later we discovered I couldn't give him children because of that earlier miscarriage. He decided that part of marriage was more important than me and he obtained the divorce. No matter the reason or person, divorce is hard. I never believed in it, still don't. Those are the facts. I'm not sure I'm ready to share the feelings."

Don sat quietly thinking about her words.

"Are you considering divorce, Don?"

He shrugged. "I'm not sure."

"Why?"

"I'm not sure."

"Tell me about your family."

He began, but too soon they arrived in front of Windy's home. "Come on up and have a cup of coffee." Windy offered. He declined, saying he still had a day's work in front of him.

"Remember, the Doc said be at his office Thursday at 10:30 and he'll decide if you can go back to work. I don't want to see you til he's released you, understand?"

Windy nodded. "Okay, but I want a couple lunch hours with you."

He smiled his consent as she opened the door with her left hand. Once inside the house, she knocked on Cora's door knowing she had to tell the wonderful little lady about her hand. But she determined to tell her no more.

Cora fussed, as usual, making Windy sit while she brewed raspberry tea. Afterwards Windy went upstairs and crawled into her little bed. Sachel, always glad to see her, curled up next to Windy and began purring. She reflected on Don's question, stirring memories she'd neatly packed away. But those memories were like pieces of ignored papers hidden in a file cabinet, and Don's questions had knocked over the cabinet spilling its unwanted contents. Windy's heart and mind sorted through the events of the last few years, opening wounds of ignored hurt and anger, rejection, fear and loss. Stephan's words echoed in her ears, *after all you have no need for them.* She turned her face into her pillow and cried.

The phone rang, waking Windy. She debated answering it but the machine kicked in.

"Hi, you've reached Jenny and Windy. We can't come to the phone right now, but please leave a message. Bye."

"Windy." Rick's voice paused. "I stopped by the store and your boss said you were home with an injury. I hope you're alright. Call me. Okay?"

Windy got up and walked into the kitchen, glancing at the clock she realized she'd been sleeping for some time. Her finger still hurt but not enough to keep her from using her hand. Expecting Jenny soon, Windy put water in the tea kettle and set it on the hot burner. On the table lay the papers Don had given her to fill out, papers that would allow her to remain home for a couple days and still receive her pay. She thought of her boss and his questions.

The phone rang again; Windy stared at it, not ready to talk to anyone. She decided to wait and see who it was.

"Um, hi. It's me again, Rick. You can call me at the station if you want to, I'll be leaving home soon, for work." He hesitated and Windy knew he was stalling, hoping she'd pick up the phone. "If you call right away you could still get me here, oh, you probably don't know my phone number, it's…"

"No, I don't," she told the machine, tuning out the young man's voice. "And don't bother to leave it; I'm not going to call you. The last thing I want or need is someone else to complicate my life more than it already is." She stopped talking as the machine clicked off.

Staring at the phone she was tempted to play back the message and listen to his number. The machine flashed a red 2 at her indicating the amount of messages recorded; two, both from Rick. She hit the off button, waited a moment and clicked it back on again. A steady 0 looked at her. "Now I won't be tempted," she said with satisfaction. She turned her thoughts back to her boss.

She'd known Don since working for him after Eddie left. She'd never thought of him in any way other than her boss; never thought of his wife or children, never pictured him in anyplace but the grocery isles or behind his desk. Now he'd added a new dimension to his life, a personal one, an unhappy one. Seeing Don as a father and husband was something to get used to. But seeing him as a disgruntled husband was more than she cared to do.

"Well, Don's problems are his problems and mine are mine. He'll have to deal with them in his own way. I'm not some counselor who can just solve people's difficulties."

She immediately pictured herself behind the desk at the Pregnancy office, Diana sitting in the client's chair. She laughed. "And when I do. I'm the one who gets the shaft."

Jenny sat across from her friend drinking a cup of hot chocolate. "It was cold at school today. The wind seemed to come right through the windows. How did you know I'd need something to warm me up?"

Windy stared into the cup in front of her.

"Win? Windy?" Jenny reached over and touched the other girl's hand, startling her.

"What?"

"Are you alright? Did something happen today?"

"I broke my finger. Isn't that enough?"

Jenny stared at her, trying to see through the wall Windy had slowly been erecting over the past few months. Jenny had hoped that Windy's New Year's Eve experience would begin to break down the wall. Give her time, she chided herself, it's only been a few weeks.

"It would be for me," Jenny replied. "I can't handle pain like you."

"What's that mean?" Windy asked defensively.

Jenny looked at her friend wondering how to answer. Should she be gentle or honest? She shrugged. "You're tougher than I am," she said, deciding on honesty. "You've been through a lot; physically and emotionally. I couldn't have handled it as well as you."

Windy eyes darkened and her chin quivered. Jenny expected an outburst as her friend's mouth opened and closed a couple times. She obviously couldn't decide what to say or if to say it.

Finally Windy stood up and took her coat from the back of the chair. She zipped it quickly and opened the door but stopped to look at Jenny. "Who says I'm handling it at all?" With that she disappeared.

Jenny started to follow her but walked into the bedroom instead and watched Windy through the window. Knowing something more than a broken finger claimed Windy's thoughts; Jenny decided to allow her some time alone. She feared her insistence might push Windy away.

"Lord, I know she's Your child, You know she's my friend. I trust You to look after her, but please, please give me the wisdom to know when to step in." Jenny saw Windy stop at the corner and for a moment thought she would turn around and come back.

Windy ran down the steps hoping Cora wouldn't hear and come out. She stepped into the cold and walked through the gathering snow. At just four o'clock the sky looked ready for bed. At the corner she stopped.

"Now where?" she asked herself. She knew she was running, but she didn't know where to or even what from. She really had no place to go. She had just walked away from her only real home; her only real friends. Suddenly Windy felt more alone than she had in years. She stepped from the curb and followed the familiar route to the Pregnancy office.

"You shouldn't have gotten mad at Jenny like you did," she chided herself. "Well, I didn't exactly get mad," she returned. The sound of her own voice in the white stillness felt a trifle comforting so she continued to talk out her feelings.

"I don't understand how anyone can think I'm strong. I'm not. I'm so weak; I can't even stand up for myself. But then, what's there to stand up for? I'm a young woman who has failed at two marriages. I have no children, nor will I ever have a child. One husband hated me so much he chose a lousy can of beer over me. The other kicked me out of his house like an old pair of worn shoes. Who do I think I am, that I'm worthy of anything? Where do I get off being angry at Jenny, Miss Perfect-Never-do-anything-wrong-always-tuned-in-to-God-Christian?"

By the time she reached the old house that contained their office Windy had convinced herself she was the saddest, loneliest, most unworthy person in the world.

She stood at the bottom of the steps, looking at the front door. She had no means of stepping through that door. The automatic porch light flickered on in preparation for the coming night but the rest of the house stood dark. Windy searched her coat pockets in the unfounded hope that her keys may have made their way there by themselves.

When her search turned up nothing, she brushed the snow from the bottom step and sat down. Where now? She asked silently. Your parents are hundreds of miles away; your childhood home belongs to someone else. You have no warm, cozy parlor to curl up in. Where now, Windy Jordan? Where now?

Chapter Ten

Just as Windy stood up to start the walk home a car pulled around the corner and stopped in front of her. The passenger door opened and Windy slid in. Jenny put the car in gear and they drove home in silence.

When they arrived home Cora opened her door. "Girls, I almost forgot. While I was getting the mail my phone rang and I brought everything in here."

She held out some envelopes. Windy quickly shifted through them handing two to Jenny and keeping two for herself. Both were addressed to Elaine Michaels with yellow correction labels on them.

Jenny smiled, "Mom," she said holding up one, "and Scott," she displayed the other with pleasure. "How about yours?"

"Eric and Lana, from Costa Rica," Windy answered.

"Why don't you girls run upstairs and read your letters. I'm just now getting supper started. We're having meatloaf tonight."

Windy smiled at the little lady. She and Jenny must have been discussing Windy's tantrum, but they acted as though nothing out of the ordinary happened.

"I was supposed to bring home groceries today," Windy suddenly remembered.

"Not to worry, tomorrow's another day. Now shoo."

Sitting at the table, the girls tore into their mail. Windy opened Lana's letter first. The envelope bore extra postage to cover the many pages she found inside.

The first page, dated August 8th, started with Lana's thoughts about their trip and the many wonderful events that took place at the camp. The following pages were written at various times, Lana saying she'd just keep writing until she received an address. As time went on Lana spoke less about Costa Rica and more about her daily life and thoughts. She reported having received a couple letters from Martin, having personally exchanged addresses with him. After Christmas she wrote:

"Martin came for a visit and we had a great time together, funny how I didn't like him at our first meeting, but he explained he always started his camps in a gruff way to let the 'kids' know they are there to work, not play. I plan to go to Central America next summer and spend it working with Martin. He'll be working on a couple sites in Guatemala. I have one more semester before earning my degree and then I'll be able to practice nursing as a missionary."

Lana went on to ask about Brad since she hadn't seen his address included in Elaine's card. The final page was written the week before, with an apology for the delay.

"I've called Martin every week since his visit at Christmas. He makes very little money and can't afford to call me. I'm not afraid to tell you Elaine, I love this man, and I know he loves me. He hesitates to say so, because he thinks he has 'so little' to give. I told him, that's true; all he has to give me is my dream—A life as a missionary nurse and a Christian man to spend it with."

As Windy finished reading she dabbed her eyes again, and blew her nose. She looked over at Jenny who sat quietly reading Scott's letter, for the third time. They exchanged smiles and Windy picked up the thin envelope with Eric's return address. It contained one piece of paper and a picture of him and a lovely young girl with shoulder length brown hair and a soft smile.

The letter said little but made Windy smile at the exuberance of it. After his name Eric wrote I Thess. 5:16-18. Windy quickly retrieved her Bible and looked up the verses.

"Boy if ever I needed this, it's today," she remarked reading the passage to Jenny. "'Rejoice always, pray without ceasing, in everything give thanks, for this is God's will for you in Christ Jesus.'"

As the girls sat in silence pondering the words just spoken, the phone rang. Jenny reached over to the counter and picked up the phone. She smiled as she recognized the voice on the other end. She spoke pleasantly for a couple minutes then said, "Here, I'll let her tell you herself." She handed the phone to Windy. "Rick," she said.

Rick stood at the station desk, his right hand held the phone while his left toyed with something in his pocket. He looked at Joe.

"Hi, Windy, are you feeling alright?"

He listened to her answer. "Joe and I thought we might drop over for just a few minutes but we wanted to see if you were up to company." A puzzled looked came across his face. "Well, Joe's my partner; I can hardly leave him here." He shrugged at Joe's questioning look. "The what? Oh, the mashed...yes, he's standing right here. I would say he's probably forgotten. You have to remember Windy; he's an old guy, prone to forgetfulness, not like us young 'kids'." He grinned at his scowling partner.

"Is that right? I believe we can make it about that time." Rick said good-bye then hung up the phone. "She says Cora has meatloaf in the oven and should be done in about half an hour. Think that'll fit into our schedule?"

"Boy, will it!" Joe grinned.

Windy had trouble keeping her eyes off Rick as the five sat around Cora's small table. She noticed how handsome he looked in his uniform, yet those two uniforms looked out of place in Cora's kitchen.

The men couldn't praise the meal enough and Cora's face stayed blushed the whole time. As she pulled out a pan of blueberry cobbler Rick told the ladies the reason for their visit.

"We would like to invite you to dinner at my house on Thursday. Joe and I will cook, and Windy can do the dishes."

"Oh my, now wouldn't that be a treat?" Cora asked, obviously not hearing Rick's teasing remark.

"I make excellent mashed potatoes," Joe volunteered, looking straight at Windy, who quickly dropped her gaze.

"What's the occasion?" Jenny asked.

"Payment for the wonderful meals we've had here, including this one." Rick answered. "Besides Valentines Day is Friday, and we couldn't think of anyone more special than you three ladies."

"Well that's sweet Rick, then maybe I won't miss my own Valentine so much."

"How's Scott doing?"

"I think he's faring better than I am. He's busy with his studies and doesn't have time to miss me." Jenny said with a pout.

"But you have your students to occupy your mind," he reminded her.

"I know, I guess I'm not as patient as some people."

"Look how long you've waited, Jenny," Windy entered the conversation. "I think you're very patient."

"It was easier before I knew for certain if this was God's will, now that I know; I can't see the reason for any more delay."

"Sometimes, it's during the delays that we learn the most." Rick said. Everyone looked at him. "Or so I think, maybe," he added somewhat embarrassed.

"When did you become one of the three wise men?" Joe asked.

Rick smiled at his partner. "About three years ago when I came under the influence of one of the other two."

Joe beamed at the unexpected compliment. "Why, thanks, my boy."

"I was speaking of Wil Packard." Rick grinned as his partner's air deflated.

"That's right, you do know Wil," Cora said. "How did you come to meet him?"

"Well, this time the credit does belong to Joe. We were fishing on Wil's property, my property now. Which brings me to something I've often wondered about, and if anyone can help me, I'm sure one of you can," Rick said. "Wil says God told him it was alright to sell his house to me. What do you make of that? Does God really talk to people, even about unimportant things, such as who to sell a house to?"

Windy and Cora looked at Jenny.

"The Bible tells us," Jenny began. "That God knows everything about us and He cares about every aspect of our lives, maybe even the color of curtains to put in our bathroom. It isn't so much the details that count, rather our willingness to trust Him with them. And yes, He speaks to us, sometimes in an audible voice, sometimes through Scripture, His Bible, sometimes through the wisdom of one of His other children. Wil, of all people, could truly hear God, because he's so God-oriented; focused. If he says God told him to sell his house to you, I for one would never question it. As a matter of fact, I'm interested in how God plans to use this whole situation."

"When I met Jenny," Cora continued. "She told me everything happens for a reason. I look back over the last couple years, since I met her and I see how things have worked out. Now, as I look back even further I see God's hand in my life, before I knew it was even there."

Windy listened and agreed with each of the ladies, then she thought of Rick's involvement in her life before her knowledge of him.

"Rick, think of it this way. You knew me, knew much about me before I knew you even existed. Yet, you did exist. My lack of knowledge of you didn't change that. So it is with God. Just because we don't know Him, doesn't mean He doesn't exist. You had an influence in my life, without my knowledge."

"And," he interrupted. "You influenced my life, without knowing it."

"I did?"

Joe looked at his partner and grinned. For years he'd been teasing Rick about not having a girlfriend, telling him that by the time he found one, he'd be so set in his ways no woman would have him. Joe's glance moved from the young man to the young woman who sat next to him.

So, Rick, my boy you've been keeping secrets from your old partner, he thought. *Here you are in love and I never knew it, never suspected.* Joe recalled their visit to the upstairs apartment so long ago, when Rick was still a cub. He saw Rick standing in that living room, holding a picture of Bilmon and his little wife. *Well, son, with all the baggage this one's carrying with her, I just wish you luck, cause you're really gonna need it.*

Chapter Eleven

Windy used her time off to answer the letters she'd received. To Lana she almost wrote a book, telling her all the things she'd left out in Costa Rica. Then she updated her on the present situation and the many changes she'd been through since last seeing her friend. She told Lana about Jenny and Scott Bradley, expressing her happiness for them. She signed it—*Your sister in Christ, Windy.*

Writing to Eric caused her more concern. Since he already knew most of Windy's history, she found it harder to admit to a second defeated marriage. So she mentioned that quickly and moved right on to her job, her church and her friends. She shared her excitement over Jenny and Scott, knowing that information would be special to him. And before she could stop herself she told him about Rick, and his moonlight rescues. Both of them. After rereading the letter she decided to add a little humor to keep Eric from wondering if she had feelings for the police officer.

On Thursday Windy kept her doctor's appointment, glad to be able to go to his office rather than the hospital. He checked her and announced her healing nicely.

"You can return to work whenever you're ready," he said, handing her a work release.

Windy stopped by the store and took all her papers in to Don. Her boss spoke only briefly and Windy felt his awkwardness. She decided not to mention their discussion of three days before, determined to pray harder for him and then just let him come to her when he felt ready.

Don informed her that since her injury happened on the job she would receive her pay for the hours she was scheduled to work. Windy hesitated, wondering if that was ethical.

"But I didn't work, Don," she said. "Is it right for me to collect something I didn't earn?"

Her concern brought a smile to his face as he assured her it was quite alright. "Not only right, it's required by state law under workman's compensation. Now, I already have the schedule finished for the weekend and you're not on it. However, I expect to see you early Monday morning. You're my best opening girl and the place just isn't the same without you. So get some rest and be prepared to make up for lost time."

With that he left his office to check on a shipment that needed unloading.

Back at the apartment Windy brought the mail in and stopped at Cora's for a quick cup of tea.

The little lady bustled around the kitchen, pulling a pan of sweet smelling wheat bread from the oven.

"We can't go to dinner empty handed, you know," she informed Windy when the girl raised an eyebrow.

"Cora, this is supposed to be Rick and Joe's treat, their turn to do something nice for you."

"Well, yes," Cora conceded. "Do you think I should leave the desert at home then?"

Windy laughed as she tore open a letter from her parents. A check fell from the folded paper. Windy picked it up and noted the amount of one hundred dollars.

"Oh, my," she exclaimed. "Oh, my!"

"Is something wrong dear?" Cora asked.

Windy showed her the check and Cora clapped her hands with delight.

Windy began reading the letter. "Mom says she's working part time for the company Dad works for. She's an assistant to their bookkeeper and is learning to use a computer. She received her first check and just felt she wanted to send me some money." Windy scanned the rest of the letter. "Everything is fine, Dad's working extra hours, and they both are feeling well." Windy smiled at her friend then continued reading the letter in silence.

When she finished she laid it down and picked up the check. "One hundred dollars. What should I do with it?" She pondered for a moment. "I should be smart and add it to my savings."

"I think you should buy yourself something nice, Windy," Cora suggested. "I'm sure she intended for you to enjoy it, otherwise, she'd have bought you a savings bond."

After a little hesitation Windy and Cora decided to go shopping.

Windy checked the mirror one more time hoping she hadn't put on too much make-up. She rarely wore any but today had decided to buy some powder and mascara.

"Maybe I should have listened to Cora and bought some of that soft colored eye shadow," she told her reflection.

The girl in the mirror shook her head. "Why," she asked. "Are you trying to impress someone?"

"Not me," Windy answered with an innocent shrug. She touched her new sweater, admiring the loose blue knit.

Just then Jenny walked in the door.

"Win?" she called out.

"Right here," Windy stepped into the kitchen and waited for Jenny's reaction.

"You're beautiful!" Her friend exclaimed. "I love that sweater. And make-up?" Jenny placed her hand on Windy's shoulder. "Really, you look nice, Win."

"Thanks," Windy smiled, accepting the compliments graciously. "My mom sent me some money and Cora talked me into spending some of it."

"Good for her."

"I have something for you, too," Windy picked up a small plastic bag from the table and handed it to Jenny.

"Oh, Wes King!" She cried pulling out a cassette tape. "Thank you, Windy." She gave the smiling girl a hug. "I heard one of his songs on the way home, I wonder if it's on here." She quickly looked through the list of songs. "Yes, see, the third one, *The Love of Christ*. It's a beautiful song;

let me play it for you while I get dressed." She popped the cassette into the small tape player that sat on the counter, fast-forwarded a little way then increased the volume. Upbeat music poured forth and Jenny nodded. "It should come on in just a minute." She disappeared into her bedroom.

A moment later the room quieted and soft music began to play. A tender male voice sang words that touched Windy's heart and she felt the song had been written just for her. It reminded it's listener of the depth of Christ's love. When it finished Windy blotted the tears from her eyes with a paper towel hoping she hadn't smeared her mascara. Jenny emerged from the bedroom also touching her cheeks.

"Isn't that beautiful?" She asked. Windy just nodded, not trusting herself to say anything. Jenny returned to the bedroom to finish dressing while the tape continued to play and Windy listened to the songs, admiring the voice she heard.

When Jenny came back out she wore a turtle-neck, flannel shirt and jeans. Windy marveled at her long honey-colored hair, and clear skin, tempted to feel envy. Jenny had a natural beauty that allowed her to look great even in a flannel shirt.

"I thought if we went a few minutes early," Jenny said, "we might walk in the woods a little. I admired the area when we went sliding at Wil's." She popped the tape out of the player. "We can listen to this in the car," she grinned.

Downstairs in Cora's kitchen Windy suddenly remembered Joe's remark about the mashed potatoes and his promise to pay her back for her 'attack'. Looking at her new sweater she wondered if she should change. *Don't be silly,* she chided herself. He was just teasing you.

"Cora, promise you won't help in Rick's kitchen, or I'll bring you back home," Jenny threatened. Windy felt a little sorry for the older woman perched in the back seat between a loaf of hot bread and a dish of frozen dessert.

Knowing Cora could never make such a promise Windy suggested, "Would you like to stop at Wil's and talk with Missy while we go for a walk?"

"That would be nice," Cora agreed. "But I didn't bring anything extra. Do you think I should take the dessert to them instead?"

Both girls laughed and shook their heads.

"Cora, if you only knew just how precious you really are!" Jenny told her.

After leaving Cora and her dessert in Missy's hands the girls continued on to Rick's.

Rick finished peeling the potatoes and wrapped the peelings in a paper towel to take them out to the frozen garden. Joe shook his head. "The critters will find those peelings long before they sink through that foot of snow."

"I know," Rick smiled. "I like critters."

"But if they're used to finding food now, they'll destroy your garden in the summer."

"I plant enough for all of us." Rick assured him.

A knock on the front door ended their conversation and Rick left to answer it.

He smiled when he saw the girls. "You're early. I hope you don't think we're going to let you help make dinner."

"Not a chance," Jenny answered handing Rick the loaf of warm bread. "As a matter of fact we just dropped Cora off at Missy's for that very reason. We want to go for a walk in your lovely woods. Do you mind?"

"Great idea! Let me check with Joe and maybe I'll join you." He headed toward the back of the house, motioning the girls to follow.

Joe stood in the kitchen doorway nodding his head. "Go on, there's not much left to do, and I'm sure I can manage to make the mashed potatoes myself." He looked directly at Windy whose face drained of its color.

"Let me grab my coat," Rick said, looking at the girls. "You look warm enough; I think you'll be okay."

"We dressed for it," Jenny assured him.

Windy just nodded and Rick wondered if she planned to speak at all. "Duke?" He called. "Let's go for a walk." A bright eyed mutt came bounding out of the living room where he'd been curled up before the fire and they all followed Rick out the back door.

Rick led them across the porch and down the steps as the dog bounced along beside him.

"We'll see if Arnold wants to go, too." Rick opened the walk through barn door and called 'kitty, kitty'. A large white cat with big pink ears strolled through the door and rubbed his master's legs. Rick winked at Windy who stopped in her tracks.

"Why Arnold?" Jenny asked.

"You don't want to know," Windy murmured, looking away from Rick. He made a mental note of her reaction.

He led them across the foot bridge he and Joe had fished off of the day Rick saw this house and knew he wanted to live here. They trudged between a few trees, across a small clearing and up a hill.

"This isn't where we went sliding is it?" Windy asked.

"Same hill, back side."

"Then your property borders Wil's?" Jenny asked.

"Yes, I bought the house and 20 acres from him. I guess all of it belonged to Missy's grandfather."

"Wil has over one hundred acres and he cuts wood to…sell," Windy's voice faded as she remembered meeting Wil at Stephan's house. She had burned many of Wil's cuttings in the front parlor. But those were memories she had no desire to dredge up. "Is that stand of pine trees on your property?" She asked, pointing.

"They're the dividing line between mine and Wil's. They're on his property though. C'mon," he said, turning. "Let me show you a beautiful little glen."

Chapter Twelve

Windy pushed her plate away. "That was a great supper. Where did you learn how to cook?" She asked Joe.

They sat in the long dining room on mismatched chairs next to an old wooden table. A white cloth had been spread out in their honor and Rick had even placed a vase of cut flowers as a centerpiece.

"I'm a bachelor, remember? I have to feed myself."

"One thing he hasn't learned is how to wash the dishes," Rick informed them, picking up his and Windy's plate.

"Well, there's not much here, I'm sure we can have them done in no time." Windy stated.

Surprisingly, Rick didn't argue but he wouldn't let Joe or Cora help. "You cooked," he pointed at Joe, "and you have the night off," he indicated Cora. "So go into the living room and enjoy the fire. There's a cassette in the player I'm sure Cora would enjoy."

Windy and Jenny followed their host into the kitchen where Windy began filling the dishpan in the one large sink. "This sink must be the original," she commented noting the one large porcelain unit that made up sink and drainer.

"Missy says it is. Most of the fixtures have never been replaced, except the refrigerator. I like the old things; they remind me of my grandparents' house."

Strains of big band music from days long gone drifted into the kitchen. Jenny cocked her head and listened.

"Is that the kind of music you like?" She asked.

"When it's suitable. I thought Cora would prefer that to anything else."

Windy washed, Jenny rinsed and dried while Rick put the leftovers and clean dishes away. When the dishwater was empty Windy washed off the counter. They finished in record time and joined Joe and Cora in the living room. Cora's eyes shined and she smiled at Rick.

"This is just lovely! I haven't heard Glenn Miller in such a long time. Clifton and I used to dance to these very tunes."

"Do you still remember the steps?" Rick asked.

"Oh yes, but I could never do them."

"Let's try." Rick took the older woman's hand and tried to help her to her feet. She resisted.

"Oh my, no! I'm an old woman; I can't dance like I did when I was young."

"Excuse unacceptable. I think if you just try, you'll find you still enjoy dancing." Rick urged. The others joined in and soon a blushing Cora rose from her chair.

Rick placed his left hand on her spacious back, gently held her hand with his other and smiled down into her sweet face. He started slowly, catching the music on every other beat until Cora relaxed and allowed her body to sway with the movement. Soon her feet were performing steps they'd never really forgotten and Cora's pleasure beamed from her face. Rick picked up the tempo, encouraging his partner with a smile and a nod.

Windy watched in delight as the couple proceeded to 'cut the rug'. Rick proved to be a perfect partner, helping Cora get used to the steps before adding a new one. He anticipated her dancing abilities and limitations.

Too soon the music stopped and a breathless Cora clasped her hands over her breast, pulling in large amounts of air. Windy jumped to her side, fearful the woman was having a heart attack. But Cora's grin revealed her excitement.

"You dance so well! Just as good as my Clifton did!" she praised the young man. "Wherever did you learn?"

"My parents." He escorted his partner to her chair where she waved a chubby little hand in front of her red face. "My first memory of my parents is of them dancing while I watched from the top of the stairs. I grew up dancing. My favorite TV stars were Fred Astaire and Ginger Rogers."

"They weren't on TV," Joe corrected.

"They were on ours. Mom and Dad always watched the old movies, and we were the first family on our block to have a VTR, video tape recorder, as they were originally called."

The tape player continued to roll out the music of days passed. Rick looked at Windy, who had returned to the couch, next to Jenny. "Want to try?"

"No, those steps are much too hard and fast."

"Nonsense, come on."

Windy just sat and shook her head.

"I'd love to learn how to dance like that," Jenny exclaimed. "I won't pass up the chance!" She stepped up to Rick and he held her as he had Cora.

Windy watched and listened as Rick slowly explained the moves and guided her friend into performing them. He showed her a couple basic steps which she quickly executed, then he went on to more difficult ones. Once she mastered those, he put it all together and they began spinning and dancing around the room the same way he and Cora had, but with much more energy. When the music stopped Jenny laughed in triumph.

"Win, it's great, you've just got to try it!"

Windy hesitated. It certainly looked fun, and for a moment she thought she might try. She started to rise but suddenly imagined Rick's arms around her, his face close to hers. Her heart fluttered and she quickly sat back down. "No," she said quietly, dismissing the issue.

"Fine," Jenny teased, "gives me a chance to learn more." She turned back to Rick who willingly took her in his arms and began moving her to the music.

Windy watched as the pair danced around the room. Jenny learned quickly and with the start of each new song Rick led her into a different step.

Rick wore a dark green flannel shirt and jeans, matching Jenny's casual outfit. They looked like they belonged together—hiking, tending farm animals, sliding down a hill. Dancing.

Jenny threw her head back and laughed, just as she had the day she and Scott Bradley stood in Cora's backyard. Windy remembered the sight vividly. That was the day she let go of her Brad and allowed him to be Jenny's Scott. That was the day she wished only the best for the two of them. Now she sat and watched Jenny in the arms of yet another handsome young man, and innocent as it was, she felt an anger rise. What would Scott Bradley say if he could see his fiancé right now? Windy tried to picture his reaction, tried to see his face scowling in anger or jealousy. But all she could muster were the kind blue eyes and the gentle understanding smile. She remembered how her Brad had looked the day he stood against a brick wall in Costa Rica and watched the bus pull away. Then Jenny stepped into the picture giving Brad a completely new identity. Now with Scott Bradley back at seminary Jenny needed someone else to entice with her beautiful blonde hair and deep blue eyes.

Tears threatened to expose Windy's thoughts but before they could she fled, finding sanctuary in the bathroom.

"You're being stupid," she whispered to the girl in the mirror. "Jenny loves Scott; she's just having a little fun; innocent fun. If you want Rick's arms around you, dance with him."

She took Brad from me, now she's trying to take Rick. A silent voice accused.

"Brad was never yours to start with," she tried to silence the voice. "And Rick certainly isn't. How can she take something from you that isn't even yours?"

Windy ran her fingers under the cold water till she thought they would turn blue. She wanted to splash her face but knew the water would wreck havoc on her carefully applied make-up. She heard the music stop, replaced with laughter. Windy stepped from the bathroom and into the kitchen. There she opened the fridge and found a two-liter of cherry cola. Having seen where Rick put the glasses, she now opened a cupboard and helped herself to a large swallow of the cold, biting liquid.

"Don't put it away," a voice said.

Rick placed his hand on her back to let her know he stood behind her. She felt the slight pressure and his shoulder as he brushed against her, reaching into the still open cupboard. He pulled out two more glasses and set them on the counter then turned the hot water tap on in front of her.

"Cora wants tea and Joe wants coffee," he explained as he filled the tea pot. Windy obediently filled the glasses without comment, watching as Rick opened another cupboard and extracted a jar of coffee and an unopened box of raspberry tea. The girl smiled.

"You're a thoughtful host," she complimented him.

"I just hope Cora comes back often enough to help me drink it all. I'm good for about one cup of tea a year."

She noticed him breaking the seal inside the coffee jar. "You don't drink coffee either?"

He shook his head. "Never could stand the stuff."

A satisfied smile rested on the girl's face.

Back in the living room, Joe sorted through Rick's pile of cassettes. "You've got some golden oldies here. Do you dance to these too?"

"I dance to everything. My parents danced as often as they breathed and to every kind of music."

Joe held up a tape. "Even Wipe Out?" indicating a 60's record with only two words and lots of fast guitar and drums.

Rick grinned. "Even Wipe Out, but not tonight, I'm too tired for that one."

Joe pushed a tape into the recorder and took Windy's hand as soon as she placed two glasses of cola on the end table. Slow, romantic music drifted from the player and an old familiar song surrounded them. Joe pulled a protesting Windy into his arms as a different 60's group sang the slow, romantic *Cherish.*

"I remember this song; I think my parents have it on an old record somewhere. It's very pretty."

Joe agreed. "Takes me back to high school and a pretty little blonde named Bonnie."

Windy smiled and allowed Joe to glide her around Rick's living room. Rick and Jenny had followed his example and now Rick tapped on Joe's shoulder and Joe responded by accepting the change in partners.

Windy now found herself in the arms of the mysterious Gray Eyes who used to come in the store where she worked. She looked into those eyes and remembered the last time she saw him before she married Stephan. Her thoughts came back to her.

She silently willed him to speak to her, wondering if he would show any interest. Would he even go so far as to ask her to dinner or a movie? Would she dare accept? Stephan's image hovered over her and she knew in her desperate heart this could be the last tie to her own life. Just one word of interest, that's all it would take to keep her from stepping into Stephan's arms.

If only Rick had spoken up then, she reasoned, if only he'd shown the interest she could see in his eyes now, she probably would not have married Stephan, never gone through the hurt and anger over their short-lived marriage.

Rick's arms tingled. His heart wanted to jump. He finally held Windy Jordan right here in his own home. The home he shared with her in his dreams. As he searched her eyes he saw the reflection of years of hurt. He saw distrust there, a terrible thing for such pretty eyes to hold. He wanted to pull her tight, to tell her he would never hurt her, that she could trust him, always. Inside he quaked with the uncertainty of her acceptance. Outside he held his emotions just as his police training had taught him.

The music faded to a quiet halt but he didn't want to let go, wanted never to let go.

She pulled out of his arms and away from his visual embrace.

"Are you about ready to call it a night?" Windy asked Jenny who looked at her in surprise.

"No," Jenny answered.

Chapter Thirteen

Friday morning Windy drove to the Pregnancy office. She knew of three scheduled appointments that day and almost hoped for more. Before leaving for school this morning Jenny talked about last night and how much fun they had. Then Cora called for Windy to come down for tea and muffins and she had nothing but praise for her dancing partner. Thankful for the excuse, Windy left quickly for the office.

When she knew she wasn't on the work schedule at the store she had called Angie and volunteered for any appointments. Last night when the girls finally arrived home, the answering machine held Angie's message.

After hanging her coat in the hall closet Windy set about the office routine. She picked up the phone and stopped the call forwarding to Angie's house, then dialed Angie's number.

"Hi," she greeted the young woman whom she knew only from the volunteer meetings. "I'm here at the office, any additions since your message?"

"No, no more. You're early. The first appointment isn't until 11:30."

Windy looked at the clock. 10:05. "I know, I thought I'd work on stats."

"Great, I'm glad you like to do that, I'm no good with numbers."

They talked for a few minutes longer then Windy hung up. She inserted a video into the player. They no longer fast-forwarded since purchasing a new tape. This one started out with a well-known former TV actress and only lasted about 12 minutes. It was made specifically for offices like THE PREGNANCY CARING CENTER. Windy thought for a moment, trying to remember what Rick called the player. Video Tape Recorder. VTR instead of VCR for Video—what? Case, no Cassette that was it—Recorder. The girl shook her head as she stood. Letters, everyone substituted letters and you never knew what was really being said. Take PC for instance. It could mean Pregnancy Center or Private Corporation or Personal Computer. You just never knew. But numbers were different. Windy liked numbers and didn't really understand people like Angie who said they were 'no good at them'. What was there to be 'good' at? 1 meant one and 2 meant two and 12 meant twelve. No guess work there. Windy opened a drawer in the desk and pulled out a blank client form. She set it on top then walked down the hall to the bathroom where she placed a small plastic cup on the back of the toilet. She checked the drawer beside the sink and noted a new box of tests next to the opened one. One line meant Negative Pregnancy Test, Not Pregnant Today, No Precious Toddlers. Two lines meant Positive.

Windy stared in the mirror behind the sink at a woman who would never have two lines. She blinked back tears.

"My, my, we're emotional today, aren't we? Just how do you propose to help the women who walk through that door if you're a basket case? Get a grip, Windy!"

Back in the office Windy pulled out January's client forms and began comparing them to the daily shift reports, checking for discrepancies. She found a couple and made the necessary corrections according to the client forms.

Last fall Windy noticed the stats weren't being done. She remembered Jenny telling her on her first visit how they kept and compiled information. Shortly after that Jean had become director and she wasn't much on numbers either. Nor did her part time job afford her much time to spend in the office.

Windy took out a blank shift report and began recording data.

43 tests in January. 10 positive, 33 negative. Less than one third positive.

29 students. 5 high school. 9 local residents. About two-thirds students.

25 against abortion. 6 for abortion. 12 undecided. More than half against.

30 would carry. 3 would abort. 10 were undecided. Windy knew the undecided didn't always mean indecision about abortion, but often whether they should get married, continue school, or even consider adoption.

When the report was complete with age, race, birth control methods and previous abortions, if any, Windy stood up and stretched. She still had a few minutes before her first client. Out in the kitchen Windy put hot water on the stove for tea, then checked the refrigerator. It was common practice for the volunteers to bring goodies in and leave them for each other. Nothing sat in the fridge except a couple diet colas. Windy checked the Tupperware container in the cupboard and was rewarded with soft chocolate chip cookies.

The kettle whistled and Windy poured the steaming water over the tea bag. She swished it around then pulled a spoon out of the drawer. She opened the lid on the sugar bowl. A person could live here, she thought. I wonder if anyone has since it became the Caring Pregnancy Center?

She strained the black tea bag and put a spoonful of sugar in it as well as a small amount of powdered cream. Herbal tea only needed honey, but Windy couldn't handle regular tea without the trimmings.

With a plate of cookies in one hand and her tea in the other Windy returned to the office. She settled into the padded chair behind the desk and listened to the quiet of the house.

The hot liquid slid down her throat and into her belly. The sweet cookies tasted great on her tongue.

"Ahh, it doesn't get any better than this."

The front door opened and Windy's work began.

Windy replaced the phone and picked up her empty cup. She'd just agreed to stay after 4:00 to see a woman who worked until then.

The clock read 1:30 and Windy's next client should be here at 2. The first two were negative—one undecided, the other a resident who wanted to be pregnant. They had talked for quite awhile, the 34 year old woman explaining the many years and procedures she and her husband had gone through. And the heartache. After several years of marriage they decided to try adoption but that proved even more difficult then getting pregnant. They weren't 'well off', her husband had high risk health, and there just weren't enough babies available.

In the kitchen Windy contemplated another cup of tea but decided against it. She wandered from the kitchen into the hallway and moved up the stairs. Two of the four bedrooms contained beds; the other two were used for storage of baby clothes and furniture waiting to be lent to a needy mom. People were always donating baby clothes.

The bathroom sounded hollow with no rugs or linen, its white walls barren. Windy went back into the largest bedroom, pulled the sheer white curtain aside and looked out over the street. She sat on the bed, surprised at how comfortable the mattress felt.

"This could be a homey little room with new curtains and bedspread." She imagined this as her own place as compared to Jenny's living room. But soon the school year would end; Jenny would fly to Florida and marry the man of her dreams. Then Windy would once again have her old room back, the very one she had shared with Eddie.

To keep from dwelling on past hurts Windy went back down to the office and pulled open the file drawer. She had a few minutes to get started on last year's statistics. At every volunteer meeting for the past several months Jean apologized for not having gotten around to compiling stats. Windy decided to save the woman any more worry. Besides, she enjoyed this type of work.

Placing all of last years records on the desk, Windy sorted through them and pulled out January's client forms as well as daily shift reports.

Windy looked at the volunteers initials on the client form. WEM. Windy Elaine Michaels. This had been her first time in the office alone. Client's name—Diana Westfield. Windy remembered their meeting. Diana sat across from her, a lovely young woman with what seemed like a heart of ice. But Windy had been able to break through and as a result of that meeting Dr. Stephan Michaels now had a baby daughter. A daughter named after Stephan. A daughter who wore the clothes Windy made for their anticipated child. Strange how life takes twists and turns and lands it's riders in the most peculiar situations. It seemed only yesterday she had a husband named Eddie who drank too much and treated her roughly when he did. But today she was the reject of two husbands, one who preferred beer over her and another who preferred children. Windy looked at the date of Diana's form. May of last year. Last year she was WEM—Windy Elaine Michaels and Diana was Mark's pregnant girlfriend.

Suddenly an outlandish idea popped into Windy's mind. Maybe Mark would want her. After all, she would never disappoint him by getting pregnant and that was the reason he left Diana.

Windy shook her head, clearing it of any such thought. She had never met Mark, probably wouldn't like him if she did. What kind of man would insist his own child be killed? Certainly not the kind she wanted to marry. Not like Rick, who himself was adopted and stood where she did on the abortion issue, even though he didn't exactly know why. Yes, Rick would make a far better husband for her than someone like Mark. Mark would probably resist marriage all together as he had with Diana; where as Rick probably wouldn't even consider living with someone. And he would adopt if his wife couldn't bear children. Men were just as hard to figure out as life itself. Eddie feared the prospect of fatherhood so much that it drove him to violence. Stephen coveted it while Mark hated it. And Rick. Rick would be willing to adopt someone else's, what was Stephan's word?—bastard.

Windy closed her eyes and rotated her head as she drew a deep breath. How long had she been at this? Surely it must be close to her next appointment.

She opened her eyes and squinted at the small desk clock. 2:30. Already? Her 2 o'clock was officially a 'no show' and her next appointment wasn't due for an hour and a half.

Windy's stomach growled and she realized the tea and cookies just wouldn't sustain her much longer. She picked up the phone and dialed her favorite Pizza Shop number.

"Hi. I'd like to order a small Cavatini, please, and can it be delivered to 712 Lincoln?" The young woman at the other end of the phone line repeated Windy's order then asked for the address again, saying it after Windy as she obviously wrote it down. Then she asked for Windy's name and spelled it back to her out loud. "No, that's Windy with an I not an E.

78

Yes, W-I-N-D-Y." The girl once again repeated Windy's order and address along with the amount.

Windy hung up and smiled at the girl's thoroughness. "Better safe than sorry," she said returning to her pile of forms.

Chapter Fourteen

Rick couldn't help but overhear the waitress' conversation. So someone named Windy was at 712 Lincoln wanting cavatini. Could there be more than one Windy in a city this size? He quickly placed his order with the same confused waitress, asking for a cavatini so it would be ready at the same time as the other one. Then he found the payphone and looked in the yellow pages under 'pregnancy'. The listing confirmed his suspicion and his mental investigation narrowed. Could there be two Windys in this city who work at a pregnancy office? He quickly dialed Cora's number. The little lady answered and closed the case.

Rick opened his wallet, "I'm also supposed to pick up a cavatini for Windy," he told the cashier.

The man looked at another slip and said, "This is for delivery."

"Right, to 712 Lincoln, she didn't realize I was coming to pick it up." He handed the ten dollar bill to the man who rang up both tickets.

"Don't matter to me, as long as yer paying for it."

Rick carried the hot bag into the cold February air. Windy might not be too happy with him. She may not let him stay and eat lunch with her, but at least he'd get to see her, even if it was only long enough to have the door slammed in his face. She certainly was hard to figure out, one minute joining him in a flirting session, the next treating him like toxic waste. But it didn't matter, he'd take his chances.

Earlier in the day he'd considered sending her flowers since it was Valentine's Day, but feared Windy would think him too forward.

He pulled up in front of the large white house with the CARING PREGNANCY CENTER sign on the outside. At the door he started to knock, thought better of it and pushed the door open. "Delivery," he called seeing movement through an open door on his left.

"Come in," answered a familiar voice.

She sat behind a desk piled with papers, her head bent over an open purse. Her soft brown hair fell forward concealing the face Rick searched for, hiding the pretty brown eyes he wanted to look into. But the small form and dainty hands gave her away, this little creature was none other than his Windy. HIS Windy, he liked the sound of that!

Pulling a bill from her change purse she lifted her head and stared in surprise, noting the familiar bag he held out to her.

"Moonlighting?" She asked, not missing a beat.

"Just looking for a lunchoen date." Inwardly Rick cringed. He had such a knack for saying the wrong thing and putting her on the defensive.

"Look no farther, my friend, but let's go in the kitchen, I seem to have lost my desk." She led the smiling young man to the back of the house where Rick pulled a couple cans of cherry cola from another bag. Windy placed the hot aluminum containers on the table and retrieved two real forks from a drawer.

By now Rick had shared enough meals with Windy to know she prayed before she ate. He sat down and bowed his head, waiting. A short silence followed then she spoke, quietly asking a blessing on their food as well as their friendship.

They talked while they ate, Rick asked questions about the house and organization. Too soon the delicious cavatini was gone and Windy rose from the table.

"I have one more client coming in. She should be here anytime. Thanks for bringing my food over. Oh, how much do I owe you?"

"Your company has more than repaid me."

She thanked him without an argument then stood waiting. Rick felt she was giving him permission to leave.

"I'm in no hurry, just going home to an empty house. I'll," he looked around. "I'll clean up while you do whatever you do."

She stood, looking uncertain.

"You don't want me here, is that too awkward with a client coming in?" He asked.

"Well, yes, in a way. She has to come back here to…" she looked at the bathroom. Rick followed her gaze, not understanding and the awkward silence grew louder.

"I tell you what; you can wait in the living room." She turned and walked away, Rick didn't need to be told to follow her back into the hall and this time through the closed door opposite the open one. "I know it's cold in here, but I'll come in a few minutes and let you out." She started to leave. "Oh, there's some literature you might find interesting." She pointed to a coffee table burdened with books and brochures then closed the door behind her.

Rick sat on the cold couch and picked up a picture of a tiny discolored baby.

The student tested negative and they had a good long talk about school and goals and changing her lifestyle. She thanked Windy, smiled and shook her hand.

"I just might call you sometime," the girl said looking at Windy's number on the business card. "When temptation gets a little too strong."

"Anytime."

"Middle of the night?"

"ANY time," Windy assured her, walking her to the front door. When the cold air blasted her in the face Windy suddenly remembered Rick sitting in the unheated living room. He sat where she left him, on the couch, head bent over the coffee table. Books and pamphlets lay open on either side of him. She noted his faded blue jeans and the flannel shirt neatly tucked in, a dark turtleneck showed at his neck. He wore dark hiking boots. As many times as she had seen him lately she was still intrigued by his face. Seeing it now in profile she realized how imperfect it was though she couldn't say just why.

"I'm sorry I took so long," she apologized. "You must be freezing in here."

He looked up then and Windy could see in his eyes the tortured thoughts behind them.

He waved a pamphlet in the air. "I uh…um…"

"Pretty rough stuff, isn't it?"

He just nodded as he stood and joined her at the door.

"Oh," he said, turning quickly and placed the scattered material neatly back on the table. He hesitated over the pamphlet he had recently been holding.

"You can take that with you if you want," Windy offered.

"No." He answered. "Thank you, but I really don't want to."

Windy started to tell him those things don't go away just because you ignore them but caught herself. She remembered how long it took her to admit what she saw. God would deal with Rick in His own time just as He had her.

They closed the living room door behind them and slowly walked into the office.

"I have just a few things to put away," Windy explained, once she reached the desk and her unfinished paper work.

"I'll go clean up the kitchen then," Rick volunteered.

A few minutes later Windy joined him. She watched from the doorway as he opened first one drawer then another until he found a dish towel and dried the few things they had used. Windy noted the table and counter were cleaned and the trash bag sat by the back door, another already in its place in the basket.

"Thank you, Rick."

He looked up obviously too deep in thought to have noted her entrance.

"Sure, glad to, thanks for the company." He smiled, but Windy could still see the trouble in his eyes. She walked over to him.

"I'm sorry you were so disturbed by what you saw and read. I've gotten so used to it; I forget how it first affected me."

"Well, it's reality, and it doesn't go away just because we ignore it."

Windy smiled at his remark. "That's true," she agreed. "But as with all knowledge, we need to absorb it a little at a time until we understand what to do with it." She stood close to him, close enough to smell his after shave, close enough to notice the stubble on his clean shaven face, close enough to see the pain in his eyes from the knowledge he'd just acquired.

She wanted to put her arms around him, to comfort him and let him know it's okay to hurt.

Suddenly she remembered another look of hurt on the face of a doctor who couldn't save a baby's life. She remembered that first kiss, the first exchange of endearment. And she quickly turned away. *I'll not fall for that again.* She told herself.

"My, it's after five already," she exclaimed, maybe a little too loudly. "Cora will be wondering about me." She turned back to her guest. The distant smile on her face faded, he looked lost. He'd just spent almost an hour in a cold room, waiting for her, reading disturbing information and now faced going home to an empty house and his unsettled thoughts.

"Come home with me," she surprised herself by saying. "Cora will be delighted to be able to feed you, and it's Friday night, neither Jenny or I have work tomorrow," she rambled. "What about you?"

"Yeah," Rick nodded. "Afternoons." He pulled his Carhart off the back of a chair and shrugged into it.

Windy opened the back door and placed the garbage bag on the enclosed porch. She looked around then switched off the light. They silently walked back to the office where Rick held Windy's coat for her. She pulled a set of keys from her purse. Rick stood beside her as she locked the front door then followed her to her car and waited until it started.

"Meet you there," she said through the closed window.

Rick watched her drive away from inside his truck before he pulled away from the curb.

Chapter Fifteen

Rick revved his truck engine hoping to warm it quickly. The moon shone brightly into the cold cab. He'd enjoyed himself tonight. After Cora stuffed him with roast and potatoes, corn and homemade bread, she placed a piece of apple pie in front of him. Of course, he had protested, but not enough to deter the little lady, and no where near as much as his stomach protested now. His late lunch of cavatini fought for its rightful place in his full belly. He wanted to hurry home and drink a couple bottles of 'the pink stuff'.

After eating, Cora and her three guests had waddled into the living room where they engaged in small talk for most of the evening. Although Rick really didn't want to talk about what he had seen at Windy's office he found the conversation kept returning to the abortion issue and he was the one returning it. The faces of the aborted babies floated in his mind as they had floated on the papers, dismembered and bloody.

Finally Jenny had popped a rented video into the VCR and they watched an excellent movie of love and sacrifice after the civil war. The three ladies openly cried for the last 15 minutes of the movie as the hero prepared to die and the heroine fought so hard to keep him. Rick managed to refrain from emotion only by mentally distancing himself from the room, its occupants and the television. But the movie left an impression on him and as he sat in his cold truck rubbing his gloved hands together for warmth he thought of the movie compared to reality.

The pictures he'd seen earlier still clamored for his attention. Babies.

Defenseless babies ripped from their mother's womb because they were 'unwanted', 'unexpected', 'unplanned'. For the first time in his life Rick thought deeply of the woman who had given him birth. Certainly he had been all of those things, a glitch in the woman's life. Like the man in the movie, she had chosen self-sacrifice for the sake of others. Because of her mistake, Rick had life, his parents had a child they truly wanted and someday a child would look into Rick's eyes and call him 'Daddy'. The tears he had refused in Cora's living room swelled into his eyes. The muscles in his jaws tightened as though he had just bitten into a lemon. Rick wondered about that woman, and why she had chosen adoption. She could have kept him, raised him with a single parent. Was marriage to the father completely out of the question? Why? He wondered if there were any way he could say thank you, any way to let that woman know how much he appreciated her decision. Knowing those answers were probably lost to him forever, he tried to dismiss them.

He shifted the truck into gear and pulled away.

Rick woke up early and rolled over in his bed. He hadn't slept well, unable to go to sleep at first he then fell into a fitful slumber. He couldn't call what he felt nightmares; there were no dreams, just a restlessness, an emptiness. He wanted to talk to his dad, needed to talk to him. He didn't intend to ask a lot of questions just wanted to be near the man whom he had always relied on, always looked up to.

Despite the early hour, despite the fact that his dad would still be sleeping, Rick turned on the lamp and picked up the phone. Then he replaced it, deciding to just go over to see his dad. Rick turned off the light and huddled back under his warm covers. A sense of loneliness swept over him. He saw in the darkness a void in his life; a huge empty hole where nothing existed but fear and longing.

"Dad," he whispered. "Dad, I need you." His mind went back to the many times he'd called out to his dad and found him there, willing to teach, to help, and in later years just to listen.

As Rick's voice called out to his earthly father, his Heavenly Father stood by waiting eagerly for the day when Rick would call upon Him. But for now, He would give this child what he needed at the moment. Peace.

Sun splashed through the window and came to rest on the face of the sleeping young man. A sigh escaped his lips as he felt the warming rays. Then his lids popped open and gray eyes stared into the passing day.

"Oh, no!" Rick exclaimed as he threw back the covers and peered into his red faced alarm clock. 12:15, it informed him.

In just over half an hour the uniformed young man jumped into his truck. He headed straight to town and his parents home, hoping they would be there.

Valerie Notts answered the door, smiling. Her short brown hair framed her face and Rick looked for the lines around her eyes that grew deeper each time he saw her. He found them, but a new sparkle in those dark brown eyes caught his attention. He then realized the sparkle really wasn't new after all. He'd been seeing it for some time without actually seeing it. Instinctively he reached out and hugged his mother.

"Rick," the surprised woman greeted him. "Come on in. Is everything alright?"

"Sure." He said too quickly. "You look really good. New hairdo?" *This is your mom, dummy, not Windy. No need to stick your foot in your mouth for her.*

"No, son, same one I've had for years now."

"Where's Dad?" He asked quickly scanning the living room.

"You just missed him; he had a teacher's meeting this afternoon."

"I knew I should have set my alarm, I just didn't expect to fall back to sleep this morning." Rick noticed his mom's puzzled look. "I wanted to see him today, spend a little time with him."

"Oh, I'm sorry, dear. But come in, I was just about to have a bowl of chicken noodle soup. Will you join me before going to work?"

Rick's stomach growled its own answer and he had to admit his mom's home made soup sounded great. He followed her into the kitchen.

Sitting at the table where his family gathered brought comfort to him, even though he'd missed seeing his dad. His mom's concerned face watched him.

"What's on your mind, son?" She asked.

Rick took another helping of soup trying to decide if anything were actually wrong, when suddenly he realized it was his mom he needed to see all along.

"Where are the girls?" He asked.

"It's Saturday, your sisters are at the mall."

Rick laughed. "Well then, we don't have to concern ourselves with privacy, do we?"

Rick told his mom about the day before, not mentioning Windy's name, afraid that just admitting his interest in her, it might jinx any chance he had for a relationship. His mother's surprise was evident.

"You never told us you had a girlfriend."

"I don't really. She's someone I like, but I don't think she feels the same way." He didn't want to go into any details. Then he asked about the events surrounding his birth and adoption.

"I wondered when you would get around to that," she said. Placing her spoon on the table, Valerie folded her hands in front of her and leaned toward her son.

"After a couple years of marriage we learned we couldn't have children of our own. That was during the 'free love' era, but before abortion became legal. Homes for unwed mothers were common then. We contacted a couple of them, filled out reams of paper work, passed a home approval visit, all that business." Valerie took a sip of water.

"Then right after Christmas of '71 we received a call. A girl had applied for admission to one of the homes. She was due in late May and we had been approved as parents. The process was very different then. There were no 'open adoptions'. Birth mothers weren't allowed to see their babies, much less pick out the adoptive parents as they can now. Records were sealed. I know it's possible to work toward getting information, but I don't know how successful it is. Do you want to find out more, Rick?"

"I don't know. I'm not looking for a different mother. You are my mom, always will be; the same with dad. I guess I just want her to know that she did the right thing. Does that make sense?"

"Absolutely."

"Mom, last night, and…and this morning, I saw an emptiness in my life I never knew existed. But I felt it so clearly that I realized it's always been there I just didn't know. I guess I thought maybe that void represented my birth, but now I'm not so sure."

Valerie reached over and took her son's hand. She ran her soft fingers over the strong skin. She hesitated and Rick wondered if she knew more but didn't want to reveal it.

"Rick, I want to tell you something. I just want you to think about what I say and whether it pertains to how you feel." She took a deep breath and slowly let it out. "I have had a very satisfying life. I love my husband, something which I'm thankful for, as I meet more and more women who are unhappy in their marriages. I never gave birth to a baby, but I gave life and love to three great children. We've always been comfortable, not rich, but not lacking. Yet, about a year ago, I woke up empty one morning. I, too, felt a void. I chastised myself for feeling that way in the midst of plenty. The guilt I felt became worse than the emptiness and I knew there had to be an answer somewhere.

"I remembered going to Sunday School as a little girl. I loved it, loved the stories and the songs. Back then in school we said the pledge of allegiance, teachers read from the Bible. God was just accepted, He was part of everyday life. But as I grew older and became involved in school activities, friends, boyfriends, I forgot about God.

"One day while standing in line at the post office I met a woman named Margie. We just entered into a conversation to pass the time and the next thing I knew we were sitting at the Coffee Pot Cafe having coffee and she was asking me if I had accepted Christ as my Savior.

"I told her I believed in God but she said that wasn't enough. We parted as friends but kept in touch. She called every week just to talk and invite me to Bible study. Finally in July I just knew I was supposed to go. I started attending weekly and really enjoyed it. When Christmas came and I thought about Jesus coming to earth to save me… Rick, I knew I had to give my life to Him completely. I gave my life back to God, welcomed Him as my Lord. And I haven't felt empty since. I've been to church every Sunday and already feel welcome.

"Son," she rubbed the back of his hand with thumbs. "Life still has its ups and downs, but I know I'm now complete. I truly believe your emptiness comes from not knowing Christ as your Savior and if you let Him into your life, that void will be filled."

Chapter Sixteen

Valerie watched her son move down the walkway. He turned and waved as he jumped into his truck. She closed the door and returned to the kitchen where she took the bowls off the table and placed them into the dishwasher.

Should she have told Rick more? She pictured the gray eyes of her friend Connie. Thought of how they lit up every time Valerie talked of her son.

"Father, You know what I believe in my heart but have never confronted in my mind. Is Connie Rick's birth mother? Have You brought all of us together at this time in our lives? If she is his mother does she need to hear the words Rick just spoke to me? Does she need to be assured that her decision was the right one?"

Valerie walked into the living room and picked up her Bible, a Bible edited with women in mind. She looked on the page that suggested verses for various situations. After looking up a couple of the scriptures she still felt unsure.

"Lord, I don't expect Doug home for a while so I'm going to call Connie maybe she'll meet me for coffee. I don't know how to go about this or even if I should, so I'm leaving it in Your hands."

She dialed Connie's number half hoping for no answer.

Valerie looked through the window of the Coffee Pot Cafe, she saw Connie sitting at a table near the front. As she entered she watched the other woman, looking for tell-tale signs. The eyes were a sure give-a-way, but were there other things that she could associate with her son?

"Valerie, I'm so glad you called," Connie greeted her friend. "I suddenly felt lonely this afternoon and in need of some company. You called at the perfect time!"

Valerie sat down opposite her friend and nodded at the waitress who held up a coffee pot in question.

"Well, Doug is at a meeting and Rick had just left the house on his way to work, so I was looking at a lonely afternoon, too."

"Where are your girls?" Valerie watched Connie lift a cup to her lips and take a sip of the steaming liquid.

Okay, Valerie, stop it right now. Relax, enjoy your friend and stop examining her.

"At the mall with a few of their friends. I don't expect them home for several hours."

The women laughed together and Connie asked, "Were we like that as teenagers?"

"We were underprivileged as young women. We had stores, but very few malls."

The waitress sat a cup in front of Valerie and filled it with hot coffee. "Anything else?" she asked.

Valerie took a quick glance around the almost empty restaurant. "No we just want to rent your table for a while."

The girl smiled. "Sure, I'll let you know when we need it."

Small talk filled the first several minutes of their conversation but Valerie easily aimed their thoughts toward her family. She told Connie a couple of the cute but unusual things the girls had done when they first arrived from Korea. They laughed with sadness as they expressed how life would have been for those precious girls had they not been adopted and brought to the states.

"I love my children so much, I wouldn't trade them for the world, but I must admit I've often wondered what a child born to Doug and I would have looked like, acted like. Not that I don't see ourselves in our kids. They have picked up so much from us. But you know, sometimes you can look at a person and see their parents, like young Molly Packard. She's so like Missy. Same walk, same mannerisms. And their boy, David, just like his dad. Even as a boy you can see Wil's gentleness, he's slow, easy, oh what's the word I want?"

"Calm," Connie supplied with a knowing nod.

"Calm. Yes that's it. If calm had a physical body, it would be Wil."

"Yes, and look at Margie's daughter. She looks just like her, no mistaking their relationship. But she's not timid like Margie."

"We've been friends for a while now, Connie," Valerie ventured. "But I really know little about you. Do you have any children?"

"I've never married. And I know I've missed so much. I would love to have a daughter. To fix her hair and dress her in lace and bows."

"They only stand for that when they're little. My girls have straight black hair that resisted anything I tried to do with it. Now they wear it long, over baggy shirts and tight jeans."

"Not that much has really changed then, as a teenager I had long straight hair, confiscated all my dad's shirts and wore tight hip-huggers."

"Well, that dates me. I was more the pedal pushers and bobby socks generation."

"But still sixties not fifties?"

"Yes, you know. I had my first pair of bell-bottoms in '66. Most people don't remember the outrageous clothes didn't come in until then."

The women's laughter died down as they both looked into empty cups, smiling at days gone by. Valerie caught the waitress's attention and lifted her cup.

"Valerie, can I ask a personal question?"

Okay, Lord, here it comes. I'm following Your lead.

"Of course." She watched the girl pour coffee into the two mugs then looked at her friend.

"What's it like having adopted children? Have they ever expressed an interest in their real parents?"

"We are their real parents."

"Oh, I'm sorry, I didn't mean to…"

"Don't worry," Valarie touched her friend's hand. "I know it's just a convenient phrase. The girls have never asked, I sometimes think Tari would like to remember a little of her childhood and Tami only wants to forget. She was 4 when they came to us, Tari was only a year and a half.

Tami's not sure what she really remembers, it's more fear and feelings, than people and surroundings. Rick came to us as a baby, a beautiful baby. Our first, he brought us such happiness. Rick recently asked about the adoption, not so much about who his parents might have been. He just said it would be nice to be able to say thank you to the brave woman who gave him life. Rick feels as Doug and I do. We're so grateful to that young woman."

The words began to flow and Valerie kept them coming. "Rick loves his dad. Doug isn't too demonstrative with his feelings, but he's always let Rick know he loves him and he's proud of him. Rick may walk like another man," she hesitated slightly, "he may have another woman's eyes, but he's our son."

A look of knowing passed between the two women in the soft silence that followed. Each woman sat with her own thoughts, her questions of whether the truth was in order at this time. They both knew the words said in the next few minutes could very well change the lives of people they both loved. Connie broke the silence.

"I know a woman who once gave her child up for adoption. She would have been pleased to know her child was happy about her decision." Valerie heard the words behind the statement, knew Connie wanted her to keep talking. "She would certainly be pleased to know she was considered brave."

"I know of few others words to describe such a woman." Valerie reassured her quickly.

After a few more drinks of coffee Connie continued the questions. "Have you ever worried about his birth mother coming back?"

"It terrified me at first. I jumped every time the phone rang. It only took one moment to fall in love with our little boy and the thought of losing him..." she shook her head. "But adoption was so different then. His birth mother didn't know who we were. I soon felt peace about the whole situation. God was working in my life, long before I even knew it." Valerie waited for the waitress to fill their cups yet another time. "I believed Rick's birth mom loved him enough to want the best for him and I just couldn't imagine her coming back into his life and upsetting it so. But now, now that he's grown, I wouldn't mind her knowing what a wonderful young man he's turned out to be. I'm proud of him, maybe more than what's good for me. But I think I would welcome his birth mother."

"Welcome the presence of another woman?"

"When she decided to release Rick she placed her confidence in an unknown couple to raise her child. I would want her to know her confidence was not misplaced."

"But how would you welcome her? As the woman who gave Rick up, or as the woman who gave him birth?"

Valerie hesitated for a moment. She hadn't thought of that. *If Connie is Rick's birth mother, am I really willing to share him?*

She answered slowly, measuring each word for truth, believing this was no longer speculation, but that she would have to live by what she said.

"I would welcome her as family. Rick is our son. But from the moment of conception he was part of her."

"And when he marries, and has children, could you share them with another 'grandmother'."

Valerie looked intently at Connie and saw her answer in the longing that poured from the other woman's eyes.

"I'll already be sharing them with another grandmother, their mom's mom. The more Grammas, the happier they'll be. And if Rick's birthmother released her only child for adoption she may never know the joy of grandchildren. Doug and I adopted because we were unable to have a child of our own. We felt empty, maybe even ununited. How could I ask another woman to feel that emptiness she saved me from?"

At this, Connie's chin quivered and though she held her eyes tightly closed her tears slipped down her cheeks. Valerie reached across the table and held the hands of her friend, her son's birth mom.

Chapter Seventeen

Rick sat behind the wheel of the patrol car, guiding it down one unseen street after another.

"Where are you boy? Gone fishing?" Joe asked, receiving no answer. "Rick!" he yelled.

His dazed partner glanced at him, then back at the windshield. Joe doubted that he'd penetrated the young man's thoughts. "Pull over." The car continued forward. "Rick, pull over. Now!" Joe reached out and slapped his partner's shoulder. "Pull over, now." He repeated in his most commanding voice.

"Huh?" Rick finally heard Joe's voice if not his words. Joe repeated his command and Rick steered the car to the curb. "What's wrong?" he asked, shifting to park.

"I'm drivin'" Joe said as he slid from the car. He opened Rick's door. "Out," he ordered.

Rick obeyed with a frown then walked around the car and took the seat Joe had vacated. "What is your problem?" he asked.

"My partner." Joe informed him. "I suppose your thinking about your little friend? Better get your mind back on your work and save her for your spare time."

The confused young man looked at the driver. "Who?"

"That sweet thing you can't take your mind off of."

"My mom?"

"Yeah, right. You're thinking about your mom, and I was born yesterday."

"Yeah," Rick agreed. "We had quite a talk before I came to work. I think she knows more than she's telling me."

"They always do. Or so they think."

"Moms?"

"What are you talking about?"

"My mom. What are you talking about?"

Joe shook his head. "Suppose we start from the beginning. You had a talk with your mom today. What about?"

"My mom."

"Is she sick or something?"

"How would I know? I don't even know who she is."

"Okay, that's it." Joe parked the car and turned to his partner. "Look, either go home and sleep this off or start making sense."

Rick took a deep breath then pushed it out. "My mom and I talked today…about me…and my birth mom…and God."

"So which does she know more about that she's not telling you?"

"I don't know. Maybe she had some kind of contact a long time ago. And she's just not sure I'm ready to hear about it."

"Contact with who, your birth mom or God?"

"Man, Joe, I wish you'd make sense, you're really confusing me."

Joe's eyes narrowed. "And you are sorely trying my patience. Look, it's Saturday night. Things are going to get crazy in this city in a couple hours. I need a partner. Are you it or not?"

"What do you think about God, Joe?"

"Oh, for Pete's sake!" He threw the car into gear and stomped on the gas but immediately let up. He didn't understand his own anger, his impatience. Rick obviously had something important weighing on his mind. Joe pushed his own thoughts into a little closet made just for that purpose and gave his attention to his friend.

"God is okay. God is nice. Sometimes he's really helpful to have around. He…he brings comfort to some people. Your mom knows God, does she?"

"She says He filled a void in her life. And I've noticed a difference in her the last couple months. She's always been happy, always cheering other people up. But it's more than that. She has this…glow, this sparkle in her eyes." The young man appeared to drift again and Joe didn't want that.

"And she says God did it?"

"Yeah, sort of. Do you go to church, Joe?"

"Used to; when me and Andrea were still together. But when she left and took my girls, well, I just couldn't go back and sit there without them."

He remembered those Sunday mornings sitting next to his wife, trying to understand what the minister talked about. He would watch his three, beautiful little girls and shush them when their giggling became too loud.

He thought of the colored pictures they would bring home to be stuck on the fridge until a school paper took their place.

He'd even bought a Bible once; saw it at a flea market; of all places. It was tattered, the binding loose. Its previous owner had underlined almost half of it and most of the margins held notes and self searching questions. He tried reading it, but could never get past the book with all the laws and sacrifices in it. Joe was a hunter and a fisherman; he gutted, cut up and packaged his deer, cleaned and fried the fish. But he still didn't care to read about it. At first he'd carried the Bible to church but the minister rarely quoted from it and only a couple other people carried Bibles. So he stuck it in a drawer until the time came for him to leave. When he packed his stuff, he included the old book. Now it lay on the dresser in the extra bedroom. That way he could show God that the Bible wasn't stuck away some where, but he still didn't have it staring at him, reminding him of days when he was part of a family.

"Joe!" Rick cuffed his partner on the shoulder. "Now who's doing the daydreaming?" He accused.

"Huh?"

"I said, 'where did you go to church?'"

"Over on the east side. Andrea picked it because many of the city's elite attended there; doctors, lawyers and such. They have a kind of ongoing competition with the Community Church, to see who can attract the best known names."

"I don't know where Mom's been going to church. I guess I'll ask her. Why don't we go together sometime?"

"Naw, that ain't for me anymore. That part of my life is far behind me, but, hey, church can be a good thing and if your folks are going, you should go with."

"You really think so?"

"Can't hurt." Joe shrugged. *Or could it?* He wondered. Going to church hadn't kept Andrea from leaving him. It never made either of them 'glow' or added sparkle to their eyes. He looked at his young partner. Would Rick be hurt by the lure of worshipping someone who might exist, but who certainly didn't care about you? Should he warn the boy of the dangers in believing, in faithfulness and trust or was that just another lesson Rick had to learn on his own?

The alarm clock, set for 8 AM, woke Rick up and he wondered why he had set it so early on a Sunday morning. Then he remembered he planned to call his mom before she left and ask about going to church with her. Now he hesitated. Would she think of it as a commitment, expecting him to go every week-end? He pictured her dear face as she sat across from him at the table yesterday. No, not his mom. For years she'd been letting him make his own decisions. She wouldn't change that now.

He picked up the phone and dialed the number. His dad answered.

"I'm sorry I woke you, Dad," he apologized. "I wanted to talk to mom, is she up?"

"Yes, she is, but you didn't wake me," his dad replied. "Mom's in the shower, can I help you?"

"Maybe you can. What church does Mom go to?"

"You thinking about going?"

"Yeah, I was thinking about it."

"Good. Then I won't feel so out of place."

"You're going?" Rick tried not to sound too surprised. He'd never known his dad to go to church. When asked his opinion of church or God, Doug Notts always said he didn't have one, didn't need one.

"Why else would I be up on a Sunday morning. So your mom got to you, too?"

Rick almost admitted it was more like he got to her, but remembered this was Dad on the other end of the line.

"Yeah, I guess you could say that."

"Good, we'll see you there."

"Dad!?" The line went dead. *Boy, Dad must really be upset about this church thing.* Rick stood and stretched, he'd give Dad a couple minutes to realize he hadn't answered Rick's question. He brushed his teeth and dropped the bath mat into the tub. Then he picked up the phone and hit redial. His mom's sweet voice answered.

Rick repeated his question, received the name of the church and easy directions.

"So," he said, his curiosity growing. "You talked Dad into going with you?"

"Actually, he rather invited himself," she said. "Last week he commented on how much I smile on Sunday afternoons and asked what made me so happy; so I told him. He said he might come with me and see what those 'Bible thumpers' were up to. I forgot about it until last night when he asked me what time I get up. He wanted to make certain we had time for all of us to shower."

"All of you? Are the girls going, too?"

"They met some of the kids in the youth group last week at the mall and were invited to a meeting. They really enjoyed it and told the kids they'd see them today."

"So, the whole family's getting religion."

"You never know. Listen, I've got to run, but we're just going to morning service, not Sunday school, so we'll be there about 10:45."

"Okay, see you then." Rick looked at the clock as he replaced the phone. 10:45 was still two hours away. It would only take him about half an hour to get ready. He thought about calling Joe and asking him out to breakfast, but he could just hear Joe's response to being awakened on a Sunday morning.

Chapter Eighteen

"Windy, I need to see you for a moment," Janice touched Windy's arm as she was about to enter the sanctuary. "You know that Jenny is my assistant teacher and, well, with her leaving to get married and all, I thought maybe you'd consider being my assistant."

"Me?" Windy asked. "Why me?"

Janice suddenly looked as though she would bolt away at any minute. Windy knew Janice just from church. She was married and had two young children and taught one of the younger classes. When Janice interacted with the kids she seemed so at ease. But around adults, Janice usually froze.

"I'm sorry," Windy grasped the woman's hand. "Tell me what I'd have to do and I'll think about it."

Relief grew a smile on Janice's face. "Not much really. An assistant is just kind of around when you're not. Like when I go on vacation or maybe if one of my kids is sick and I can't come, which doesn't happen very often."

Windy knew that was true. As an assistant, Jenny had rarely been called upon.

"Janice, let me pray about it, alright? It's good that you're asking this early though, it gives me time to think it over."

Janice was all smiles as she left to find her husband who had two children crawling on him. Windy thought they must be the perfect family. As she stood watching a familiar voice sounded behind her.

"Windy, I'd like you to meet my family."

Windy turned and smiled at Valerie, trying to think of her last name. She remembered meeting Valerie and her husband at Mary's New Year's Party and thought it would be nice to greet him by name and make him feel more welcome.

Then her eyes meet a set of lovely gray eyes, smiling at her. She smiled back and moved her attention to Valerie.

"This is my husband, Doug." Valerie indicated the tall dark haired man beside her.

Windy reached for his hand. "We met at Andrew's party, though I'm sure you don't remember," she said.

"Indeed I do," he took her hand and shook it. "Seems you were attached to some big blond guy at the time."

"Jenny's fiancé," she spoke up quickly looking back at Rick. "Scott Bradley, you remember him."

"You know this pretty young lady, Rick?" His dad asked.

"Yes, I do, we do. I mean Joe… Yes. I do."

Valerie smiled at her son.

"And these are our daughters, Tami and Tari."

Windy shook hands with each of them. Hadn't Rick talked about two adopted sisters? Oh, yes, when she sat in his truck accusing him of, of what?

"Shall we go in?" Windy asked. Doug started to follow her but Valerie placed her hand on his arm, allowing Rick to go first, then she motioned for the girls to follow.

Like a lost puppy, Rick followed Windy into the pew and sat down beside her, his family eased in next to him, taking up the rest of the space and pushing Rick tight against Windy. For a moment she considered moving to the empty pew in front of them but thought that might be rude. She glanced around the people to her right and looked at Valerie just as the other woman leaned forward to look at her. A smile spread across Valerie's face. Windy started to return her smile when she realized Valerie looked not at her, but Rick who also leaned forward looking at his mom. He sat back quickly, a red glow moving from his collar and tie up into his clean shaven cheeks. Windy eased back into the little bit of room left for her and opened her bulletin, pretending to look at it. She could feel Rick's arm against hers, his hip against hers, his leg against hers. She breathed deeply, trying to keep her composure but the action summoned his after shave closer for a better smell. She caught the familiar scent and remembered it from the day at the office, when they shared a late lunch and she'd wanted to comfort him after leaving him with the pictures. Was that only two days ago?

Windy took another deep breath, this time through her mouth, trying to avoid that heady smell. With her lungs inflated, her arm pushed into Rick's and she quickly let her breath out, trying to make herself smaller.

She leaned forward and placed her purse on the floor since she couldn't set it beside her. Her Bible she left in her lap.

"Shall we stand and turn to number 43, What a Mighty God We Serve." Some one said from the pulpit. Windy looked up, surprised that Margie wasn't song leader today.

Placing her Bible on the seat she vacated, Windy pulled a hymnal from the rack in front of her. Rick reached for its mate but one of his sisters grabbed it before he had a chance. He cleared his throat and spied the rack in the seat in front of them. Reaching over the pew he pulled an unused hymnal from its place and dislodged the one beside it, sending it to a crashing death on the uncarpeted floor. In trying to catch it he lost the one he held and executed it beside its twin.

Windy cleared her throat and moved her hymnal toward him. "We can share," she whispered as she joined the congregation on the chorus. Rick quickly picked up the tune and Windy listened to his smooth voice. She knew little about music, couldn't tell a tenor from a bass, but she knew quality when she heard it. Throughout the song, the girl sang the words from habit as she concentrated on the sound flowing from the young man next to her. He held his side of the hymnal and Windy noticed how the book stayed even, not raised on one side as it would have been if Rick were much taller then her.

The song rolled to a halt. Rick took the book from Windy to set it back in the rack, just as she reached behind her to pick up her Bible. A loud thunk echoed through the sanctuary as their heads collided in mid-bend.

They both drew their breath in, stifling the 'ouch' they wanted to say, but knowing it would draw still more attention to their situation.

Windy saw this as her opportunity to move into the next pew, using the fallen books as a good reason. But before she could move, Rick whispered.

"Why don't we sit up there? It'll give us a little more room and me a chance to redeem myself."

Windy nodded and scooted around the bench, aware that everyone else had sat down and the whole congregation watched their progress. Rick slipped in beside her and quickly revived the dead hymnals.

Windy moved over so none of her touched any of Rick; she didn't need another bumping episode. She said a quick prayer asking God to keep them graceful until the service ended.

Will stood up behind the pulpit, welcoming everyone including the visiting minister. Half way through his greeting, an older man and woman slowly moved into Windy's pew. The woman pushed a walker in front of her and when she settled in, moved the walker between her and Windy, causing Windy to back up slightly, but just enough to make contact with Rick. He shifted to accommodate her movement and Windy sighed with relief. She then moved to see the pulpit better, turning slightly away from Rick.

They stood for another song, and managed to get through the prayer and offering without any more incidents.

Rick took a measure of comfort in seeing his friend standing up front. Wil smiled and nodded to him. Soon the preacher stood. Rick watched Windy thumb through her Bible. She stopped and turned slightly toward Rick, her finger indicating where the preacher said he would read.

He felt a shiver move through the girl. She quickly pulled a Kleenex from her purse and dabbed her eyes. Rick swallowed, hoping this wasn't one of those TV type churches where people got all emotional and jumped around, yelling '*Praise the Lord*' and '*Halleluiah*'. He glanced back at his mother and saw her looking at her Bible. He caught his dad's eye as the older man pulled the tie away from his neck and swallowed. Seeing his dad in this situation brought a smile to Rick's face. He knew exactly what was going through his dad's mind.

Windy leaned toward him a little and whispered.

"This is a beautiful scripture."

Rick looked down and watched the delicate finger point out the lines.

'Like a shepherd He will tend His flock, in His arms He will gather the lambs, and carry them in His bosom; He will gently lead the nursing ewes.'

'Who has measured the waters in the hollow of His hand, and marked off the Heavens by the span, and calculated the dust of the earth by the measure, and weighed the mountains in a balance, and the hills in a pair of scales?'

None of it made sense to Rick. He read the words over again, then noticed some were underlined and in the margin of her Bible, Windy had written something. *New Year's Eve.*

He remembered that night, would never forget it. But what did it mean to Windy? Why had she written it in this particular place? He studied the small face that looked up at the preacher, attentive to his every word. Who was this little creature sitting next to him? He knew some facts, even some trivia. But he didn't know her. Did she always write in her Bible? What did she write? What did she pray about? Had she ever prayed about him? Did she go to church with the Doctor or had she gotten religious after their divorce? And what was this preacher saying that deserved her close attention?

Rick closed his eyes and drew in a breath. She smelled good, like…hummm. Like candy, sweet but not sugary. He drew another breath, trying to capture that smell. It was familiar, but elusive. Like his mom's kitchen, like ice cream. He breathed again. What was that smell? He eased himself a little closer, his shoulder bumped hers and she jumped.

"Sorry," he whispered, determined now to discipline himself and listen to the preacher. He managed to hear a few sentences before his mind wandered and he found himself studying the rafters of the building and the two large ceiling fans that pushed the heat back down toward the people.

'Okay Rick,' he chided himself. *'What's the sense of coming here if you're not going to figure out what's happening?'* Once again he caught a couple sentences

but without context he had no idea what the preacher talked about. He turned so he could see his parents and his arm naturally moved to the back of the seat. His mom caught the movement and smiled at him, a distracted smile meaning she too, listened to the words of the preacher. His dad sat studying the rafters before his gaze moved to the fans. Rick chuckled to himself.

Then he realized his arm was draped behind Windy. His attention moved back to her. His hand lay just inches from her head. She looked down at her Bible and when she lifted her gaze, her hair brushed against his skin.

He imagined caressing the silken brown strands, running his fingers through her hair, pulling that head close to his own, brushing a kiss across her forehead.

He shook the vision from his mind and looked straight at the preacher, determined to stop those thoughts before they got him into trouble.

Windy shifted her weight, crossing her legs left over right, and settled back toward him a fraction of an inch. He looked at the flowered material that covered her legs. His gaze moved up the dress she wore to the lacy collar around her neck. He'd never seen her in a dress. His eyes wandered down the covered arms to the dainty hands that rested on her open Bible.

God, she beautiful. The thought startled him. Had he just prayed?

Chapter Nineteen

"Windy, would you join us for dinner?" Valerie asked. They stood in the middle isle, ready to move toward the back of the church.

Windy hesitated, remembering her desire to know Valerie better, but not sure if she wanted to spend an afternoon at her home, especially if her son were there.

"I don't know," she replied. "Cora usually has dinner in the oven and..." Her eye caught a movement and she looked across the sanctuary. Cora stood waving her handkerchief, trying to get Windy's attention.

"Don't forget," Cora called over the pews. "I'm going to my nephew's today."

Oh great, Windy thought, she'd almost forgotten about Cora being gone. *It had to be today, didn't it?* She nodded to Cora and looked back at Valerie. The woman just waited, obviously not pushing.

"Let me check with Jenny and see if she had anything planed. With Cora gone, Jenny may be counting on my company."

Windy noticed a moment's hesitation before Valerie offered. "She's welcome to come, too"

"I'll tell her." Windy moved away quickly before Rick could escape Wil's handshake. She found Jenny talking to Janice and waited until they finished their conversation before telling her about Valerie's invitation.

Jenny thought for a moment.

"Cora's going to her nephew's, right?" Jenny asked.

Windy nodded. "If you had plans for us, it's quite alright. I know that we don't have all that much time left to spend together before you leave."

Jenny looked at her curiously. "Well, only about four months, and we see each other every day." Jenny stood silent, looking from Windy to Valerie, her gaze shifted to the young man beside her. "Isn't that your police man?"

"He's not mine," Windy quickly defended herself. "But yes, it's Rick. Doug and Valerie are his parents."

Again Jenny remained silent and Windy knew she was piecing the puzzle together. "Valerie said her kids were adopted…Rick said he and his Korean sisters…" Jenny mumbled to herself.

Windy grew impatient, but knew better than to interrupt. Then Jenny looked back at her and Windy could still see her friend's brain working behind her perceptive eyes.

"Do you want to go?" Jenny asked, not one to mince words.

"I don't know," Windy stammered. She had never admitted her attraction for Rick to herself, much less to Jenny. But Jenny already knew, and Windy knew she knew.

Jenny breathed deeply, looking from Windy to Rick. Windy understood the hesitation. Jenny was praying. Jenny always prayed, about everything. Right now she was probably praying for God's will in Windy's life. Windy knew the exact thoughts filling Jenny's mind. Jenny liked Rick, but didn't want Windy getting involved with a man who wasn't a Christian. She also thought Windy needed more time to develop her faith and relationship with the Lord before handing her life over to another man. Windy knew what Jenny prayed. She was curious to hear God's answer.

"Okay," Jenny said. "We'll go."

Windy realized Jenny saw this as an opportunity to scrutinize Rick in the family setting, see if he shared his mother's faith.

Windy smiled. *Poor Rick, you don't know what your mother has just gotten you into.*

Valerie placed Windy across the table from Rick, with Jenny at her right. Doug sat on the end between Windy and Rick; Valerie sat at the other end, enjoying a conversation with Jenny. The sisters sat across from

Jenny. At first Windy felt relieved not to be seated right next to Rick where they could accidentally brush elbows. But it didn't take long to realize that might have been safer.

Rick had lost the suit coat he wore as soon as they all walked in the door. The tie went next then he rolled up his sleeves and let out a sigh. Windy noticed the elder Notts had done the same thing.

Now he sat in front of her, white shirt open at the collar, strong hands holding his fork. His arms were visible half way up to the elbows. He'd shaved that morning and his face looked just a little blotchy from the razor. Windy found herself imagining him shaving his face with the razor blades he'd bought from her. His sandy-brown, close-cropped hair didn't even come near his ears. But the longer part on top that was supposed to be combed back kept falling over his forehead.

Friday he'd looked like a lumberjack, okay, a short lumberjack. In his uniform he possessed dignity and authority, but today, today he looked like a little boy. He caught her studying him and smiled. She looked down but felt the redness creeping up her throat, toward her cheeks. And every time she looked up she saw him.

Saw him smile at some remark his youngest sister made. Tari appeared to be the comedian of the family although each of the Notts had an admirable sense of humor. Rick even showed his when he relaxed enough to be natural.

Windy saw him blush at his mother's praise; which seemed to be Valerie's role in the family, praising her husband and children.

Windy watched him slop gravy on his white shirt and spill water on his mom's good table cloth. Doug questioned Rick's sudden clumsiness.

"I couldn't help but notice your wrestling match with those heavy-weight hymnals," Doug commented. Tami snickered and Tari laughed suddenly, spewing lettuce dangerously close to her mother's plate.

"I really enjoyed the guest speaker," Jenny appeared to rescue Rick. "What did you think, Val?"

"Excellent. I followed everything he said. He really made the truth plain, even for those who aren't familiar with the Bible. What did you think, Doug?" Doug was caught in mid-bite; he quickly shoveled his fork into his mouth then made exaggerated motions about his mouth being full.

"How 'bout you, Rick," Jenny asked innocently. "Anything catch your interest today? The sermon, the songs?"

Again the color began to spread and Windy wondered if there was anything that didn't embarrass this poor guy.

"The uhh…uhh," Rick stammered. Tami snickered. "Yes! Um…the um…, his voice." Tari laughed and Valerie covered her plate. "Nice voice. I could, um…, I heard it. Plainly."

Doug jumped in. "He's right; the acoustics in that place are great for as old a building as it is. Did you notice those fans, sons? Good fans. Great ventilation."

Rick caught his dad's leading and took off with it.

"Really great fans. And those rafters, did you see them? What do you think? Hard wood or pine?"

"Definitely pine. You didn't see the knots in the boards?"

"Now that you mention it, I did. I agree, pine."

Windy admitted to herself that she liked what she saw.

"That woman ought to be a detective," Rick told the mirror in his old room, on the second floor of his parents' home. He finished tucking in his uniform shirt and straightened his tie, adding the official city police tie clip. He'd brought his uniform this morning so he could change and go straight to work at three o'clock.

"Why did she ask mom all those questions about her faith and her thoughts on the sermon?" He asked the reflection. "I'll tell you why, she's checking you out, buddy, making certain you're good enough for her helpless, little friend. Poor Windy knew it, too. And so did, Mom." Rick shook his head in defeat. "Moms, they know everything."

He dropped his rear end onto the bed and stuffed his foot into a shoe, pulled it back out and stuffed it into the other shoe. He reached down to tie the laces.

"What does she think I'm gonna do? Treat Windy like that arrogant Dr. Michaels did? Yell at her for hitting a volleyball the wrong way? Doesn't she know Windy is more important to me than that? Does she know how long I've waited to hear Windy say my name?" Rick sat up and cocked his head to the side. "No, she doesn't. How could she? Jenny's doing just what she feels she should be, protecting Windy. Hummmm. Guess she cares enough to ruffle a few feathers; even the feathers of a guy who carries a gun." Now he laughed at his silliness. "Got to admit, the lady has courage."

Rick stood and pulled his gun belt around his waist, adjusting it. He picked up his suit from the bed and arranged it on a hanger which he hung on the back of the closet door. Maybe next week he'd just come here on Saturday night and stay. He smiled. Guess that meant he intended to go to church again next Sunday. And why shouldn't he? Windy would be there, he'd have yet another opportunity to show her what a clumsy boob he could be.

If you're going to church just to see Windy, don't bother.

Rick spun around. "Who said that?" No one answered. No one was there. "Great. I'm talking to myself and myself is starting to answer."

He moved toward the door as the statement he'd just heard struck him again. He quickly defended himself. "I didn't go today for that reason, did I? I didn't even know she'd be there."

A knock sounded on the door and Valerie Notts voice followed it.

"Rick, you're going to be late." Rick opened the door. "Who were you talking to?"

"God," He answered. As soon as the word left his mouth he knew he spoke the truth. He placed his arms around his mom and pulled her into an embrace. "And I have a feeling it's going to be the first of many such conversations."

Valerie laughed, her eyes lighting up as she beheld her son. "Well, the next time you talk, tell Him I said 'thank you'."

They walked down the stairs laughing and rounded the corner into the kitchen where four women chatted as they washed dishes. Windy stood in front of the sink, her dress sleeves pushed up and her hands covered with soap suds. She looked up at him. Several strands of hair had pulled away from the little bun thing she'd wrapped her locks into. Sweat from the heat of the dish water beaded on her forehead. She smiled and Rick felt love shoot through him harder and faster than any bullet ever could. He wanted to rush over to her and take her in his arms. He wanted to kiss every strand of hair, every freckle, every drop of sweat. If Rick Notts had any doubts about his love for this woman they vanished in that one second of realization.

He caught himself and cleared his throat. "I see you've taken over my job, Windy." He thought he should say something to the other workers, but she was the only one he could see at the moment. The only one he wanted to speak to.

Windy just continued to smile and he hoped she'd been struck in the same way he had, taking away her ability to speak. Jenny brushed past him on her way to the table to retrieve more dirty dishes at the same moment Tami drew Windy's attention.

"Jenny," Rick said as quietly as he could. She looked up at him. "I know what you're doing." He said. Once again he was the self-assured police officer, in charge of the situation.

Funny, he thought, *how can I be this calm and sure around the beautiful Jenny, but lose it when I'm near Windy?*

Jenny lifted her eyebrows in feigned innocence.

"And I approve. As a matter of fact, I'm grateful. I want to protect her just as much as you do."

The woman stared at him for a moment, her deep blue eyes piercing his gray ones. Then she smiled, and he knew he would soon have an ally. He decided to summon his courage and make his first real 'move'. He walked over to the sink and placed his hand on Windy's back.

"Walk with me to the truck?"

Without an answer, Windy rinsed her hands and dried them on a dishtowel. They moved through the kitchen, Rick's hand still on her back, every eye in the room on them. Jenny caught Rick's attention and raised her eyebrow. But he didn't back off. He was staking his territory. And Jenny needed to learn right now who was included in it.

Chapter Twenty

Windy watched the black pickup drive away. She pulled her coat closer to her and shivered. She hadn't noticed the cold minutes ago when Rick stood close to her in his creaking leather jacket, his eyes looking into hers, his breath touching her cheek, his smell robbing her of her senses.

She'd hardly said a word to him all afternoon, just kept staring at him sitting across the table from her.

But what really knocked the wind of out the girl was when she turned from the sink and saw Rick standing in the doorway, decked out in his uniform. Hat in hand, gun strapped to his side. She'd never experienced anything like she did then. Not with Eddie, certainly not with Stephan.

He'd spoken to her and she couldn't answer; couldn't make her brain work, much less her mouth. She just stared at him. Then he moved toward her and the room ceased to exist. All she could see was Rick moving closer, darkness all around him. She'd thought for a moment she might pass out. She could still feel his hand on her back; hear his words and the invitation in his eyes.

Windy knew in her heart she accepted more than just an invitation to say good-bye at his truck but she could not have refused if her life depended on it.

They made small talk, mostly about the dinner and his mom's cooking. Then Rick looked at his watch and said he'd probably be late. She thought he was going to kiss her. She felt the movement of his body leaning toward hers; heard his intake of breath and his eyes closed for a moment.

Then he smiled and touched his fingers to her cheek. She'd waited, unaware that she held her breath, willing him to put his arms around her and let her lose herself in his embrace.

He asked for permission to call her and quickly outlined his work schedule. Windy mumbled something about opening everyday except Tuesday or Wednesday, always with Sundays off.

So with no other promise than a phone call, he left.

Windy wandered back to the door, uncomfortable with entering a house she'd only been in that day. She hesitated, debating whether she should knock. A harsh wind almost blew her off the porch and she quickly opened the door and stepped inside. Valerie greeted her.

"You girls aren't in a hurry to leave are you?"

"Well, I don't know." She honestly didn't. For Windy the day had just ended. She couldn't see past the man sitting across the table and now that he was gone so was her day. She tried to focus. What was today? Oh yes, Sunday of course. What happened on Sundays? Church; over with. Dinner with Cora; not today. Cora drove her own car so the girls weren't responsible for seeing her home. Sometimes Scott Bradley called Jenny on Sundays. Then it was church again in the evening although since Pastor Burke left Sunday evenings were rather sporadic.

"Jenny may be expecting a call from her fiancé, and we usually go to evening service if there is one."

Valerie nodded. "We have family time on Sunday after dinner. We might do any number of things from playing monopoly to dancing."

Windy brightened. "Rick told us how he grew up dancing." She saw Valerie's questioning look and went on to explain about their Valentine's dinner. "Cora danced like a professional once she got started and Jenny picked up the steps right away."

"And you, did you learn them?"

"Well, I, no. I guess I was being shy that day."

Valerie laughed and surprised Windy with a hug. "You are a treasure, Windy! I hope my son…" Valerie stumbled on her words, "…my son…brings you…here, a lot. But you needn't wait for an invitation from him, you're welcome anytime."

Tami pushed through the kitchen door.

"Mom, Jenny says she loves word games and she can draw a fairly decent picture."

"Okay, Tami, you girls pick the game, I'll get Dad." Valerie turned to Windy. "Looks like they've talked Jenny into staying."

"Then you'll have to put up with me, too, I came in Jenny's car." Windy followed Tami as Valerie headed toward the living room.

"Did you have a good time?" Windy asked as she and Jenny headed for home.

"I sure did. Being with a family like that makes me miss my own."

"So, did they pass the test?"

Jenny tried to look innocent but Windy shook her head.

"I know what you were up to. Don't even try to pretend with me."

"Do you like him, Win?"

"Of course I like him. So do you."

"You know what I'm asking. He's not a Christian."

"Neither was I when we meet, but you didn't turn me away. You helped me to see God."

"And you think you might be Rick's guardian angel, sent to convert him?"

"No, I don't. I've tried to avoid him often enough. We just seem to keep being thrown together. Do you think it was coincidence that he showed up at our church, that he's Valerie's son?"

"You know I don't believe in coincidence."

"Well neither do I. Jenny, I appreciate your concern, as a matter of fact I welcome it. I like being looked after and cared for. I'm glad you love me enough to worry about me. But let me assure you, God comes first. If He wants me to have someone, He will have to supply the person, because I'm not looking. I now have certain criteria and the next man I marry, IF I ever marry again, must fit the bill."

"And what does your list of requirements include?"

"Number one—Christian. Not church goer. I want a Biblical Christian man. Spiritual head of the house, all that. He must be dedicated to God. God must be more important to him than I am. Number two— understanding about my not being able to have children. I want so much to be a mom, hold a baby in my arms. I'll never forget how I felt when I cared for the babies at the hospital. So if any man wants to marry me he'll have to be willing to adopt. Number three—pro-life. I could never love someone who considered killing babies a choice." Windy hesitated. "Good looking would be nice, but not important. Fun. I'd want a relationship I can enjoy. And I hope he's poor. At least poor enough that money wouldn't be an issue." Again she hesitated. "And not too tall, hugging height would be nice." She smiled and cast a look at her friend. "And he should smell like the outdoors, and sound like a horse saddle, and," again she peeked at Jenny who began to frown. "And look good the day after he shaves, you know, manly in his stubble."

"Windy! Do you realize who you're describing?"

"Yes, I just wanted to see if you were paying attention."

"Just remember, Win, you've only known him for less than two months. You've shared a couple dinners and danced together once. Take it slow okay?"

"Actually, Jenny, I've known him for quite a while, it all started one cold, snowy night." Windy gave Jenny a brief history of their encounters.

"Remember the volleyball game at Wil's," Windy snickered. "When I hit the ball right into Stephan's face?"

Jenny didn't smile, obviously remembering the man's reaction.

"I never told you what distracted me. It was seeing the 'Razor Blade' man, Gray Eyes himself, at Wil's." She hesitated a moment then decided to open up to Jenny. She told her about seeing Rick in the store the day Stephan 'gave' her the little blue convertible. How she'd been attracted to him then, hoping he would say one word, give one sign of interest.

She concluded with, "Don't worry, Jenny. I'm a big girl. I know I've made mistakes in the past, but I have no intention of repeating them. I told you before, I want God. It really is that simple. I want God."

February slipped into March. The blue haze of winter stood over the two women who lived in the little apartment on Maple Street. Jenny had begun marking off days on her calendar, anticipating the moment she would hold her husband-to-be in her arms. She truly wanted Windy and Cora to fly with her to Florida and attend her wedding but that appeared to happen only in her wishes. Neither could afford the venture and although Jenny would have loved to pay their way she knew that would not be feasible. Besides they were planning a small wedding at her parents' church with just the family attending. She and Scott weren't even planning a honeymoon.

Windy reported to work every scheduled day. A couple times she cornered her boss and insisted on spending lunch with him. Her resolve to let him worry about his own problems lasted as long as her indifference to some one in need. Don appeared to be going through some doldrums and he knew if he just rode it out, things would get better. He admitted there was nothing amiss in his marriage or family life, he just heard time ticking away and felt dissatisfied with life itself.

Windy spent at least one day a week in the Pregnancy office. She felt drawn there. She read everything that came in and soon began ordering brochures and other educational material she thought would be helpful. Jenny talked to Windy about taking over the directorship. Jean's job demanded more of her time and Jenny believed she would gladly relinquish her responsibility. As Windy thought about the idea she became more and more comfortable with it. In March she attended the meeting of the board of directors to meet everyone and become familiar with them. Jean approached her afterwards and asked Windy about being the director. Windy admitted she'd been praying about it, and although God hadn't told her yes, He hadn't told her no either. Jean promised to give the matter serious prayer time.

Rick joined his family at church for several weeks. Although he sought Windy out after the service, he made it a point not to sit near her. He recognized her as a distraction and wanted to see what the services were actually about. He enjoyed the warmth and friendship he found there. He encouraged Joe to join him but Joe declined.

Late in March Andrew approached Rick and Doug as they stood waiting for Valerie and the girls.

"We're getting a group together to attend Man 2 God Ministries conference in June. I'd like to encourage you to join us." He told them a brief history of the Christian men's movement and its successes. Then he gave each of them a small booklet that explained it in better detail. Andrew showed them which conference he planned to attend and who the guest speakers would be. Rick had never heard of any of them but one name caught his dad's eye.

Doug promised Andrew he would consider attending. Rick agreed.

When the April sun cleared the last of the ice from the inland lakes, Rick saw his opportunity. Trout season was quickly approaching and Joe enjoyed fishing from Rick's creek.

Chapter Twenty-One
August, 1975

Jason filled the tub with warm water, he liked taking baths but wasn't sure why Devy wanted him to take one today.

"Can Jeremy and Josh take a bath too?"

"No, them boys ain't old enough to be registered."

"What's registered?"

"So you can go to school and not be so stupid."

"I'm going to school? What's it like?"

"I never liked it, but you probably will. It's where you learn things like how to read and use numbers."

"Oh." He wanted to ask more but could tell Devy would only get mad. He put the washcloth and soap by the tub. He wanted to be extra clean to get registered.

"When you get done, get dressed and let me know." Devy informed him.

"Who's taking me? How we gonna get there?"

"I gotta take ya cause I'm yer mother, and we're walkin, it's only a couple blocks away."

"Are you Jeremy and Josh's mother too?"

"No, stupid. Darly is Jermy's ma and Deeny is Josh's."

Jason crawled into the tub and grabbed the soap and washcloth.

So that's how it worked.

The other kids in the building lived with their mama's too. Some lived with other old people, but Jason was the only kid who lived with 3 girls, a gramma and a gram, plus two boys. He knew the 3 girls were sisters and Gramma was their mama, so he thought Jeremy and Josh were his brothers. He smiled thinking he had his own mama and so did the other boys. *But,* he reasoned, *since us boys got sisters for moms, I guess that still makes us brothers.*

Jason ran home from school, he couldn't wait to show his papers to Devy, his mama. He hoped she would be proud. Tomorrow he would walk with the other kids who lived in the building but not today.

"Mama look!"

"Shut up!" came several girl voices from the living room. "Go see what the boys are into."

Jason put his papers in his room, the one he shared with the boys, then peeked into the living room. The women were watching soaps. They watched soaps a lot and the boys weren't allowed to bother them during that time. Jason had hoped the soaps would be over by the time he got home from school. He ran out the back door, knowing the boys would be playing at the playground. That's what they always did when it was warm outside. When it got cold, they played in the halls until the other old people made them be quiet, then they went in their room.

Jason saw the two boys. 3 year old Josh sat in a swing, holding tight and crying. Jeremy pushed as hard as he could and laughed at the little boy. Jeremy could be mean. Jason ran over to them.

"Quit pushing so hard." he grabbed the swing and brought it to a stop, helping Josh down.

"Sissy!" Jeremy yelled. "Yer a sissy, yer a sissy."

"I'm not." Crying, Josh rubbing his eyes.

"Yer a sissy, you wear girl clothes." With that Josh began to cry in earnest.

Jason wanted to hit Jeremy, but knew the boy only repeated what he heard. Devy and Darly teased little Josh. They put his long curly blonde hair in pigtails and dressed him in girl clothes. Deeny didn't join them and Jason just realized why. Cause she was Josh's mama. But why didn't she make the other girls stop being mean to her own son?

"Yer older 'n Josh, yer supposed to take care of him." Jason reminded Jeremy.

119

"Just cause yer oldern me, don't mean yer the boss."

"I am the boss and you know it. Did you put any clean pants on Josh today?"

"No, yer the boss, you do it."

"I told you when I go to school you got to put clean pants on Josh when he gets up." Jeremy stuck his tongue out and ran for the building. Jason checked the little boy's pants. They gooshed when squeezed. "C'mom, I'll give you a bath. You eat anything today?"

Josh shook his head and hugged Jason. "I wuv you, Jacy."

"Yeah, I love you too."

Jason led a clean, dressed Josh into the kitchen and sat him at the table. He opened a low cupboard door and pulled out a box of macaroni and cheese. The pan, with a large spoon in it, sat beside the other boxes. Jason pushed the chair to the sink and filled the pan with hot water and set it on the counter. Walking to the stove, he pushed the pan ahead of him. He retrieved his chair so he could reach the top of the stove, opened the box and poured the hard noodles in, stirring them with the big spoon.

"How you know what yer doin?" Devy asked from the doorway.

"It tells you on the box."

"You can't read."

"No, I just follow the pictures, but today in school we looked at the alfbet, it's letters."

"I know what the alphabet is, I ain't stupid."

"Most of the kids already knew it. If you knew, why didn't you already tell me?"

"Cause I knew they'd teach you in school, why should I bother?"

Jason turned the heat down when the water almost spilled over. He wanted to hurry and eat supper so he could work on his letters. He determined to know them all the next day, so he wouldn't look stupid in front of the other kids. He would teach Jeremy and Josh too, if Jeremy would listen.

"Git out another box, that ain't enough for all of us." Devy said as she walked away. "Gram got her check, but the old witch she said she ain't buying us no pizza today."

Jason liked when Gram got her check. Usually. She would go to the store and buy a big box of beer and pizzas that the girls put in the oven. The boys got one slice each. Jeremy always tried to take Josh's but Jason wouldn't let him. Later, when the girls were all lying around the living room drinking beer, the boys could sneak another piece of pizza if there was any left. It didn't taste as good cold, but they didn't mind much. Sometimes the girls would start fighting and that's when Jason was sorry that Gram got her check. They would say mean things and call each other bad names; names that Jeremy tried to call Jason, till he got belted for it.

Once the girls all went to sleep Jeremy would check the beer cans and drink up the ones that weren't empty. Jason tried to stop him cause he knew Jeremy would be sick the next day and he would have to clean up after him, but Jeremy usually got drunk like the girls.

Chapter Twenty-Two

Easter came late that year, the second Sunday in April. Windy loved April, the trees budded, the grass began to green, and hearty flowers peeked through the brown earth. And she loved Easter this year; her first since becoming a Christian. Easter held a whole new meaning for her. She looked at Christ's death and His resurrection in a different light.

The church had confirmed the visit of soon to be Rev. Jason Shane. He would arrive on Thursday; Maunday Thursday Margie called it, and would stay throughout the following week. The Pulpit Committee had activities and meetings scheduled that whole time. Windy hoped to attend as many as possible. She wasn't too sure about the Thursday night foot washing service; that sounded a little bizarre to her. Jenny tried to explain the concept.

"It's following Jesus' example when He washed the disciples feet before the last supper. He humbled himself, did the chore of a servant, to show His love for His followers." Jenny went on to recall instances of foot washing that had really touched her life. "Just come, Win. If you're not comfortable participating in the foot washing, just watch, no one will pressure you."

An afternoon service was scheduled for Good Friday between 1 and 3 pm. Windy intended to ask Don if she could get out of work early so she could attend that one. Saturday Pastor Shane would meet with the committees, and Sunday was a marathon day with the sunrise service, breakfast and an Easter egg hunt instead of Sunday School, then the regular worship service. This church would find out quickly just how much stamina young Pastor Shane had.

Windy and Jenny hopped out of Jenny's car and Windy reached for the back door handle to let Cora out. As they headed for the church Cora echoed Windy's uneasiness.

"Now, if I don't want to do this, I can just watch?"

Jenny nodded. "No one wants to make you uncomfortable, Cora, we just follow Christ's example." Once inside every one gathered in the sanctuary. Wil and a nice looking young man stood at the front behind the wooden table that always stood before the pulpit. On the table were the familiar items for communion, covered silver trays that held the small pieces of unleavened bread and another set of taller trays that held the tiny cups of grape juice. These items represented the body and blood of Christ.

Windy looked over the young man who came to candidate as their next pastor. He was taller than Rick, but shorter than Scott Bradley. Windy shook her head. Why did she always compare one person to another? Couldn't she just accept them for who they were? She tried again. Pastor Shane stood about 5'9", he was quite slender in build, maybe even a bit too skinny. She looked at his hands but he held a Bible and she couldn't get a good look. He had short, dark hair that acted as if it would curl if he let it. His face was handsome, but from where she sat she couldn't see much of it. *In time*, she told herself.

At exactly 6:30 the organist sounded two quiet chimes. The room was already hushed with reverence. Several people had come for the service, far more than Windy thought would show up. Maybe it was because this was Pastor Shane's first appearance.

"Thank you everyone, for coming," Wil began. "This here is Pastor Jason Shane, he will be serving communion with us tonight. Will the elders please come forward and help us serve."

Solemnly four of the elders moved to the front of the church and accepted the silver plates which they passed down the rows to the people. Some placed the bite size piece of bread into their mouths right away, others waited. Windy preferred to wait until the pastor, in this case, Wil, partook of his bread.

When the elders returned, Pastor Shane looked at the open Bible he held in his hands and began reading a familiar passage, the passage used every first Sunday of the month when the congregation partook of communion. Windy hadn't thought to bring her Bible so she sat back and relaxed, listening to the young man's smooth voice.

"And when the hour had come He reclined at the table, and the apostles with him. And when He had taken some bread and given thanks, He broke it, and gave it to them saying 'This is my body which is given for you; do this in remembrance of me'."

Windy placed the thumbnail size piece of bread in her mouth just as Wil and Pastor Shane did. She chewed on the dry morsel, then swallowed.

When the tray of juice came to her she held it while Cora choose a tiny cup then handed the tray to Jenny before choosing her own. Everyone held their cups while Pastor Shane read again.

"And when He had taken a cup and given thanks, He gave it to them, saying, 'Drink from it, all of you; for this is My blood of the covenant, which is poured out for many for forgiveness of sins.'" Pastor lifted his cup to his lips, the congregation followed his example.

Margie then led the church in another song.

"We'll separate now," Wil instructed. "The men downstairs and the ladies in the Youth room. Let's pray. Dear Lord, I ask that you bless this time we have together. I pray that Your Holy Spirit would touch each of us tonight and that we would be able to share openly with one another. Amen."

Windy took Cora's hand and together they followed Jenny into the Youth room where several dishpans were sitting next to a stack of towels on a table. Chairs were arranged in a circle and the ladies sat down, Windy counted 12; herself, Cora, Jenny, Margie, Mary, Valerie, Connie, Kim, Janice, Missy and her two daughters. She knew Ruthie was only 6 and Molly couldn't be more than 10. She wondered at their presence in this solemn event.

Margie read a short devotional about older women being an example to the younger ones. Windy thought of Cora and how this older woman had certainly been a good example for her.

"Does anyone want to share about a specific foot washing experience?" Margie asked.

Missy spoke first remembering the first foot washing she had been to and what it meant to her. Mary then told of the celebration she and Andrew were part of in Costa Rica and how they used water from the Pacific Ocean.

Then the ladies began to take off their shoes. Windy gulped. The moment had come, she must make a decision.

"I will, if you will." Came Cora's uncertain whisper.

Both ladies slipped off their shoes and returned their attention to Margie who had risen and was at the sink putting warm water in a dishpan. She had a long white towel draped over her shoulder.

"You may fill your dishpan with warm water and use a towel for drying. The Bible says Jesus was girded with a towel, but ours aren't quite long enough to tie around our waists. Empty your pan and start with clean water each time." She walked over and knelt down in front of Kim.

"Kim," Margie began and she placed one of Kim's feet in the water and carefully poured water over Kim's foot with her cupped hand. "You are such an inspiration to me. I know you're still finding your place in God's Kingdom, but I have seen such growth in you these last few months. Thank you." When Margie finished both feet the ladies stood and embraced, each with teary eyes.

Windy looked over to see Valerie washing Connie's feet. Neither said anything but both were visibly crying. She once again noticed Connie's gray eyes, so like Ricks. Rick is adopted she reminded herself, what if he's really Connie's son and Valerie knows it? The idea that both women would wind up in the same city and the same church was too far fetched for Windy to believe. *Rather like two men being the same one who happens to know both her and Jenny but in two different worlds?* A voice seem to whisper.

Before she had time to give the idea much more thought little Ruthie appeared before her sloshing water in a pan almost too heavy for her little arms. Windy looked around almost in desperation, was this little girl going to wash her feet? Why?

Ruthie seemed very comfortable with the routine; she placed one of Windy's feet in the water and slowly poured the warm liquid over it.

"Miss Windy, thank you very much for knitting mittens for us kids. It was a real cold winter and I loved my pretty pink mittens they kept my hands real warm and I can still wear them even though they are gittin kinda tight. I think of you and God every time I put them on." Windy continued to watch that precious little girl as she dried Windy second foot. Though Windy tried to hold them back, tears poured down her face in awe of this child. Ruthie stood and Windy pulled her into her arms.

At that moment Windy felt a huge pang of sorrow as she realized she would never hold her own little girl in this way.

Windy helped Ruthie carry the pan back to the sink and refill it. Ruthie then moved over to her mother, a gesture so beautiful yet so sad for Windy. A second revelation hit her. Although she would never hold her own daughter, she could hold her own mother. Her own mother, who didn't know the Lord, had never attended church that Windy knew of. Her own mother, who needed the salvation only Christ could give. Windy vowed at that moment to call as soon as she got home and tell Mom and Dad about the Lord. But for right now she had a very important mission. She picked up a dishpan and poured warm water into it, then placed a towel over her shoulder. If she was going to get her feet wet with this new experience, she might as well jump right in. She walked over to Jenny's chair and waited till her friend had finished washing Janice's feet.

Jenny sat down quietly, aware of Windy's uncertainty in this situation. She had seen so much change in Windy since they first met at the Community Church less than 3 years ago. And now her friend was about to reenact the serving gestures of their Lord and Savior. Jenny's eyes already held unshed tears from the conversation she'd just had with Janice. Now those tears spilled over and new ones came quickly to join them.

"Jenny," Windy began. "I believe God has loved me since before I was born, just as the Bible tells us. I believe He loves me enough to have come to me no matter where I was or who I was with. But I truly thank Him for allowing you to be the one to introduce us. As Paul said, I planted, Apollos watered and…well, some one else harvested. Jenny, you planted, you and the whole church watered and the Costa Rican group harvested.

I love you Jenny McCourt and I am going to miss you desperately when you leave. But at least I know you and Scott Bradley will be in good hands." When Windy finished drying Jenny's feet they both stood and embraced.

Jenny thought of leaving this wonderful friend, of walking out of Windy and Cora and Mary's lives to start a new one wherever God led her and Scott. Though she counted the days till she would join her fiancé and unite with him in marriage, she dreaded leaving this little family she loved so dear.

As the emotion threatened to overtake her, Jenny pulled away from Windy and they both looked at their surrogate Grandmother. Kim was in front of the little old lady speaking her appreciation. It looked like Jenny and Windy weren't the only 'grand daughters' Cora had.

Chapter Twenty-Three

Windy attended the Good Friday service along with Jenny and Cora. Only Jenny was involved in the meetings on Saturday, since she served on the Board of Christian Education. All three got up early to attend the first Sunday morning service, stayed for breakfast and the regular morning worship.

After Margie led the congregation in a couple songs, the offering was taken and Wil stood up.

"Friends," he said from the pulpit. "I am proud to introduce Jason Shane to you this morning. Some of you have already met him and know he'd rather we didn't call him 'pastor' till he graduates from the seminary in a couple weeks. He also prefers us usin' his first name to his last. So folks this here is Jason, the young man we are seriously considerin' as our new pastor."

Wil sat down in one of the small pews on the platform and Jason came forward.

"Good morning." The congregation repeated his greeting.

"Over the last couple days I have had the privilege of meeting several of you." His eyes searched the flood of faces before him and made contact with several familiar ones. "You have been very gracious and have welcomed me without reserve. I already feel as though I am one of the family."

Many heads nodded and several 'amens' were heard.

"I have refrained from telling you my story, my testimony, because I planned that for this morning and didn't want anyone to have to sit through this twice. You'll be able to see how miraculously God has moved in my life."

"I was raised in a home with three generations of women; three younger ones, Devy, Darly and Deeny, and two older ones Gramma and Gran, and with two other boys; Jeremy and Joshua.

"Our home was not a good environment for anyone, especially three little boys. Men came and went, few stayed long enough for us to learn names, but even they were not good role models.

"When I was five I found out Devy was my mother, Darly was Jeremy's and Deeny was Josh's. Though we were cousins we were raised as brothers and that's how I see them.

"I took care of my brothers, I cooked for them, bathed them, got them up and to school. I even washed some of our clothes by hand. The women, all five of them drank and used drugs.

"My life changed when I started attending school. I loved school, and I met Mr. Jarvis, the janitor. He began taking us boys to church. As much as I loved school, I love church even more. Then Mr. Jarvis paid for my way to youth camp one summer. That's where I accepted Christ as my Savior when I was eight years old.

"I realized how much I needed God. But I also realized my brothers and the women in my family did too. Gran, my mother's grandmother was my first convert. I talked to her many times about the Lord. She admitted she lived a bad life, but it was the only life she knew. When she turned 70, she decided to die. She stopped eating and refused to come out of her room. She looked like a skeleton, could barely breathe and wouldn't go to the doctor, but she still let me tell her Bible stories.

"I spent all the time I could with her and she finally broke down and asked for forgiveness, turning her life over to the Lord. She died in her sleep later that night.

"Next I turned my attention to Gramma. She is, and always will be, a very angry woman. Her three daughters have different fathers and none of them know anything about their dads. My brothers and I have different fathers. We know nothing about them.

"Devy and Darly have hardened hearts. They have followed in their mother's footsteps, hating all men, but using them as much as possible.

"Deeny died a couple years ago. She had a good heart and if I could have communicated with her away from all her bad influences, I believe she may have turned to the Lord. She is the only woman in our house who tried to be a mom to her son. I know that Josh prayed for his mother constantly, he kept in contact with her and I hope that maybe his love got through to her, if it did, neither of us know.

"When the time came for me to go to college, Mr. Jarvis worked with our church, our state office and the University itself for my tuition. With all that support, grants and scholarships I have been able to complete 8 years and owe nothing. The same with Joshua. He and I were welcomed into the home of some wonderful Christian people where we lived the whole time. Joshua just finished and is preparing to enter the missions' field. He will probably go to South or Central America.

"As good as we tried to be, our brother Jeremy tried to be bad. Today he's in prison. He has two children with different moms. I've never seen them, don't know where they are.

"I tell you my story, of the heartache and hurt, not for your pity or even sympathy but rather so you can see how God has worked in my life and how he can work in yours and your loved ones. I know each of you has someone you love very much and desire them to come to the Lord. I want to say to you, believe in miracles.

"Jeremy, Joshua and I have almost the same blood, we were raised in the same house, by the same women, yet look how differently Jeremy turned out. We can only blame our parents, our upbringing, our environment so much. Then we have to accept the consequences of our choices. Jeremy also attended the same church, heard the same Bible stories. Jeremy chose not to listen to God's voice.

"I have prayed continually that God would lead me where he wants me. Joshua feels called to the mission field outside this country, I feel called to the needs of young people like Joshua, Jeremy and I. We live in a great country where opportunity abounds. Mr. Jarvis opened so many doors for me, now I want to open some for other kids lost in a home of hopelessness. If God leads me here, I will be the best man of God I can.

I will actively look for the Joshuas and Jeremys in this community and I'll ask you to support me in this ministry. So I warn you now, life will change.

"I have had a chance to visit with you, get to know you as well as anyone can in such a short period of time. I am asking that you prayerfully consider me as your next pastor. I look forward to the rest of this weekend."

Chapter Twenty-Four

The following Sunday a meeting was held after the church service. A unanimous vote elected Jason Shane as the next pastor of this welcoming congregation. Margie, as secretary of the pulpit committee, sent young Mr. Shane a letter with the good news. He replied that after his mid May graduation he would arrive ready for the task.

"I thought we might go fishing this week," Rick approached his partner. They stood just inside the station ready to start their afternoon shift.

"You fishing?" Joe looked at Rick. "You hate fishing."

"I don't really hate it, I just don't enjoy it. But, for some strange reason, I enjoy your company."

"What's the catch?"

"Fish. Maybe. Just show up at my place and we'll drown a few worms in my creek. This Saturday is the beginning of trout season, isn't it?"

Joe nodded. "Okay, I'll be there early." He stressed the last word.

"I'll be awake."

Saturday morning Rick stood in his kitchen asking himself why he was up so early. He intended to ask Joe to church, again. For some reason that Rick couldn't understand, Joe coming to church became important to him.

He put hot water in the tea pot to boil and pulled the jar of instant coffee from the cupboard along with a box of tea bags. He didn't care much for Cora's fruit teas but found a strong cup of black tea enjoyable. This morning he needed something to keep him awake, he knew the fishing wouldn't. Rick set two cups on the counter and dropped a tea bag in one then he sat down on the kitchen stool to think of the best way to approach Joe, again. He planned to stay at his folks' house tonight and join them in the morning. Rick had been thinking about this Man 2 God thing all week. He'd read the brochure several times. It looked interesting and he felt certain he and his dad would enjoy it. But would Joe? Rick recalled Joe's experience with church. It sounded like a social club rather than a worship service.

"Look at you," he told himself. "You're starting to sound like your mother!"

"Good," his self replied. "She's a great lady to sound like."

His conversation was interrupted by a knock on the door. Joe walked in, not waiting for Rick's answer, three fishing poles in his hand.

"I don't believe it," he announced as he walked into the kitchen. "You're up, awake and you've made coffee. This is a little scary, you know."

"Did you have breakfast?" Rick asked. "It would only take a minute to whip up some pancakes and eggs."

"Later. I hear my name being called by some hungry fish." Joe grabbed the steaming cup Rick offered and opened the back door. Rick followed him.

"Why all the poles?" he asked.

"One for me, one for you and an extra, in case one decides to break."

Rick poured the last of the batter into the hot frying pan. He still hadn't asked Joe to church tomorrow. They had sat side by side all morning, talking about everything but church. Rick even opened up a little about Windy. He could feel, more than hear, Joe's negative attitude about the girl. But he knew it was women and relationships in general that Joe didn't trust.

Maybe he would just wait until a special occasion arrived to invite Joe to church. Having made the decision to procrastinate, Rick sighed in relief and flipped the pancakes.

Windy awoke to Jenny singing in the kitchen. This was the first Monday in May. In six weeks school would end and Jenny would fly off to Florida to marry the man of her dreams. Windy's excitement and jealousy fought each other once again, as they were doing more often lately. She wanted Jenny happy, knew Jenny and Scott Bradley belonged together, but a tiny voice deep in her heart still claimed the happiness she felt in Costa Rica when Jenny's Scott was her Brad. Would she ever feel that contentment again?

Windy's thoughts turned toward Rick. They had seen each other several times in the last couple months. She was delighted to see him attend the church services with his family. And Valerie's face lit up every time she sat down and her family filled the pew. Windy had made it a point not to sit any where near Rick for fear of being the Sunday morning entertainment committee. Besides, she found she could concentrate better on the sermon if that good-looking, great-smelling, red-faced hunk wasn't sitting beside her.

"Hush," she whispered. "No need to start daydreaming the minute you wake up. Besides, he doesn't really fit 'hunk' criteria. He's not tall, not muscular in an obvious way, his hair messes easily and his face, well, it's a strong handsome face, but Rick Notts is by no one's definition 'hunk' material."

Jenny popped her head around the corner. "I see you're up," she said. "I'm leaving now. What time do you go to work today?"

"Ten," Windy replied. "But I think I'll stop by the office first, see if there's any mail."

"Have you given Jean an answer about taking over the directorship yet?"

"Not officially, but I have been making deposits and taking on more responsibility. So it's just a matter of time, I guess."

"Do you enjoy doing all that?"

"I really do. I like working with the girls, but I look forward to the managing type work."

Jenny smiled, "Gotta go, see you tonight." Her pretty face and swinging blond hair disappeared.

Windy climbed off her little bed and padded into the kitchen. She downed some orange juice, showered and was soon walking down the street enjoying the bright morning sunshine.

At the office, Windy opened several letters, some containing checks; others were newsletters or pleas for support of other organizations. She wrote out the necessary thank you notes and slipped them into the outgoing box for the mailman. She arrived at work 10 minutes early and sought out Don, asking about him and his family.

"I talked to my wife," Dan said, not entirely happy with her answer. "She sounded interested in visiting your church. She said it would be good for the children. You know, Windy, Colleen and I met at a church picnic. Our parents are fairly religious, but my mom always told me I had to make my own decisions, that I couldn't get to Heaven on her beliefs. She said I had to develop my own. I have. I'm not sure I want to join the so-called Christians, but my kids can't make their own choices unless they know what they have to choose from."

"Well, I would be honored if you and your family come."

"Are there any other black folks."

Windy hesitated for a moment. "Yes, Don, there are. But in God's church there's no distinction. I understand why you're asking, but please don't come looking for differences, come looking for God."

Don smiled as he would if his daughter said she'd visited the moon. He humored her for the effort she put forth.

"I've got work to do," Windy said and left his office.

Yes, Don thought. *We'll come to your church and you'll see how blacks are treated by 'Christian' white people.*

Rick stopped in that afternoon on his way to work. Windy felt a pang of disappointment that the warm weather had caused Rick to leave his leather jacket in the closet. But at least he smelled great, even if he didn't creak. This time he wore a short sleeve shirt instead of a long one and

Windy noticed his bare arms for the first time. They weren't skinny but he'd never win arm wrestling with Schwarzenegger.

"When's your next day off?" Rick asked her.

"Thursday," she replied. "I usually spend those days at the office."

"Can some one else cover for you?"

"I don't have any appointments yet, I could just tell Carrie not to schedule any. Why?"

"I'm going down to South Haven, walk on the beach, build sandcastles that sort of day. Will you come with me?"

Rick's invitation took her by surprise although she'd been hoping for something like this for a while. The last few months their friendship had been nothing more than a couple dinners at Val and Doug's. She had begun to think Rick was losing interest.

"I'd love it," she replied. "Wait, you just happen to have the same day off?"

"I will have," he grinned and winked at her.

Windy's heart jumped. There was something about a wink, that private communication between two people that Windy loved.

"I'll pick you up early, before eight, so we can really make a day of it."

"How long does it take to get there?"

"Just over an hour," he said backing away. Suddenly Windy didn't want him to go. She didn't want to lose what little communication existed between them right now.

"RRRick," she stuttered. "How about coming to Cora's for supper tonight?"

"Joe, too?"

"Of course."

"What time," he asked as he neared the end of the aisle.

"Seven, I don't get off until six."

"We'll be there," he promised before disappearing.

At Windy's next break she called Cora and asked if the guys could come.

"That will be lovely, Windy, I have a new dish I've wanted to try. But you might bring home some salad fixings."

Chapter Twenty-Five

Windy looked into the mirror again. The same face stared back at her.

"Just what do you wear to a sand castle construction?" she asked her reflection. She pulled the comb through her hair one more time. Should she tie it back away from her face? Windy shrugged, it wouldn't matter how she fixed it, the wind would be victorious in the end anyway. Should she wear make-up, or would she wind up with black blotches under her eyes?

She stepped into the kitchen and looked at the clock. 6:30. Jenny wasn't even up yet. Rick said before eight, he didn't say how long before eight but she doubted he was even out of bed yet. Windy put a kettle of hot water on the stove. "How about some caffeine to calm you down?" she asked herself, pulling a tea bag from the canister.

"Win? Who are you talking to?" asked a drowsy Jenny from the bedroom doorway. Her golden hair stood on end, and her lovely blue eyes squinted in the light. School started at 9 am and although Jenny always got there early, she needed little time for preparation in the morning. *That's one of the many nice things about being naturally beautiful'* thought Windy.

"I'm sorry, Jen, I didn't mean to wake you."

"Who's here?" Jenny croaked, her voice box still asleep. "What time is it? Why are you up so early?"

Windy guided her friend back to bed. "I'm going to South Haven for the day, remember? But you still have an hour to sleep."

Jenny nodded into her pillow as Windy pulled the covers over the girl.

She tip-toed out of the room and closed the door behind her. She glanced at the clock but time hadn't moved yet.

After fixing her tea Windy sat down at the table to wait. Should she wear hiking boots or tennis shoes?

"Thanks again for dinner the other night." Rick said.

He had knocked on the door just as Jenny's alarm sounded and Windy poured her third cup of tea.

They had been in the truck for about 15 minutes and hadn't spoken except for their initial greeting.

"You're welcome." Windy looked out the window and watched the new spring leaves fly by. She'd been to the beach before, when Stephan took her for the three day—try to get pregnant trip. Why had she agreed to come with Rick? Was this relationship going anywhere? Did she want it to? Did Rick? Maybe she should back off, refuse to see him for awhile. Being friends didn't require seeing each other on a regular basis. Maybe she should just ask Rick what he wanted from her. Without realizing it, she voiced her question.

"What do you want from me?" She asked the window.

"Windy? Are you talking to me?"

"Well, I wasn't talking to the window."

"In that case, all I'm wanting is a day of fun and relaxation."

"Then why ask me to come along?"

"What fun would I have building sand castles by myself?"

"I'm afraid my sand castle building skills are right up there with Hymnal retrieval." Now why had she brought that up?

"Good, I'm pretty rusty at it myself," he laughed. "We can learn together."

"Tell me about South Haven."

"Most beautiful place in Michigan," he began. "I was born there. Mom and Dad and I lived in a little brick house right on the Lake Michigan. I thought every kid had a lake in their back yard. We lived in a little community, a couple dozen houses, every one knew each other. Every summer day the kids would head for the sand hill. Dad's a teacher and he never worked during the summer so he could spend time with Mom and

I, usually they were the only adults out there playing with the kids. I was one of the youngest, but then age didn't seem to matter." He smiled with his recollection. "It was a great place to grow up."

"Why did you leave?"

"I was eleven when we moved. Mom and Dad were in the process of adopting the girls and we knew we'd need a bigger house. Then one of Dad's friends contacted him about a job in Grand Rapids, even knew of a house near him for sale. None of us wanted to leave, but it seemed like the best thing at the time. It all just worked out, you know. Almost as if we had no say in the matter," again he smiled.

"Thirsty?" Rick asked, exiting the expressway. He pulled in to a gas station and jumped out of the truck. "Cherry Coke, okay?"

"Sure," Windy answered.

In a moment he was back in the truck handing her a bottle of cherry coke and a chocolate bar. "A woman's two best friends," she commented as she accepted his offering.

Rather than return to the expressway, Rick stayed on the back road, driving through a couple small towns until he turned west and came to the Lake.

"This is a beautiful drive down here; part of the reason for going to South Haven is the trip." The road took them right along the lake shore; at times Windy wondered what held the road in place, the erosion obvious as they drove along. Rick continued to talk about his childhood and soon Windy found herself eager to see his cherished sand hill.

Before long Rick turned his truck west onto the main street of South Haven. Windy looked at the quaint shops and wondered if they would have time to go into a couple of them.

Rick surprised her by pulling into a parking space.

He jumped out of the truck and walked around to her side and opened her door. When he took her hand to help her she felt every one of his skin cells next to hers, felt the soft roughness of his knuckles under her fingertips, and loved the ease with which he grasped her hand, as though it was the most natural thing for him to do. Standing beside him she smiled into his face and was rewarded with a grin.

"Come on," he said, guiding her toward the store.

They entered a delicious smelling bakery.

"There is no place on earth that has pastries as good as they have here." Rick informed her.

"Hey, Ricky!" a woman behind the counter called out to him.

"Hi, Rose." He nodded and smiled as he pulled a small bit of paper from a skinny stand just inside the door. The number read 53.

He released Windy's hand and walked over to the cooler pulling out two small jugs of chocolate milk then he returned to the pastry case.

"How's the folks?" Rose asked.

"Doing great."

"I sure miss your mom. You'll tell her hello for me?"

"Of course. As soon as schools out, they're planning a weekend here."

"Oh, that'll be lovely. 53." She called out.

Rick handed her his slip of paper.

"I called an order in." He informed her.

Rose walked over to the shelf and looked at the bags.

"I don't see you name here, Rick."

"It's probably in the refrigerated case," he suggested. "I ordered custard filled long johns."

She opened the case. "There's two bags here."

"One for us, one for the folks. I don't dare go home empty handed."

She rung up the order on the register and handed Rick his change.

"What are you up to today?"

"It's beach time, I miss the lake."

"Supposed to be a lovely day, too. Enjoy yourselves!"

Rick took Windy's hand and guided her to the door.

The street angled down. Black River stretched out before Windy as it emptied into Lake Michigan. They drove along the river and into a parking lot. Windy noticed the beautiful red light house at the end of the pier. Across the channel another pier jutted out into the large body of water.

"This is the South beach," Rick explained. He pointed quite a ways down the shore to the south at a large expanse of sand, "and that's my sand hill. Just beyond it you can see Palisades Nuclear Plant. Dad remembers when it was being built in the late sixties."

Rick placed the truck in park and opened his window slightly. "Still a little chilly out," he commented.

They shared a long john, Windy expressing her doubt that she could eat a whole one, and each sipped on a jug of milk.

"This is so good," Windy licked chocolate icing from her fingers, hoping she hadn't made too much of a mess.

Rick nodded, his attention on the blue expanse that lay in front of them. Various boats dotted the lake, sail boats, fishing boats, yachts.

"When I was a kid, we rarely watched the sunsets on the lake, took them for granted, you know? This summer I'm gonna grab a tent and sleeping bag and spend a weekend on the beach."

"Sounds relaxing."

"You're invited." He said, then suddenly turned red. "You'll have to bring your own tent, though, mine only holds one person." He stammered. "Pup tent they call 'em."

Windy smiled, glad for Rick's obvious innocence. For the first time she found herself wondering about his previous relationships. A man as good-looking and kind hearted as Rick must have had many girls in his life.

Again her mouth took over before her mind had a chance to veto the words. "Why aren't you married?"

Rick looked a little surprised but didn't hesitate. "I'm waiting."

"For the right girl?"

"For the right time."

"Oh, okay, money in the bank, own your own home, which you do…find the right girl," she repeated.

"Windy," he looked so insecure for a moment that Windy wished she hadn't pushed the issue, why had she anyway, what did she want him to say? Rick reached over and took her hand, suddenly looking very confident. "I've found the right girl. I'm waiting for the right time. I want her, you, to know me as your friend, someone who won't hurt you or reject you. Someone you can always count on. I want us to develop a relationship, a comfortable one. I've been waiting for over 3 years. I thought I'd lost you once. But here you are, with me now. I may not be good looking, or smart or rich, but I am patient." He stopped as though he'd run out of words and confidence.

Windy wanted to say something to put him at ease, but didn't know what. Didn't he know just how good looking he was? Didn't he know by now that she was interested? Part of her wanted the relationship he spoke of; part of her wanted everything, right now. Part of her wanted to run. How could he be interested in a used woman like her? Some one tossed aside by two husbands, one for a can of beer, and one for a family. Did she really have anything of value to offer this wonderful young man?

A quiet thank you was all she could murmur.

Chapter Twenty-Six

Rick pointed the truck up the street, exiting the parking lot, then turned right, following the lake. Heading inland, Rick pulled into a grocery store. "Be right out, do you want anything?" Windy shook her head and moments later he returned carrying a bouquet of cut flowers. He pulled a pink carnation from the bunch and handed it to her, winking.

That simple gesture caused Windy's heart to skip a beat. Again. She used to watch her dad wink at her mom and knew there was a special connection between the two of them. Eddie had never winked at her, and Stephan...

"Oh let's not go there," she mumbled to herself.

"Pardon?" asked Rick.

"Well...where are we...going there...now"? She tried to hide her embarrassment.

"To Aunt Shirl's" he replied.

In a couple minutes they were headed south on the main road and Windy saw rows and rows of berry bushes.

"What kind of berries?" she asked.

"Blue. South Haven is the Blueberry capitol of the world. Every summer we have a Blueberry festival in late July. The city is crazy with all the tourists. People have been coming here from Chicago for decades. My friend's grandfather used to tell us about his dad working on Al Capone's cars back in the 30's."

"Blueberries and Al Capone, what more could a town ask for? "Mom's sister or your dads?"

"What?"

"Aunt Shirl."

"Neither. She was my Gramma Pearls' best friend. Every one called her Aunt Shirl. My mom would tell me how she would pick wild flowers every spring and take them to Shirley and Lil. Lil was Shirley's mom, lived to 105. Anyway, I've tried to carry on Mom's tradition and bring flowers to Shirley. I've missed a few years, but she understands."

Soon they made a right turn and headed down a short paved road. Rick pointed at the towering, wooded hill in front of them.

"I thought it was a sand hill?" Windy asked.

"You just can't see the sand yet."

Rick drove down a short sandy driveway and pulled up to a small brown house. He handed the bouquet to Windy, and grapped the two bakery bags.

"Come on," he said. "You're gonna love her." Again he took Windy's hand and she followed him to the door which he knocked on, then opened slightly. "Aunt Shirl, you home?"

"Who is it?" a voice called from inside.

"Ricky," he called back. He grinned at Windy, then winked again.

"Oh Ricky, come on in!"

He led the way through a small clean kitchen, tearing a paper towel off the roll and placing in on the counter under a cheese Danish then put the two bags in the refrigerator. He retrieved the flowers from Windy and they entered a little room, encased with windows. Windy felt she had entered an indoor screen house. On all the windows frilly curtains pulled back to reveal a small active yard. Birds fluttered on feeders while squirrels ran up and down the trees. Aunt Shirl sat in a large wicker chair that matched the rest of the furniture. A green sweat suit covered her body; gray brown hair framed a delightful face. She reached up; hands lightly adorned with rings, and captured Rick's face, bringing it down for a solid kiss on his lips.

"It's so good to see ya!" She exclaimed in her slight Chicago accent. "Who's this little doll ya got with ya?"

"This is Windy, my…"

"Windy, oh I love it! Sit down, sit down. Do yas want a soda, there's some in the fridge, help yerselves."

Rick brought his hand from behind his back and presented her with the flowers he held.

"Oh, yer so sweet!" she looked at Windy "I can always count on this guy ta bring me flowers, isn't he just wonderful? You got yerself a good man here, don't let him get away." She smelled the flowers then handed them back to Rick. "There's a vase under the sink there, Ricky, put em in some water for me will ya? And get you and yer little girlfriend a soda while yer there."

Her gaze captured Windy and Windy felt herself pulled into Aunt Shirl's smile. "You have a very welcoming home." she said.

"My wonderful niece comes up from Chicago and cleans for me. Go look around." Aunt Shirl invited.

"Well, I do need to use the bathroom since Rick has filled me up with Cherry Coke."

"That way," Aunt Shirl pointed.

Rick reentered the room holding two cans of root beer and the paper towel with the Danish.

"Oh ya been to the bakery, I love these things…"

Windy left the room through an open archway into the living room. The small house was lovely with many antiques which Aunt Shirl had probably purchased when they were new. Windy checked out the darling purple bathroom, crossed back through the living room and entered the dining room with its Oriental rug and amazing glass chandelier. Windy peeked into the one bedroom, noting its partially cylinder shape, windows along the rounded wall were adorned with fluffy pink curtains that matched the bedspread.

Windy made her way back into the sunroom where Rick sat on the edge of the couch leaning toward Aunt Shirl, his hands holding both of hers.

"I sure miss Pearl; life just ain't the same since she passed away. All my friends are gone now," she shook her head. "Guess that's what happens when yer as old as I am. But God gave me a big family and lots of kids to keep me young!" The smile returned.

Windy sat next to Rick and picked up the pop can sitting next to his. She listened while Rick and Aunt Shirl talked about his childhood and all her nieces and nephews from Chicago. Rick asked about one after another pleased when he heard they were doing good, offering condolences when the situation warranted. Soon their cans were empty and Aunt Shirl's smile appeared a little tired.

"You kids run along and play," she said. "Wake me up before yas leave, I'll be napping right here."

Not allowing her to stand up Rick gave Aunt Shirl a strong hug, followed by a softer one from Windy. They said their temporary good byes and headed out the door, Rick retrieving one bag from the fridge.

He jumped into the bed of the truck and pulled a backpack out of a built-in carrier, handing it to Windy. Next he pulled out a medium size cooler also handing it to Windy before he jumped down. Windy helped him position the backpack. He picked up the cooler and captured Windy's hand with his free one. Leaving his truck next to Aunt Shirl's house they headed out. He pointed to other houses as they walked along, told Windy about the kids that lived there and how they had fit into his life as a child. In moments a huge sand hill loomed before them.

"We don't have to climb that, do we?" She asked.

"Can't make sand castle in dry sand," he answered.

"We need to get across that to the lake. Climbing is the only way I know how. Any better ideas?"

"Mmmm," Windy contemplated. "Why don't I carry the cooler and back pack?"

"Sounds good." He grinned. "What do I carry?"

"Me."

Chapter Twenty-Seven

Windy sat on a towel, sipping ice cold water, amazed, but thankful for all the items Rick had pulled from his back pack and cooler. She sifted warm sand between her toes, glad she had worn tennies instead of hiking boots. Her hair had reacted just as she knew it would, flying free with the wind. A few feet away stood the most pitiful sand castle she had ever seen. Its edges kept sliding down, so they settled for the 'dome look'. Finger pokes represented windows and tiny pieces of driftwood made the drawbridge. The moat, which Rick was still trying to fill with water, was surrounded by small rocks. A pretty seagull feather graced the top of the dome.

She watched as Rick poured another bottle of lake water into the moat, then grinned as the sand absorbed it. Short hair stuck up at the crown of his head and muscled arms extended from his t-shirt. He had rolled up his jeans which got wet on the cuffs anyway and his bare feet and ankles were covered with wet sand.

"Hang it up, Rick, you're never going to get that thing to hold water. It's a defective moat. Acme Moat Company will be recalling it any day now."

He dropped the empty water bottle and sunk to his knees in front of her.

"It's because you don't believe," he explained. "Sand castles only work if the Princess believes in them."

"So that's my castle, huh? And I suppose you're my Prince

147

Charming?" She looked into his beautiful gray eyes and her stomach lurched. There it was, the Andrew look, emanating from Rick and piercing her soul. Wasn't this what she had longed for, dreamed about? And now it had become reality. Or was she imagining it?

He moved slightly closer, Windy could feel his breath on her cheek, see little droplets of moisture on his forehead, hear his intake of air. In a moment she recalled all the times of seeing him; at the grocery store—breaking her fall; at the Pizza Shop—smiling at her over melted cheese; in Wil's driveway—stepping from his truck. The very man she had admired from afar now kneeled inches away from her.

"Yes, Windy," his soft voice floated to her ears. "I am your Prince Charming and I have come to rescue you and take you away from the mean old witch that keeps you captive."

In one fluid movement Rick stood and scooped Windy up in his arms, surprising her with his strength. "I'm going to take you to my underwater hid-a-way where you will be safe."

He began running toward the water.

"No!" Windy screamed. "Don't get me wet, the water's too cold, I'll catch pneumonia, I didn't bring extra clothes." She kept yelling reasons why Rick should not continue his journey to his underwater hid-a-way but in seconds he had reached the shore. She tightened her arms around his neck, determined to take him down with her if need be.

He splashed into the water then twirled around, laughing.

"Oh, Windy, I lo…" he stopped short, cutting off whatever he intended to say. "I won't get you wet, not very, anyway." He set her down, her bare feet swallowed by the next wave.

"Rick this water is freezing."

"When I was a kid," he caught both her hands in his. "We were swimming by this time of year. As soon as the ice melted, we would climb that hill and reclaim our lake. By June it was all Mom could do to keep me…"

Windy broke free of his hold and began walking backward out of the water.

"Rick Notts, you're crazy!!" She yelled. "You're gonna get pneumonia and I'll have to drive home and I can't drive a stick shift!"

He followed her to the sand trying to capture her hands but she held them behind her back. Before she could react, he reached around her, grabbed her hands and pulled her close to him. He looked deep into her eyes, every fiber of her body was acutely aware of his closeness; the smell of his breath, the color of his eyes, the shadow on his jaw. She felt his bare arms against hers. His silly grin faded and seriousness spread over his face.

"Windy," he breathed. "Windy." He tasted her name a second time.

She wondered if he expected a response. Wondered what his next move would be, what she wanted it to be.

"Windy, would you do me the honor of becoming..." she held her breath. Was he going to propose? Right here? Right now? He hadn't even kissed her yet. Maybe he wouldn't like the way she kissed, would he really take the chance of being stuck with her kisses for the rest of his life? What should she say? Did she want to be his...his... "interior decorator? I...I need a new couch and you're the only one I trust to help me pick it out."

Had she heard right? She shook her head, trying to clear her thoughts.

"No?" he asked. "Why? I think you have excellent taste. You have a great sense of style and an ability to envision what my living room could look like with just the right touch." He still held her hands behind her back, hadn't moved at all. His voice, his actions had led her to feel his seriousness; yet here he was talking so casually about a couch.

"You..." she began. "You really are crazy."

"Why? You've sat on my couch. You've even complained about the springs sticking you in the back. Don't tell me you're so attached to my couch you can't bear for me to get rid of it. Well, I'll give it to you then, but I don't know what you're going to do with it. I suppose I can store it in my barn till you decide."

What was he doing, why was he playing with her like this. Was he making fun of her, or just teasing? She tried to pull her hands free but he held tight.

"Let me go." She said quietly, firmly. He did.

She turned and walked away, heading south along the shore. Why did she do this to herself? Why did she get into situations with crazy men? Hadn't she learned her lesson with the first two? She moved over into the wet sand, allowing the waves to barely touch her toes. She stopped and looked out across the beautiful blue expanse of water. *Lord, help me. All I want is You. And here I've gone and allowed my heart to be captured by this crazy man. One who carries a gun and brings me to this secluded place. I'm sorry, Father.* She watched the seagulls floating on the water, bobbing up and down with the tiny swells. *Here's the deal, if You get me safely out of here, I'll tell him to take me home and leave me alone. I won't see him anymore. I'll concentrate on You; not let myself get sidetracked by good looks and charming words. Please, just get me safely out of here.*

He'd really done it this time. How in the world was he going to explain this? A couch!? Where had that come from?

When standing there holding her so close he felt the rise and fall of her chest against his, he sunk into deep trouble. This little girl, this beautiful woman had suddenly consumed him. He could see nothing, hear nothing, feel nothing but her. He was words away from bearing his soul to her, asking her to be his wife, pleading with her to fulfill his longings, his dreams, when the terror of pushing her away, losing her completely because of his impatience welled up within him. He heard the dumb words, he was committed and then he rambled, digging himself deeper, convincing her he really was crazy.

He looked up and saw her standing about 20 feet away. Slowly, fearing she might bolt, he covered the distance between them. He stood quietly by her side for an eternal moment.

"I'm sorry." He whispered. She didn't respond. "Titched. That's what dad calls it. He says all the Notts men are titched in the head."

"Titched isn't a word." She informed him.

"It is now. Dad added it to our dictionary."

"I'd like to go home, please." She requested, showing no emotion. He stared ahead at the seagulls a few feet from them.

He didn't know what to do. Why did he always say the wrong thing? Now she wanted to go home. He had completely spoiled this perfect day. Maybe lost the relationship itself. He felt tears sting his eyes. *Oh no*, he told himself. *The woman will really think you're a raving lunatic.*

"Windy, I am so sorry. I...I..." Dad always said honesty was the best policy. "I wanted to kiss you." He looked down as the next waves slapped his toes. "I want to kiss you. But I told you I would be patient, give you time. I didn't want to scare you off and yet I did just that. Windy?"

She turned and looked at him. He saw no fear, no anger in her eyes. But no trust either. *Honesty* he told himself.

"I knew...I know...the moment I kiss you, I will never let you go."

Chapter Twenty-Eight

Windy's desire to turn and run deserted her. Her resolve to eliminate this man from her life fled and her voice silently called out to God. *Lord, here he stands before me, apologizing. What am I supposed to do? I won't deny that I'm drawn to him, that I want to throw aside all caution and ask him to take me in his arms and never let go. But Lord, haven't I learned anything in the last four years?*

Have you learned to trust Me?

I think so, I hope so.

Then trust me now. Do not flee. Accept his love.

But Father he's not a Christian.

It that your responsibility?

I don't know, maybe. I believe I am to follow Your commandments and tell everyone about You.

Have you told Rick about me?

Not really. But I don't want him to consider You as a way to reach me.

Do you see honesty, integrity in this man?

Yes, there's no doubt about that.

Then trust me and tell him.

Windy reached down and gripped Rick's hand, she moved back toward the south and together they walked along the shore.

After several minutes Windy spoke. "Rick, why do you go to church?"

The first words to his mind were light and teasing, *my mom makes me go.* An answer a child would give.

"I'm not really sure." Again he chose honesty. "I go because of my mom. Because of the difference I see in her life. I go because, although I already have so much, I know there's more. I guess I believe I owe it to God. My life I mean. My birth mom could have aborted me. She chose instead to give me to a loving couple and I'm very thankful for that. I love my parents, my family and I guess I want to say thanks to God."

For once, Rick didn't second guess his answer, for once, in Windy's presence he wasn't worried about her reaction. He realized in that moment he wanted to please God more than Windy. He liked that feeling.

"Just last year I walked along the water's edge in Costa Rica." She stopped and looked at Rick. "May I tell you about it?"

Rick listened intently as Windy described her time in the small Latin country. He felt the same envy she did when talking about the closeness of the group. He heard a familiar desire in her voice when she described the emptiness in her heart. He rejoiced as she took him to that quiet beach where God filled her longing and renewed her soul.

"Until you come to know Jesus, you'll never understand the peace and contentment He can give. My prayer is that some day you'll surrender your life to Him."

Rick nodded. He knew in his heart that day would come, he felt deep inside an assurance that God held his life, that God gave him life for a reason. But right at that particular moment he didn't really feel the need for surrender. *God*, he thought. *When You want me, just tell me.*

The couple continued their walk in silence, after a while, Rick turned them around and they headed back to the sand castle. Still in silence he pulled a baggie of veggie sticks, a couple hunks of cheese and the bakery rolls from the cooler. They sat quietly on the towels, watching the waves and finishing off the flavored water. When Windy thought she couldn't eat another bite, Rick handed her half a cheese Danish.

"I see what Aunt Shirl means," she commented after the first bite. Their meal finished, Rick stood and pulled Windy to her feet, inviting her into his arms and held her lightly for several minutes.

"Thank you for coming today." he whispered.

She nodded.

"I'm sorry I was an idiot."

"Idiots have their place in this world."

"I hope you'll accept my place as being next to you. I need you. I think after a little practice you'll do very well extracting my foot from my mouth."

"Oh I don't know; you look kinda cute that way."

He gave her a little squeeze, then released her. "We have to be going. Gotta stop back at Aunt Shirl's."

They quickly packed up their stuff and said goodbye to their sad castle. Trudging over the hill tired Windy who just wasn't used to that type of physical strain. Rick climbed slowly, carrying all the gear, waiting as Windy rested often. When they finally reached the top she stood catching her breath.

"I feel like an old woman," she said. "I always thought I was in pretty good shape, but this tells me I need to start exercising." She noticed her surroundings. "Where'd all this prickly grass come from?" she asked.

"I'm not sure, it's always been here, I just accepted it as part of the hill." He spread his arm out, encompassing the huge sandy area. "This has changed so much, even in the last 15 years. The wind is always pushing the hill east." He explained as they walked along the top.

When they reached the other side Rick said, "My mom tells me Aunt Shirl's house used to be right about here. She had it moved to its present location when she could no longer keep the hill at bay. Mom remembers when the house was only three rooms and Aunt Shirl had an outhouse. The kids used to climb on top of the outhouse and jump into the sand, but don't tell Aunt Shirl," he whispered. "Anyway, there was even a road in front and behind her house, but the hill just kept moving east, so she moved the house and added on the living room and bathroom and some years later the sunroom."

"You have great memories of your childhood, don't you?"

"The best, I can't imagine any better place to grow up."

They stared down at the expanse of sand before them. Rick grinned.

"When I was a kid playing on this hill, we would roll down like hot dogs." He shook his head. "I doubt I can do that now, I'd probably make myself sick." Instead they ran down, hand in hand, falling when they reached the bottom. Rick picked himself up and tried to brush some of the sand away, shook his head and laughed.

"Mom used to say sweeping the floor was a waste of time." He took Windy's hand and led her away from the hill, through a small cluster of sycamores to a sandy one lane drive. Across from them sat a short double wide mobile home.

"That's where my house used to be. It was a very small, one bedroom brick house. Built in the 50's it had a flat roof, no basement, only an attached carport. Mom's parents built it, she lived there as a kid and when she married dad, Gramma and Grandpa gave it to them as a wedding present. I loved that house. I still dream about it. Grandpa built a split stone fire place in the west end of the living room. I remember standing next to him in front of a blazing fire; feet slightly spread apart, hands behind our backs."

Rick smiled. "I had two of the best male role models in the world."

Chapter Twenty-Nine

Rick quietly opened the screen door and slipped into the kitchen when his second knock brought no response. Windy could hear the TV on, but no other sound came from within. Rick tiptoed through the house and peeked around the corner at the sleeping form in the chair.

"Isn't she beautiful?" he whispered.

Windy nodded, feeling like an intruder.

"Aunt Shirl?" He reached down and gently touched her arm.

"Aunt Shirl, it's me, Ricky."

Her eyes flew open in a moment of confusion.

"I didn't mean to scare you." Rick apologized.

"Oh, Ricky, no it's okay, I didn't hear ya come in. Did yas have fun at the beach?"

"We had a great time," he said, moving to the couch and sitting on the edge like before. He gently pulled Aunt Shirl's hands into his. "We're headed home now."

"Thanks so much for droppin by. You know how much I love ta see yas."

"I know and we'll be back. I think Windy's beginning to love our sand hill." He grinned at the girl, drawing Aunt Shirl's attention to her.

"You sure are a little doll. Where'd you find her Ricky?"

"Oh, at the grocery store, razor blade aisle. I swept her off her feet the first time we met."

"Yes, and then he left me high and dry, walked out of my life for two years. Now he thinks he can just waltz right back in, expects me to be standing in the aisle, just waiting for his next razor blade purchase."

"Well if he's got any sense, he'll walk you down another aisle. It's about time you settled down and got busy with a family, you know."

Rick's face turned slightly red as he nodded. He leaned close, "I'm working on it Aunt Shirl, don't scare her off."

"Oh, pshaw, she's a sensible girl; she knows a good thing when she sees it." Aunt Shirl captured Rick's face in her hands. "If I was a younger woman..." she brought her face close to his and kissed him quickly.

Rick helped her to her feet and she walked them to the door, giving Windy the same kiss. "You drive careful now and tell yer folks I said hello." After a couple more kisses and a few more goodbyes Rick helped Windy into the truck then jumped into the driver's seat. He maneuvered the vehicle through the sandy drive back to the blacktop where he stopped and turned off the engine. He got back out and walked over the passenger side, opening the door.

"Slide over," he said.

"Rick, I can't drive this thing."

"Not yet," he responded.

"I thought we had to hurry and get home?"

"We have time for one lesson." He gave her a little nudge. She eased her legs under the long floor shift.

"It's your funeral," she said. "I hope you have good insurance and I'm the beneficiary."

Rick's patience shined as he explained how the shift worked and the location of each gear. He had Windy hold in the clutch and run through the gears a couple times. Then he instructed her to put in the clutch, slip the transmission into first and start the engine. She grinned at him when the truck came to life.

"Now ease the clutch out just a little as you place gentle pressure on the gas pedal."

Windy complied and the engine died.

"Maybe that was a little too gentle," he said. "Try again."

That time the truck lurched forward before kicking itself off.

"Okay, now you know the extremes, try for the middle ground."

Windy slipped in the clutch, pressed lightly on the gas and then eased off the clutch, bringing the truck to a slow roll forward. With Rick's guidance, she successfully moved the shift into second gear and drove the short distance to the stop sign where she turned off the engine and moved back into the passenger seat.

As Rick slipped beneath the wheel she commented, "That was fun, when's my next lesson?"

"Tomorrow; on the road between my house and Wil's."

She grinned all the way to town.

Back on the northbound expressway, the box of treasured sweet rolls on the seat between them, Rick put a cassette of 60's music into the tape player and serenaded Windy on the drive home.

They arrived at the Notts residence just after 7pm and Valerie welcomed them in with a big hug.

Rick replayed their day for his parents, giving them Aunt Shirl's well wishes. Valerie dabbed at her eyes with a tissue.

"I sure miss her," she said. "We're going down for a weekend as soon as school's out."

"Speaking of the end of the school year, son," Doug began. "I signed us up to go with Andrew to that men's gathering in Detroit. Last weekend in June, he said. He's going to get back with me on the details, but said he'd take care of getting a room and tickets to the event. Sound okay to you?"

"Of course, I'd heard some talk about it and I was meaning to ask if you wanted to go. Can I foot the bill for your birthday?"

Rick eased his truck along the curb in front of Cora's house. His switched off the engine and turned his body toward Windy, hidden in the darkness.

"Thanks again for coming with me."

"Rick, I had a wonderful time. Aunt Shirl is the greatest, I really would like to visit her again."

Rick took a deep breath. There was so much he wanted to say to this girl. She was a part of his life, he thought about her all the time, couldn't imagine life without her now that she was finally in his company.

"Windy," he began, then stopped. Was he about to make a fool of himself again? Push her away from him like before? He just couldn't risk it. Maybe he needed to shut his mouth and settle for telling her goodnight.

Windy reached over and took his hand. "Rick, please forgive me for my behavior today. Sometimes I just get so...I don't know...paranoid. I'm afraid to care about someone. What do they say? Once burned, twice shy. So I've been twice burned, guess that makes me a little titched. But if that's the case then I guess we have some common ground, don't we?" She interlaced her fingers with his. "I want to be very up front with you. When I was married to Eddie we had an honest relationship until a...situation occurred. We both reacted in our own way. He started drinking and became a completely different person. I just chose denial. With Stephan, I determined to be honest with him, but our concept of honesty wasn't the same. We both saw honesty from our own point of view.

"Rick, you told me earlier that you want a relationship with me. Well I want one with you. But I also want honesty. Real honesty, not perceived. I'm a Christian now. I have a whole different set of priorities than I did a year ago. This last year has brought so many changes that I think I need time to adjust to them all. You said you're patient. Well, I'm asking for that patience.

"Rick, will you pray with me?" She held his hand a little tighter, bowed her head and sought her Lord.

"Father, I don't know what your will is in mine and Rick's lives. I only know You want us to be as close to You as possible. Right now, Father, I pray for that closeness for both of us. I pray for our friendship, our relationship if You so will. Lead us, guide us, continue to love us. In Jesus name Amen."

They sat quietly for a few moments, then Windy broke the silence. "Don't forget about my driving lesson tomorrow."

"Oh I won't. In the morning? I work at three."

"Mmm, no. I work at 7 tomorrow and Saturday. How about that afternoon?"

"No, I'm scheduled all week."

"Well, I guess it's not our problem. When God wants me to learn to drive a stick, He'll be the one handing us the keys. Goodnight, Rick." She leaned over to give a quick hug. "You smell like fish." She whispered in his ear.

Chapter Thirty

Windy cornered Don the next morning in his office, handing him a folded paper.

"Here's last week's bulletin, it has all the information you'll need to find the church and understand the schedule. The Sunday School class I attend is watching a series of videos about the founding of our country. I know you'll find them interesting. So, will I see and your family in the morning?"

"Sure, I already ran it past my wife and kids. They're looking forward to it."

His answer surprised Windy who expected to have to convince her boss to come. "Great. Great! I'll just get back to work."

Sunday morning Windy, Jenny and Cora all arrived early to make certain they were there when Don and his family arrived. By 9:30 Windy was beginning to get a little nervous thinking Don may have decided not to come but then a tall black lady surrounded by four children walked though the door. Windy had met Colleen King at the grocery store and knew her instantly. She had seen a picture of Don's children but wasn't that good at remembering faces.

"Mrs. King," Windy stepped toward her and offered her hand, which Don's wife grasped. "Welcome."

"Oh, Windy, call me Colleen, don't go getting all formal on me just cause we're in church." She smiled brightly at Windy showing perfect white teeth.

As Windy introduced Colleen to Cora and Jenny little Ruthie Packard caught the hand of the little girl standing next her mom.

"I'm Ruthie, I just turned seven. How old are you?"

Colleen quickly turned to introduce her children. "This is Jaela, Ruthie. She's six years old."

"Then she goes in my class. Come on, we have a fun class, you'll like it." Ruthie tried to drag the little girl away from her mother. But Jaela grabbed her mother's coat and started to cry.

Colleen knelt down. "It's okay baby, Ruthie wants to be your friend and daddy and I will be here, just in another room. You go along and have fun."

Jaela wiped her eyes. "I want to go with you."

"Listen, I'll bet Kenan goes in the same class, him being eight and all." She looked to Ruthie for confirmation.

"Oh, yes, six, seven and eight goes in my class," she spied the boy Colleen was talking about and reached out for his hand.

He gave her a scowl and looked unhappily at his mom.

"I ain't holdin no girls hand." He informed her.

"'I'm not holding any girls hand'" she corrected. "Run along Kenan." She turned her attention to her older children. "This is Adonna and J'mon."

By then Don appeared behind his wife and Windy began the introductions again.

"Sunday School has already started, so why don't we head to our room?" She nodded at the two older King children, judging them to be preteens. "We'll show you two your class on the way."

The group moved down the stairs and along a hall, Windy indicated an open door where music could be heard and the two remaining children stepped inside. Windy could hear a chorus of hellos.

The group ended up in the fellowship hall where about 30 people were seated, watching a gentleman on the television. Windy found a place near the back for all of them and turned her eyes attentively to the speaker. At ten o'clock the teacher turned off the video and addressed the class.

"We'll have about 5 minutes for discussion."

Several people stated that they had never known some of the things the video pointed out.

"They certainly never taught me that in school," commented a man near the front. Many others agreed with his statement.

"Now, I would like to take a couple minutes to meet the newcomers." The teacher indicated a couple sitting near the front of the room. They stood and introduced themselves, identifying who had invited them to join the service.

"Windy, looks like you've brought some guests."

Windy stood. "Most of you may already know Don King who owns King's Grocery over on Erie Street. This is his wife Colleen. I have the privilege of working for Don."

The couple stood when asked but quickly sat back down.

"Okay, there's a few minutes left before the bell rings so please make our guests feel welcome before moving to the sanctuary." Don and Colleen were quickly surrounded and Windy asked Jenny to wait for them.

"I'm going to the kids classes so they see a familiar face when they come out." She peeked in the junior door and saw Adonna and J'mon standing with the rest of the group, hands held, heads bowed in prayer. She eased past and found Ruthie's class.

When the class dismissed, Ruthie exited with her new friends. "Hi, Miss Windy, is it okay if Kenan and Jaela sit with me?"

"Sure it is, you'll be going into Kid's church, won't you?"

"Oh, yes," she turned to the other two. "We have a lot of fun in Kid's church, too." She took Jaela's hand and they headed for the sanctuary.

Windy returned to the other class just as Don and Colleen arrived.

Both kids were busy talking to their classmates, so the adults moved on.

For the next half hour Windy tried to be a good hostess and still lose herself in worshiping the Lord. Colleen was very attentive and joined in the singing. Don seemed easily distracted until the guest speakers stood.

The church supported missionaries in three different countries, the ones from Uganda, East Africa, happened to be in the states this spring and were visiting their sponsor churches. Brother Tom Stevens spoke first; he skillfully took the congregation across the Atlantic and into the heart of the Wild continent. He explained about the wonderful Ugandan people, their culture and lifestyle. He mixed humor with sorrow and kept the congregations attention. Then Cindy Stevens brought updates on their family. She spoke about the new school which was being built, the amount of students it would service and the ongoing skills training. Together they talked about life in the villages and the very real everyday needs of the Ugandan people.

"Please come and visit us." Cindy asked. "We would love to have you. We've built a very nice compound in Kampala, and can easily accommodate large groups. There are many, many projects that need to be finished. Right now we have several buildings without roofs. The first roof always take 3-4 days, the last one only takes one day."

The Stevens then asked for questions from the congregation.

"Wouldn't it be more practical for us to send money, rather than spend it on air fare?" One gentleman asked.

"It might seem more practical, but it certainly doesn't make an impression on you or the people you minister to," Tom answered. "Once you sign a check and drop it in the offering plate you don't usually think about missions till the next offering is taken. But if you visit the country, meet the people, learn their names, feel their hugs and their gratitude, your life is changed. You come back excited about what you've learned eager to do more."

Windy thought of her time in Costa Rica. It was hard to relate to what Tom was saying. Her time had been spent working on a Youth Camp with very little contact with the Costa Ricans.

Monday morning Windy meet Don at King's Grocery as he was unlocking the door. His face lit up as she neared him.

"Windy, when you went to Costa Rica, how did you find out about going? Did you travel with the church? What did it cost? Yesterday when the missionaries said we should visit, did they really mean it?" Don continued his questions as they moved through the stock room and into Don's office. They knew their morning routine so well they could hold a conversation while readying the store for business.

"If you'd stop talking for a moment I would try to answer your questions." Windy laughed. She explained how Jenny was the one slated to go to Costa Rica and had to change her plans. She suggested that Don talk to Pastor Shane next Sunday.

"Who's Pastor Shane?"

"He's our new pastor; he's graduating from seminary this week. Next Sunday is his first official day in the pulpit. You'll like him, Don. He's young and this will be his first pastorate."

"Okay, okay," Don agreed. "We'll be there. By the way, I wanted to tell you we really liked your church. The people were so friendly, the kids have already made friends and Colleen was very impressed with the Sunday School lesson."

"And you," Windy nodded her head at her boss and grinned. "Want to go to Uganda."

Chapter Thirty-One

Windy kept wiping at her eyes, trying to see the directions out of the airport parking lot. Cora sat beside her, not bothering to stop her tears.

"I can't believe she's gone." Cora whispered.

Windy sniffed in reply.

"I do wish we could have gone down and attended the wedding," Cora continued. "Jenny will make such a beautiful bride. Did you see the picture of her wedding gown?"

"Many times," Windy said, thinking of the simple satin gown Jenny's mother had purchased with Jenny's approval.

"I know it was more practical to buy it in Florida so Jenny wouldn't have to ship it, but oh, I wish I could have seen her in it."

"Jenny promised to send pictures and a video," Windy reminded the older woman.

"I know. It just isn't the same."

'No.' Windy thought. 'Life will never be the same'. The last couple weeks had flown by. She had helped Jenny pack her things in a trunk to be sent down ahead of her. Jenny's everyday clothes, toiletries and a few other articles would go on the plane with her. Jenny decided to fly down to Florida and sold her car to Windy for a ridiculously small amount. The girls tried to find time together but it just wasn't there and suddenly Jenny was gone. Windy remembered the day she had taken off for Costa Rica, thankfully Jenny did not share Windy's tendency for motion sickness and actually looked forward to the flight.

When the two crying women reached home, they silently retreated into their own apartments for some reflection. As soon as Cora was safely behind her door, she wiped her tears, blew her nose and started baking, the one thing she could do in any mood.

Windy walked into Jenny's apartment and realized it was now hers again. She walked into the living room and began to disassemble the little bed. She placed the bedding in the dirty clothes basket and started to take the mattress down to the basement when an idea hit her. Why not put the twin bed in the bedroom and the full size in the basement, after all, she wouldn't be sharing her bed with any one.

"No," she told herself. "You have been left behind once more; left alone by two parents, two husbands and a best friend."

"Your parents didn't leave you," herself corrected. *"You left them, for Eddie."*

"Yes, and he left me for a can of beer."

Pulling herself out of the gloom she decided to ask Jenny to help take the big bed downstairs because she knew she couldn't do it alone. But she was alone. Jenny was gone and she was alone.

The phone rang.

"Hey girl," Rick's voice sounded on the other end of the line. "Mom thought you and Cora might be a little sad tonight, she wants you to come to dinner."

"I think we would welcome a few laughs tonight." she accepted. "I'm sure Cora's baking something she can bring. Hey, are you working right now?"

"No, got the day off and just visiting the folks"

"I wanted to do some rearranging, you know bring the couch back up from the basement, take the bed down..."

"I'll be right there."

Rick wasted no time getting to Windy's house. He wanted to see her, but more than that he wanted to reassure her that she wasn't alone. He could understand why she might feel that way, but determined she wouldn't if he had anything to say about it. He pulled into her drive, turned off the ignition, pulled the key and opened the door in one swift movement. He smiled to himself as he thought of how Joe had taught him the importance of swift, sure actions. *"You have to be in control, of yourself, your situation and your actions,"* Joe had told him. Well, he was going to be in control now. He peeked into Cora's kitchen as she was closing the oven door.

"Hey sweet lady," he said, startling her.

Rick took the stairs two at a time and knocked on Windy's door. He imagined a time when there would be no door between them.

They spent the afternoon moving, rearranging and laughing. Rick loved the easiness of their relationship, loved how they touched in an effort to squeeze something through an almost too small door.

By five o'clock the apartment had taken on a new look.

Windy glanced around and sighed.

"I feel as if I have moved Jen out of my life."

Rick came up behind her and pulled her into his arms, taking in the fresh scent of her hair as he kissed the back of her head.

"Jenny chose to move out of this apartment, but neither of you have left each other's lives. She is still here, in our hearts and our laughter."

"My, when did you get so wise?"

"I think it's the company I keep." He released her, resisting the desire to turn her around and pull her into his heart. "C'mon, let's grab Cora and be on our way."

They headed down stairs and popped into Cora's apartment where she was placing two pies in her old double pie carrier.

"We received this as a wedding gift," she informed them.

Rick nodded, he had heard this tidbit before but Cora reminded them as much as she reminded herself. He picked up the carrier and pulled his keys out of his pocket. Tossing them to Windy he said with a wink, "Here, you drive." He placed his hand on Cora's back and guided the little lady out the door,

Windy's protests followed him.

"Really, Rick, I should take my car, it's easier for Cora to get in and out, and then you don't have to bring us back later."

Rick continued to guide Cora to his truck parked at the curb, "Cora loves a little adventure and who said I minded bringing you back?" He stopped for a moment, thinking of Windy's time with Stephan, the guy who always had to be in control.

Turning to Windy, he said, "If you want to take your car that's fine, but I'd like to give you a little more practice in the truck and I really don't mind bringing you home."

Windy marveled at how easily Rick relinquished control and gave her a voice in the situation. For that reason alone, she chose his idea. Dropping her house keys back in her purse she accepted his challenge by trying to wink at him. Both eyes closed part way as her nose winkled. He laughed.

Windy slipped in the clutch like Rick had taught her, started the engine and shoved the gear shift into first. She eased the clutch out ever so slowly, the truck lurched and stalled. Cora laughed. Windy sighed and looked at Rick.

"I think it's in third." he suggested.

She repeated the routine; this time making certain the shift was in first gear. The truck glided forward and away from the curb. Each time Windy neared a stop sign, she held her breath, but the black machine just purred as she pushed in the clutch and eased it back out again. By the time they reached Doug and Valerie's, Windy felt quite confident if not a little proud.

Great conversation took place over the excellent meal. Valerie surprised Rick by inviting Joe over saying they hadn't seen him for quite a while. Cora and Windy were reminded that they had many friends and were definitely not alone. Later Tari and Tami cleared the table and put the leftovers away as Rick and Windy completed their usual task of washing dishes.

The other adults sat in the living room, enjoying a time of relaxation. Soon the four younger folks sat on the floor in front of them and played their favorite word game, but this time with a twist. The girls had found a Bible edition of the game. Rick immediately called for Windy as his partner. His two sisters had been attending youth group and Sunday School and he knew they would be better at this than him, but he also knew Windy would probably knock their socks off. She could win the game all by herself and carry him along with little effort of his own.

Windy proved him wrong. They won the game but with lots of effort on all sides.

Doug Notts watched his precious children, especially the way his son interacted with the cute little lady sitting across from him. Doug's first instinct had been to warn his son off. This woman was barely in her twenties, yet married and divorced twice. How could two marriages go wrong without her being at fault in some way? Rick always talked to his parents before making any decisions; before entering the military, before joining the police force, before enrolling in college, before buying a house. But he hadn't confided in his parents about Windy. And Doug couldn't help but wonder why.

He had to admit, he really liked the girl. She spent enough time around his family to show her true nature. Doug could see nothing bad about her, except for the marriage and divorce thing. Doug didn't believe in divorce and from what he heard at their church, yes, he admitted to himself, it was his church too, neither did God. But because Rick had never talked to Doug about the girl, he didn't know the details. He did know his son was definitely in love, obvious to anyone who could see.

Doug knew that Cora thought the world of Windy. She would probably fill in some details on Windy's life if they ever had some time alone. Yet, he hesitated to place Cora in that situation. No, he would wait on his son. When Rick felt the time was right, he would come to his Dad as he always had.

With the game completed, Rick joined his parents on the couch, Windy sat in the vacant chair and the girls went upstairs to get ready for bed. Doug smiled as he thought of the girls nightly routine. Exercise, cream their faces, set out their clothes and recently, read their Bibles. Although more than two years apart in age, his daughters' actions would convince anyone they were twins.

"Say, Windy," Valerie asked. "Did you know Doug and Rick are going on an adventure?" Doug smiled at his wife's phrasing. The girls had picked that up when listening to Windy talk about Costa Rica. Now it seemed that anything his family did out of the ordinary was deemed an adventure.

Windy smiled at Doug. "A father son time? That's great. Where are you going?"

"Well it's not just us, we're joining a group from church that's attending a men's rally in Detroit. Man 2 God, they call it. As I understand some pretty big names will be there as speakers, although none are familiar to me."

"If you read those new magazines we've been receiving you would know the names." His wife informed him.

"Hey, school just got out. Now I'll have time for magazines."

"When are you going?" Windy asked.

"End of this month." Rick volunteered. "As far as I know there's four of us with Andrew and Pastor J. I'm looking forward to it. There's room for more, Joe."

Rick's partner shook his head, refusing to be drawn into the conversation.

Doug wished he shared his son's enthusiasm. He truly wanted some special time with Rick, but was a little unsure of a 3 hour trip confined in a vehicle with a preacher. He liked Jason, but could hardly picture him as pastor of a congregation. Pastors are supposed to be old and wise, not young enough to be your child. But he supposed the boy had to start somewhere and their church seemed to be the best place. Established in the 1930's the people that attended there were well grounded in their faith, if Jason needed a family, this was the best. They would raise him right for certain.

Chapter Thirty-Two

Rick helped Cora from the truck as Windy went to unlock the front door. He placed his hand under her elbow and steadied her pace. Had Windy noticed any difference in Cora? Did she see what was obvious to him? The sometimes unsteady walk, the slight trembling of her hand, the same stories told over again?

He knew the little lady was getting older, everyone was, he just prayed that she wouldn't lose her health too soon. He'd become quite attached to the sweet old girl.

After getting Cora settled in, the two young people went upstairs.

"Do you want a cherry cola?" Windy asked.

"That stuff is bad for you." His answer stopped her in her tracks. "Well, it is." He defended himself. "Now you take the well water at my house, good, sweet, spring fed water. No chemicals or additives…"

Windy reached up and touched her finger to his lips.

"You're rambling." She warned.

He kissed her finger.

"That's twice in one day." she said.

"What, that I've rambled?"

"No that you've kissed me."

She stood so close; he could just reach out and pull her in for a real kiss. He looked into those eyes, saw the trust, even the admiration. He looked over her cute little face with its freckled nose and thin, pouty lips. He could do it. He could kiss her, she'd let him. But somehow he knew it wasn't time.

He wanted that first kiss to be so special they would both remember it for the rest of their lives.

"Mom's been talking to a lady at church that eats organic food and drinks lots of pure water. I have a feeling Dad and the girls are in for one of Mom's new lifestyle changes."

"Does she do that often?"

"No, but when she does, she takes it very seriously."

"So…do you want a glass of water rather than cherry cola?"

"Hmmm," he shook his head. "Not city water, it's full of chemicals. Now if you want to go to my house, we can drink all we want."

Windy popped the top on her can and wrinkled her nose.

"Your folks live in the city, what do they drink?"

"My water, they fill jugs and take it home with them."

"She is serious, isn't she?"

"Why are we talking about water when we could be talking about you and I?"

"We are talking about you and I—drinking water."

"You run my head in circles, woman."

"Quite an achievement considering that point on the top."

He grinned and lifted her chin with his finger, kissing the end of her nose.

"Make it three."

Windy stood at the bedroom window and watched Rick pull away. The man fascinated her and irritated her at the same time. Was he ever going to kiss her? It seemed he just toyed with her like a cat with a mouse. He'd told her he was patient, that he wanted a good solid friendship first. She admired that, wanted it too. But she thought she might be ready for more.

Rick's words flashed in her mind echoing Stephan's words.

'That stuff isn't good for you.' Was she going to hear Stephan in everything? What if Rick said, 'What did you do today?' or 'it looks like rain?'

When would she allow Rick to be who he is and not a comparison to Stephan or even Eddie?

That night she slept in her little bed in the room she had shared with Eddie, thinking of the crazy police man with the lovely gray eyes.

Sunday morning she drove Cora to church where Rick waited for them at the front door surprising Windy.

"You're here for Sunday School?"

Rick nodded. "My sisters shamed me into it. Said dad would come if I did and wouldn't that make mom happy?"

Windy grinned, silently thanking God for the wisdom of younger sisters. They escorted Cora to the seniors class then descended the stairs into the basement fellowship hall. Sure enough Doug sat beside his wife. Valeria watched the younger couple enter, she smiled a *thank you* to her son.

Rick sat next to Windy and held her hand as they watched a continuation of the gentleman who spoke about the Christian beginnings of our country. Windy was so pleased to see Don and Colleen for the third Sunday in a row. When class ended the foursome walked up stairs. Windy retrieved Cora and Rick guided them both to the pew beside Don. Windy looked around for the King children and found them assimilated in the congregation.

Adonna sat with Tami and Tari, Jaela with Ruthie, Kenan and J'mon were integrated into a pew filled with boys.

Worship music played softly over the speakers, preparing the congregation for the service.

Rick placed his arm on the pew behind Windy and whispered in her ear.

"I invited the Kings out to my place this afternoon."

"You're cooking?"

"Grilling!" he replied raising his eyebrows. "Don's bringing the steaks. Think Cora could whip up a special desert?"

"Are you inviting us out?"

Rick touched his fingers to her hair and played with one of the curls.

Windy wrinkled her nose. "Behave. Don't you work at three?"

"One of the guys needed a day off during the week so we traded. I soaked corn overnight in the hopes that I'd have company."

Windy's mouth watered as she thought of Rick's special corn on the cob. He soaked it overnight in the husks to moisten it, then placed it on the grill until the outer leaves burned, which are then peeled down into a handle of sorts and the hot corn cob is dipped in a can of melted butter.

"Steaks, corn on the cob and Cora's specialty of the week. Hmmmm. Anything else that might entice me to say yes?"

His fingers found the back of her neck and he softly stroked her skin. Then he leaned closer to her ear, "How about some sweet, spring water? Clean and clear, no chemicals, no additives."

Windy laughed quietly.

She leaned into him brushing her hair against his cheek.

"Sold," she whispered. "What time?"

"I told Don 2 o'clock; that gives them time to go home and change, find some good thick steaks. But you and Cora should come as soon as possible. Have Cora bring her ingredients with her and she can use my kitchen."

Windy nodded her okay as Margie walked to the podium and repeated the number from the hymnal.

Windy enjoyed the afternoon with the King family. After eating outside on the picnic table, Rick called Wil's house and within minutes his children appeared from a path in the woods. Soon all 8 kids had disappeared across the bridge, seeking adventure.

The adults eased into patio chairs in Rick's back yard, listening to the soothing music coming from the creek.

"Where's Joe?" asked Cora, accustomed to seeing the partners together.

"He's working today, I took a special day off," Rick explained.

"Where's your mom, then?"

"She's probably at home with the rest of the family."

"They have children?"

Windy sensed the confusion in Cora's mind.

"Cora," she said gently. "Joe is Rick's police partner.

His mom and dad are Doug and Valerie."

"What about Connie?"

Windy shot a surprised look at Rick and shrugged.

"Connie's just a friend Cora, she's not Rick's mom."

"Oooh," the lady nodded. "Well, he's got her eyes."

"Rick, this is a lovely old house, you said you bought it from Wil Packard?" Colleen gracefully changed the subject. "I tried to snoop when I used the bathroom but didn't see much."

"There's not much to it, but I'd love to give you a tour."

They all headed inside where Rick showed them the downstairs. Don liked the fireplace, stating one day they would have a home with a large one. Rick assured him he could get plenty of firewood from Wil.

They moved to the upstairs where Windy was just as curious.

Rick looked over at her. "You've never seen this floor." He stated. She shook her head.

The stairs opened into a small landing with three doors.

Door number 1, on the left, led into a room as long as the house itself situated over the dining room and kitchen. The room contained a large, old metal frame bed adorned with a chenille bedspread. Three old dressers and a vanity shared the room.

"My goodness Rick, where did you find these antiques?" Colleen admired.

"They belonged to Missy's grandparents and came with the house."

"You're kidding?" She approached each item and gave her guestimate on its age.

"Do you know much about antiques?" Windy asked.

"Only enough to get me into trouble. I know a little about style, but nothing about wood."

"Really?" Don asked. "That's cherry right there, and this piece is made from oak."

"Look at there, you two have a special knowledge that neither of you knew about. You should start an antique business." Windy suggested. Everyone chuckled, but Windy could see a new appreciation for each other on her friends faces.

The second door revealed a full bath, right over the downstairs bath and the third door, on the right opened into a second, smaller bedroom, the length of the living room. Obviously Rick used this room. Although very tidy, it had a man's look to it.

"Rick, why aren't you using the master bedroom?" Don asked.

"Not until I have someone to share it with." Don and Colleen both looked at Windy and she blushed.

"When I bought the house, I knew it needed some work."

He pointed out the old wallpaper, missing in some spots. "The floors are beautiful hardwood and I have redone those. But as for decorating or new furniture, I decided to wait until there's a lady of the house who has much better decorating sense than I do. My mom told me how wise a decision that is."

Chapter Thirty-Three

Rick showed up at the store the next morning. He headed straight for Don's office in the back of the building and waved at him through the window. Don motioned for him to enter.

"Thanks again for those steaks yesterday."

"My pleasure. We really enjoyed ourselves. I heard about your woods and the creek and the trees all the way home."

"Sounds like you should move to the country."

"Naw, then it wouldn't be a treat, or a reward that I can hold over their heads." Both men chuckled.

"Hey, I'm going to harass one of your employees."

"Go right ahead, if you get out of line, she can handle you."

Rick found Windy in the baby aisle, her favorite. She placed the last bottle of shampoo on the shelf as Rick strode up next to her.

"You're up early." She commented without turning to look at him.

"What time do you get off?"

"6. I didn't come in until 10 today."

"Well, Joe and I usually get hungry around that time. I thought I could pick up some things today, take them to Cora's and we'd have dinner together."

"Is this going to be a habit, officer Notts?"

"I hope so." A frown quickly replaced his smile. "Is Cora up to cooking a meal?"

"Oh yeah. Cora may forget some things, but she'll always remember her way around the kitchen. I'm sorry about what she said yesterday, that was awkward."

"Don't worry about it. Now help me pick out tonight's meal."

She sent Rick back for a shopping cart, then proceeded to help him fill it. When looking at an item on the shelf he asked if they carried the organic equivalent. By the time they finished it appeared that Rick attempted to completely restock Cora's pantry.

"Mom says chemicals in our food can cause early dementia. If something this simple can help Cora, then we'll get it."

Before heading for the checkout, Rick stopped at Don's office again.

"Hey, Don. Besides the health food stores there's no place to buy organic food. Thanks for stocking some. Just to let you know, the more you stock, the more we'll buy. My mom's got our family on organics and supplements now."

"You know Rick; I have actually looked into providing an organic section, if I knew it would move; I'd do it."

"I'll tell mom." Rick volunteered then added, "she's got friends."

Joe slid into the passenger seat of the patrol car, glad that Rick volunteered to drive. He wasn't sure he'd be able to get behind the wheel. As with every one of Cora's meals Joe tended to eat too much. He was sorry for the belly ache, but not sorry for the delicious food.

Joe looked over at his partner. "You're really serious about this girl, aren't you?"

"I want to marry her Joe; she has become my whole life."

"You know I like Windy, she's a sweet kid, but you've got to watch out for yourself. Two bad marriages can't be solely her husbands fault."

"I understand what you're saying, but both of us know the deal with Eddie."

"Yeah, but what drove him to drink? I'd never heard of him as a teen. He was already married when his drinking started."

"Some day maybe Windy will tell me. I do know that Dr. Michaels intention was a family and Windy is unable to have children. When he found out he made her leave."

"Did she know that when she married him? Did she deceive him?"

"Even you know the answer to that. She could have made a stink and tried to get some money out of the guy, but she didn't. She got nothing from that marriage but heartache."

"But now she's got religion. How are you gonna handle that?"

"You're right there, she deserves someone with the same beliefs as herself and I'm not going to 'get religion' as you say just to get a woman. I'll have to see how things play out."

Joe shook his head. At least he had tried to warn his young friend.

Rick had to work out his schedule to accommodate the Man 2 God trip. So he wound up doubling back and working days the next morning.

He went straight to Windy's after his shift ended. He knocked on Cora's door first as always, but received no answer. Then he took the steps two at a time to Windy's apartment. She opened the door after the first knock.

"Where's Cora?"

"Spending a couple days with her nephew. They just had another baby and they asked Cora to stay and help with the cooking."

"Just her cup of tea. But that means you'll go hungry this week."

"I know how to cook, I may have forgotten, but it'll come back."

"So how about coming to my house and put your memory to the test?"

She frowned. "Aren't you on your way to work?"

"No, just got off. I don't work tomorrow but then straight through until we leave for Detroit."

"That is next week, isn't it?"

Windy put food and water down for Sachel then retrieved her purse. "What's for supper?" She asked

"So your mom's getting pretty heavy into this healthy eating?" Windy asked as she handed Rick another pan to rinse.

"Yeah, took Dads bacon away until she can find a pig farmer that doesn't feed his pigs garbage. She really surprised us with what she's been learning. I have to admit, once I heard what pigs eat, pork chops don't sound as appetizing as they used to."

"Good thing for you she found a beef farmer who doesn't use chemicals and such."

"She mentioned raising her own chickens until Dad told her she would have to kill and pluck them herself."

Windy laughed. "Your mom couldn't kill anything."

"She limits herself to mosquitoes and flies."

He stacked the last pan in the drainer as Windy cleaned out the sink and dishpan.

"You're not going to replace this old sink are you?"

"Do you like it?"

"Yes, I do. I can't imagine how old it is."

"Okay then, I'll keep it, just for you." He winked and grabbed her hand. "Movie or music?"

"Hmmmm... Music. Then we can talk."

"Talking music it is," He agreed as they headed for the living room. He put on some slow oldies, the romantic type, and they sat down on the couch.

"I think it's time I told you some of the things you don't know about me."

"You mean there are things I missed?"

"Yes, even things a good police detective couldn't find out."

Windy began with her last year in high school, dating Eddie, receiving a scholarship, mom and dad moving, and her marriage. Then she told him about the pregnancy and miscarriage. She surprised herself by crying.

"I denied what happened. Told myself it was just a couple missed periods, not a pregnancy, not a baby. Then I started seeing the pictures of babies of the Pregnancy office, I was drawn to those at eight weeks; amazed at the little people I saw. It wasn't until Stephan told me I couldn't conceive that I realized I had. I never visited the hospital so my insides became infected and now I can't have children. Once I realized that, I remembered why I miscarried and why Eddie started drinking.

"He was thrilled at first, when I told him I thought he might be a dad, then scared, and said he didn't know how. I assured him he would be a great dad. But a few days later he came home drunk for the first time and the drinking escalated. On the fourth of July he became violent and knocked me around. I…I started bleeding.

"Months later his dad and siblings came to visit. Mr. Bilmon is a mean, hateful man. Eddie had actually stopped drinking for a little while, but his dad's visit started him up again. He was afraid of his dad, and probably afraid of being one.

"You know a little about my marriage to Stephan. It was a mistake, pure and simple. It should never have happened. I didn't even care for him, though I told myself I did. Now, I find it hard to believe I was ever his wife."

They sat for a while, Rick's arm around Windy, his hand gently rubbing her shoulder. The soothing music continued. He pulled her a little closer so her head rested on his shoulder.

"Now I know more about your past, so tell me how you see your future."

Windy smiled and looked up at him.

"I see children, not of my womb, but certainly of my heart. I see my husband and family spending time with each other and with our Lord. I see happiness, even in adversity."

"Do you see me?" he whispered.

She nodded and turned her face into his neck, drawing in his earthy scent. She sighed and placed her hand on his other shoulder, nestling in, nice and comfy. Rick reached down and pulled her legs over his. Settling her on his lap, he scooted down into the softness of the old couch.

Chapter Thirty-Four

Hours later Rick awoke. His neck and back hurt and his leg had fallen asleep. He considered twisting his body until he could lay Windy on the couch, then go upstairs to his own bed, but one look at her peaceful face, one sound of her even breathing stopped him. He could sleep anytime, but for right now he held Windy, here in his own home and he wasn't going to give that up easily. He shifted his weight, tried to scrunch a throw pillow under his back and then closed his eyes. She stirred and pulled herself a little closer, for a moment he felt as if she might kiss him. He moved his head away. He didn't want a kiss that might belong to someone else. They had never been together while she slept and if she kissed him now, that kiss might not be intended for him and he wouldn't take that chance.

Windy patted Sachel, wondering who shaved him. She loved sleeping with him, loved the heat he exuded. He was certainly warm this morning. She sighed, feeling her bed move beneath her. Beds don't breathe. She held her breath. Some one was in her bed. Or was she in someone's? Where? Who? *Wake up Windy*! she screamed. Flowers, she could smell flowers, but her eyes were closed, why couldn't she open her eyes? *This isn't a nightmare. I smell flowers and grass; I don't have flowers in my nightmares.* She drew in a breath and felt a twig stick in her back. Was she in a tree? Trees don't breath, well not so you can feel them anyway. The bed moved or the tree. Whatever breathed, now moved. Why couldn't she wake up?

"Morning." The moving thing whispered. It sounded like Rick, why would Rick be in the tree? *Morning? How could it be morning? There's no sun.*

"I'm going to sit you up, Honey. My back didn't fare very well."

Finally she opened her eyes and looked into his beautiful gray ones. His lashes weren't very long. Could someone have beautiful eyes without long lashes?

"Hey," he ducked his head, "you in there?"

She started to yawn, quickly covered her mouth and nodded. "I think so," she mumbled. "I was dreaming."

"About me?"

"Kind of. Mostly about Sachel and breathing trees."

"Well I'll tell you what, little missy, after we have breakfast, we are going to the furniture store." He stood and stretched, heading for the kitchen. "If you insist on falling asleep on me, it won't be on this couch again."

Then she remembered. Her eyes flew open in horror. She'd stayed the night at Rick's, on his couch, in his arms. What would she tell Cora? What would everybody say? Jenny would kill her!

Jenny.

Jenny wouldn't know, Jenny was gone.

Serves her right for leaving me unprotected.

She slipped through the kitchen and opened the bathroom door, hoping to scrub her teeth with her fingers.

Rick stood at the bathroom sink, his toothbrush in his mouth. He winked at her.

"Oh! I'm sorry! I didn't! Oh my, oh my goodness!"

"It's alright," he laughed, spewing toothpaste on the mirror. "If I wanted privacy, I would have locked the door."

He held up another toothbrush still in its wrapper.

"Anticipating company?" she asked, trying to regain her composure.

"No, I buy them on sale, got several more if you don't like the color." He opened a drawer in the vanity revealing more little packages. "You can choose your own flavor toothpaste too." He rinsed his mouth using the top Dixie cup from the upside down stack, pulled a rag from under the sink to wipe off the mirror, then walked over to her, handing her the brush.

"What am I going to tell Cora?" she whispered, looking at him.

"About what?"

"About being here, about not going home last night."

"Tell her we talked and listened to music and fell asleep. I think that's about all there is to tell."

"What will she think of me?"

"She'll think no different than she always has. Besides why do you have to tell her anything?"

"Oh, she'll catch me as soon as I walk in the door." She stopped, puzzled. "I wonder why she didn't call last night when I didn't come home?"

"Maybe it's because she didn't come home, either."

Windy looked at him, mystified.

"Her nephew, the new baby…cooking…she's staying the weekend…"

"Oh," Windy sighed with relief. "Praise God."

"I do," he answered, dropping a kiss on her forehead. "Now, I have organic eggs, organic bread and real butter. Sound good?"

"Organic milk? I gotta have my milk."

"How about organic surprise?"

"Do you have this is pink?" Windy queried, smiling at Rick's wrinkled nose. She ran her hand over a very expensive sofa, complete with recliners on both ends.

"We might be able to order it in rose." The young salesman responded, trying hard not to look repulsed.

"What do you think, Rick, will Rose go with that orange and green shag carpet?"

He snickered as the salesman lost his battle.

"We have a full line of floor coverings, I'm sure we can match whatever you choose."

"Well," Rick pondered. "Can you order this in orange and green?" He looked at Windy. "Honey, that way we won't have to change the carpet."

The young man finally caught on. "I hear those great colors are coming back into style, I might just be able to fix you up." He stretched out his hand to Rick. "I'm Mick. We've got some very nice furnishings. Let me know how I can help you."

Rick grasped the man's hand and introduced himself. "I bought an old farmhouse a couple years ago. Haven't changed a thing yet and I know I need help in that department; serious help."

Windy had moved on and now sat in a comfy rocker.

"And your wife is partial to pink."

"She's not my wife, yet, but I figure if she helps me with the decorating she'll love the place so much she won't be able to say no."

"Smart man." They watched her move on to another couch, checking the price before sitting down.

"You know, if you're looking to do an entire room, we have specials. When purchasing a grouping; couch, love seat and chair, we can usually include a couple end tables. Maybe throw in a pair of lamps."

Rick nodded, watching Windy. She was enjoying this, he could tell. He was glad he'd heeded his mother's advice when he bought the house. He'd asked her to help him choose some replacement furnishings and she simply said, "Let your wife do that. It'll make her feel better about moving into your house." At the time Rick wondered how his mom could possibly know about Windy, then he realized, it was just a mother's wisdom speaking. He took her words to heart and every pay day placed a percentage into his house fund. He had a nice little nest egg now and knew he would follow the young man's advice.

"Well, Mick," he said pulling a paper from his wallet. "Here are the dimensions of my living room. Guess it's time to start redecorating."

Chapter Thirty-Five

Rick threw his duffle bag into the back of the SUV next to his dad's canvas bag. He hopped in the back seat and shook hands with Jason Shane. The four men agreed that Doug could drive, since he had the nicest vehicle and knew a little about the geography around Detroit. Andrew would act as navigator.

Rick knew his dad preferred that. He liked to drive.

The trip held many surprises for father and son. They found out their Pastor Jason knew almost as much about sports as he did the Bible. He liked swimming and actually held a couple records in his high school. Like Rick, he had no desire to hunt animals with a gun but enjoyed taking pictures of the wildlife. He even thought building a deer blind on Rick's property would be a great idea, with a camera as a weapon and film as ammunition.

Doug and Andrew, both high school teachers had already established a friendship which solidified during the 3 hour drive.

The men arrived at their destination with Andrew giving directions to the hotel. They settled in with little fanfare, and Andrew quickly guided them to a nearby restaurant for dinner. They had arrived at the silver dome in plenty of time before the evening session began.

Rick ordered a steak and French fries while his dad ordered chicken and salad.

"Mom got you on a diet?" he teased.

"Son, one thing you must learn and you might as well learn it the easy way, by my example; if a woman loves you, she wants to take care of you, keep you around for a while. If she says you should eat certain foods to stay healthy, listen. If she says she'd rather have you fat and happy, watch out!"

They all laughed.

Then Andrew ordered chicken.

"Now that's a man with a wife who loves him." Doug stated.

Jason looked at Rick and grinned.

"Steak and French fries," he told the waitress. "Till Rick and I find ourselves well loved, we're gonna eat what we want, when we want!"

After their hearty meal the four men jumped back into Doug's SUV and headed for the super dome. A place that often packed out with excited, beer drinking football fans would now be a place of excited, spirit filled God fans.

The African American preacher told it like it was.

Rick could see the glory of God through the man's words in one minute and the agony of Hell the next. His voice picked the young man up out of his seat and dropped him back in again, he felt pinned to the chair and in a wave of utter emotion feared he would fall off his seat. What power did this man of God possess to have such a physical impact on him?

After 2 hours of riding a roller coaster, Rick bowed his head as the black man finished in a prayer so intimate Rick thought for sure that God must have been on the platform holding the speaker's hand.

The MC thanked the speaker after 3 solid minutes of applause from the audience. The speaker, wiping his face with a sweat filled hanky, just kept repeating, 'thank you Jesus'.

30,000 men orderly filed out of the stadium amazing Rick at the lack of noise and confusion. Each man seemed to be in his own world, reflecting on the message drilled into them.

The foursome joined the slow moving tide and eventually made their way to the vehicle. No one said anything on the drive to the hotel. Rick showered after Jason; the teachers saying they usually showered in the morning before heading to school. They expressed one very nice thing about summer vacation; they only had to shower on Sunday morning.

Rick crawled, exhausted, into the king size bed beside his dad. How would they ever make it up in time to pack, eat and attend the 9am session?

Doug's internal alarm went off at 6 am, as it always did, summer was no exception. He quickly showered. Andrew obviously had an internal clock too, as he was up and waiting when Doug came out.

The older man woke Rick and Jason. They packed and had the SUV loaded by the time Andrew dried his hair. Breakfast at a morning café across the street and they walked into the stadium by 8:15.

At nine sharp a tall, impressive man stood behind the pulpit wearing polo shirt, kakis and deck shoes. He spoke well and held everyone's attention. The pastor of an enormous church that just kept growing, the man talked of God's love, Christ's sacrifice, man's need for a Savior and the absolute necessity of Christians working together, ignoring denominational boundaries, becoming brothers and obeying God's command to go into all the world and spread the gospel. Then he got into the meat of his talk.

"Husbands!" he said. "You've all read that wonderful scripture about a wife being submissive to her husband." He waited while the applause died down. "Great scripture. Truly great, for God ordained man to be the head of the household, to provide for and protect his family. If we are being proper husbands, that is what we do; provide and protect. I've always believed that when a man beckons for his wife to come to him. She should come." Again he waited for the approving noise to diminish. "However," audible moans filled the stadium. "HE MUST BE WORTH COMING TO!" Each word stated sharp and crisp. "A man's right to beckon for his wife only stands if he deserves her response. So let me take you a little further into that great scripture. Paul goes on to say 'Husbands, love your wife as Christ loves the church, being willing to die for her."

Rick looked over at his dad and saw utter concentration. His dad watched and listened as though the speaker talked only to him. But Rick paid attention to the words also. He wanted to be that kind of husband to Windy.

Rick had never heard such a great speaker. He thought of the enthusiastic man of last night's session and the calm determination of this gentleman.

Time was allowed for the thousands of men to stand and take a break. Bag lunches of turkey, ham or roast beef sandwiches, a small bag of chips and a granola bar were passed down the aisles by program workers. Bottles of water followed.

Workers picked up the trash in record time and the third and final session began.

A short, balding man shuffled to the pulpit. He hunched, his head bent forward between his rounded shoulders. Rick felt a tinge of disappointment. How could this little guy compare with the previous speakers? Why would they save this guy as the speaker to send them on their way, back into a mundane, daily life?

In a feeble, droning voice the man began telling of his childhood, one spent in fear and terror; of an abusive mother and a parade of live-in men. He watched adults eat hearty meals while he was allowed to eat whatever was left on the plates before washing them.

He suffered taunts and beatings from school bullies, could never find a place to fit in. He was "Not". Not athletic, not popular, not smart, not good looking, not talented, not a druggie, not a rebel, not any teacher's pet. Not accepted in the service because of his underdeveloped frame and sickly continence. Not accepted into college because of his extremely low grade point average. Not eligible for scholarships or financial help. Not healthy. Not disabled. Not hired. Not wanted. Not anyone's friend, not anyone's enemy. Not hated, not loved. He wandered through life, not really living. Just not.

Rick found the man's story almost unbelievable. How could anyone be nothing? Have nothing? He simply couldn't comprehend such a life.

"I had heard the phrase, 'Jesus loves you.' who hasn't?" the man said, lifting his head a little. His gaze went from the pulpit to the first row of seats on the playing field. "I figured He probably did; love you, not me. I lived on the streets, saw the filth and anger, lived in fear and poverty. I never kept anything good. Found a real nice pair of boots one time, I took them from the dumpster, traded 'em for a loaf of bread. My shoes were worn through, I needed those boots but I knew they would get me knifed in my sleep.

"As time went on I began to think that not being alive could be better than the existence I had. One day I walked along the river bank wondering why I still lived. Why not just step into the water and sink to the bottom? I would not be missed. I would not be looked for. So I sat on the concrete wall getting up my courage when some one sat beside me. He was the man from one of the downtown missions."

The small man lifted his head a little more, looking at the first row of bleachers.

"He asked what my intentions were and I told him I planned to fall into the river and not come out. 'Why?' he asked me. So I told him about my life; how I had no place in this world and the world had no use for me. He began to tell me about another Man the world had no use for. A Man the world rejected and despised, a Man denied and abandoned by His own friends. This Man was spit upon, mocked, beaten almost to the death, then cruelly nailed to a cross. The world saw this Man as nothing and treated Him as nothing. But in truth He was the very Son of God and nothing the world said or did could rob Him of His identity."

The small man looked up into the crowd, he stood straighter. "The man beside me explained that Jesus allowed Himself to be crucified on a cross so I could have an identity not given me by the world, but given me by my Holy Father in Heaven. By dying for me, Jesus shared His identity with me and bought my life with His blood, adopting me into the family of God."

The man lifted His head high, tears streaming down his face. "Jesus became nothing in my place, in order to share His Father, His identity, His eternal glory with me. All I had to do was accept His love. That day I acknowledged and repented of my sins, I asked Jesus to forgive and cleanse me, make me a new creature in Him. When He did, I felt His love pour into my being, I felt release from the world who would not have me. I experienced His amazing grace and mercy."

Rick watched as the man on the platform stood to his full height and lifted his hands toward his father in heaven. His voice filled the stadium, his emotion permeated the air.

"I no longer wander through a world fearful of those who reject me, now I rejoice with a family who loves me, whom I share a wonderful Heavenly Father with. I have brothers and sisters who I will spend a glorious eternity with.

"I am no longer a NOT, I am a son of God, a child of the Most High, an heir in the greatest family. I have more wealth than the richest man, I have more knowledge than the most educated man, I am well fed on the Word of God, I am accepted, I am wanted, I AM LOVED!!!"

The crowd stood as one. Rick heard the shouts, the praise, the worship. Suddenly everything became clear—where he was and why, the things he had done and hadn't done; resisting the temptations in the service to join the guys for a night at the local bar and a trip to the house where young ladies waiting to rake in the servicemen's extra cash.

Rick knew without a doubt he heard God's voice in his ear. The stadium rung out with choruses sung by thousands of men singing praise to their creator, but a small, powerful voice, one that held all authority, whispered in his ear. These words came from God, the God who created Rick, saved him from an abortionist's instruments, placed him in a loving home and gave him strength to endure the taunts of his fellow soldiers. This voice spoke to him in a dark apartment about a young woman who needed him, who would one day be his bride. This love, God's love, ordained the stars in the heavens, the seasons, the tides, the miracle of birth and growth. This Lord who spoke to him—no, called him, asking for his alliance, his commitment, his life. This God he wanted to follow, to make himself not just available, but totally completely dedicated to a mission of God's choosing, a life of serving the God who died for him.

Rick knew his identity didn't depend on an earthly family, adopted or birth. His identity lay in his Lord.

Rick had not accepted the ways of the world because God had a much better way, a much better plan and God had kept Rick close enough to lead him, while still allowing Rick to make his own choices. Without even knowing it, he had chosen God and now that he knew it, he had to make a conscience choice to do so.

"Dad, Dad?!" He needed his dad, needed to share this moment with the one man in his life that he loved dearly, that he wanted to emulate. He needed to feel his Dad's presence; to hear his voice, touch the shoulders that had always bore Rick's burdens. He wanted to turn all those burdens, all those fears and doubts over to God, but he needed his dad with him when he did. This was too big, too important, not to have his dad right there.

"Rick, Rick," Doug reached out to his son, the boy he had always adored, the man he would gladly give his life for, he needed Rick right now, he needed Rick to be a part of this momentous occasion, when he would become one with his God, his Creator, he needed Rick to share this moment with him.

They grabbed each other and embraced as tight as they could, they felt their love surging, felt their oneness with each other and their Lord.

Jason stood beside the two hugging men, feeling the excitement flow through them. For a moment he felt jealous. Some where out in this big world stood his father; the man who sired him and left. Doug and Rick had each other, they were one as far as their relationship was concerned, Doug had taught Rick so many things that only a father can. He had been there throughout Rick's childhood, caring for him, teaching, guiding, loving. Why hadn't his own father stepped forward to do those things for him?

Jason knew it wasn't his own fault. He knew that a tiny baby is not at fault for anything. Either his father wanted no part of them or his mother wanted no part of his father. He wondered how life would be different if his mother had chosen adoption as Rick's mother had.

Yet the words of the speaker rung true in his mind. He knew where his identity lay, had known since the first day he walked into church with Mr. Jarvis, God's family was his family.

Then Jason felt a nudge on his shoulder and turned to look. No one was close enough to touch him but a small voice whispered in Jason's ear. *I am your Father and I love you.*

Tears welled up in the young man's eyes. He had the best Father any man could ask for.

Doug grasped Jason's arm.

"Jason, Rick and I want Jesus in our lives, will you pray with us?"

Jason placed both arms around the father and son and began the prayer.

"Dear Heavenly Father…"

They repeated his words.

"We come before You today, seeing the sin in our lives…"

"We confess to You all the wrong behavior, wrong attitudes…"

"We acknowledge our need for a Savior…"

"Thank You for sacrificing Yourself on the cross…"

"That we may enter into Your kingdom…"

"On earth and throughout eternity…"

"Please forgive us and enter our hearts…"

"Jesus, come into our lives as Savior and Lord…"

"Be a part of everything we do from this day forward…"

"Help us to be the men You created us to be…"

"Make us Godly men, husbands and fathers…"

"Help us be an example to our families, friends and neighbors…"

"That You may be glorified. In Jesus Holy name. Amen."

Chapter Thirty-Six

Doug wanted to call Valerie. He wanted to tell her about the life changing decision he and their son had made.

But Rick stopped him. "Dad, I really want to tell mom in person, I want to be next to her so she can hug the stuffing out of me."

Doug agreed.

Then Jason suggested, "I haven't planned a sermon for tomorrow, I thought that sharing our time here would be more interesting. Are you willing to wait until tomorrow and tell your family at the same time you tell your church family?"

The men considered it, stating how hard it would be to contain themselves, but agreed it might be a good thing.

The three hour drive ended far too soon for Doug who had plied Jason with every question he could think of. Sometimes the young man admitted he didn't know the answer, but suggested they start a men's bible study and find the answers together. Since Doug and Andrew were on summer break, they only needed to work around Rick's afternoon schedule.

Rick couldn't believe he sat in front of the whole congregation. What was he thinking when he agreed to this idea?

His dad and Andrew stood in front of a classroom of sometimes unfriendly teens; this should be a piece of cake for them. And Jason, well, no need to even go there.

Last night he really had to keep himself from telling Windy. He wanted so bad to call her, invite himself over, and tell her of his experience with his Father, his God, his Lord and Savior. Now he searched the congregation for her, but she and Cora were both missing. He hoped everything was okay.

Jason spoke from behind the pulpit. "Brothers and sisters, as most of you know—on Friday I traveled to Detroit with these three men to a Man 2 God conference. We would like to share our experiences with you. But first would Mary and Hannah, Valerie, Tami and Tari join us?"

The women moved up to the platform, Valerie sat between her husband and son. Rick couldn't look at her, he knew if he were going to get through this he had to keep his emotions completely in check.

Jason spoke for a few minutes about his reaction to the whole event, stated how awesome it was to be in a huge stadium filled with men worshipping their Creator. He smiled and said "I believe there is hope for this country, when Godly men are not afraid to stand up for their faith and tell the world about our need for a Savior." He then turned to Doug who rose from his seat. Rick stood also. They hadn't talked about how to go about this but one thing he knew, he and his dad did so much together, and they would do this together too. Doug placed his hand on Rick's shoulder then turned and motioned to his family to join them. Rick heard his dad's words, understood and agreed with them, but remained nervous. His mom's arm tightened around his waist as Doug explained their mutual decision to ask Christ into their hearts. The congregation appeared to sit on the edge of their seats, most of them crying, several praising God with a loud thank you Lord or a soft Amen.

When Doug finished his family embraced, all of them in tears. Then Rick's mouth opened and he began to speak.

"Most of you know that my sisters and I are adopted. My birth mom loved me so much," Rick noticed many heads turn and look at Connie, he noted that she, too, was crying, "that she released me from her life so I could be raised by the most wonderful parents in the world. A couple months ago, I became aware of the emptiness in my life. I thought maybe I needed a wife," he grinned and received several smiles in return. "Or maybe I needed to know more about my birth parents. So I went to the man who always helped me find answers, but he wasn't home. As soon as I saw my mom, I knew it was really her I needed to talk to. She told me about the emptiness she had experienced and how God had filled it. So I came to church with her and met some pretty wonderful people. This weekend God's Holy Spirit spoke to my dad and me, we asked Christ into our hearts just as he told you. I now realize we are all adopted. Our earthly parents are very important, but our Heavenly Father is the One through Whom we receive our identity."

Rick knew those words came straight from God, because he could never have done this on his own. He pulled his mom into his arms and they cried openly. After a few moments his family returned to the chairs behind them and Andrew stepped to the pulpit with his wife and daughter. Rick listened with a thankful heart, looking over his brothers and sister in the Lord.

Chapter Thirty-Seven

Rick met Windy on his porch and handed her a pair of pink water shoes. They sat down on the steps and she slipped off her sandals.

"What are these?" She asked.

"We're going for a walk. How's Cora?"

"She's much better. A walk where?" She pulled the tight stretchy fabric over her foot, surprised it fit.

"Down the creek. What was wrong with her?"

"She didn't sleep well and seemed a little disoriented this morning. Along the creek?" She pulled the second one on.

"No, down the creek. Have you noticed this sort of thing before?"

"A little, she repeats herself a lot, but I figured it's old age, you know? You're wearing these too." She noted the tight dark shoes at the bottom of his tanned hairy legs. She'd never seen him in shorts before. He looked pretty good.

"Yeah, you're not the only one who can wear jean shorts."

She blushed.

He stood and pulled her to her feet. He wore a light blue sleeveless t-shirt and Windy noticed the muscles in his arms. "Has she talked to her doctor about it?"

"No, but I told her we're making an appointment tomorrow, I used the excuse about her not sleeping." He really did look good; there was something different about him today. "I don't like to miss church, but I just didn't feel I could leave Cora alone."

"I'm sure she shouldn't have been. You did the right thing." He held her hand as he led her around the house and through the back yard.

She cocked her head. "Good sermon today?"

"Jason didn't preach."

"Who did?"

Rick chuckled. "Guess you could say Andrew did."

She stopped and looked up at him, wrinkling her nose.

"What's going on?"

He continued the walk. "You've forgotten?"

"Forgotten what?"

"I was gone for two days, and you didn't even miss me."

"Oh, that's right, your men's conference. Did you have a good time?"

"A great time. So we shared with the congregation today."

"We? You said Andrew preached."

Instead of walking onto the little bridge that spanned the small creek, Rick headed down beside it, stepping into the water. "It's a little rocky but the shoes will protect your feet."

Windy stepped in beside him. "It's cold!"

"Of course it's cold, it's a trout stream. All of us said something, but Andrew summed it up; did a great job too. He and dad just got up there and talked like it was the most natural thing in the world. I didn't do as well. I mean, how do you say 'license and registration please,' to seventy people?"

Windy laughed. She could just imagine Rick standing at the pulpit, stumbling over his words. She almost stumbled over a slippery rock.

"Just walk on the bottom, it's fairly sandy. I actually got out a couple sentences, and I didn't even have to flash my badge to get everyone's attention."

"You probably wore your gun for insurance. What about snakes?" Small trees and bushes lined the creek as the land farther away sported large poplars.

"Oh there's some in here, but they won't bother you."

She followed him up the creek against the flow.

"Are you going to tell me about your trip?" Her foot sunk into a gushy spot. "Do you do this often?"

"No. Just once last year, when I wanted to see where it led. Yes, I'm going to tell you." They rounded a sharp bend and came upon a large rock right in the middle of the creek. A couple smaller ones circled it. Beyond them the land cleared a little but looked muddy.

"I think someone had a dam here once, looks like this was a pool." He gestured ahead of them. "I've thought about building it back up, but I'm not sure how it would affect the wildlife."

Windy smiled. Leave it to Rick to be concerned about the fish and snakes and whatever else used the creek.

He sat down on the rock and motioned Windy to join him.

They had to sit almost back to back, their sides touching. She leaned against Rick, pulled her feet out of the cold water and secured them on another rock.

She wanted to pump him about his experience, yet, she wanted him to tell her in his own way, knowing the recitation would be much better.

"Windy, I told you I want to be your friend, earn your trust. I told you I want a relationship with you, a long term one. But I've held back, because, well, I wanted to deserve you." He took her closest hand and turned so he could see her face. "But I also believe God was holding me back, telling me in His own way, that it wasn't time yet."

She looked into those beautiful gray eyes and saw the 'Andrew look.' She wanted him to love her, wanted him to need her. But more than that she wanted to love him.

"I know you're a Christian and I know you should marry a Christian man, one who shares your faith. I admit, I never thought about getting religion just to get you. That wouldn't be right. Some time ago, I felt this huge emptiness in my soul. I wondered what it was. What would fill it?" He lifted her hand to his lips and tenderly kissed it. "I though maybe you would fill it or maybe knowing my birth parents. I talked to my mom and she said only God could fill that void. So I started going to church. I felt good about being there. But I knew there was more."

He turned and pulled Windy into his arms. She heard his intake of breath, felt wetness on her forehead.

"Windy, yesterday I asked Christ into my heart…" he swallowed.

She felt her own tears cascade down her cheeks.

"Dad and I together, we were drawn into God's love by His Holy Spirit," his voice cracked. "Windy, I have become a new creature in Christ. I'm actually glad you weren't in church today because this is how I want to tell you. Just you and I here, in God's presence surrounded by His love."

"Windy Jordan, I have also come to realize I will never deserve you. If I am so blessed to have you as part of my life it is because of God's amazing mercy. I am undeserving of anything good; especially His grace, His sacrifice." He hesitated. "But Windy, I now have to confess, even after all this time of wanting to be with you, if God suddenly said no. Well, I'd follow Him; even if it meant following Him without you."

She buried her face in his shoulder and released a torrent of thankful tears. She had never told Rick of her selfish daily prayer for his salvation. She wanted to be with him, but she would never allow him to come between her and God. It just couldn't happen. Now he was telling her of his birth into God's family. This had to be the happiest moment of her life. But oh how she wished she had a Kleenex.

Rick pulled back a little and tried to look in to her face, but she kept her head down. Then he laughed, reached into his back pocket and handed her a handkerchief.

"You don't think I'd let a drippy nose get in the way of our first kiss, do you?"

Chapter Thirty-Eight

He waited for her to wipe her nose, then placed his hands gently on the sides of her head and carefully smoothed her tears from her cheeks with his thumbs.

She looked at those beautiful gray eyes, his tanned cheeks and the sandy colored mustache that graced his moist lips.

He grinned.

"I know," she said, realizing he studied her face, too. "My nose always gets red when I cry."

"I like it." He softly kissed her red nose. She closed her eyes and leaned her forehead against his cheek, drawing in his scent. He smelled like fresh cut grass, pine trees and creek water. She loved his smell, wanted it to be the only scent she recognized.

"Windy, I have a confession."

She laid her head on his shoulder. Confessions were often bad things and she wanted nothing bad right now.

"Is it a good confession?"

"Hmmmm. Maybe it starts out bad, but ends up good?"

"Hmmm. Maybe I don't want to hear it." She slipped her left arm behind him and placed her right hand on his chest, feeling the rhythm of his heart. She tucked her head a little deeper into his neck. She didn't want confessions right now. She didn't want anything, just this moment, Rick so close to her and the knowledge that they both pledged their lives to the same Lord and Savior. She thought of his words about a first kiss. That would be nice, but really the anticipation was pretty good, too.

He spoke softly into her ear, his voice caressing her soul.

"We weren't a church going family, but my parents and my moms parents are very moral people. When I hit that awkward age, my dad sat me down and spoke very directly to me about being a man. He left out nothing. He talked about the physical, the moral, and the responsibility aspects of manhood. He had always taught me right from wrong. But this was so much more. That talk shaped who I became. What I did, and didn't do from that point on, I based on his direction.

"Whenever I had a decision to make, I always asked myself 'what dad would do?'. Would he accept that joint offered by the kid next door? Would he steal a kiss under the bleachers from a girl he wasn't really interested in? Would he attend that party?

"When I entered the service, those questions became a lot harder. But I always used my dad as a measuring stick. Because I wanted to. Because I wanted to make him proud, but I also wanted to be a good man.

"At the conference, God opened my eyes and I saw all those years, all those situations from His point of view. I knew my Heavenly Father had watched over me, instilled His will in my life without my even knowing it."

He once again reached into his back pocket. Windy knew he held something in his hand for her to see, but she didn't want to open her eyes. She wanted to stay in her secure little dream world.

"Windy open your eyes," he whispered. She shook her head. *What if it's a ring?* She thought. *What if it isn't?*

"Please?" his breath touched her hair and she did as he asked. He held a broken pencil. She squinted. A familiar broken pencil. Memories flooded back, Eddie had left, she tried to call him, found her broken pencil on the floor. She'd thrown it away years ago. How had Rick found it? Then she realized it was the matching end. She sat up and looked again. *Windy Jordan class of*—the eraser end was missing. She looked at Rick, waited for him to explain.

"Three years ago last month Joe and I were dispatched to a residence where a woman had been transported to the hospital. A scared, sweet old lady asked us to check the upstairs apartment. We did. On an end table I found a picture of a young couple. I couldn't put it down. I kept looking at that girl's face, knowing she lay in a hospital bed, not knowing the extent of her injuries. I turned to leave and almost tripped. Under my foot I found a broken pencil. I put it in my shirt pocket…"

Windy looked into Rick's eyes, she saw tears, but she saw more. The Andrew look. He'd stolen her pencil. Still had it after all this time and all she could think of was the Andrew look.

"…I've thrown it away many times, only to retrieve it again. When I read of your marriage to the doctor, I felt like this pencil, broken. I chided myself for keeping it. But I have carried it in my uniform pocket every day I work. It reminds me that the people I am called to assist, are people, broken people who need my help. They're not just another routine situation.

"Windy," his eyes caressed hers. "I believe I fell in love with you that night. Joe reminded me of my first night on duty—fixing your tire and taking your husband to jail. I saw your effort to change that tire, saw the wet tennis shoes, one wet jersey glove. I admired you that night, and loved you after seeing one picture."

He placed the pencil in her hand.

"I stole your pencil. I'm sorry."

She looked at the object; a simple piece of wood with lead in the middle. Yet it meant something to this man; this crazy, who could possibly figure him out, man. She opened his hand and put the pencil back where it belonged then reached up and stroked his loving face.

She felt his slight movement and shifted her weight toward him. She raised her head and closed her eyes. She smelled the woods, the grass, the water, felt his bare arms on hers, heard his intake of breath and touched her lips to his. He tasted fresh and woodsy. With Ricks' mouth against hers, she felt the tickle of his mustache, and the slight movement of his lips.

This was right, this was the perfect kiss, she felt his emotion enter her mouth and move slowly down her body; every fiber of her being collected in that strong, sweet kiss.

She reached her hand behind his head, worked her fingers against his close cropped hair. He caressed her face holding on to the kiss, before allowing it to end.

She stared into his eyes and he stared right back at her. She felt no embarrassment; just looked at him as though it were the first time.

"I wanted you to ask me out."

"When?"

"At the store. In the fall, just before I married Stephan."

"I remember. I wanted to ask you out."

"Why didn't you?"

He pulled her close, breathed deeply and exhaled.

"I don't know. It was definitely my intention but I just couldn't get the words to come. I kicked myself all the way home that night. Wondered what was wrong with me. There you were, in front of me, I could see your answer in your eyes and I couldn't make my mouth say the words."

"That evening when I got home there was a little blue convertible parked on the street, the keys on my table. I..." Windy hesitated, she would not tell Rick what happened that night, in no way wanted to relive it. "I felt obligated. I told myself I felt love, but it was fear and loneliness. He was a doctor, a wealthy man and he wanted me."

"What ended the marriage?"

"My inability to have children. He wanted a family. I couldn't give him one. So he kicked me out and married a woman I had counseled at the Pregnancy office. I talked her into keeping her baby not knowing my husband would marry her. Weird, huh?"

"Yeah. But I've heard weirder."

"I don't think that's a word."

"A Nott's specialty, Dad added that one to the dictionary too."

"Rick, at one point I was really angry with you for not asking me out. That was a turning point for me. One word from you and I would probably not have married Stephan."

"You're joking?" he pulled away and looked at her.

She shook her head. "I wasted two years of my life on him. I thought you could have prevented that." She smiled and touched her lips to his. "I was wrong. Later, on New Year's Eve, when you stopped beside the car and I had that flat tire, I was listening to the radio and the guy quoted

Isaiah 40:12. 'Who has measured the waters in the hollow of His Hand…' I didn't hear the rest of the verse because those words spoke directly to my heart and I realized God had everything under control. I thought of all the water in the earth in the hollow of a hand, His hand and thought of how big He really is. That I, one human being, compared to all that water, compared to the whole world, could still mean anything to a God that big amazed me. None of my years were wasted. They were the roads that brought me to God; that brought me here to you."

He kissed her again and it still felt like the first time.

"Windy, you may think this is too soon, but my heart tells me it's right. I love you." He kissed her nose. "I love you." He kissed her cheek. "I love you." He kissed her forehead. "I love you." He brought his mouth to hers and whispered the words again. She breathed deeply, pulling in his scent.

"I have one question." She whispered back.

"What?" He pulled on her lip with his own.

"What makes your breath smell so good?"

"Sassafras," he answered, not missing a beat. "I've been chewing on the tree roots just for you."

"You chew on tree roots? Isn't that a bit strange?" She kissed the corner of his mouth letting his mustache tickle her upper lip.

"Not if you like the smell of my breath."

"Hmmmm. Well…" she looked into his eyes and smiled. "I love it." She kissed him. "I love you."

"Windy, I want to spend my life with you; I don't want anymore wasted days, much less months or years. You are the woman I believe God has chosen for me. Will you marry me? Will you be my wife?"

She knew this would happen; knew this question was inevitable. She wanted this question; wanted his love. But now that it was actually spoken, her doubts began jumping around in her head.

"Rick, you just heard me tell you that I can't have children."

"Yes, and you're wondering if I really want to marry a woman who can't bear my offspring?"

"Of course, that is something very important."

"Hmmmm…I understand what you're saying. But I ask myself what would my dad do?"

Windy smiled.

"When my parents realized they weren't going to have children of their own, they didn't have tests done to see who was at 'fault'. They just adopted. They are my parents and I am their son, the girls are their daughters. It really is as simple as that. Windy, I would marry you no matter what; if you weighed 50 pounds or 500 pounds, if you already had 12 children, if you were born on Saturn and had bumps all over your head and three fingers on each hand. The question, if you recall, was not if I would marry you, but rather will you marry me?"

"Yes?" she whispered.

He pulled her close and sighed. She wrapped her arms around him, willing herself to move into his being. They sat this way for several minutes. Windy heard the gurgling of the creek as it passed over the rocks, heard the leaves on the poplar trees, listened to the songs of passing birds. She felt Rick's arms around her, felt his heart beating against hers, heard his slow even breathing. She smelled the grass, the trees, Rick.

Could God really be blessing her this much? To allow her happiness with this man whom she had grown to love and need. Life couldn't be more perfect now that he had accepted Christ as his Savior.

"Rick, I believe we need to sit down with your parents and talk with them about this."

Rick smiled and shook head. "How do you know my thoughts?"

"Because you always ask yourself 'what would dad do?'"

He laughed. "You already know me too well. I'll never be able to hide any secrets from you; not that I would want to."

They walked slowly back to his house where Rick called his parents. They had just finished their Sunday meal but invited Rick and Windy over for ice cream and cake.

"Who's birthday?" Rick asked.

"Yours and Dads. Your spiritual birthdays."

Chapter Thirty-Nine

Rick and Windy arrived at his parents around seven, noting a strange car parked in front of their house.

Valerie met them at the door, hugged them both and ushered them into the dining room where his family sat around the table, joined by Connie.

Doug rose to receive a hug from his son. A very special looked passed between them.

A cake sat on the table along with plates and utensils.

Tami came in from the kitchen bringing the ice cream. Valerie cut the cake and the girls helped serve to everyone.

"Rick," Connie spoke up. "I was so pleased and proud today when you stood before the congregation and gave your testimony."

"Thank you, but I have to tell everyone, I was so nervous, I stood up there, my mouth opened and words came out. I would say I have no idea how, but I do know. God did it."

Connie smiled and nodded. "I understand, since I gave my life to the lord almost four years ago, He has accomplished things through me that I never could have alone."

Windy kept looking at Connie. They'd been in the same room many times, for church or a meal afterwards, but she had never really been close enough to observe the woman. There was something so familiar about her.

"If you don't mind, I would like to share a little of my testimony."

"Of course." Rick invited.

"When I was a girl I fell in love with the boy next door, though I wouldn't tell anyone. He had become my older brother's best friend and I followed them every where. They were 3 years older than me and didn't like me around. Tommy, my brother, started calling me 'dandruff' because they were always trying to brush me off.

"When the guys graduated, Jimmy went into the service and Tommy to U of M. When I graduated I planned to go to Western. That summer, Jimmy came home for a while before leaving for Viet Nam. I surprised him by being all grown up. Being young and naïve, I decided to make Jimmy love me back for those couple weeks he was home. I threw myself at him and finally wore him down. We were together only once and I conceived our child in August the week before I left for college. I was so happy at first, the thought of Jimmy and I and our baby together, that's all I really wanted. But for some reason I kept quiet. I wrote to Jimmy and hinted about a future together but I never received a reply.

"Jimmy had been engaged when he was home, engaged to another girl while I did everything I could to get his attention. He resisted, but he never told me he was engaged. I'm not really sure if that would have even made a difference. I wanted Jimmie and nothing would have gotten in my way. Of course, my family was clueless, I'd always been mean to Jimmy and everyone thought I disliked him.

"As soon as Jimmie returned to his base he got married. Mom wrote and told me only because Tommy went with him to be his best man, before returning to Lansing.

"I couldn't tell anyone I was pregnant then. I knew my parents would be terribly hurt and I wanted them proud of me, not ashamed. So I hid my pregnancy. I had a job which, along with school, kept me too busy to make friends. I took no one into my confidence. I couldn't go to the doctor because my parents would find out, so I contacted a home for unwed mothers. I spent a lot of time there, only going back to the dorm to sleep. In late May, classes ended but I didn't go home. I used the reason that I wanted to keep my job and bank some money for next year. The people running the home were wonderful to me. I saw their doctor and he took care of me through the delivery. I then gave my beautiful little boy up for adoption. No one knew. They still don't.

"I was devastated. And scared but I never once considered abortion. I had heard of girls at who made the trip to New York where abortion was legal, but I knew I would never do that.

"By August I felt it safe to visit home before classes started again. That's when Jimmy died, less than three months after his little boy was born. I just went numb. My life ended but the world kept moving around me. I left early, found a second job, threw myself into my studies. But all I could think of was that I had given away Jimmie's son. I had given away Jimmie.

"I contacted the home and they told me there was nothing I could do. Adoption records were sealed, I had already signed off my rights and I no longer had any claim to my child."

Throughout the recitation, Rick kept his eyes on Connie.

Rick then looked at his parents, swallowing his emotion he asked. "How long have you known?"

Valerie reached over and took her son's hand, "Since that day you spoke of in church. After you left our house I called Connie, I'd had my suspicions but I needed to know."

"I don't look anything like you."

"Except your eyes." Everyone replied.

Connie pulled a picture from a cloth bag and handed it to Rick. It was an 8x10 of a young man in army dress standing next to a flag. He could have been Rick with deep blue eyes.

"Why now? Why didn't you tell me sooner?"

The women exchanged looks. "Your mom felt from your conversation that it wasn't a priority for you. And as soon as I realized who you were, I began asking God if or when I should say something. Today in church, He said 'Now'."

"If I had thought it was a priority, Rick, I would have told you sooner." Valerie assured him.

"I don't want to interfere with your life in any way, my hopes and prayers for you have come true. All I wanted was for you to be loved, and you are, immensely."

"Today, after what you said in church I felt the Lord nudge me. I talked to your dad and we agreed to call Connie."

Silence reigned for several minutes, then Rick looked at Connie. "Did Jimmie have any other children?"

"No. Our moms are still good friends so my mom kept me posted. His wife remarried a couple years later and now has three children."

They sat for a long time, talking and eating cake. Connie told Rick about her family, about Tom, Carol Anne and their children. Her parents were still alive although they had divorced and both remarried.

Connie had never married, never had any more children. Then she told the Notts' about her own conversion and her walk with the lord.

It was already dark outside when the conversation lulled.

"Well," Rick stated. "This seems to be a day of revelations and new beginnings. Windy and I have news for all of you." He looked at Windy.

"But we wanted to talk it over with you first."

"I guess I should be on my way." Connie stood to excuse herself.

"Connie," Rick reached out and grasped her hand. "If you can stay I would be honored to have you here."

Connie's eyes misted as she sat back down.

Windy took the floor.

"Doug, Valerie, you know a little about me, probably enough to be leery of your sons interest in me." Very briefly, Windy explained the many events that had taken place in her life in the last five years.

"Being 23, married and divorced twice was something I never planned on. If you had told me this is how my life would be I would have told you how wrong you were. I don't believe in divorce and am embarrassed of my past. Yet God has my life now and I really believe everything happens for a reason. I wish I could change things, but I can't. I just know that I love your son very much. I have fought it. But I have also prayed fervently for God's will. I felt almost safe that Rick wasn't a Christian because that gave me a reason to fight, at the same time I have prayed for his salvation; for his sake of course, but also for mine. There's been a little battle in my heart for months and today God let me know the battle is over and He won."

Doug smiled, "God has had a very busy day."

Connie dabbed her eyes with a tissue. "Rick, Windy, since the day I gave my life to Christ I have prayed for my son, asking God to watch over him, show him the love and peace I have found. But I've also prayed for his girl, asking God to bring them together in his time. It's nice to know it's you I've prayed for."

"Windy knows that I gauge everything I do by what you would do, Dad. We both want your input on our decision."

"Doug, I was once told that too many changes in a short period of time can be hurtful. Part of me says not to rush into another change, not to bring Rick down with me. Yet I feel so at peace about all this. We do need your input, your wisdom."

"Mom, you have spent more time with God than anyone else in this family, we need your spiritual guidance."

"So I'm thinking you two want to have dinner together?"

Everyone looked at Doug. "For the rest of your life." He finished with a grin.

"Yes, we're going to get married." Rick answered grinning at his dad. "When?"

"She says April."

"It's a beautiful month, spring time when all life is getting a fresh start. And that would give us the winter to," she smiled at Rick, "court."

"I've been 'courting you' off and on for three years."

"In your mind," she laughed.

"Yeah, so what?" He leaned over and kissed her lightly then remembered they weren't alone. "I suggested next Saturday."

Rick's mom rolled her eyes while his dad nodded in understanding.

"We want to get married at Rick's house, outside by the creek, so it should be warm out, and we want something very simple."

"What about your parents Windy?"

"I'll call them; they live on the east coast, and ask them to make a visit."

"So when is it? April or Saturday?" Doug asked.

"Well, we compromised, and settled on August."

Chapter Forty

Windy picked up the phone in anticipation of this special conversation. She talked with her parents weekly but today was different. She would ask her folks to come home to her wedding. She had just written to Rob and didn't know when to expect a reply. She was glad now, that her parents had not been here when she married Stephan, she really didn't want him to be part of their memories. But she truly wanted them here now.

Her mom picked up on the first ring.

"Mom?"

"Windy, honey girl, I was just about to call you. How are things?"

Windy had told her mom about Rick, confided her concerns and hopes about their relationship.

"Everything is wonderful, mom. Rick asked me to marry him."

"I knew it, how could he not love you and want you by his side? When's the date?"

"I suggested April, he suggested Saturday, so we compromised on August." She smiled using Rick terminology. "Late August though we haven't set the date. I want you and dad here, I can help with gas money…"

"Don't be silly, Sweet heart, we'll be there. We need to see our favorite daughter."

They both laughed.

"Have you heard from Rob lately? Shouldn't he be due for some type of leave?"

Mom hesitated. "Actually he is. Because he's been over seas for quite a while, he's eligible for an extended leave. It's lucky that everything's coming together right now."

"Oh, it's not luck, mom, it's the Lord."

Ever since Windy gave her life to the Lord, she'd talked to her parents about Him. Rob received long letters from his sister but his replies never mentioned any interest.

"I know honey girl." Windy detected a tiredness in her mom's voice. "Is everything okay?"

"Everything's fine. Dad's work has run out again and we decided to return to Michigan for good."

"Oh, Mom, that would be wonderful. Are you planning to come back soon?"

"Truth is, we're already packing."

Windy hung up the phone and immediately called Rick. When he didn't answer, she realized he had probably just arrived at work. So she called the station to leave a message.

"So this is the infamous Windy?" the officer on the other end of the line asked.

Windy blushed. "I guess you've heard about Rick and me?"

"Girl, for four years that kid hasn't said one word about females. Kept you all to himself. Now that the cat's out of the bag, he won't quit talking about you."

Again she blushed, but shivered with excitement. "Is he still there?"

"Just left with Joe."

"Will you give him a message to call when he can?"

"Do you one better, I'll radio him right now."

Minutes later she heard a knock, Officer Kozininski stood at her door. "You've reported some kind of emergency, Ma'am?"

Windy stared wide eyed.

"I've got my partner checking the parameter now."

"Hey, Joe?" Rick called from the bottom of the stairs.

"Cora's got warm cinnamon rolls."

Joe tipped his hat. "New emergency, Ma'am, can't let my partner handle this alone." He grinned.

Together they descended the stairs and joined the other two in Cora's kitchen.

"Raspberry ice tea," Cora explained as she placed a glass in front of Joe, Rick had already downed half of his.

"We're having salad for supper, if you boys want to come back later." Cora invited.

"Salad?" Joe sounded skeptical.

"Well, it is a bit too hot to have the oven on, but if you'd rather have meatloaf."

"No, you're not making meatloaf, Cora; these guys will do just fine on one of your special grilled chicken and strawberry salads."

"Oh, that kind of salad." Joe nodded. "I guess we could make our rounds back this way later."

"Around 6," Cora said, checking the time. "Should I start the chicken now?" she asked Windy.

"No, it's too early. We'll wait a couple hours." She looked at Rick who watched Cora. They exchanged concerned looks when the little lady turned around.

Windy reached over and took Rick's hand. "I called my mom, dad's last job just ended and they've decided to move back to Michigan." She let Rick hear the excitement in her voice.

"That's great, when are they coming?" He leaned over and kissed her, causing her to blush, but one look at Joe told her he was far more interested in his cinnamon roll.

"Their apartment is rented till the end of the month and she asked me to start looking for a place for them. I told her mine would be vacant in late August, so they should just stay with me and then take mine over. That way Cora can keep an eye on them." She smiled at the old lady who nodded her head.

"I'd be happy to have them here, I don't want an empty house, but don't want to look for new renters either. I knew God would work everything out."

Rick smiled at Windy, "So this means the bed and couch have to be moved again."

"Just the beds, I can sleep on the couch for a few weeks."

"Rick's got two bedrooms and you're gonna move in there anyway," Joe looked at the couple staring at him. "Just kidding."

The next morning Rick and Joe showed up while Windy was at work. They moved the furniture around and spent an hour cleaning the basement and hauling trash out for Cora. In appreciation she made sandwiches and invited them back for dinner.

"You know Cora; all the guys want to be Rick's partner. He thinks it's because he's such a great guy but I know it's because they're jealous and want to share our personal cook."

"Well, one day this summer, I'll have Windy take me out to Rick's house and I'll cook for everyone. There's not enough room here you know."

The guys laughed. "Seriously?" Joe asked.

"Oh, yes, I don't want to play favorites."

That evening Windy read the paper as Cora finished cooking their meal.

"Eddie's Aunt Darla died." She said. "She was such a sweet lady; she's the one who got the church and preacher for our wedding. I think she hoped that would start Eddie and me going to church with her. It's a shame we didn't."

"Now Windy, if you had, you wouldn't be marrying Rick."

"THAT would be the real shame." she grinned at Cora. "Anyway, I'll go to the funeral tomorrow, to pay my respects."

Chapter Forty-One

January 1976

Mama was throwing up in the bathroom again. She threw up a lot, and Eddie could smell it everywhere in the small house. Beer smelled bad, but it smelled worse when it came back up.

Daddy drank beer, too, but he didn't throw up.

"I thought you went to that clinic?" Daddy yelled.

"I did!" Mama yelled back.

"You did not, you took that money I had for Christmas presents for them boys and you spent it on yerself!"

"If gittin rid of yer kid is spendin it on myself, I guess I did."

"You lyin little…"

Five year old Eddie pushed open the front door and ran as hard as he could. He didn't care that he had no coat or shoes on. He didn't care that the snow and ice froze his socks the minute his feet touched the sidewalk. He just ran. He wished Aunt Darla didn't live so far away. He could run there and stay at her house and sleep on her couch where nobody yelled and cussed at each other.

He reached the end of the block and stopped. His stomach growled and his feet hurt terrible. Christmas presents. So that's why the only present they got was from Aunt Darla.

Eddie turned the corner, knowing he should go home. Maybe he could slip back in while they were still fighting and they wouldn't know he'd gone outside. He ran down the alley and stopped by the back door, easing it open. He listened and heard the argument continue in the front of the house. He squeezed through the door and ducked into the bathroom. They would never know. He stood on the heat register trying to thaw out his frozen toes.

"Git oudda here," Mama threw the door open. "I gotta p…" Eddie made it out just as her hand smacked his head. He ran to the bedroom and closed the door, throwing himself on the bed he shared with his two brothers.

Six year old Kenny sat eating a piece of bread, while Johnny huddled under the covers.

"Don't let her find me, Eddie." Johnny begged.

"I wonder which kid theys gittin rid a?" Kenny asked. "Prably the little cry baby."

"Shut up." Eddie warned.

They heard the toilet flush and Kenny opened the bedroom door.

"I'm hungry." He stated.

"Tell yer ole man," Mama said. "I gotta go ta work."

"Don't know why ya bother, ain't no man gonna pay to see yer fat belly." Daddy said.

"Well if you knew how to keep yer pants up, it wouldn't be fat." Mama came back at him.

"Weren't my pants that was down."

"Why you son of a…"

Eddie put his hands over his ears tucking his head to his knees.

June 1996

"Hi, Babe."

Windy jumped at the familiar voice. A jumble of emotions ran through her mind; fear the strongest, yet she was aware of an anticipation she couldn't explain. To see him again, especially now, brought a tingle to her spine. Would he be the old Eddie, the one she fell in love with or would he still be the stranger she had learned to fear? Windy glanced at the near empty room wondering if he would dare to touch her here. Haltingly she turned to confirm her fears or excitement.

Her head moved slowly on its own power. She wanted to run but she could only anticipate what she would behold.

"Hi, Eddie," she whispered as her eyes looked into his. "I'm sorry about Darla."

"Yeah, me too. She was probably the only decent one of the whole family. No wonder she always liked you."

Windy nodded, willing but unable to pull her gaze away. Eddie's dark complexion looked sallow, his face thin. She passed it off as the lighting in the dreary room.

"You look great, Babe. Different, but great." He smiled his half smile that first melted her heart and she felt a tug deep within.

Just like any friend I haven't seen in awhile, she told herself. *It's good to see him again.*

"So do you," she lied.

"Naw, I know I look pretty rough." Their gaze finally broke when he shook his head, allowing Windy a quick look. "I been out of circulation awhile."

"Oh?" Windy's survey revealed a very thin Eddie in what appeared to be his oversized father's shirt.

"Yeah, that little girl I brought to the apartment..."

"Crissy."

"Yeah. Yeah, Crissy. Well, she was a bit young and, uh once she found her way back to her ol' man they called the law. I did six months fer takin a minor over the state line."

"Six months? In jail?"

"Yeah, Babe, that's a..." he laughed nervously, "that's usually where ya do time, ya know."

"So that's why you're so thin and pale."

"Well, no, not really, I guess. See..." he looked at the floor then scanned the room. "Let's sit over here a minute, okay?" He guided her to a small sofa in a quaint little alcove. When they sat he started to place his arm around her shoulders, pulled it away, then nervously laid it across the sofa behind her. He tried to pick up her hand but she gripped her purse tightly.

"Windy, I'm sober now. Dried out while I was inside. Haven't touched a drop since I got out, either. That's eight months total. Eight months on the wagon, Babe. And I know I can stay this way, with help, with some one who cares."

"Eddie…"

"I know I was wrong, Babe, I know I hurt you. Bad. Admittin all that stuff, well, it's part of goin straight. Oh, man! I had it so good. Had the best wife in the world and I blew it. I can't believe I was so stupid. I can't believe it. But it was the booze, Babe. I never hurt you when I was sober, did I?"

Windy shook her head as she watched tears form in his puffy red eyes.

"I didn't think so. I didn't remember ever hurtin you when I was sober. But I do remember the good times. They were great, weren't they? You remember that first year, don't you? It was good, wasn't it?"

"Yes, Eddie, it was. For awhile."

"Babe, I need you. I really need you now. I'm sure you've got a new life," he looked at her left hand. "Not married, though? but…I came back to see you, to ask you,…oh, I know, Babe, I know what yer thinkin, I wouldn't ask you to take me back, I can't, not like I am. But I need you. I need to hear you still care…"

"Eddie, I…"

"I'm sick, Babe, really sick, dying sick. There was a lot of Chrissys, ya know? There was one too many, and now I'm sick. The family, my own family, they're afraid to have me around. Afraid of me, afraid I'll make them sick. Oh, Windy, ya gotta help me, please."

As the realization of what Eddie meant hit her, Windy fought the urge to run. Repulsion welled up inside, her throat constricted, she tried to speak, tried to breath, but nothing happened.

"Are you sure?"

"Look at me. What do you think?"

"I don't know. I mean, I don't know anything about, well about…"

"It's called AIDS. You can't catch it by saying it."

"I know that, Eddie. But are you really sure? Is that what the doctor said?"

"Haven't seen a doctor."

"Then how do you know for sure?"

"I'm dying, Babe, inside and out, what else could it be?"

"Do you know which girl…"

Eddie shook his head and looked away.

"Then Eddie, you have to go to a doctor. It's silly not to go. Maybe he can help."

"There's no cure, Babe."

"I know. But there's medicine they can give you so you don't feel so bad. Besides, maybe that's not what it is."

"What else could it be?"

"I don't know, but listen. The health department does free testing for this kind of thing. We'll go today, after the funeral. There should still be time after we leave the cemetery. Okay?"

"Don't really feel like visiting a cemetery right now. Wish I didn't have to be here, but I owe it to Aunt Darla and Mark."

Organ music began and Windy led Eddie over to a seat. She sat beside him throughout the service, wondering why Eddie would show up now. Just when life starting looking so good.

Windy pulled into the driveway and turned off the ignition.

"This yer place?" Eddie asked, looking at the impressive two story house.

"No, no I work here. We do free pregnancy testing…"

"You pregnant?"

"No." *And I never will be, thanks to you,* she wanted to say.

"Eddie, listen, I have some things I need to do here, it'll take a few minutes." She thought of the pictures in the office, and how they had first affected her. Suddenly she wanted Eddie to be affected too. "Come on in…"

Inside the office Eddie busied himself with looking at pictures and pamphlets. Windy looked over the appointment book, called Angie and checked on any new dates and messages. She then called the health department to make an appointment. When she hung up, Eddie handed her a picture.

"Six weeks, huh?"

Windy took the picture of the tiny baby still in it's sack held between a doctor's thumb and forefinger, and nodded.

"It's already got fingers and stuff," he noted. "Like a real person."

"It is a real person."

"So, this kid's mom missed one period?"

"Just one."

Eddie looked slowly around the room, noticing the display of fetal models. "Which one would it be if she missed two?"

Windy picked up the smallest one. "This is eight weeks, it's complete; all organs are formed and functioning. All this baby needs now is time to grow." She noted the troubled look on her ex-husband's face. Was this a good time to talk about their own lost baby? Was Eddie realizing what had actually happened or was he still denying as she had for so long?

"Babe, when we were together…and you missed those two…did you ever think, maybe…"

"Yes, Eddie, I was pregnant."

"And you lost it?" Windy nodded. "And…and I caused it, didn't I?"

Windy took a slow breath, a lump settling in her throat. She wanted to scream at him, *you killed our baby, my baby, the only baby I will ever conceive.* She wanted to hit him and hurt him just as he had hurt her. She wanted to take away his ability to have children, allow him to feel the pain and heartache.

"Yes, Eddie, you did. And now I am unable to conceive another child."

"I knew, I always knew. Ever since that night. I tried to pretend, just like you. But I knew what I'd done, and I hated myself for it."

"I suppose we should talk about this, get it settled?"

Eddie nodded.

The words spun through Windy's head, questions, accusations. She could form none of them. Tears slid down her cheeks and she stared into the eyes of the man who had given her so much love and so much pain.

Eddie shook his head. "I've lived that night over a thousand times, changing the ending. I never meant to hurt you or the…the baby. When you told me about the kid I got scared Windy, I got so scared. You met my ol' man…I thought I might turn out to be like him…"

Eddie's eyes shifted away from Windy and back in time.

"My dad wasn't always mean and hateful. Kenny and I are close in age and for a while the three of us made kind of a family. Johnny came and things changed. But mama never tried to be a mama. She worked at a bar, dancing for money. She drank and used drugs. She hated us kids, Aggie the most.

"Mama and Daddy fought all the time. I remember them talkin about mama 'gittin rid' of the kid. I thought they meant one of us, probably Johnny since neither of them liked him. Mama was home sick for a few days and daddy was almost nice to her. Then she started getting big in the belly and they fought even more.

"Aggie was born. I didn't think things could get worse, but they did.

"One night Mama never came home. She wasn't there when we left for school in the morning, still wasn't there when we got home. Daddy really changed then. I think he blamed us kids for mama leavin. Specially Aggie. He was powerful mean to the two little ones. One day I stood up to Daddy told him to leave them alone. Before long I was taking their beatings. I became the hated child.

"When Aunt Darla asked if she could take us kids home Daddy went crazy, but Aunt Darla just stood, unafraid. He kicked her out. But she didn't stay away. She always came for birthdays and Christmas.

"After that I just waited til I could quit school and move out. One day Daddy said we were movin to Iowa where his brother lived. I think he left because someone turned him in to the state. It was probably Aggie's teacher cause she always had bruises. I choose to stay here; made him real mad but I stood my ground. Aunt Darla said I could stay with her while I finished school. You know the rest, I quit school, got a job and moved in with a buddy, then I met you.

"I didn't want to be a father. Ever. Soon as you told me you missed yer period and we might have a kid, I started sweatin. All I could think of was my ol' man. I kept waiting and waiting for you to tell me you weren't pregnant. Then you said you were late again. That's when I got scared, afraid that you might leave me, afraid of what kind of father I would make. I went out and got drunk for the first time. Even in high school, I never got drunk, seen my dad like that too many times. I never meant to hit you. I never wanted to hurt you. Never.

"When I made you lose the baby I hated myself more than I ever hated my dad. He may have knocked us around but I had killed my own kid. I knew I was crap that I didn't deserve you; that I deserved my daddy and all his meanness. I just couldn't go on facing you."

Eddie's face twisted in the torment of his words. He closed his eyes as the tears poured from them, unwilling to stop.

Windy stroked his shoulder, wanting to relieve some of his agony but he turned away. "Don't touch me, don't offer me your kindness, I don't deserve it. After all I've done to you, you gotta hate me."

"But I don't. I did for a while but not any more. You never talked about your family, I never knew Eddie. If you had told me, if we'd talked it out, all the hurt and heartache could have been prevented." Windy thought of how different her life would be if he had only told her. They could still be married with a baby, maybe two by this time. She wanted to hate him, to blame him for screwing up her life, robbing her of her womanhood.

The words caught in her heart. That was the phrase Stephan used when he found out she couldn't have children. She looked at Eddie and thought of all he had gone through. He made some good choices in life, but he made some bad ones too. She thought of Pastor Jason who said we can't blame our failures on someone else, many people are given a raw deal and they can use it as a excuse or for learning.

"Eddie, what's happened can't be changed no matter how badly we want it. Anger only makes it worse. What you have to do now is decide what the rest of your life will be like. It's your choice, no one else's."

"I need you to forgive me, Babe. I know it'll be hard, but I really need to know it, that you forgive me."

"Of course, I do, even before you asked." She patted his hand surprised that it felt bonier than it looked.

"Say it please."

"I forgive you, Eddie."

"For everything?"

"For everything."

They left the office and Windy drove Eddie to his cousins' home.

Chapter Forty-Two

As soon as Windy arrived at her apartment she called Rick letting him know what happened and her plans to help Eddie.

"Why you? He has a family, let them help."

"But he's not close to them, I'm surprised they even let him stay there. He didn't tell them he was sick, or they probably wouldn't have."

"So...he's a grown man, Windy, he can see the doctor on his own. He doesn't need you playing nurse to him."

"He doesn't have a car, how can he get to his appointment?"

"City transportation?"

"He has no money."

She heard Rick's frustration, felt it herself. Her life was finally coming around; she believed God's blessings were showering her right now, why would He let this happen?

"Windy, I don't like the man, he hurt you. You're my responsibility now and I don't want you near him."

"Rick, don't misunderstand. I have no feelings left for Eddie, except pity..."

"Which is a very strong feeling, especially for some one as caring as you." He interrupted.

"He's sorry for all that happened, he asked my forgiveness."

"You're playing right into his hands."

"No, I'm not," she became impatient. "You may need to learn a little about trust."

"And you need to learn a little about reality. He abused you, he sent you to the hospital, he ran out on you, he killed your ba…"

"Stop it!" she yelled.

Silence reigned for several moments.

"Windy, I'm sorry. I shouldn't have said that, but please look at it from my point of view."

"If you'll look at it from mine."

They had come to a stand off.

"Rick, I'm not happy about this either. My life is suddenly wonderful, we're planning our wedding, you've accepted Christ, my parents are moving back. Now this…"

"It doesn't have to be 'now this', you can refuse to help him."

"Is that what Jesus would do? Is that what your dad would do? I don't want him back in my life, Rick. I didn't invite him. Maybe God brought him back here, to refine us; to make us stronger. Maybe Satan brought him back, because he doesn't want us together, walking with the Lord. I don't know why. But I assure you this is not permanent, this has nothing to do with you and me. But I can not, with a clear conscience, turn my back on him; not in the shape he's in."

"Fine. You do what you have to do." He hung up.

The moment the phone was back in its cradle Rick wanted to kick himself. He couldn't believe he'd hung up on Windy. But then he couldn't believe what she'd just told him.

At least she told you, she could have hidden it and you would never have known.

But she shouldn't have gone near the guy in the first place. Why is she jeopardizing our relationship because of this scum bag?

Why would you let a scum bag come between you and her?

I'm not! She is.

Enough of talking to himself, this would get him no where. He had to talk to his parents.

"It appears to me, son," Doug held his coffee cup as steadily as he held Rick's gaze. "That Windy has enough faith in herself to be near this man without it being a problem and she has enough confidence in your love to allow it."

Rick closed his eyes and lowered his head. He wanted his dad to tell him it would be okay to demand Windy not see Eddie again. That's what he wanted, but he knew long before he got here his dad would do no such thing.

Valerie reached for her son's hand. "It is a test Rick. I don't know who initiated it, but it's up to you to pass it. Certainly Satan doesn't want you trusting the Lord…"

"But why now? All these years, I've lived a good life, resisted the temptations set before me. Why didn't he try to entice me then?"

"He didn't need to. You were happy just being a good person, and being good doesn't get you to heaven. You were no threat to him then. Now you are."

"But why would God allow it, now that I've given my heart to him?"

"To make you stronger, to help you solidify your beliefs, your trust in Him."

Rick shook his head and finally lifted the glass of water to his lips that his mother had placed there some time ago.

"Rick, you are the only one who can let Eddie come between you and Windy." Doug stated. Rick knew his dad spoke the truth and he almost begrudged him for it.

"So what now, I should call the guy and invite him to join Windy and I for dinner?"

"Rick!" Valerie admonished him but Doug just smiled and called his son's bluff.

"If that's what God is telling you to do."

For the next week, Windy jumped every time the phone rang. Would it be Rick wanting to talk this over? Would be the health department with Eddie's results? She had given them her number and promised to contact Eddie as soon as she heard. He was staying in Darla's old camper. Darla had given the house to her son Mark and now he and his family lived there. Eddie didn't want Mark to know about his suspicions and wouldn't use his cousins' number for messages.

When the phone rang on Friday and the woman calling identified herself, Windy's heart stopped beating.

"You've got one sick fellow on your hands."

"How serious is it?"

"Oh, it's serious. He has got to get treatment before there's any more damage."

"Then something can be done for him."

"Sure, hepatitis is treatable, but it's not something to fool with. I recommend you contact a doctor today and get him started on medication. It may be best to even have him hospitalized till it's under control."

"Did you say…hepatitis?"

"Yes, but let me warn you, it is hepatitis B, the more serious form. It's sexually transmitted, and it's highly contagious."

"Hepatitis, not AIDS?"

"No, at this point, not AIDS."

"Could it turn into it though?"

"He tested negative on the HIV test. However, it's not uncommon to test negative in the beginning stages of the disease and it can lay dormant for years. Since he already has Hepatitis B, AIDS is a future possibility."

"But he's negative now."

"Yes, now."

"Where should he go?"

"How about your doctor?"

"I guess I don't have one."

"Well, take him to the health clinic, they have a doctor on call and can see that he begins the treatment."

"Thanks, so much, I really appreciate your help."

After Windy hung up she debated her next move. Stephan probably still worked at the clinic. She had no desire to run into him, especially with a sick Eddie. But why should she be the one to take him? He could now tell his cousin and Mark could take him. *Would that be okay, Lord?* She asked. The Lord remained silent.

She found the clinic number in the phone book and started to dial. She missed a number and started over, missing another number. On her third try she heard a busy signal so she set the phone down, staring at it. She frowned then redialed, this time the call didn't go through and she was rewarded with an obnoxious buzzing. She rechecked the number with the phone book, dialed and heard it ring.

"Hello."

"Hi, I'm call…"

"Hello? Hello?"

"I'm sorry, I'll speak up…"

"Hello? Nobody's there."

Click.

Frustrated, Windy slammed the phone down. How could she make an appointment for Eddie if she couldn't get through?

Call Eddie.

"Why?"

Call Eddie.

"But I should make the appointment first, then I only have to call him once."

CALL EDDIE.

"Fine." She answered, picking up the phone and dialing Mark's number. She waited while he went to the camper to get his cousin. She informed Eddie of the results and the possibility of being seen at the clinic.

"Eddie, if it's okay with you, I'm going to call my pastor." *Now where had that come from?* "I'm sure he'll be happy to take you to an appointment. He's a good man and it would do you well to talk to him."

"Sure, Babe…"

"Eddie, don't call me babe."

"I'm sorry, using your name seems so…I don't know…not…you. But go ahead and call your preacher, that'd be fine."

After hanging up Windy dialed the parsonage and Pastor Jason answered on the first ring.

"Sitting on the phone?" she asked.

"Nice thing about these cordless, you can carry them anywhere. What can I do for you Windy?"

"Got a minute?"

"Got all day."

It was such a simple solution to turn Eddie over to Pastor J. Eddie would not only get to his appointments, he'd get the spiritual medicine he needed. Windy could feel secure in his care and Rick could have his fiancé back; if he wanted her. She hadn't heard from him all week; began to wonder if she would ever hear from him again.

Thinking Rick would turn his back on her, that his love was so fragile this little situation could shatter it was more than Windy could handle.

"Why, Lord? You give me a man whom I can truly love, who I thought truly loved me and one little trial sends him running. Guess that makes me a little better than nothing. Rejected for a can of beer, rejected for a family, rejected because of compassion."

She spent the better part of the day in a pity party, deciding to let Rick make the first move. She loved him, wanted him but not if he couldn't trust her, not if he didn't want her.

Chapter Forty-Three

"It's not uncommon to catch something and find out you really didn't want to catch it, you just enjoyed the chase." Joe reasoned. "You weren't really in love with the girl, you didn't even know her. You saw a pretty little girl in a picture, thought of her in a hospital bed, beaten up by her husband and you felt sorry for her. But now that you've gotten to know her, you realize it was the chase you wanted, not the catch."

"But it's just the opposite, Joe. I do love her. I want her. I miss her so bad. Man, I thought everything was going great. Found the Lord, experienced that with my dad, proposed to Windy, she said yes, I meet my birth mom at my parents house and find out what a great lady she is, that she's a Christian and has prayed for me everyday for four years. I find out my Dad didn't know about me and probably would have been in my life if he had, if he'd lived."

Joe silently kicked himself. He'd had opportunities to warn the kid; had thought about it many times. You just can't rely on religion and women; two of the most dangerous things in the world.

"It's this God stuff, it was never meant for you." He said. "You put faith in something that doesn't exist and you get kicked in the gut."

"No, Joe, He exists. I know in my heart and my head that He does. Everything came together at that conference…"

"Now everything is falling apart."

"Sure feels that way. But…Windy said something about two many changes in your life at one time could be confusing." He shook his head. "Believe me; this past week has brought nothing but change."

Windy read the passage again. How had she missed this? She'd read Luke before but didn't remember this verse. She read it again. And again; then noted the reference verses, quickly looking those up. So that was why God brought Eddie back into her life before she and Rick could marry. The verses were clear, all too clear.

She grabbed her concordance from the small book shelf and moved to the kitchen table where she could open both books. She found that hateful word and looked up every scripture reference. She reread the ones in the New Testament especially those spoken by Jesus. She retrieved the notebook and pen she kept on her bedside table and began writing down her thoughts, the ones God revealed to her.

Then she looked up the other word.

How could she have been so blind? How could she not have known this? Why didn't someone tell her? But no one knew about her and Rick's plan to marry except Cora and their immediate families. Doug wouldn't know this verse, he was a brand new Christian and hadn't even picked up a Bible until last week end. Her parents certainly had no clue. But what about Valerie and Connie? Why hadn't they said anything? And Cora, how many times had she read this passage? Did they all just not understand?

Well, she had no intention of reuniting with Eddie, but at least she could save Rick from hell.

Sunday morning Windy tried to force herself out of bed. She didn't want to go to church. Didn't want to face family and friends, tell them the wedding was off. She certainly didn't want to face Rick. She'd have to find another church after this, she was only one person, Rick's whole family went to this one, they shouldn't have to leave because of her sin. She rolled over but could hear Cora singing in the kitchen below. How could she spoil everyone's happiness?

She remembered THE night, the one she often thought of, when she stood beside Cora's car in the snow telling God she only wanted Him. No one else. Had she really meant it when she said, *'Lord, I want to be Yours and Yours alone. I want no one but you. I want nothing and no one to come between us, no one, Father. You are all I need, all I desire. There isn't a person in this world I would choose over You, no matter how secure and comforting his arms may be. I don't want those arms, Lord, I don't want them in my life, if it means losing You.'?*

Maybe, like Abraham, God was just testing to see if she meant it. "Well, Father. I meant it. I love Rick, and I want to be his wife, but I love You more and eternity with You is more important than a temporary life with Rick, no matter how wonderful it would be. But Father, Jesus also said that there would be no marrying or giving in marriage in heaven. So that means I won't be a divorced woman. Would You mind if in heaven…would You allow Rick and I…I mean could we at least be near?"

Maybe, like with Abraham, God would also find the right sacrifice at the last moment.

She mustered herself out of bed and plodded to the bathroom. One look in the mirror reminded her of the hours spent crying the night before. The long night that would never come to an end. She would never really experience sunshine again.

She thought of Stephan. Serves him right. Now she could get revenge on him without doing a thing. Tears welled up in her eyes, she didn't want revenge, didn't want to live in a dark world without love, didn't want to live without Rick.

"Oh Father, why did you let me fall in love with him, just to take him away? I wasn't looking for anyone, he came to me and You… You told me to invite him to Scott Bradley's party. It was You wasn't it? Or was Satan working his evil and ruining our lives?"

Windy stepped into the shower and let hot water cascade over her body. She cried harder and felt she would never stop.

When she finally turned the water off she heard an insistent knocking. Slipping into her robe she went to the door afraid of who she would find. Could she face Rick or even Cora right now?

"Who is it?" she asked meekly.

"Mom and Dad."

Windy flung the door opened and pulled her mom into her arms allowing the tears to start all over again. Her mom held her tight as she moved them aside letting Dad in.

Windy realized Mom cried too, she pulled back and looked into that dear face and suddenly realized how much she missed her mom these last few years.

When the crying subsided a little, Debbie Jordan looked at her daughter.

"How did you know?"

"Know? Know What?"

Her mom's face paled.

"Know what? What mom?"

"Why were you crying?"

"That can wait." She heard the fear in her own trembling voice. "Know what?"

"That dad has cancer?"

Chapter Forty-Four

How dare He? How dare He do this to her dad, how dare He do this to her and her mom. Where was His mercy? His love? Where was the God she had given her life to, the One she had just reaffirmed her love and devotion for? How could He expect her loyalty after throwing her whole life into turmoil? After taking everything she held dear?

She could understand Him taking Rick away from her. After all she was an adulteress. In God's eyes she was still married to Eddie, had no right to leave him. Yet she had, and she'd remarried and now she would be a sinner for the rest of her life, unable to ever be a wife and mother. She could handle that, she told Him she could. And now He was giving her this? Her father dying of cancer? What did He want from her?

Her mom was leading her into the living room, sitting beside her on the couch, talking to her in soothing tones, speaking words Windy didn't hear.

"Windy!" Her mother's voice became firm and her hands tighten on Windy's shoulders. "Windy, please. I need you to look at me, I need you to listen to me."

Her mom's eyes bore into hers, demanding Windy's attention. "We've come back here because we need our kids to help us through this."

So mom thought she was strong. Why did people think that? She remembered Jenny's words. *'I'm not as strong as you.'*

'I'm not strong,' she wanted to yell. *'I'm scared and angry but I am not strong!'*

Then her dad sat beside her and pulled her into his arms. She remembered the times as a little girl when he would lift her, carry her. She felt his arms again, holding her now, comforting her, letting her know he was still there.

"I'm not going anywhere, Baby Girl. We're going to fight this and win, but I need my family around to help me through it."

Windy looked into her dad's eyes and saw his promise, his honesty. They needed her. Let God throw whatever He could her way, she didn't care what He did now. She would be strong, for them. God could take anything from her, but not her parents, she would fight Him tooth and nail on that.

Rob Jordan felt his little girl relax in his arms; he leaned back on the couch and pulled her with him. This was what he needed, to still be strong for his family. The moment Debbie heard the word cancer she panicked. Debbie, his sweet little wife, went ballistic, drilling the doctor on everything, from the type of cancer and its fatality rate to the treatment options. She was ready to put him in the hospital that day and start injecting him with whatever poison might kill the cancer. When the doctor used the words, *'give him a little more time'* Debbie came unglued.

"That's not an option." she had yelled at the poor man. "More time is not an option. We want an end to the cancer."

She said it so simply that Rob thought it might actually happen. The doctor assured her everything that could be done would be. He gave them several papers, explaining the cancer and the treatment.

Once they arrived home and looked over the information Rob made a decision. None of them were an option. His choices were; poison it, burn it, cut it; none of which seemed like they would do the rest of his body any good. So he told his wife he wouldn't commit to anything until his family was back together and they could all decide what to do.

Then Windy called all excited about her upcoming marriage. He and Debbie decided to wait until after the event took place to tell Windy about the cancer. They were as truthful as they could be. Rob's latest job had just ended and it seemed the best time to reunite the family. They had been right upfront with Robbie though. He knew what was going on and knew what to expect when he returned. In a few days they would all be together.

A knock at the door sent Debbie into the kitchen. Windy heard Cora's voice and her mom's introduction. Moments later Debbie returned.

"What a sweet lady. She didn't remember meeting us before we left, but that was a while ago and we only visited you and Eddie a couple times." Debbie almost smiled. "Cora is fixing breakfast right now and says we are all to come down in 15 minutes. So Windy, how about getting dressed while Dad and I bring up our luggage?"

Rob followed as Debbie led their daughter out of the room. He stopped in the kitchen and looked at the books open on the small table, picking up Windy's notebook and reading the words she had scribbled there. Many were indiscernible because of the dried water splotches.

She hadn't come. Rick thought maybe she chose to attend a different class to avoid him. Windy just didn't miss church, especially two Sundays in a row. Maybe Cora was ill again. He hoped not, but it seemed a better excuse than Windy not wanting to see him. He sat through Sunday school not hearing a word.

In the sanctuary he looked in vain for the two women. He couldn't bear to sit with his parents, not today; they would ask questions he didn't want to answer. He tried just standing by the coffee pot, but everyone who came by wanted to talk, so he went outside and took a deep breath of fresh, hot June air, hoping he might see them drive up. After the first song ended he decided to go back inside and found a chair just inside the sanctuary.

At the beginning of morning worship Jason repeated some of the things mentioned last week for those who hadn't been there. Last Sunday was so different than this one. It amazed him how life could trudge on for an eternity and suddenly everything is different in a matter of days. As he listened to the young man behind the pulpit and thought of all Jason had been through Rick felt very selfish. God had granted him a wonderful life, given him parents that many kids could only dream of. Surely God would see him through this seemingly insignificant trial concerning Eddie. Rick determined to grab Jason after church, hoping he didn't have dinner plans with one of the families. He needed to talk to this godly man and glean some wisdom from him. It would be great if it could be done at his parents house where Rick could also have his dad's input.

When the next song started everyone stood, Rick's cue to move forward and take his place beside his family. Valerie threw a questioning look at her son. He could tell by her expression she knew something was up. Moms. You just couldn't slip anything past them.

Cora chattered as everyone placed fluffy scrambled eggs and sausage patties on their plates. Windy looked at the meat and wondered what this particular pig had been fed.

Cora reached out and grabbed hers and moms' hands, Windy automatically grasped her dad and her parents followed suit.

"Windy, would you pray?"

She shook her head no.

"Oh," her refusal surprised the little old lady but she jumped right ahead. "Dear Heavenly Father, thank You so much for this food You've given us, thank you for Windy's parents' safe arrival and especially for upcoming events. We ask Your blessing on us all. Amen."

She had to stop this now before it went any further.

"I'm not getting married." Windy stated.

Cora's hands went to her mouth, while Mom and Dad just stared at her.

"Windy, if this is because…" her dad started.

"No," she interrupted. "It's not." She looked at her mom. "That's why I was crying when you arrived." She placed a bite of tasteless egg in her mouth, willing herself to chew.

"Did you have a fight?" Cora whispered.

"No, yes, I…maybe. There are other reasons. I don't want to talk about it now. I just don't want you thinking otherwise."

They ate in stunned silence for a few moments, then Rob looked at Cora.

"Cora this is a wonderful meal, thank you so much for providing it for us."

"There's just the two of us, until now that is, so I cook and Windy washes dishes, it works out very well you know. Now that you're here I would love to continue cooking for you; that is unless you prefer to do your own cooking, Mrs…"

"Debbie, and no, the truth is, I'm a really bad cook."

Dad picked up the conversation. "Cora, it appears you're family too, so we need to let you in on what's happening. I have recently been diagnosed with cancer."

The little lady once again covered her mouth, silencing a gasp.

"Debbie and I decided to return to Michigan because we feel much more at home here and we want to be with Windy. Once our son arrives we are all going to sit down and discuss the situation." He looked at Windy and smiled. "We weren't going to say anything until after the wedding, but it's out in the open and we might as well deal with it. And," he continued. "It looks like more needs healing than just my body."

Rick finally took a bite of his meal. The meatloaf, though cold by now, was delicious.

"Rick, why don't I warm your plate?" Valerie asked. "Your foods got to be cold."

"Can you just warm it in the micro…" Valerie shook her head no.

"We don't do Micro anymore." She took his whole plate and placed it in the toaster oven. Rick pulled a still warm roll from the covered bread basket and looked questioningly at the two men seated with him.

Jason swallowed. "Well, the situation with Eddie isn't really a consideration. He's had no contact with Windy all week."

Rick stopped mid-chew. "How do you know?"

"She called me on Friday, gave me a brief history and an update. I took Eddie to the hospital where they admitted him. I've visited with him and he says he hasn't seen or talked to Windy. They released him yesterday, he's staying at his cousins. He and I have had some very good conversations. In light of his situation I feel he may soon accept Christ."

"Oh, now that would be good, we can all sit in the same pew, Windy in the middle."

"Rick!" Valerie admonished him, but Doug smiled.

"If that's what God is calling you to do."

"What? You have an echo in this house? You said the same words just a few days ago."

Jason laughed, "I don't think God will ask that of you. Mark and Heather attend church; I guess Darla was a very fine Christian lady. Anyway, Eddie gave the indication that he might go with them. They were certainly happy at the prospect."

"So now you and Eddie are chums, huh?"

"Rick, what has gotten in to you?" Valerie asked. "I've never heard you be so sarcastic. It's not like you."

"I know, mom, I'm sorry. It's just…but if…" he sighed. "If Windy hasn't been around him, why hasn't she contacted me? Why didn't she come to church today?"

"Tell me again how your last conversation ended." Jason asked.

Rick nodded, "Okay, right, I hung up on her. I need to initiate the conversation."

"I think there's a grave matter of trust here, Rick. Windy thinks you don't trust her and I'm wondering that myself. How would you react if Windy had continued to help Eddie?" Rick opened his mouth to speak, but Valerie set his plate in front of him. "Eat, it's my turn to talk.

"First point, Windy didn't follow through with him, she handed him over to Jason. My guess is she didn't want him back in her life, didn't want him to come between the two of you, so give her credit there. Second point, even if she had helped him get to the hospital and visited him while he was there, that doesn't mean she still wants him in her life. Remember when she told us about Costa Rica and how she gave her past to God. She said she watched it roll out into the ocean along with the waves. She has put that behind her Rick. She's living in the present, you need to join her."

Rick placed a forkful of sweet tasting mashed potatoes in his mouth and let them melt before swallowing.

"Okay, points taken. Now what about the God aspect?" he looked at Jason.

"We all face trials, questions. Some are brought on by God, some by Satan and some are even a cooperative effort on both sides."

Doug and Rick looked surprised while Valerie nodded.

"Job." She said.

"Exactly. Whatever the reason, the situation is not nearly as important as the outcome. Do you trust God? Do you trust Windy? Can you trust them in the future? Dr. Micheals still lives in the city, practices medicine here, works at the hospital. He hurt Windy too, in a different way than Eddie, but no less painful. What are you going to do move to another town to avoid ever seeing him?

"Satan does not want you to walk with the Lord, and God wants to refine that walk, bring you closer to Him. I have some suggestions on where to go from here. Pray. Pray alone, pray with your family, really seek God's will in this. If He says give up Windy, are you willing to continue to follow Him? When you get direction, act on it. Call her, apologize, reassure her."

Rick remembered the conversation he and Windy had while sitting on the rock in the creek. He told Windy he would choose God over her. He meant it then. God asked if he meant it now. Rick reached for his parents hands and bowed his head.

"Lord, I love You. I love You more than life, I love you more than Windy or anyone, even those at this table. But I am weak and I need Your strength. Forgive me for my attitude this week, forgive me for doubting You and Your will in my life, lead me, direct my paths and show me what you want me to do. In the name of Your precious Son, my Savior, Jesus, Amen."

Eight hands released, six eyes looked at Rick, three voices said, "Call Windy."

Tami stood behind her brother and handed him the phone.

He dialed her number, silently asking God for the right words. When he heard her voice the words started to pour out.

"Rick," she interrupted. "Thank you for calling. I intended to contact you today. My parents arrived. My dad has cancer and we won't be getting married. Please ask your family to say a prayer for us. Bye."

Rick pushed the talk button and looked dazed at those around the table. "Her dad has cancer and we're not getting married." He repeated.

Chapter Forty-Five

Jason knocked on the apartment door, praying for God's guidance. As soon as Rick said cancer, Jason knew his parishioner needed him and he immediately left the Notts home. He promised Rick they would meet later in the week.

A petite lady, an older version of Windy, opened the door.

"I'm Windy's Pastor, Jason Shane." She took his offered hand and let him in.

"Debbie Jordan, I'm Windy's mom."

"I can tell," he smiled.

"Come in, can I get you some thing to drink, tea or pop?"

"No thank you, I just had a full meal and don't dare add another drop."

Jason had visited Windy and Cora, remaining in Cora's pleasant smelling kitchen, but had not been in Windy's apartment. He followed Debbie to the small living room where Windy sat on the couch beside her dad. Debbie indicated the chair to Jason then sat on the other side of her husband.

"I hope you don't mind me barging in, I was having dinner with the Notts when Rick called you. I want you to know, I and your church family are here to help you in any way possible."

"Thank you, Pastor J. This is my dad, Rob," Jason reached out and grasped the man's hand. "and my mom. We are...well...I am still trying to get past the initial shock. We hear the word cancer everyday but refuse to connect it with our own family or those we love."

"Of course, but cancer isn't something to be feared. It is treatable and there are new alternatives that can be considered."

"It's interesting you should say that." Rob spoke up. "Because I have already informed my girls that I'm not going to make myself sicker in the hopes of getting better. Debbie and I have been researching the internet and finding options other than the usual accepted treatment."

"I understand that. I spent the last several years in a church of many people and some battled cancer. I have to admit that after watching them go through all the agony of chemo and radiation and then die, I vowed I would never go that route if faced with the disease. Please know that I am here to help in any way. Are you folks Christians?"

Debbie looked at her daughter then back at him.

"Not in Windy's definition. We believe in God, but Windy's been telling us for years about her experience. It's different than ours but we're very proud of the young woman she has become."

"Well, I'm not a doctor and can only give opinions on medical issues, but now, the Lord, that's my field. I would be very glad talk with you, answer any questions…

"Windy, in light of all that has happened this week, could we get together and talk, tomorrow, maybe?"

She appeared hesitant, she knew of his presence during Rick's phone call and now of his knowledge of the cancelled wedding. But she trusted him with her past and with Eddie, he hoped she would trust him with her future also.

"Yes, I believe that would be a very good idea. Tomorrow would be great. I'm scheduled to work, but have already called Don to let him know I won't be in, so anytime would be fine."

"Good, let's say eleven."

"Okay." She saw him to the door and thanked him for his concern.

Jason descended the stairs and stopped at Cora's door, knocking lightly. The sweet little lady greeted him, her nose and eyes red from crying.

"Oh, hello," she said. "you must be Windy's brother, they're right up the stairs."

"Cora, it's me, Pastor J."

"Who? Oh my, where are my glasses? I think I left them by the Kleenex box," she toddled away leaving Jason standing in the door.

'*Poor Windy*', he thought, '*she certainly has a lot to deal with.*'

Cora returned a moment later, glasses perched on her nose. She squinted at the young man. "Now who did you say you are?"

"I'm Pastor Jason, from church."

"On my goodness, you must think me an idiot. Come in, come in, I have water on for tea."

He took a seat at the table. His meal having settled enough that a cup of Cora's raspberry tea and maybe even a special roll or biscuit sounded good.

Monday morning Jason arrived at the church by 9 am. He walked around the building, still amazed that God had blessed his with this wonderful congregation. He thought back to those years growing up in a dirty rundown house. Who would have thought that one day he would have a degree and be the pastor of a wonderful, thriving body of Christians? He knelt at the altar and offered his daily praise to the God Whom he served so willingly and lovingly.

In the kitchen he started the coffee pot using the organic coffee Valerie had given him the day before. He thought of all the events taking place right now. So much had happened over the past week, it made his head spin and he was the observer. He couldn't imagine being caught up in all this. He poured his coffee and walked to the office. He still had difficulty calling it 'his' office. Pastor Burke had been so well loved here in this place and had obviously enjoyed his service to these people. Jason just prayed he wouldn't let them down. He didn't have Pastor Burkes experience or wisdom, but he prayed God would use him anyway.

He looked over the attendance records from yesterday and the previous month, noting a slight decrease in numbers. In seminary they were told that major changes can occur when a pastor leaves and again when a new one arrives. Jason checked the file cabinet for the previous year. According to records, attendance remained the same after Pastor Burke left, in fact it looked like the regulars in the church were even more regular during the time between pastors. Attendance had dropped a little in June, but from the looks of it, that could be due to traveling and vacations.

Soon people began to arrive, the part time secretary, Betty, worked 10-2 everyday, Margie always showed up on Mondays, he wasn't sure exactly what she did, but she always appeared busy. He knew she liked to be totally prepared for the song service each Sunday.

The cleaning crew preferred Saturday, so Jason often had appointments then also. People who worked all week seemed to appreciate that.

At 11 o'clock Windy tapped on the open door and Jason invited her in. He had not dismissed what he'd learned about being alone with female parishioners and always made certain his appointments coincided with other church activity.

"Come in Windy, sit down." He motioned to a comfortable chair. He remained behind the desk, preferring to be the authority in a setting like this. People would open up more if they felt they and their problems merited respect.

She sat and looked at him expectantly.

He lifted his cup. "Would you care for some coffee? It's organic." He assured her. Windy smiled.

"I'm afraid even organic couldn't tempt me to touch that stuff."

"When I was a kid, we had pop and coffee in the house. Cold pop on a cold day just didn't do the trick." He set the cup down and looked straight at the young woman. "Well, I asked you to come because there's been a lot happening to you in the last week."

She nodded.

"Can I just ask some questions? Would that be okay?"

Again she nodded.

"Windy how old are you?"

"23."

"And you have been married, twice, divorced, twice. You had two abusive relationships..."

"Stephan didn't hurt me."

"Physically."

She looked at him and he knew she understood. "Windy, let me help you see where I'm coming from. I don't encourage people to wallow in victimization. Everyone, absolutely everyone, in this town, in this state is a victim of abuse of some sort. Whether it be physical, personal, work related, political, financial. We pay taxes to our state which in turn gives our money to programs we don't want to support, programs that may go completely against our beliefs, yet there's little we can do. That constitutes abuse to me. Our society is always looking to blame someone or something. Stuff happens. We determine not what happens but how we let it affect us."

Windy nodded her understanding.

"Windy, when you enter into another marriage…"

"That won't happen." She stated clearly.

"Why?"

"You of all people should know why. You are the one who should be telling me not to get married."

"Why?"

"Because I'm an adulteress and I don't want to send anyone to Hell."

Chapter Forty-Six

Her words took him completely by surprise; he expected her issue to be trust. He never suspected adultery. He pondered for a moment.

"So you're not going to marry Rick, to save him from hell?"

"Yes." She answered matter-of-factly.

"When did you become the Messiah?" *Where did that come from?* He asked himself.

She gasped at him and started to stand up. She sat back down and covered her mouth, stood again and headed for the door. But she stopped before reaching it, returned to the chair and pulled a Kleenex from the box on his desk. She wiped her eyes and caught her breath.

"I'm here to find out how to help my parents through this hard time. Why are you here?"

Startled, he stared at her wide-eyed; He mulled her words over in his mind. Windy being an adulteress wasn't the reason, or so he thought. He invited her here to talk about the sudden events in her life. Then it came to him.

"You've been reading Luke."

"Yes, and Matthew and Romans and Mark and First Corinthians...and I haven't yet gone near the Old Testament."

Jason nodded. This young woman's thoughts went far deeper than he expected. He wasn't sure if he was up to tackling this. He arose from his desk and sat in the chair next to hers.

"Windy, I've started out all wrong. Let's pray."

He took her hands in his and bowed his head.

"Father we come before You now, seeking Your truth and wisdom, Your forgiveness and healing. You have called Windy into Your fold and You desire her to have a full abundant life walking with You, trusting You and leaning upon Your strength. Please open Your Word to us now and help us see what You have planned for Windy and her family. In the precious name of Your Son and our Savior, Jesus. Amen"

He sat back and looked at Windy. She needed a friend right now, she had already found the authority.

"Do you deny that I am an adulteress?" she asked.

He shook his head. "According to the verses you have read, the meaning is clear. I will not deny that. But Windy, Jesus never stopped with hopelessness, he never condemned without offering forgiveness, he came to give us hope, not heartache."

She touched the tissue to her eyes and he pulled the box from his desk, handing it to her. Then he stood and retrieved the wastebasket, placing it by her chair. He didn't want a simple thing like a runny nose to hamper this discussion.

"Windy, how big is Your God? Is He bigger than your sin, is He bigger than your past?"

She nodded, sniffing.

"Then let me share with you another scripture." He reached for his Bible and opened it to 2 Corinthians and read "Therefore if any man is in Christ, he is a new creature, the old things passed away, behold new things have come.

"Were you a Christian when you married Eddie?"

She shook her head.

"Stephan?"

"No, but I accepted Christ while married to him."

He set the Bible down and picked up her hand, "The day before you asked Christ into your life, you were an adulteress. But on that wonderful day God took your sins and threw them as far as the east is from the west. The Bible assures us God is faithful to forgive us of our sins. From that day on, you were a new creature, void of all your past."

She swallowed and sucked on her bottom lip, he could see the fear in her eyes, wanting to believe what he said.

"But now, you are a divorced woman. If you marry without confessing your sin to God, you're right, you would again be an adulteress. God has brought this passage to you, not to condemn you, but to release you from that past.

"Are you ready to let go?"

She nodded, tears streaming down her face.

Once again he closed his eyes. "Lord, you have made our way clear. You have shined a light on Your Word and brought us into a better understanding of Your love, Your precious child needs a word with You…"

"Oh Father, forgive me, forgive me for doubting you, for seeing my sin as something You couldn't handle. I denied Your saving grace and power, I tried to void your death on the cross by grasping my sin and holding on to it. Forgive me and cleanse me, make me wholly Yours, Father, a new creature, not forged from my past but made in your likeness. This day, I relinquish my sins, my sins of commission and of omission. Give me new birth today, new life, new hope. In Jesus name, amen."

Jason reached the tissue box before Windy and blew his nose, dropping the tissue in the basket. They sat for a few moments, each with their own thoughts.

"Do we need to deal with Eddie?" he asked.

She nodded. "He is no longer my husband, nor is he a rock around my neck, keeping me from the Lord, but he is a soul, someone who desperately needs God. Is that my responsibility?"

Jason thought for a moment silently asking for a little more wisdom. He was finding Miss Jordan had a knack for hard questions.

"No. You did the right thing by asking me to step in. Eddie is very needy right now and could easily look to you to fill his needs. He has me, and Mark and Heather. Now he needs the Lord. Leave that to us."

"Rick's salvation."

"What about it?"

"It's one of the changes. I've prayed for some time that he would find the Lord. I tried not to pray selfishly. I know his conversion is real, but should I back off? Give him more time with God and his new walk of faith?"

Okay, Lord, I need an answer here.

He looked at Windy and shrugged, "I don't know. We have decided to start a men's prayer and study group. He's attending both Sunday school and worship service. He has his dad. And his mom is a very strong Christian."

"And Connie." she added, then looked up at Jason.

"And Valerie's friend Connie, yes. Maybe the question is do you need more time to feel secure with Rick's new faith."

She breathed deeply, pondering his words.

"This could come back to the trust thing and him being so upset about Eddie."

"Oh," she almost laughed. "If I find myself not trusting God, how can I condemn someone for not trusting me?"

Jason raised his brow, he needed this girl on the spiritual advisory committee.

"We'll talk," she said. "If he still wants to talk to me. He has reason to be upset the way I've acted."

"I think Rick would echo your sentiments about trust and the Lord."

"Yeah, I think he would."

"Okay, next issue?"

"My dad."

"Well that has to be taken one step at a time. The first step is none other than trust. If you can trust God with your life are you willing to place your dad in his hands too?"

She smiled and nodded. "In the hollow of His hand. Yes."

"Okay, next step, where are your folks staying?"

"With me."

"Do you have room?"

"Yes, they can have the bedroom, I'll sleep...oh...I had planned to sleep on the couch until Rick and I got married, then let mom and dad take over the apartment."

"What about your brother? Where will he stay?"

"I…I really hadn't thought about…how did you know my brother was coming?"

"Cora thought I was him yesterday, which is something else I want to talk to you about." Windy nodded.

"Listen, the parsonage has three bedrooms. I'm not using the two upstairs. I'm certain the church would have no objection to your folks and brother staying with me for awhile. We don't want them feeling like they're intruding on you, in that small apartment. They need a little more space than you can provide, it sounds like they have a computer to set up for their research and you really have no place for one. And we don't want you pushing yourself out of your apartment to make room for them. They'll still be close enough for you to see them everyday. I just think it'll be better if they're not worried about inconveniencing you."

Windy listened intently and he could tell she mulled over the idea. "You believe the church would okay it? I mean, I guess Mom and Dad could pay room and board…"

"Nonsense, this church is here to help its family. I don't believe Jesus would charge them to stay and we are supposed to be the arms of our Lord. There happens to be a board meeting tonight, we'll discuss it and I'll call you tomorrow. Next issue?"

"Dad's decision not to have treatment."

"Well, what I heard is that your dad doesn't want conventional treatment. They seem to be on top of this thing. They're doing their homework and I know there are doctors around who look at treating cancer differently. Can you trust them with this decision?"

Windy nodded again. "I think so. I guess I wish they would have asked Robby and I first."

"I think that's why they're here. They could have just pursued this where they were living and never even mentioned it, if they didn't want your input."

Windy smiled. "You're right, again."

"We can't sit here and solve all the problems you're going to encounter, but we take them one at a time and deal with them as they come along."

"Thank you, Pastor J, I certainly feel a lot different than when I came in."

"A new creature; not Eddie or Stephan's ex-wife, not even a divorced woman and certainly not as adulteress."

They stood and embraced. "I'll call," Jason volunteered, "or better yet, I'll come by, maybe Cora will have…Cora…"

"I know." Windy nodded. "We're aware of her…situation. But it's still in the early stages and Valerie believes an organic diet for Cora would do wonders."

Jason eye brows rose again. "Can you make organic cinnamon rolls?"

Windy laughed. "If anyone can, Cora can."

Chapter Forty-Seven

Windy's next stop had to be the little house out in the country. She owed Rick an apology, and she intended to give him one. She pulled into the driveway, behind his black pick up and walked up to the door. Just as she started to knock, Rick opened the door and stepped outside.

"Hi."

"You knew I was coming?"

He nodded.

"Pastor called?"

"No, why would he?"

"Because I just left the church. He and I had a very good talk."

"Good."

He stood between her and the door, looking very suspicious.

"I'd like to talk, Rick, I have much to say. Can I come in?"

"Or we can talk out here, it is a nice day, a little on the hot side, but then it is summer in Michigan and you have to expect…"

"You're rambling…"

"Then stop me."

She stepped into his arms and pulled his head down to hers, seeking the sweet taste of his kiss.

They sat on the steps talking over all that had happened in the last several days, exchanging apologies and promises.

Windy shared her reaction upon finding the verse on divorced women and how she didn't want to cause him to commit adultery.

"I can see why you were upset." Rick used his thumb to smooth away the tear that escaped down her cheek. "That's pretty heavy duty, too heavy to bear alone. Is that why you went to talk to Pastor J?"

"Yes, it is; and he led me through some other verses where Jesus offers hope rather than condemnation. Rick, I want you to know that today I prayed and claimed the verse in Corinthians where we're told we are new creatures and old things are passed away. Before that, I felt..." she hesitated unsure if she wanted to cover this ground with Rick. Should she speak so intimately with a man, even the one she wanted to spend her life with?

"I felt that I was coming to you as damaged goods. Used. I wanted to offer you so much more. I wished that I had never been married, never been with anyone else, but I couldn't change that. Today Pastor J showed me, that God can change it and though I'm..." she closed her eyes and fought for the right words. "Through the grace of our Lord I can come to you as a new creature. By the world's definition, I am no longer a virgin, but in God's eyes, I am. He has thrown my past away, never to remember it."

Rick smiled and lifted her head so he could gaze into her eyes. "It's interesting. What you were worried about concerned me too, but in the opposite way. God kept me from the 'normal' temptations. I won't say that I never wanted to be with a woman. Sure I have. But somehow the desire was never strong enough for me to follow through. My army buddies used to get drunk, then go looking for women, but I didn't drink and had no desire to go with them. God kept me for you, but I feared that my inexperience would disappoint you."

Windy threw her arms around this man, this God-given, God fearing man whom she loved. "I could never be disappointed in you."

Finally Rick stood, helped Windy to her feet and eased her into his embrace.

"I have to go to work."

"I know."

"I talked to your folks, I'm really anxious to meet them."

"When did you talk?"

"Earlier today, I called to talk to you, but your mom answered. She sounds just like you, here I was—pouring out my love to this total stranger who finally interrupted me and informed me I probably wanted to talk to her daughter."

Windy laughed. "We used to be mistaken on the phone even when I was kid, people would call, she'd answer and they'd ask if her mom was home. Sometimes it proved convenient because she could honestly say no."

"Come on inside while I get ready." He led her to the door. "Close your eyes."

"Why?"

"Trust me?"

"Unconditionally." She allowed him to lead her into the house where he turned right, taking her into the living room. "Oh, you got your new couch."

"Sort of. Open your eyes."

Windy looked around at a completely different room. Her feet sunk into the new variegated Berber carpet. The couch they both liked, one of soft blue, sat against the inside wall, opposite the fireplace, while the matching love seat and chair graced the other walls. New coffee and ends tables of beautiful cherry sat arranged properly, with blue glass lamps on the end tables.

"Rick, it's beautiful! I didn't know you were going to refurnish the whole room."

"They gave me a great price and really I couldn't just buy a new couch it would have been out of place. I've been measuring that back wall and I'm planning to put a book shelf on the whole thing. Would you like that?"

"Then the wedding's still on?" she asked.

"It was never off for me." He led her to the couch and pulled her down beside him, kissing her softly. She melted into his arms, surprising him with the intensity of her response. He gently pulled back and kissing her forehead reached over to the end table.

"This is for you," he whispered, handing her a small velvet box.

She sat upright and smiled. He loved that smile.

Trying to hide her excitement she opened the box and pulled out a diamond ring from a quarter machine.

She looked at Rick.

"Soon as we can, we go to the jewelers and pick out our rings. I didn't want to buy you a ring you wouldn't want to wear forever."

Her look softened and tears welled up in her eyes. Was there anything that didn't make this woman cry?

"I don't deserve you." she whispered.

"How about we save that argument as our first one after the ceremony?" He welcomed her kiss in answer but didn't allow himself to get caught up in it. "Do you work tomorrow?"

"I open. I'll ask Don if I can leave early."

"I'll pick you up at noon, we'll go to the jewelry store."

"I'd like that."

The next morning Pastor J showed up at Cora's apartment.

"You're just in time…"

"Cora, I believe that everyone who walks up to that door is, 'just in time.'"

"Valerie gave me a new recipe and Rick and Windy had bought me several organic items. Well this morning when Windy headed out for work, she suggested I make cinnamon rolls for you."

"Now that is very kind of both of you." He stepped into the kitchen which was already 10 degrees hotter than outside and sat at the small table.

"Do you drink coffee?"

"I do, but I'll have that at church when I go in."

"Then you'll need milk with your rolls."

Jason hesitated for only a moment before he took a big bite of the first roll Cora placed in front of him. His eyes lit up.

"These are organic? I thought organic food would taste like straw or green stuff. These are delicious."

"I'm so glad you like them, maybe you could take a few to Windy and her nice boss when you leave."

"I'd be glad to." Jason made short work of his share of the rolls and milk then headed upstairs to tell the Jordans the board had okayed them staying with him.

Windy had spoken to her parents the night before and they sincerely thanked Jason for his thoughtfulness. They admitted to being quite worried about having Windy so close as her dad's illness progressed. A short time later Debbie finished the note to Robbie with an explanation and directions. She left it on Windy's table. She and Rob followed Jason the several blocks to the church parsonage where he helped them settle in. Then he drove over to King's Grocery to deliver Cora's rolls, while there he decided to check out the organic food isle.

At the church he sat at his desk wondering what the next move was in the Rick and Windy saga. He thought about taking the family out to dinner, but the family kept growing. He didn't like the idea of Cora cooking for everyone; it seemed too much for her right now. The phone interrupted his thoughts.

"Pastor," Valerie Notts started. "We'd like to invite you to dinner, we thought it would be better for the Jordans to come here tonight, hopefully their son will arrive by then."

"You have solved my dilemma, but, I insist on helping with the food, what can I bring?"

Hours later Jason observed the family gathering.

The newest addition, Robert Drake Jordan Jr, had stolen Rick's teenage sisters hearts the moment he walked in the door. Tall with short brown hair and a walk that exuded confidence, Robbie looked every bit the marine; even in civilian jeans and short sleeve yellow t-shirt. His family resisted keeping him all to themselves, knowing their turn would come. Jason noted the same smile on Robbie's face that graced Windy's.

Rick and his partner, Joe, showed up minutes before dinner started. Jason could see Rick and Windy sending silent messages the minute he walked in.

Rick went straight to Windy's side.

"We'd like everyone's attention, please." He waited until every eye was on him and his fiancé. "Life has been a little chaotic lately, to say the least, but we want everyone to know that we're back on track." He pulled a small box from his pants pocket and handed it to Windy. Jason watched the look that passed between the two people, so obviously in love.

Windy opened the box and took out a ring. Jason stood too far away to see it, but common sense told him what it was, that plus the women's reaction. All the females in the room swarmed Windy with oooh and aaahs. Rick stepped back, wisely knowing a man's place at that moment.

"We picked it out together today," Windy explained. "Our wedding bands too."

After the appropriate time of admiration the ladies commenced putting a huge meal on the table.

During the meal discussion Debbie thanked Jason again for inviting them but when put on the spot she did admit, they would still be pressed for space once they set up the computer. In the next moment Robbie was moved out of Jason's house and into Ricks.

"I don't want to steal him from you," Rick told Debbie. "But I have an extra bedroom and you could use Jason's third room for your computer, then you can let loose and relax."

Anyone approved the plan and Rick gave Robbie directions and the key to his house. Robbie had already paid for a room in a nearby hotel but promised to find his way out tomorrow.

Chapter Forty-Eight

Wednesday morning Rick received a phone call much earlier than he cared to. He figured Joe probably wanted to go fishing and wondered why he hadn't asked about it last night.

"Yeah, whadayawant?"

"Rick?" came his mom's puzzled voice.

"Oh, I'm sorry mom," he quickly sat up and switched hands grabbing his alarm clock with the newly freed one.

"No, I'm sorry, I didn't mean to wake you."

"Ten o'clock? Wow, I really slept hard. It's okay, I should have been up minutes ago."

She laughed. "Connie and I want to come out and talk to you."

"Oh." It was usually bad enough when your mom says she wants to come to your home and talk to you, but when both your moms want to— it's dangerous.

"You don't want me to come there?"

"No."

"You sure?"

"Yes."

"Well, I guess by the time you get here, I'll be dressed."

"Okay."

And Mom talking in one word sentences always scared him. He pulled himself out of bed, grabbed a pair of jeans and headed for the shower.

Minutes later he stood in his kitchen, barefoot and shirtless watching steam shoot from his tea kettle.

He was glad Mom and Connie got along so well. He knew they'd been friends for a while, so they had time to get used to the idea of Connie being his birth mom. He hadn't. He figured if he had a choice in birth moms she'd be his first pick...

He heard their laughter from the front and turned as they entered the kitchen.

Connie stopped, hand in mid-air, he heard her intake of breath and saw her chin quiver as her eyes filled with tears. Then he remembered the picture she showed him of Jimmie. He knew, by the look on her face he was a duplicate of his birth dad only with gray eyes. Well, a short duplicate.

The three stood there staring at each other. Rick thought of a couple dumb things to say. He managed "I'm sorry."

"Don't be. Don't ever be sorry."

Guess that was the dumbest.

"I mean...I'm not really...I didn't mean..."

Connie laughed. "Well, at least that's something you got from me, saying dumb things and having them taken wrong."

Oh, his life might as well be over. Two moms. Two moms who knew what he was thinking.

"Alright ladies," he decided his best chance of survival lay in the cop routine, take charge, demand an answer. "What am I in for?"

The women joined him at the counter, both talking at the same time. "He has herbal tea, how thoughtful." "I think the water's boiling, Rick." "Where does he keep the cups?" "In that cupboard." "Isn't this sink a treasure?" "My gramma had one just like it."

Grabbing a can of cherry cola from the fridge he sat at the table. He rarely drank pop anymore, what with mom's new organic regiment, but he knew he would need one today.

"Rick, that stuff..."

"Mom, no, no." He held up his hand and shook his head, something he learned from his dad. "If you want me sane through out your...whatever it is you women are planning, let me have my poison."

"While the tea is brewing let me show you Rick's new living room set,"

Valerie said, amazing her son with that woman ability to change the subject when threatened. "He and Windy picked it out together…" He followed them through the dining room and bounded up the stairs as they entered the living room. Those two were acting more like Tami and Tari than two grown women. He could hear them chirping below. Chirping. He pulled a t-shirt over his head. That's what Dad called it. Mom chirped when she was nervous. The thought of his mom nervous sent chills through his body. What were these two women up to? He quickly looked out the window, but mom had already anticipated his reaction and parked right in front of the garage door. He might as well go down and get it over with.

"We want to talk about the wedding." The threesome sat at Rick's small kitchen table, their comfort drinks close by.

The wedding. Too easy.

"Shouldn't you be talking to Windy about that, I mean isn't that a chick thing?"

"Well, yes." The women exchanged looks.

Why couldn't they read his mind right now and just spit it out?

"We don't want to butt in, but with Windy's dad ill and her mom so wrapped up in his situation, we want to help, but we don't want to do so without Windy asking us first."

"So you want me to ask Windy to ask you to help?"

"Couldn't you be a little more subtle?" Valerie asked.

He shook his head. "Men don't do subtle." He referred back to one of his dad's favorite phrases. "Besides, we're going to have a LITTLE wedding, with very FEW people and NO fuss."

"Well, if Windy asks you if you think we might want to help…"

"I'll tell her you'd love to. There that wasn't so bad. Guess you two need to be about the next thing on your list."

"Yes. We do."

So that was the practice round and the real ammunition is about to be fired. He sat back down and took another draw from the unhealthy aluminum can.

"Do you work tomorrow Rick?" Valerie asked, trying to look nonchalant.

"It's a holiday; I get stuck on midnights with the new guy."

Connie picked up the conversation. "My family has a get together every July fourth. I plan to tell them about you. And I'm wondering if you would come with me. To meet them."

"Tomorrow?!"

Connie nodded. "I know it's short notice…"

'A week is short notice.' He wanted to yell. *'Tomorrow is out of the question!'*

"I intended to ask you last week and things seem to fall apart, a little, but you and Windy are okay now…"

Birth mother, birth family. This whole thing was becoming complicated. Why couldn't he just go back to being Rick Notts? He didn't need more grandparents and uncles and cousins. He needed a wife and his home. And his pink cat of course. But how could he disappoint this very sweet, very patient lady. After all, she'd known who he was for a long time and kept silent. Didn't he owe her something?

"Let me think…better yet, let me pray about it. Okay?"

"That's the best answer I could ask for." But Rick knew it wasn't the one she wanted. "It's at my brothers house near Kalamazoo. I'll leave here around noon, be home by six." Connie shrugged. "If you decide to come, I'll drive."

"If I go, I want Windy with us." He could tell by her face she took that as a yes.

"Of course. Of course. You can drive. My car."

Rick smiled, he did like that little red sports car.

"I'll call you in the morning."

The chirping stopped and the ladies finished their tea. As he walked them to the door, his mom turned to him.

"But, Rick," *Oh, oh she's coming in for the kill.* "We would like to come over and clean house for you, not that it's dirty…"

"Mom, I would welcome your help cleaning the house." *Finally, something that would make them happy.* He kissed his mom's cheek and gave Connie a hug; but held his breath until the car had actually backed out of the driveway.

He had to admit, they brought up a legitimate point. Even simple weddings required a certain amount of work. He would be sure to let Windy know of his mom and Connie's desire to help.

Rick sat the clean, soapy cup next to the dishpan and yelled "Come in," to the knocking on the front porch. He'd almost forgotten about Rob and breathed a sigh of relief that his mom had already left. He wouldn't want his brother-in-laws first opinion of him to be formed while he dealt with the two ladies.

The screen door squeaked shut and he heard something hit the floor, Rob's duffle bag, he assumed. But he never heard the footsteps fall behind him.

"Nice place. Do you fish the stream?" Rick listened for peculiarities in the voice; he prided himself on being able to recognize most people with just one word.

"My partner does." He turned and greeted his new house guest. They took a short walk around the place, Rick showed Robbie the weed garden that looked like it might produce a couple tomatoes and a few dozen Zucchini.

"Joe told me to plant just a couple seeds, but I scattered a handful. Joe's actually a pretty smart man. Some day I'll start listening to him," *but not about women and religion*, he thought.

"I've been in the service so long, I forgot what it's like to live in a house. Barracks are cheaper and since I don't have a family I could see no reason to invest in property."

They discussed their time in the service, with a few similarities.

"Hey, Robbie," Rick stopped. "You don't mind that? Being called Robbie? I mean very few people get away with calling me Ricky."

Windy's brother laughed. "Dad is Rob, I am Corp. Jordan, or Jordan. I guess while I'm here, I can buck up and take the well intended abuse."

"Well, make yourself to home, Jordan. I report to work at three and I wanted to stop to see Windy before I go in. My moms were just here and I have to let Windy know about the newest bombshell."

"Moms?"

"No one's told you? You've been here a whole day and still don't know the family history? The way my sisters were looking at you last night, I figured they would tell you just as an excuse to keep your company."

"I think your dad saved me."

"Dad's are great."

"You know, I haven't been around mine enough lately to know what you mean. But that's changing. I've been in 11 years and although I intended to retire after 20, my plans may be completely different. I have an extended leave right now, 3 months to see how Dad's treatments go. If he's good, I'll return, if not, I won't leave them."

Rick found Windy in her favorite aisle, sneaking up on her. He grabbed her from behind and nipped her ear.

"I wish you guys had to wear your leather in summer. You can't sneak up on me when you creak."

"Well, just wait a few years and you'll be able to identify me by my creaking joints." He used his silly old man voice.

"Not if your mom and I keep you healthy."

"Speaking of mom… Can we go in the break room or something?"

"I need to be sitting down for this?"

He nodded as he placed his hand on her elbow and she led the way to the back of the store. Windy grabbed a cherry cola as they passed the cooler and once they settled on a couple chairs she opened it and offered Rick the first swig.

"No, you go ahead. I already had mine for the day."

"So what's your mom up to now?"

"She and Connie came over today; they are itching to get their hands on the wedding." Windy smiled and nodded. "They thought if your mom isn't up to it, they could help. I told them, it's a simple wedding, but I'm sure there's something you could use some help with."

"Sure there is. My mom says she has a great program on the computer for printing cards and stuff. She wants to make invitations…"

"Windy, we can just invite people by asking, there's not going to be that many."

"I know, that's what I told her. But she feels like she has nothing to offer. I mean, they have only a little money saved and Dad has no insurance. Which even if he did, it wouldn't pay for alternative medicines. They can't buy us anything, even as a wedding present, so she wants to do this. If your mom and Connie would help her get familiar with names and faces, give her addresses, make her and Dad feel less like outsiders."

Rick nodded, he could see where she was going with this. After all Windy had been around his family for months, and the church family for years.

"Then Cora insisted on doing the cooking. I told her we weren't having a meal, but a picnic. If the ladies want to help her, she could sure use it."

"Wow, that was simple, and they will be very happy, oh yeah, they plan to clean my house."

Windy laughed. "Good; that way it'll be like a brand new house and we can move in at the same time." She thought for a moment and bit her bottom lip. "I don't want to sound pushy…"

"Oh don't worry, I had two moms in my house today, nothing could sound pushy after that."

"I…I wonder, about the bedroom…"

Rick grinned. "Next day off we go to the furniture store and get that squared away. I'll tell the ladies it's off limits."

"Okay…Rick, how about if we take the smaller bedroom and use the larger for…the…future? You never know, we may adopt a passel of kids someday."

Rick stood and pulled her into his arms. His lips found hers and he lost himself in the pleasure of holding her, kissing her. She finally pulled back.

"I'm on duty." she whispered.

He moaned. "Isn't it September yet? I just want to be yours, completely, and have all this behind us."

She pushed him lightly, "I have to get back to work."

"Oh, wait, I haven't even gotten to the hard part yet." He looked into her eyes, hoping she would understand his concern and help him through it. "Connie wants us to meet her family."

"Uooo," she shook her head. "Big step, too soon."

"That's what I'm thinking. I told them I would pray about it and let them know, but I'm not doing it alone, you have to be with me on this one."

"Okay, I will pray about it. When does she want you to meet them?"

"The fourth of July."

"That's tomorrow."

"I know. Do you work? Because I told Connie I wanted you with us, so if you work we won't go."

Windy remained silent for a moment. She shook her head. "I was on the schedule and a few minutes ago Don came up to me and said he's giving me the day off. When I asked him why, he said," Windy swallowed and tears welled in her eyes. "He said God told him to."

"Maybe we should eat over at Jason's from now on, your kitchen is so little." Debbie suggested.

"I know, I'm so sorry." Cora nodded.

"No, don't apologize, it just seems so inconvenient for you."

"Oh, it's really easy here. You always know your own kitchen best."

"Well, as long as you let Windy and I do the clean up…'

Windy, Cora and Debbie finished putting the food on the table and were just about to call the guys in to get their plates when Cora's phone rang. The little lady answered it but quickly handed it to Windy who scooted out the door and sat on her steps.

"Hi Honey, are you and Joe coming over for supper?"

"Windy, as I've prayed today," Rick began, without hearing her question. "about meeting Connie's family, I keep thinking about Jimmies. I believe I want to do this, get it over with. Then I'll talk to Connie's mom about Jimmie's family, she knows his mom and would understand better what should be done."

"Why his family, did Connie bring them up?"

"No. I guess God did. I put myself in their place. Connie's family still has Connie. They're just getting another member, if they want one, that is. But Jimmie's, well they lost him. Maybe they'd like to have a little piece back again."

Chapter Forty-Nine

They met at Windy's the next morning at 11 o'clock. Connie handed Rick the keys and moved to the back seat. She enjoyed being with Rick and Windy. They were great kids and a real cute couple. Conversation felt awkward so she retreated from time to time and sought her Lord, asking Him if she had done the right thing. She just couldn't imagine not telling her family. She had robbed them of two grandchildren, now God was giving her a chance to at least know one of them.

'Lord,' she ended her silent prayer as Rick stopped in front of the house she indicated. *'All I ask is that Your will be done.'*

"Okay, give me about half an hour." She instructed before closing the door.

"You're still sure?" Rick asked. She nodded, took a deep breath and closed the door. She had previously suggested the kids drive around but Rick said they would probably just sit and pray.

Connie surveyed her family as she walked around the house to the back yard. The six adult couples sat in lawn chairs, the men drinking beer, the women drinking wine coolers. Connie thought of all those other July 4ths when she would join them, sometimes indulging in a few coolers two many. Tom's three children took their places around the back yard.

James, the oldest at 20, stood at the grill, already fitting the male stereotype. Jessica and Kaitlyn sat by the small in-ground pool, their bathing suits revealing far too much. Jess had one more year in high school, Kaitlyn two.

The younger people followed suit in their drinking habits. Tom and Carol Anne, in their worldly wisdom, allowed their children to drink at home. A practice Connie had never approved of even during her drinking days. She took her spot in an empty chair near her parents, refusing the cooler Tom offered her.

"Still not drinking? What's this make, four, five years?"

"Four," she answered.

She savored the peaceful moment, knowing she was about to shatter her family's world. They engaged in small talk for awhile, catching up on jobs and schooling.

"I have something important to tell you." She started in her best *I've got everything under control,* voice.

"Are you getting married, Aunt Connie?" Jessie teased.

Connie's lack of a partner was always at least one topic of their holiday conversation.

"No," she smiled, '*but I am about to add a family member. Take it slow girl, do this the way you practiced it.'* "But I do have a very interesting story for you."

The girls giggled, but drew their chairs closer to their aunt. Connie loved Tom's kids, had often wondered what it would be like to have a couple of her own, but she was the only one to blame for this void in her life.

"Well as you all know, my life has taken many twists and turns…"

"Oh, Aunt Connie's going to give her 'testimony' again."

"No, not quite. I know you're all tired of hearing it, but today I have something different to tell you; something none of you have ever heard before." She gathered her courage and looked at her watch. In 20 minutes Rick and Windy would arrive. She wanted this timed just right.

"Remember that summer before I started college, when Jimmie came home for leave?" The older adults nodded, and her parents took a couple minutes to remind their new spouses of Tom's best friend, the boy next door who died in Viet Nam.

"I spent a lot of time with Jimmie, then," now she received silence.

"You never liked Jimmie, Dandruff."

Connie smiled at the almost forgotten nickname. "The truth is, I loved Jimmie from the moment I saw him." She waited to let that sink in.

"I wondered," Connie's mom, Linda, admitted but Tom just gave her a 'yeah, right' look.

"Well, after I arrived at Western, I found out I was pregnant." All eyes shot opened and Kaitlyn actually gasped.

"By Jimmie?" Tom asked.

Connie nodded, suddenly afraid this wasn't such a good idea, but she'd already started and couldn't turn back.

"I wrote to him, hinting that maybe we could have a future, but he didn't respond and the next thing I knew, Mom's telling me Jimmie's married."

"What happened to the baby?" Her dad, Paul spoke up.

"I…I ga… I released him for adoption."

"You gave up Jimmie's son?" Tom leaned forward in his chair, and glared at her. "Jimmie's only child?"

"I didn't know what to do, he was married; I couldn't suddenly announce he had a child, we had a child."

"Why didn't you tell us?" Linda asked. Connie saw the hurt in her mom's eyes at being left out of such an important part of her daughter's life.

"How could I? I didn't want you to be ashamed of me. Jimmie already had a wife and well, I took what appeared to be the best road for the baby and myself. I didn't know how to be a mom, or how to finish college with a child. I figured I had brought my situation on myself and I would be the one to take care of it." She fought the tears, knowing they would flow soon enough and wanting to keep them at bay as long as possible.

"Jimmie's only child." Tom repeated. "Lost to us."

"Well, no," Connie contradicted him. "I wouldn't have brought this up if I didn't have a good reason."

Connie feared her brother's eyes would pop from his head. She reached over and took his hand. "I know you loved Jimmie," she tried hard to hold the tears back. "But I had already signed all the papers by the time Jimmie died. I tried to get the little boy back, but adoption was different then. They wouldn't tell me anything." She swallowed and regained her composure. "But God was in it all..."

"Don't bring up your God stuff now,"

"I have to, Tom, because God is the One Who brought us back together."

Rick sat between Connie and Windy. Supported by two women who loved him, he felt a little less uneasy.

He held his bottle of water tightly, hoping he wouldn't send the cap flying in the air. His cousins had looked at him as if he were from another planet when he refused the alcohol they offered.

He silently went over the names again, Connie's mom and step-dad, Linda and Wayne Stoltman; her dad and step-mom, Paul and Terri Cooper. Tom hadn't stopped staring since he and Windy made their entrance. Tom's wife Carol Anne was civil but distant, where her kids were openly friendly. James made a comment about him getting Rick's name, being Jimmie's namesake and all. The girls, well, they were girls, a bit less mature than his sisters. They made him feel welcome, but at the same time it saddened him how young people are so open to sin. People could call it tolerance if they wanted, but sin is sin and when people stop calling it that they open themselves to a world of hurt. Not that he condemned Connie, not at all. He admired her, but she had confessed her sin, received forgiveness from the Lord, these kids, his cousins, saw no sin.

He fielded a number of polite questions from the grandparents, his grandparents. He almost felt as if he defended himself and Connie, and his parents. He tried to look at the situation from her family's point of view. They must believe he rightfully belonged to them. They gave him the impression they thought he had been wronged by being 'given away'. And although all of their lives had suddenly changed, he was still Rick Notts, Doug and Valerie's son and he always would be. He loved his family; he felt he could find room to add these people as his friends, in time.

"So you're religious too?" Terri Cooper asked.

"I recently asked Christ into my heart, just a couple weeks ago actually.

My dad and I attended a men's conference and we were both saved. I don't know about being religious. But I am a Christian."

"Your mother must have coaxed you on that answer." Wayne Stoltman responded. "It's what she always tells us."

"I didn't know you'd met my mom." Rick stated before he had a chance to think it through.

Wayne's face grew red. Rick wondered how many beers he'd had and how they were affecting his reaction to this news. He did feel concern for this family, just finding out that not only had their daughter given birth and released a child without them knowing it, but now that child walked back into their lives. He wasn't sure that he would act much differently.

Windy sat next to him, like a secure little rock. She answered when spoken to, treated everyone very well, just as he knew she would. Now she reached over and placed her hand on his shoulder, an 'I'm right here' gesture.

"Well, sir," Rick sat up straight and assumed his position. "Your daughter is a lovely woman and I am proud to know her as my birth mom. She made a very hard decision 25 years ago and allowed me to be raised by a wonderful family. My mom and dad could not have loved me more if I had been born to them; the same with my sisters. I admire Connie and I am very thankful that God has brought us back together." He reached over and took Windy's hand. "One of the reasons for our visit is to let you know Windy and I are getting married on August 24th and we would be honored if you would attend."

Windy felt Rick's cold, clammy hand in hers; heard his little speech that ended in the unexpected invitation. She felt so proud of him right now. He was just how God intended man to be—a provider and a protector. He protected Connie from her own family, at the same time defending his parents. God must really love her to have sent this man into her life. Now she had to deserve him.

The three drove silently to Cora's house. Windy invited them in but both declined. Connie hugged them and said goodbye then jumped back into her car and eased down the street.

"I need to get some rest before work tonight." Rick said.

"I know." Windy slipped her arms around him and held tight, wishing they were already married and that she would be waiting for him when he arrived home in the morning. "Why don't you take a nap here instead of driving home, it'll give you a few more minutes of sleep."

"I couldn't sleep knowing you're in the next room."

"I'm going over to Pastor J's and do some work with mom."

He took a deep breath and pulled her a little tighter. "My uniform is at home and I need to feed the animals."

"I can take care of that for you."

He kissed the top of her head. What she suggested made sense. But he had no desire to sleep in the same room, the same bed she had once shared with Eddie "We should have gotten married on Saturday, like I wanted."

She snuggled into his neck. "Maybe you're right, but it's too late now."

"No it isn't, we could get married THIS Saturday."

"And disappoint everyone? Time has a way of moving too quickly. Before you know it, we'll be standing in your backyard exchanging wedding vows and you'll be wondering how to back out gracefully."

"No, no, never." He lifted her chin and looked into her eyes. "If there is one thing I am sure of in this crazy changing world, it's that I love you and I want to be with you forever." He kissed her softly and Windy knew that if she added just a little passion he wouldn't want to leave. She pulled away slightly.

"Go get some sleep. I want you alert on the job."

Chapter Fifty

The ringing irritated Windy. She wasn't used to hearing that particular noise in her sleep. It stopped and Windy sighed. A moment later is started again. If she wanted to get some rest she knew she had to stop that ringing. She pulled herself from the bed and trudged out to the kitchen looking around for the noise. It came from the phone. She looked at the clock 3:15.

Why would someone be calling her at 3:15 in the morning?

Dad!

Quickly she grabbed the phone and hit the talk button. "Mom?"

"Windy, this is Officer Blackmon. Joe's at your downstairs door. Will you let him in please?"

"Joe?" She couldn't understand why anyone would be at her door. "Joe who?"

"Kozininske."

Why would Joe be here at this time of night? Did Rick not report to work and Joe thought he might be here? Rick. Rick?!

She dropped the phone and ran down the steps, unlocking the door for Rick's partner.

"Joe," he stood in front of her in a rumpled t shirt, his hair uncombed. "Why are you here?" She didn't want him here; she didn't want him at her door in the middle of the night it could only be for a bad reason.

"Let's go upstairs, Windy." He touched her arm and guided her up the steps. "I don't want to wake up Cora."

"Sit down," he gently directed her to the table and eased her into a chair. "Windy, I need you to listen to me, I need you to pay attention."

"What?!" she yelled. "What?!"

He stood her back up and put his arms around her. She seemed to calm a little.

"Windy, there was an accident…"

"NO! NO!" She shook her head and looked at him, refusing to acknowledge what he had to say. "NO!"

"He's alive."

She sagged against him.

"But he's hurt and he needs you."

"My purse…" she pulled away and looked around.

Joe grabbed her shoulders and made eye contact. "Rick is alive, he's hurt, he needs you to be strong for him. Stay with me Windy."

She looked into his face and saw the fear he tried to mask.

"You need to go into your bedroom and get dressed. Brush your hair. Then we'll find your purse and I will take you to Rick."

"He's alive?"

"Yes."

"Is he okay?"

"He needs you to be okay."

"He needs me?"

"Yes."

"He asked for me?"

"He needs you, go get dressed and brush your hair so you look presentable for him."

She couldn't think. She didn't dare think. *Get dressed. Do as Joe told you. Get dressed.*

She pulled on the jeans she wore yesterday, slipped a t-shirt over her head and began looking for her bra. She pulled the covers back, looked on the floor. No bra. *Brush your hair.*

She rushed into the bathroom and grabbed the brush, yanking on her unruly locks.

"Windy lets go." Joe held her purse and her tennis shoes. "You can put these on in the car."

"He's alive?" she asked.

"Yes, Windy, he's alive."

She couldn't ask any more questions. They thumped through her brain; but she feared the answers. *He's alive.* That's all she needed right now.

Joe drove too fast, even for this time of night. Joe was scared. She didn't want him to be scared. She wanted him to say these things happen all the time and everything is okay. Rick is okay. She watched the street lights go by quickly. She wanted Joe to drive slowly, not because she feared the speed but because he wouldn't drive so fast if everything was okay.

Joe parked the car in the hospital lot and intercepted her before she could get to the emergency doors. He turned her to him and held her head in his hands, firmly, gently.

"I don't know what he looks like. I'm not even sure what happened, I was told an accident. I don't know what kind. I need you to be strong. Rick needs you to be strong."

Strong. She hated that word, why did people think she could be strong. She didn't have to be strong anymore, she had Rick and he would be strong for her. He would protect her and take care of her. He said so.

She nodded and Joe released her head. He placed his arm around her and they calmly walked into the hospital emergency room. While Windy paced, Joe went to the desk but could glean no information. He pulled his badge and showed it to the nurse who still shook her head.

"You can not go in there, you'll distract the doctors. The patient is the priority, not your need to see him."

"Can someone just let me know what happened, how badly he's hurt? Was another officer brought in with him?"

"An uninjured officer, yes."

"Where is he?"

"I believe he is in the cubicle with your friend."

"If he's in there, why am I out here?"

"Because the other officer witnessed what happened and is relaying that information to the emergency staff."

"Who's the doctor?"

"Dr. Roeden is on duty tonight, but they called in the internist."

"Who?"

"Dr. Michaels, of course."

At that moment Doug and Valerie burst through the doors. Windy ran up to Valerie and the women embraced. Doug joined Joe at the desk.

"I know nothing." Joe said, glancing at the nurse.

She frowned.

"You must know something, who called you?"

"Same officer who probably called you. Said a patrol was involved in an accident and the officers had been taken to Community General."

Doug nodded at the familiar words that kept him company on the way to the hospital.

Valerie had talked Windy into sitting down and the two men joined them. Joe sat for a moment then stood.

"I need coffee, anyone else?"

Doug nodded. "A little cream, please. I'm going to call Pastor J, I know he'll want to be here."

Joe walked behind the desk and disappeared into a doorway, quickly returning with two mugs of coffee.

"One perk of being a cop," he explained as he handed one to Doug. The four slipped into silence.

The hospital had recently redone their emergency rooms and those waiting could no longer see into the trauma area. Up till this point Joe felt that was a good idea. But now he was the one stuck in a room across the hall from the action and he didn't like it one bit.

The outside door opened and a striking woman walked in. She went straight to Valerie who stood and embraced the newcomer.

"Joe, this is Connie, Rick's birth mom."

So this was the lady Rick had spent a lot of time talking about lately. He'd pictured someone older, although Rick did say she was only 18 when he was born. Joe shook her hand and felt her soft skin against his rough calloused flesh.

"I'm Rick's partner, he's mentioned you...a lot. I'm pleased to meet you, just wish it was under better circumstances."

"Yes, me too."

He liked her voice. It was soft without being weak, yet very distinct.

"Would you like some coffee?"

"No thanks, something a little stronger, and cold…is there a pop machine?" she glanced around.

"Be right back." Joe sat his cup down and disappeared behind the desk again, returning a moment later with a can of Coke. She thanked him then opened it with a perfect nail.

Joe noticed her hands. She wore her own nails, painted a soft purple, *what was that called?* Joe knew the primary colors, anything beyond that didn't have purpose as far as he was concerned. But he knew there was a name for this particular color and he determined to remember it.

An opening door caught everyone's attention and Dr. Stephan Michaels strode up to the now standing group. Joe noticed the doctor's hidden surprise at seeing Windy.

"Family of Rick Notts?"

"Yes," Doug spoke up, "all of us."

"Officer Notts is not in immediate danger."

The group breathed a collective sigh.

"Right leg is broken in a couple places. He has major trauma to the right side and I detect internal bleeding. A surgical room is being prepped as we speak. Officer Notts is awake but in significant pain. He has given permission for the surgery. As long as we have him sedated we will go ahead and get that leg set." He looked over the little group, ignoring Windy. "One of you may go back and sit with him until we're ready."

Four voices whispered "Windy."

Chapter Fifty-One

Windy followed Stephan across the hall and into a cold, dimly lit room.

"Dr. Michaels, I'm glad it's you doing the surgery." she managed to say.

"As well you should be." He replied as he walked away.

Windy made her way to the bed and found Rick's hand. A blood pressure cuff surrounded his left forearm. She locked her fingers in his and leaned close enough to kiss his cheek.

He lay slightly on his left side, his right leg in an air cast, a pillow propped behind his back. "Windy?" he whispered.

"I'm right here. Right here where I belong."

She kissed his dry lips, trying go give then some moisture, she knew he couldn't have anything to drink. Not before surgery.

She closed her eyes and opened them a couple times, trying to adjust to the semi-darkness. A soft glow came for the muted light above the bed. The monitors, heart rate, respiration and blood pressure, added a red eeriness. She felt the IV in the back of his right hand.

She thought of the day in Costa Rica when she gave Eddie up. It was hard, but not painful, not when she knew Who waited for her. There was no giving up Stephan, he was never hers and seeing him now, she once again marveled that she had even been his wife. Her marriage to him seemed impossible; like watching a bad movie till the finish just to see if it gets better, and feeling great relief when it ended.

But she couldn't release Rick. She wouldn't give him up, not without a fight.

"Lord," She spoke out loud. "I know he's Yours and I know I told You just months ago that I didn't want anything coming between us. Now it would appear that my love for Rick could be that stumbling block. I don't want that. I am selfish, I want you both. Please, Father I beg of You, don't take him away from me. Spare him, Father, please, please. If not for me then for his family. I ask for your healing touch on him."

She gently laid her hand on his right side. "In the name of Jesus I ask that you stop the blood flow in Rick's side. Touch the organ that bleeds, Father, repair it." She reached down and placed her hand on the air cast. "Just as You knit Rick's bones together in the womb, I pray You would knit them once more. Bring the fractures into alignment, fuse his bones back together stronger than before. Let him walk again. Let him dance for Your glory."

The tears came in a flood and she felt unspeakable sadness well up from her soul.

"Oh, please Father, please don't take him from me." She sobbed. "How could I bear it? How?"

With Me.

Tears continued to stream down her face and drip off her chin. "But Jesus You said, 'we have not because we ask not'. I am asking, I am begging, please allow Rick to live, please allow us to continue our lives together, serving You, glorifying You. Oh Lord I think of my dad who is also fighting for his life. It's so easy to not realize that, because he's not in the hospital, not trembling with pain. But Lord, don't let me take his illness lightly. Help me to pray for my dad, touch my heart and soften it toward him and his needs. Please Father, don't let my prayers for my dad commence when he is gravely ill. Lord, if it be Your will, touch these men. These wonderful, important men You have placed in my life. Thank you for them, and if You decide to take them home, thank you for the time you gave us. But Lord, please, please, speak to my dad's heart, bring him into your kingdom before he leaves this world, whether soon because of cancer or later in old age. His salvation, not his health is what I desire most."

Rick's soft moaning and labored breathing had become the backdrop of Windy's prayer. He moved his head slightly.

"I love you," he whispered. "Windy…Windy…"

She placed her cheek on his and let her tears mingle with his sweat. "Oh, Rick, I love You, too, more than I can tell you. Just remember God loves you more then I ever could, trust Him, Rick. Call out to him, not me. He's here, He's by your side waiting to heal you."

"Father." Rick's voice was barely audible. "Jesus…"

Windy pulled back a little, feeling her heart would break and she didn't want Rick to feel her hopelessness. Joe said she must be strong. But she wasn't.

When you are weak, then are you strong.

"Father, you know me so well. I need Your strength right now, because I have none without You. I need to be here for Rick, to give him courage and hope. But I can only do that by Your grace." the tears poured again. "Oh Father, please don't take him from me. How could I go on?"

With Me.

A peace settled over her. A calmness she knew could only come from God.

"Alright, Father, if it means letting him go I will. I would release him to keep him alive. He is Yours, not mine. I am Yours, not his. Father, let Your will be done."

Joe watched Windy as she sat with each of Rick's relatives, holding their hands, praying with them. The young pastor had arrived minutes after Doug's phone call, he appeared too young and Joe wondered how this kid could minister to a grieving family. After Windy returned to the waiting room saying Rick had been taken to surgery, Joe noticed a difference in her demeanor. Her red, swollen face held a look of peace. Immediately upon her return the family grouped together, pulling Joe and Jason in with them, and prayed. Each took turns, speaking aloud, asking for Rick's recovery, the doctor's knowledge and skill, their own comfort during this time and most importantly God's will.

Joe was most touched by Connie's prayer. She said she had released Rick once to a better life, since she had just found him, she didn't want to let him go, but was willing to release him once again into God's care, trusting his will and his love for their son. When the group finished praying they all sat down and quietly talked among themselves. No mention was made of the past or the future. Time seemed to be on hold for this unusual family.

Joe excused himself, grabbed the empty coffee pot he had confiscated earlier and came back with a full one. He also carried two cans of cold cherry cola.

As he watched Windy, a new respect began to grow. She had been a basket case when he first entered her apartment. Now, still not knowing the extent of Rick's injuries, but knowing that surgery was needed to save his life, she appeared calm and peaceful, giving her strength to those who shared her grief.

He grudgingly gave Rick credit where this little lady was concerned. Maybe, just maybe, she wouldn't rip the young man's heart out and stomp on it as Andrea had done to him.

Try as he might, Joe couldn't keep his eyes from wandering back to the lovely blonde. She had appeared distraught when she first came in, but now shared in the serenity so prevalent in this room.

Windy looked up as Dr. Michaels walked into the room. He refused to look at her and directed his attention to Doug.

"Mr. Notts?"

Doug strode forward and gripped the doctor's hand.

"Your son is doing very well. Once we opened him we found a tear in the kidney, a rather long tear that required several stitches. This is where the internal bleeding originated, however we found no bleeding. I can not give you a reason for this. By all rights that kidney should have been pouring blood, yet it was not. We have closed the tear, it should heal without incident. We also set his leg. What appeared on the first x-rays as two clean breaks now appear to be fractures. Again I have no explanation. Officer Notts will make a complete recovery, I expect him to have no long lasting health concerns."

Doug pumped the doctor's hand, nodding. His smile grew with each sentence.

"Dr. Michaels, we truly thank you for your expert work this night. I have to tell you that our prayers have been answered, but I think you know that."

"Well, I'm glad you found comfort in your prayers."

"We found comfort, Rick found healing."

Dr. Michaels nodded slightly. "Your son will be taken to recovery for the next couple hours. You may visit him once he has been settled into a room. I wish all of you well."

With that he departed.

Doug immediately dropped his head.

"Father, our hearts are filled with joy and thankfulness," Windy bowed her head and reached out for the hand nearest her, in moments everyone stood in a circle and prayers of praise and worship filled the room.

After the last 'amen' Valerie walked over to her husband. "We need to get home and be with the girls."

"I know it's out of the way, but would you go by Cora's and let her know what's going on?" Windy asked. "If I don't show up for breakfast she'll be beside herself."

After they left, Windy walked over to the window and looked at the beautiful sunrise. The hospital had good sense placing this room on the east; the sunrise of a new day always gave encouragement. Jason joined her.

"I'm going home, Windy. I'll talk to your parents and see that Robbie knows what's going on. Then I'll get the prayer chain started." He pulled her into a comforting embrace.

"Thank you, Pastor. I really appreciate you being here. And thanks for informing my family. Please, when you start the prayer chain would you add my dad?"

"Of, course."

When he left, Joe and Connie joined Windy and for several minutes they just watched as the sun rose and its light spread through the sky.

"Joe?"

Windy turned and saw a bedraggled officer standing in the waiting room door. Joe covered the distance in seconds and pulled the man in, dropping him into a chair.

"What happened?" Joe demanded.

Windy noticed the officer was about Rick's age, probably the newest kid on the force, that's why he wound up on midnights. He stared wide-eyed at Joe, his fear apparent.

Windy sat next to the man and introduced herself. He apologized verbally but his eyes told of his real sorrow.

"Rick will be fine." She assured him. "He's out of surgery and the doctor says he'll make a complete recovery."

Joe fidgeted until Windy finished talking. "What happened?" he demanded again.

The man swallowed. "We were chasing what appeared to be a drunk driver. Man, he was all over the road, 50 miles per hour in a residential. We followed him to the express way, had already called the state boys. Then he took an exit, headed onto a busy street, places open 24 hours, you know. Rick told me we had to put a stop to it. He radioed for permission to engage. We received it.

"I headed for his left rear fender, to push him over, ya know, but he cut it sharp to the right and instead I caught his right rear fender, spun his car around and it smashed right into Rick's door.

"The guy got out of his car and started walking around, I got him, threw him in our back seat. Back up was there in minutes. Rick tried to slide over and get out my side, he couldn't move, they actually backed up the guys car and pried Rick's door off to get him out.

"I'm so sorry." He looked at Windy and she smiled.

"You were doing your job, you had to keep him from hurting anyone and Rick is the one who told you to do it. You're not to blame, Officer…"

"Morgan, Clay Morgan, Miss Jordan." He took her hand and squeezed it lightly. "He'll be alright? He'll walk again?"

"Oh, yes, he'll walk, and the internal bleeding had stopped even before they got inside. He's all sown up and we're just waiting till he's able to see us."

Officer Morgan excused himself, Windy thought he wanted to get away from Joe and she couldn't blame him. Joe's anger was very apparent.

At that moment Nurse Laswell appeared. She smiled at Windy.

"Is the family of Rick Notts here?"

"We are," Windy said. "How's he doing?"

"Good. I just came on duty and that's the first thing I heard. One of you may come into his room, we just settled him in."

Joe and Connie both smiled at Windy. They didn't have to tell her twice, she quickly followed Bernie.

Joe looked at the pretty blonde, the last remnant of a night filled with grief and hope.

"How about breakfast?"

"Sure, I'd love to hear a little more about this amazing son of mine. I'm sure you have some stories to tell."

"Boy, do I." He placed his hand under her elbow and they left the room.

Chapter Fifty-Two

Windy sat beside the bed watching the man she loved. He breathed easy, though not deep, he lay slightly on his left side a pillow behind his back. His short hair sparkled and Windy thought there might still be tiny slivers of glass from his broken window in it. His face was a little discolored, if not for his summer tan he would look ashen. His poor lips were dry and cracked. She placed an ice chip on them then searched her purse, finding a tube of lip gloss. At least it had no color to it. Windy carefully spread the gloss on his lips, then placed another ice chip on them.

She thought about all that had happened in the last two weeks. She remembered thinking just a short time ago how perfect life was. It seemed it all came crashing down after that. Yet they had survived.

Rick and Doug had come to know Christ as their Savior, and Rick met his birth mother.

He'd proposed and she'd accepted, setting their date.

Eddie was under a doctor's care, staying with his cousin and even going to church with them, according to Pastor J. Mom and Dad had already been in contact with a Christian doctor who believed in natural ways of curing cancer. She herself was no longer a divorced woman but a new creature in Christ. Rick had met Connie's family and they had welcomed him in a cautious sort of way. He had survived a serious accident with no long lasting complications. They had been busy, God had been busy! This must have been one of those 'shadow of death' valleys.

Honestly, they weren't out yet. Dad still had to decide on what treatment to try. Rick had some time in a hospital bed and later on crutches. Oh how he would hate that.

Eddie's illness, though treatable, remained serious.

At least they knew God controlled the events in their lives and even the things they considered bad, could be worked to good in God's time and wisdom.

Rick moved his head and licked his lips.

"Water?" he whispered.

Windy held a glass near his face and touched the straw to his dry lips.

He drank gratefully but she only allowed him a little then pulled the straw away. He licked his lips again and moaned.

"More?" she could barely hear his voice.

She complied.

After swallowing, he turned his head and a drop fell on his neck. Windy used a Kleenex to blot it.

"Windy?"

"I'm right here."

"Mmmm, kiss me."

She obeyed, touching his lips gently.

He tried to lift first one arm then the other. The left still had a blood pressure cuff, set to read his BP every few minutes, the other sported his IV.

"I'm handcuffed." he murmured.

"Yes, you're my prisoner for the next couple days."

"Oh, no."

"What's wrong?"

"I want to get married at my house, not in jail."

She laughed. "Oh, sweetheart, when you wake up, you're gonna get teased good."

Pastor J showed up around 9 and insisted Windy go home for some sleep. When she refused he suggested a quick breakfast in the cafeteria. Windy thought of the few times she'd visited that room when married to Stephan, she didn't want to take any chances of running into him. '*Dummy,*' she thought. "*You're going to see him at some point, he's Rick's doctor, he'll have to discharge him and give follow up instructions.*

Yet, she just couldn't make herself go down there.

"I want to be here when he wakes up. I figure it'll be good practice for when we're married. I mean, now, in his state I'm probably gonna look pretty good, hopefully that'll make an impression for all those mornings when he wakes up normal."

Jason laughed. "If that was supposed to make sense, I have a lot of learning to do."

"What's so funny? You people are sitting around a seriously injured man, and you're laughing?" Don King's voice almost blew them off their seats.

Windy and Jason looked like kids caught being naughty. Jason recovered first.

"He's going to be fine, Don, and I'm well, I'm just trying to keep Windy in good spirits; she's had a hard night."

Don strode in and set a couple grocery bags on the table. "I brought him some spring water, he doesn't like this city stuff." He pulled out a bottle, emptied Rick's cup in the sink and refilled it. "And I brought you some breakfast cause I know you won't leave the room." He held out a granola bar and a jug of chocolate milk to Windy who promptly stood up and hugged the big man.

"Hey, that's my girl."

All three visitors turned toward the bed where Rick lay with a frown on his face.

"If I weren't cuffed, I'd arrest you." He moaned softly and closed his eyes.

"Yeah, he's gonna be all right, now eat." Don commanded.

Windy unwrapped the bar, noting it was her favorite kind. "Hey, how'd you know we were here?"

"Well now, who was supposed to open this morning?"

Windy gasped. "Oh Don, I'm so sorry."

"Don't worry, this little preacher boy woke me at 5 am to let me know what happened and that you wouldn't be in." He frowned at Pastor J, "That's the last time I put my home phone number on some church new visitors card."

Windy held her hand over her mouth to keep from spewing its contents over the laughing men.

"Does he act this tough at work?" Jason asked.

"He tries, but everyone knows better. He gets away with it with new employees for a little while. But they all figure him out eventually."

"Speaking of new employees; I hired some timid little girl to take your place next week."

"What?"

"Yeah, I can't have you working in the aisles thinking about your young man up here in this bed. And when he gets out, he's gonna be restricted in his movement, so you're probably gonna be waiting on him hand and foot."

"Don, I don't think I can afford to take any time off."

"You can if it's paid."

"No," she shook her head. "No."

"Yes. How long have you been working for me? You've rarely taken any sick days or personal days. Never had a vacation. Now's the time to collect on all that."

"But you said you had to hire someone."

"Yeah, a timid little girl who's been pestering me for years about coming to work at the store. When she found out about Rick, she told me she was taking your place and if I ever wanted another meal in her house, I would agree."

"No, my house." The patient interrupted. "We're getting married at my house. Wish you'd take these cuffs off, I wasn't the one driving."

Windy leaned over the bed and gave Rick a kiss. "No honey, you weren't driving. Do you remember what happened?"

"Yeah, chasing a car, it hit us." Rick tried to lift his hand then moved his head. "Get this…I can't…"

"What, honey?" Windy asked.

"My head itches." Windy reached over and gently scratched his head, fearing she might implant some glass slivers in his scalp.

"Mmmmm…" Rick smiled. "I tried to get out the other door. It was open and I wondered why I couldn't scoot over. Gets pretty sketchy after that."

"Well, you have a broken leg and lacerated kidney. You had surgery, everything is stitched and set. You're going to be fine, confined for a while, but fine."

"Did anyone else get hurt?"

"No. You stopped him in time and Officer Morgan was not hurt."

An unfamiliar face appeared in the doorway, he held a magazine in his hand.

"Rick?" the gentleman asked.

"Yes, come in," Windy invited. Now she placed the man, from Connie's picnic yesterday. She hesitated. He was one of the older gentlemen, and since it was doubtful that Connie's stepdad would come on his own, she figured it must be Mr. Cooper.

"Mr. Cooper?"

"Yes, you remember me?"

"Of course. Rick's awake, come on in."

The older man handed Windy the magazine. "I...uh... I don't know his interests." He apologized. "He said he had a house in the country and some acreage...so..."

Windy saw a tractor on the cover. "He'll enjoy this, he does have a small garden, it's mostly for the animals and birds, I think."

Mr. Cooper stared at the air cast suspended from a pulley. "Are you in a lot of pain, son?"

"No," Rick answered. "I guess I haven't been awake long enough to feel anything yet."

"I can come back."

"No. Please stay." Rick invited.

"You've driven a long way; we certainly want you to visit for a while." Windy added. "Mr. Cooper, this is Don King, he's my boss and very good friend and this is Jason Shane, our pastor."

The men shook hands.

"Well, it's time for me to get back to work, no telling what kind of trouble that timid little girl has gotten into. I brought plenty of food, so you be sure to eat."

"I will, Don, promise. Oh, and give this to that timid girl." She hugged him tightly. "Thanks again, for everything."

"And I have a church to run, I'm sure the calls are coming in now that the prayer chain's been started." Jason noticed Windy start to say something. "I'll check on Cora, and bring your parents up this afternoon."

"Thank you Jason, you're a treasure." She hugged him also.

Mr. Cooper had walked over to Rick's bed looking quite uncomfortable. "She always hug everybody like that?" He asked Rick, smiling.

"Oh yeah, don't think you'll get out that door without getting a hug yourself."

"Well, I was up here on business, thought I'd like to talk to Connie after our party yesterday." The man looked away, tears welling up in his eyes. "You two are Christians, like Connie?"

Rick nodded, his eyes closed.

"Yes," Windy answered. "I gave my life to the Lord a year ago, Rick and his dad accepted Christ at a men's conference just last month."

"But you both seem so...sure, I guess."

"Walking with the Lord brings wisdom and understanding, we're still babes in Christ, but we have complete faith in Him."

The man looked around the room, Windy could tell he had something to say.

"Mr. Copper..."

"Call me Paul, please."

"Paul, you're already here and we're glad you've come." She sat in the chair closest to Rick's head and indicated the one next to it. "Please, sit down and tell us what's on your mind."

Paul patted his grandson's shoulder before sitting.

"Yesterday, I had a hard time accepting what Connie told us. I mean, you think you know your children. I just didn't understand how she could have gone through all that, and not come to us for help and support." He nodded. "We would have been disappointed, but not ashamed. She's our little girl."

Windy grabbed a tissue and wiped her eyes.

"I think of all she's gone through since then. We wondered why she never married, we knew of a couple men friends, but she always said she wasn't the marrying kind.

"I noticed a difference in her a few years back, four I think she said. She found the Lord. She was so excited, couldn't wait to tell us about it. Tom just scoffed at her, and the rest of the family followed his lead. But

I saw my little girl again, the way she used to be. Happy. I wondered about her new beliefs but I never asked her. Then I found out about a men's Bible group at the office, so I started going out of curiosity.

"Those men knew what they were talking about. I didn't want to admit that I didn't. So I listened and learned from them but I still don't know…well, they call themselves Christians, I don't know what they mean.

"I've tried reading the Bible, all those laws and sacrifices, I just don't get those. But I found the Psalms. I like them. One in particular.

"Rick, yesterday, you stood up for your mother, for your faith. You made me see what a coward I've been and I'm sorry, but I'm glad that God led you to us, to make a difference in our lives. I called Connie's work this morning. They told me about your accident and that Connie wasn't coming in today. I called her house and she wasn't there so I figured she'd be here. I hoped she would be because I wanted to tell both of you what was on my mind. Has she been here this morning?"

"No," Windy shook her head. "I left her and Joe in the waiting room just after sunrise when they told me I could come in here."

"Okay," Paul Cooper nodded. "Okay, well."

He reached over and touched Rick's hand. "I'm very sorry about the accident. Glad things look good for you…" He continued to nod. "You're a fine man, I'm proud to have you in our family."

Windy could see the older gentleman had more to say, but felt unsure of himself.

"Paul, would you mind if we prayed before you go?"

"That would be nice."

Windy grasped his hand and took Rick's in her other one.

"Dear Heavenly Father, thank you for the miracles You performed last night. Thank you for healing Rick and we praise You now for his quick recovery. Thank You too, for Paul and for bringing this family together. I ask that You allow us all to grow closer to each other and to You. In Jesus' name. Amen."

They released hands and still Paul hesitated.

"Tell us." Windy said.

"Well there is a Psalm and I think I'm supposed to read it to you." He pulled a pocket Bible from the suit coat he carried and opened it at a bookmark.

"It's Psalm 121. 'I will lift up my eyes to the mountains, from whence shall my help come? My help comes from the Lord, who made heaven and earth. He will not allow your foot to slip, He who keeps you will not slumber, behold, He who keeps Israel will neither slumber now sleep.'" Paul looked up checking their reaction. Windy nodded and he continued.

"The Lord is your keeper. The Lord is your shade on your right hand. The sun will not smite you by day, nor the moon by night. The Lord will protect you from all evil; He will keep your soul. The Lord will guard your going out and your coming in from this time forth and forever more.' I don't know if that means anything to you."

"In light of all that has happened lately, that is the most appropriate verse you could have read." Windy grasped his hand. "You know we'll want to talk to you about the Lord again."

"Yes, I know. I would really like that."

"Dad?" Connie and Joe stood in the doorway.

"Connie. Hi, sweetie. I...I tried to call you." Paul answered nervously.

Chapter Fifty-Three

"Where have you two been?" Rick asked, delighted to see the two of them together.

"A night of worrying about you worked up our appetites." Joe explained. "And since you were in no shape to extend hospitality to Connie; that left me."

"It's a dirty job, but someone had to do it. The poor man took pity on me and fed me." Connie reached for her dad and gave him a sound hug.

"There's a lot of hugging going on, and I'd like to know why I'm not the recipient." Rick said.

Connie turned to him and kissed his forehead, "Quit complaining, you're the one who's going to be getting special treatment for a while."

"Well, I should."

"I don't know about that, you're the reason no one got any sleep last night and everyone's missing work today." Joe pretended to grouch.

"You can sleep anytime and we all know I simply supplied a good excuse for everyone to take a day off work."

"Are there really any sick people in this room?" A voice asked from the door. Two uniformed policemen stood there surveying the crowd.

Rick laughed. "Looks like the only way I'll get any more sleep is if they knock me out."

"Now that can be arranged." Joe promised.

Windy bent over her husband to be and kissed him. "I'm going home and get some of that sleep you mentioned. I also need to check on Cora and my folks. I think you'll have enough people coming and going today to wait on you properly."

"Guess that means I'm out of here too." Joe said. "Since I'm the one who brought the little lady here." He grasped Rick's shoulder. "Glad you're doing okay."

Connie gave Rick a second forehead kiss. "I think Dad and I need some time together." Rick nodded his agreement.

He watched as the foursome left the room, then turned his attention to his buddies.

"We brought contraband," Russ held up a bottle of cherry cola.

"Sounds good, guys, but it just might dissolve my stitches."

Windy collapsed on the bed. All loose ends were tied and she really needed some sleep. Dad's first appointment was set for Monday, since she didn't have to work next week she planned to go with them. Cora was busy downstairs making muffins for everyone who might happen into Rick's room. Pastor J took on the responsibility of fielding questions and her call to Rick assured her he felt great and had many visitors. Looking at the clock she realized that just twelve hours ago she had feared for Rick's life and now everything had fallen back into place, a little misshapen perhaps, but it could have been much worse.

She reached for her Bible and found the chapter Paul had read to them. Psalm 121. She read it over twice, stopping both times at the words 'the sun will not smite you'. She certainly felt as if they had been smitten, she would have Doug add that word to their dictionary, and God had seen them through time and again. Windy fell asleep with the words "thank You Lord" on her lips.

Windy awoke to a knocking on the door. She reluctantly pulled herself off the bed and made her way into the kitchen.

"Your supper is ready and don't tell me you're not eating, you must eat to keep up your strength."

Windy gave a Cora a hug. "I'm not just hungry, I'm starved!"

Cora's kitchen contained more people than Windy thought possible. Her parents and Robbie were there, Joe and Connie, and Pastor J.

She received hugs all around.

"Who's with Rick?" She asked.

"Rick is at Doug and Valeries." Jason answered.

"How can that be? How'd he get out?"

"They did a battery of tests today. Took another set of x-rays, his leg is doing great, as long as he keeps it up, he's fine."

"But his side, his kidney?" Windy asked.

"They took x-rays of his lungs to make sure there was no water in them, his kidney looks fine."

"Who released him?"

"Dr. Roeden, the ER doctor who admitted him."

"Did Dr. Michaels okay it?"

"I assume."

Windy shook her head; she just didn't think he should be out so soon.

Joe put his arm around her. "He's fine, Windy, the ambulance transported him, he has a bed in Valerie's front room, she and the girls are answering his every call. There's nothing they can do in the hospital that can't be done at home."

Windy could think of a lot of things, medication, IV, wound cleansing, bandaging.

"After you eat, we'll go over and you can see for yourself."

"Okay." she said. She would see alright and if she had to raise a fuss, so be it. "But I'm making one phone call." *'probably the hardest one I'll ever have to make, well, to date anyway.'* She picked up the phone and dialed the hospital.

"Is Dr. Michaels on duty today?"

"One moment please."

"Emergency room."

"Is Dr. Michaels on duty today?" she repeated.

"Dr. Michaels no longer works emergency room duty. Is there someone else you'd like to speak to?"

"Yes, Dr. Roeden, please."

"He's off duty."

"Thank you." Windy punched the off button and took a deep breath. She dialed Stephan's home phone.

"Michaels' residence."

"Diana?"

"Yes, this is Mrs. Michaels. Who's calling please?"

Windy swallowed.

"Mrs. Michaels, this is Windy Jordan. My fiancé was in an accident last night and Dr. Michaels performed surgery, is he there by any chance?"

"Yes, he is, just a moment." Windy heard Diana call to her husband.

"This is Dr, Michaels, how can I help you?"

"Dr. Michaels, this is Windy Jordan. You operated on Officer Rick Notts last night after he was involved in an automobile accident."

"Yes, that's right."

"I just heard that he has been released from the hospital and I wanted to know if you were aware of that."

"That information is confidential."

"Please, Rick is my fiancé and I am concerned that he's been released too soon."

"Your fiancé? Hmph. So you don't trust the opinion of his doctor?"

Windy felt her face burning; she wanted to remain civil, but found that growing hard to do. "As much as it pains me to say so, yours in the only opinion I do trust."

"As it should be. Yes, Mss. Jordan, I approved the release of Rick Notts from the Community General this afternoon at 5 pm. Good day." He hung up.

Windy ate a very good, very informal meal in Cora's living room. Everyone mentioned how wonderful that Rick was doing do well. Connie and Jason kept sliding in comments about God's grace and healing but Joe and her parents pretended not to hear.

When everyone had finished eating, Connie and Debbie headed for the kitchen sink, insisting Cora sit and relax.

Windy watched the two women and thought of the night she and Rick first washed dishes together, the night Scott Bradley proposed to Jenny.

Jenny!

Jenny would be furious if Windy didn't enlist their prayers for Rick's well being. She would call as soon as she arrived at Doug's house. They had a lot of catching up to do.

Joe appeared at her side, "Ready?"

"Ready."

Once in the car, Windy felt slightly uncomfortable. She didn't know how to have a conversation with Joe.

"I want to tell you," he began. "How proud I am of you. I was a little concerned when I first picked you up, thought I had a basket case on my hands, but you met the challenge head on and I saw how you comforted everyone else. You really are a strong little lady."

"I truly wish people wouldn't use that word to describe me. I am not strong. I never have been. It's only through God that I can accomplish anything at all."

"Yeah, I've heard a lot of similar talk the last several hours."

"It's true Joe. I don't know where you stand in your faith, but God really is there to take care of us."

"Faith helped me lose my wife and family."

"I'm sorry. But, Joe, God doesn't tear families apart."

"Well, He didn't keep mine together."

"He gives all of us free will to make our own choices. If your wife made a bad choice, that doesn't mean God told her to."

"Could He have stopped her?"

"I'm..." she hesitated knowing her words were very important. "He could have, yes. Just as my parents could have stopped me from marrying Eddie, but they knew I would only hold it against them. God loves us as much as my parents loved me, even more. They allowed me to have my way, not to hurt me, but to let me grow up."

Joe pulled into the Notts driveway, turned off the car and looked at Windy. "I want to believe. I just don't think there's anything to it."

"And I want you to believe, but in God's time. I will pray for your understanding, but I won't push my beliefs on you."

"Thanks."

They exited the car and walked to the house together.

Sure enough, in the middle of Valeria's beautifully decorated living room sat an imposing hospital bed, with a laughing Rick in it.

Windy handed the phone to Rick who personally assured Jenny of his well being. "I just don't understand why all these people asked God to heal me, then don't want to believe He did." He said. "I know I'm new at this stuff, but it seems pretty straight forward to me."

He nodded to Jenny's remark. "Yeah, that'd be great. Hey, big guy. How's Florida?"

Windy listened to his conversation with Scott Bradley and marveled at all that God had actually done in her life. If anyone had told her a year ago that Brad would be married to her best friend and having a conversation with her fiancé she would have said they were crazy. *God does have a sense of humor!* She thought.

As soon as she hung up the phone, it rang. Wil and Missy were calling to give Rick their love and prayers. Valerie told Windy the phone hadn't been on its cradle all day and they had run two phones out of juice and were now using the den phone. It pleased Windy to know of the love and prayers headed Rick's way. It pleased her for Joe to see this also.

At ten o'clock Valerie shooed Tami and Tari upstairs, leaving Windy and Joe alone with Rick.

"I hope you don't mind us going to bed, Windy. It's been a long day." Valerie said.

"Of course not, I'm sorry we're here so late."

"No, no problem, just lock the door when you leave."

"I'm going out to get some fresh air," Joe excused himself.

Windy sat beside Rick on his bed, careful not to touch him. She didn't want to knock anything loose and send him back to the hospital. But he pulled her close and kissed her longingly.

"If I had known I would garner all this attention, I wouldn't have told Morgan to get that guy."

"Well, honey, God uses all things to good. Look at the wonderful example we now have for my folks and Robbie and Joe. They're seeing God's goodness first hand and all we had to do was break you."

"The sacrificial lamb, huh?"

He kissed her again and she settled down beside him.

"Tomorrow's Saturday. We could still get married."

"Oh no, I have it made right now. You're here with 3 women to wait on you; I'd be crazy to take that on myself. Besides I want you totally pain and medication free when you say 'I do'. I'm not taking any chances of you crying incoherency later on."

He pulled her a little closer and she was almost glad for his cast. She wanted to be close to him, very close.

"I need you to do something for me." He whispered in her ear.

"Hmmmm?" she bit at his lip, rubbing her tongue against it.

"You can stop that anytime."

She pulled back. "Okay, I'll be good." She looked into his eyes and saw her longing matched there. "For now."

"I have a special bank account for the house, for decorating. Mom's name is on it. I want the two of you to refinish the bedroom while I'm here. Take your mom, take Connie, whoever you want."

"But Rick it's not my house it's yours.

"You silly woman! Why do you think I bought that house?"

"For the fishing."

"I bought it intending to share it with you."

"How could you? I was...I wasn't even single when you bought it."

"Well I had high hopes. And look what happened. You're here aren't you?"

She kissed him again, thanking God that she was indeed here.

"Well, I have always wanted a pink bedroom with a canopy bed."

"Lilac." Came an intruding voice. "That's the name of that color. Lilac."

"Joe, what in the world are you doing?"

"Came in to get your silly woman and take her home so you can get some rest."

Windy gave Rick a quick kiss and a big smile. "We're not bringing him on the honeymoon!"

Chapter Fifty-Four

Sunday morning Doug wheeled his son down the center aisle of the church, parking the chair next to the front row.

"Dad, I wanted to be out of the way."

"You are; no one ever sits up here."

Rick placed his hands on the large wheels and tried to maneuver back down the opening, but too many people stood before him. Everyone wanted to wish him well, to let him know they had prayed for him. Rick nodded and smiled and said thank you a couple dozen times and Sunday School hadn't even let out yet.

He felt a hand on his back, thinking it might be Windy as he hadn't seen her yet. He turned and looked at Joe's smiling face. Rick grinned.

"Don't get too excited. Connie shamed me into it." Rick laughed remembering how his sisters shamed him into coming to Sunday School.

"It's a start, Joe, a great start." He watched Joe sit next to Connie. Seeing them together seemed so natural, he could only hope Joe felt that way too. He wondered why Windy hadn't come up from class yet, when he saw her enter the sanctuary with her parents and Robbie. She found an open pew near the back and left them there to come up to him.

"I'm going to sit with my family, okay?"

"You just don't want to share center stage with me." He accused.

"Well, there is that." She planted a quick kiss on his cheek in answer to his wink.

The service finally got underway, Wil leading the worship and Margie the singing. Soon Jason took his place at the pulpit.

"Friends, two weeks ago, Rick Notts stood before this congregation and told us of his decision to accept Christ as his Savior."

The congregation clapped and Rick watched Joe's reaction. Not only had he just learned about Rick's decision, but he looked uncomfortable with the display of enthusiasm.

"Three days ago this same young man was involved in a car accident that could have claimed his life. Instead his family and friends claimed God's healing." Again the congregation burst into applause. "And here he is, after spending only 15 hours in the hospital and having major surgery. Is our God awesome or what?!"

People stood, still clapping, with shouts of 'Alleluia' and 'Praise the Lord' mixed in.

When everyone returned to their seats and quieted, Pastor J continued. "It could have been very different. We could have been gathered together to commemorate a young man's life.

"We would all have something very fine to say about him, about his friendship, his loyalty, his love, his example.

"Far too often we wait until it's too late to express our appreciation and love for one another. We say those words, over a casket or at a graveside. Why? Why don't we spend more time appreciating each other while we can?"

Rick heard the sniffing, one person blew his nose, and many more whispered an agreeing 'amen'. He began to think of how he would have felt if some one he cared about was suddenly taken from him. His immediate family all knew the Lord now, but what about Joe? What about the other guys who put their lives on the line every night, but have no Savior to welcome them into His arms. *'God, show me, use me. Allow this accident to not be an accident, but an opportunity to share Your grace.'*

"Is there a loved one that you're at odds with? Is there a friend you've been meaning to speak to? Tell them you care, tell them God cares. Show them. Show them just how amazing your Lord is, by allowing Him to use you."

Pastor wrapped up his short sermon and Margie led them in a closing hymn.

"Next week we'll have a pot luck dinner here at the church. We want to have a time of fellowship and getting better acquainted with our church family, so this will begin a monthly tradition. Please plan to stay next week and bring a dish of your favorite food."

Margie stood as the piano began to play the doxology and Pastor J moved to the rear of the sanctuary.

On the last 'Amen' Rick saw Windy moving toward him, and his heart skipped a beat. Everything hit him at once, the excitement, the turmoil, the fear, the pain, the relief. He just wanted to take Windy in his arms and spend a quiet day holding her.

She sat in the pew next to him and reached for his hand. He knew she understood as he wiped a tear from his own cheek.

Valerie joined them.

"Windy, I wonder if you would mind Ricksitting this afternoon. Doug and I thought we'd take your folks out to dinner and the girls are going to a friends' house."

"I'd love to. Thanks so much, Valerie. It'll be good for my parents to know how much you care."

Valerie kissed Rick on the cheek. "Dad's bringing the car around, he'll be in as soon as the way clears a little."

Many people came up to Rick expressing their thankfulness, for him and for the Lord.

Don and his family waited patiently for a chance to express themselves. Wil and Missy waited until everyone else had their say.

"Son, while you're laid up, don't be worryin about anything. And if you need something, I'm just a holler away."

"Thanks, Wil. I'm still on the payroll; it just comes from a different account while I'm not working. So I'm fine there. Windy's brother, Rob Jordan, is staying at my place and will take care of it and the animals. But I may just be hollering, so keep your window open."

Missy hugged Rick, then pulled Windy into an embrace. They exchanged tears and smiles.

Once settled into the back of the car, his right leg extended across the seat, Rick finally let out a sigh.

"Tired, son?" Doug asked.

"Exhausted."

Rick slept most of the afternoon and Windy was content to sit and watch him.

Monday morning Windy accompanied her parents to her dad's first doctor's visit. She listened to all he had to say, understanding in the moment, but knowing she could never recount what she had been told.

Her mom asked lots of questions obviously having done much research on the subject. They finally decided on the next step and even though Windy still felt unsure, at least they were going forward.

After seeing her parents settled in at the parsonage Windy called Valerie and they planned the rest of the day; first to Rick's house to measure and determine how to redecorate the bedroom, then off to the furniture store.

"We both like blue," Windy told Valerie, "but that's the color in the living room now. I don't think we want the whole house blue. When the time comes to paint the large bedroom I want to use a light green."

"Well, there are so many variations of blue, you could do the whole house and not have two rooms the same."

Together they picked out the carpet. She and Rick had decided to keep the old dressers. Windy had a hard time deciding on a bed. She couldn't get Rick to tell her anything about what he preferred. He just kept saying, 'anything you want as long as you're in it'.

"My girls have feather beds." Valerie offered. "Doug and I don't because he likes a firmer bed. We've thought about getting a new one, with dual controls for firmness. Maybe one day we will. Rick's bed at our home has a nice mattress, but after his time in the service and having slept on that worn out mattress that came with his house, I believe the boy could fall asleep on just about anything."

They finally settled on a mattress with a nice thick 'pillow top'.

Windy picked out the bed frame to match one of the dressers already in the house. Don had told her which types of wood the dressers were made from and she decided on the oak. Don, Doug and Robbie all volunteered to take the bedroom furniture outside, sand it down and refinish it. Windy couldn't wait to see the end product.

Next she and Valerie went to Buy-mart and picked out the linens for the bed along with matching curtains. They decided to paper up the wall halfway and looked for a design both Windy and Rick would like.

When the ladies returned to the house, Doug and Robbie already had the furniture in the front yard, sanders running at top speed.

"I do believe they're enjoying themselves." Valerie observed. "Your brother is a very nice young man. He certainly fit right in, didn't he?"

"Yes. He says if Dad is better in 3 months he'll return to duty. I want dad better, but I wish Robbie wouldn't leave. I just hope he finds the Lord before he goes."

Tuesday while the men sanded, the women papered. Windy had never done anything like this, but Valerie was an old hand, having papered most of her home.

The next day the carpet arrived, Doug and Robbie assured Windy they could lay the carpet themselves, freeing up more money for other furnishings. On Thursday the two men, joined by Andrew and Pastor J, laid that carpet as if they did so everyday of the week.

The bed came on Friday. The dressers stayed in the garage where they were sanded again, varnished, sanded and varnished a third time.

Windy spent her usual Thursday at the Caring Pregnancy office. Summers were slower than the rest of the year. She had only one client, but that one client took all her energy. She spent time in the office, praying over the ministry, it's workers and the women who would come in for help.

Rick's recovery sped along, but she didn't know what lie in store for her parents. She anticipated keeping her job with Don and wanted to still volunteer at the office but should she really spread herself so thin at this time?

Windy marveled at how quickly Rick healed. Two weeks after the accident she accompanied him to his doctor's appointment, thankfully with his own doctor and not the one who performed the surgery. Dr. Winton pronounced Rick 'a fine specimen of health'.

"All x-rays show great improvement. I'm going to put you in a fabric, walking cast. Wear it constantly except to bed." He informed them. "Ultrasound shows that kidney working perfectly. I'd like to attribute it to modern medicine, but I have to admit something else was at work here, too."

"Yes, He was, doctor. My family and friends petitioned the Lord on my behalf; and He answered."

Windy smiled at Rick's new found confidence. She thought of the young man who stood in front of her, slapping a package of razor blades on his palm. They had come so far, down a difficult and sometimes muddy road. She looked forward to where that road would lead them.

"I want you off work for 6 weeks," Rick started to protest and the doctor held firm. "6 weeks, not a day sooner. In the mean time find something to do with your hands, and stay off the leg as much as possible."

Her dad's health was another matter, as Rick improved, her dad seem to lose his vitality. He tired so easily. Every week he went for a new treatment that worked by strengthening the healthy blood cells. She respected her dad's decision not to have chemotherapy or radiation, she just hoped and prayed this new medicine, or whatever is was, worked.

The doctors had offered surgery but his cancer was spread to several lymph nodes and they admitted they couldn't get all of them. So her dad said no.

Valerie diligently worked with her mom on organic foods. All the worry, the doctor's appointments, the treatments and Dad's condition tired her mom, but she said she felt physically better than she had in a long time.

After her week off Windy wanted to return to work. August 24th seemed so far away and she wanted the time to go quickly.

Days rushed by, Valerie had her hands full trying to keep Rick busy and out of trouble. The girls spent hours playing games with him till he had tired of every one they introduced.

An early August evening Connie showed up.

"You look great!" she commented, kissing his forehead. She sat next to him on the couch. The hospital bed had long since been removed and Rick slept in the den on the hid-a-bed.

"My mom and I have discussed the possibility of telling Jimmie's parents about you. We both feel it's unfair, to leave them out. It could bring them more grief or peace. We don't know. But I've also spent a lot of time in prayer over it. If you want to, I would like you to meet them. Mom has spent some extra time with Julie and she thinks now would be a good time."

Rick nodded. He'd given the matter much prayer himself and did want to meet Jimmie's parents, but he didn't want to push the issue.

"I'm ready to set a date to go visit Mrs. West. I'll play it by ear as for what to say. I assume anytime is good for you, since you're still playing hooky?"

"I'd prefer a Sunday; that way I know Windy can be with me."

"You've got it." She kissed his forehead then stood to go.

"Connie, what's with the forehead?"

She smiled. "When I was a little girl my dad always kissed me on the lips. When I turned 13 he said I was growing up and he'd only kiss my forehead from then on." She wiped a tear from her cheek. "I missed your childhood, Rick, so I have to go straight to the forehead."

He stood and embraced this very special woman. He placed his hands on the sides of her head and gently brushed her tears away with his thumbs before kissing her cheek.

Chapter Fifty-Five

Sunday after church, Connie, Rick and Windy piled into Connie little sports car and headed west. Jimmie's parents still lived in the same town, same house as they had years ago, next to the Coopers. Connie felt it better to visit the West's home rather than bring them to Rick. They would be in their own element and be more comfortable throughout this unusual meeting.

As when Rick and Windy visited Tom's home, the pair stayed outside and waited for Connie to motion them in.

"Are you nervous?" Windy asked, looking over at the man who would soon be her husband. When he turned and met her eyes, she bit her lip. Rick's gray eyes caressed her, letting her know, without words, how much he loved her.

He shook his head slightly.

"For them maybe. They're what? In their sixties. That's not necessarily old, but this is going to be a shock to them. I just pray they handle it well."

"Me, too." Windy took his hand and bowed her head. Together they asked the Lord to be with Connie and the West's as she broke the news.

"Connie, it's so nice to see you dear." Julie West took Connie's hand in both of hers. "How have you been? Come, sit down." She led Connie into a homey living room. Connie noticed some minor changes, but for the most part it looked as it had 25 years ago, bringing back a flood of memories.

"You're both looking very well." she commented.

"We're managing to stay healthy. We walk everyday."

"Yes," James West joined the conversation. "To the Dairy Queen."

"It's a mile one way; I figure we deserve a treat." Julie smiled.

"Do you both still work?"

"Oh, yes, neither of us are ready to retire, I can't imagine sitting around the house all day."

"I would drive her nuts." James said.

"Oh, you would golf every day and leave me sitting at home." She looked at Connie. "He tried to teach me once but he's too impatient, and I'm too indifferent. Who cares how many times you have to hit that little ball, as long as you get it to the hole in the end."

Connie laughed. This wonderful couple reminded her so much of Jimmie; their enthusiasm for life, their sense of humor.

"What have you been up to these years? We never see you visit your folks. Your mom tells me you've never married."

"Don't you like men?" James asked.

Connie took the bait.

"I used to. I had one special fella in my life."

Julie nodded. "It must have broke your heart when he got married."

"You knew?"

"Of course I knew. Your love was evident from the first time you saw him." Julie looked back into her memories. "That last summer he was home; you spent a lot of time together. I rather hoped..."

"Who are you talking about, old woman?" James asked.

"Your son, who else."

"No, you're mistaken. She didn't like Jimmie and those boys always got mad when she hung around. Had a name for you...what was that?"

"Dandruff." Connie volunteered.

"That's right, always trying to brush you off, Jimmie said." James too, looked back into his life, "He was a good man, a brave man, a son anyone would be proud of."

"Yes, he was." Connie agreed. "Mrs. West, you mentioned that last summer."

"Yes, dear."

"We did spend a lot of time together. I was still young and a bit spoiled, wanting my way you know."

"Every teenage girl looks at life as if it has something to give."

Connie nodded. Regret swelled in her heart, if she hadn't chosen adoption, if she had come home with her baby, her parents and Jimmie's would have had the privilege of knowing her son.

"Well, I have some news for you, I'm afraid it's going to come as a surprise, so I hope you're up to it."

The older couple gave her their attention, Julie nodded.

"I think we are." She said. "I always wondered, Connie, wondered about you and Jimmie, wondered why you never visited that first year in college. You were home that next summer when we received the news and you left immediately, didn't even stay for the funeral. You loved him, didn't you?"

"Very, very, much, Mrs. West."

"Why didn't you tell him?"

"I wanted him to say it first. I was so foolish. But it's probably a good thing, because he was already engaged."

"He came to me." James entered the conversation. Both women turned toward him. "The night before he left. Said he was having doubts about getting married. He said he cared for her, loved her, in a way.

"I told him he was just nervous, understandably so. Going off to Viet Nam and all. I asked if the arrangements were made, he said they were. The wedding would take place shortly after his return to base. Said he'd wanted to bring her home for us to meet, but she was in the service too, and couldn't get leave." James hung his head. "I told him, he'd made a commitment and should live up to it. He never said he had fallen in love with you. I didn't know Connie." He shook his head sadly. "I just didn't know."

"Oh, Mr. West," she took his hand. "We can't relive those moments, we have to accept our decisions as they were and go on from there."

"I kept you two apart."

"No, I can't believe that." Connie wondered if there had ever been a chance for them. What if Mr. West had advised Jimmy to wait? Would Jimmie have contacted her? Would they…she shook those thoughts out of her head. "There is a much stronger force working in our lives. One of the new things I have experienced is a relationship with the Lord. He's taught me not to look back, but to look forward." She took a deep breath, "That's why I'm here today, to give you a little of your past back, but with a promise of a brighter tomorrow."

Julie began to weep. He husband pulled her close.

Connie had to continue now, or she might not have the courage to go on.

"I became pregnant that summer, but after I found out about Jimmie's marriage, I released the baby for adoption."

"You what?!" James bolted upright. "Jimmie's child?"

Connie nodded, the tears flowing freely. She wanted to be strong for these wonderful people, not fall apart in front of them.

"Yes, Jimmie's son. When he...when Jimmie died, I contacted the agency, tried to find out where the baby was, if I could get him back; but I'd already signed the papers. Everything was final."

Julie wept openly, not even trying to control her sobs.

"Why are you telling us this?" James accused. "Why now? Why?"

Julie looked at her husband. "Because she's found him." she whispered.

James' mouth dropped open, tears sprung from his eyes. "You've found him? You've found our grandson?"

Rick looked at the couple sitting on the couch, holding hands. Somehow he connected with them the moment they met. He saw himself in the gentleman. The shape of his face, his brow and especially his nose. Funny, he even had the same little mustache. He watched the couple as Connie explained how she and Rick had been brought together, slowly, in God's time.

"The day after I accepted Christ as my Savior, I began praying for my son. And his girl, or wife, whoever God had intended for him. When I met Valerie and heard she had an adopted son the same age my son would be, I secretly hoped, knowing the odds were totally against me. I avoided asking anything about him, not wanting to be disappointed, at the same time, wanting so much to find him. Then one day Valerie showed me a picture of her son; and I knew.

"I believe God was preparing me to meet this young man, and to bring him into our lives. Actually, Valerie is the one who made the first step. She had already guessed, having looked into those gray eyes for 25 years. She and Doug are wonderful people. They are the ones I would have chosen to care for and love my child."

Julie and James West never took their eyes off Rick. He found himself staring as well. He thought about the man who connected them. The man he looked like. The man who gave his life for his country. What would life have been like if Connie hadn't released him for adoption? No doubt Rick would have been welcomed into this home, probably put to sleep in his father's bed. He would have run through that front door a hundred times, yelling, 'Grandma, Grandpa'.

But that's not how life happened for him. He just couldn't imagine any other life than the one he had. Doug and Valerie Notts were his parents. That would never change. They had loved him, cared for him, instilled their good values into his life.

But now he had a birth mother, three more sets of grandparents and cousins he had not grown up around. What did God want from him? Why had He orchestrated this reunion? Where did they go from here?

Chapter Fifty-Six

Her head hurt. It had been bothering her more lately; she knew it was stress. The stress of Rob's illness, of not having insurance, of not having an income, of knowing their son was spending his savings on his dad's treatments, of not knowing how they would manage the rent once Windy moved out of her apartment, of seeing her daughter married again and not being able to help, of choosing between her men; if her husband gets better, her son leaves, if her husband gets worse, her son stays. She wanted them both, nearby and healthy.

She rubbed her neck and massaged her temples.

"Are you okay, Mom?"

Debbie nodded. "Just a little headache.

She looked over the dresses again. Pink, of course. Windy loved pink. Her daughter had asked Cora to stand up for her and the little old lady's reaction was priceless. Debbie wished they had a video camera to record her surprise. Tami and Tari Notts would also stand up for Windy, while Rick had asked Joe to be his best man, Robbie and a young man from church, Andrew, would also stand up for Rick.

This little back yard wedding had turned into a huge family reunion. Now Debbie understood that Connie's family would attend as well as Rick's birth father's parents.

Rob would walk Windy down the aisle, or in this case the path, but Debbie worried about that. After 5 weekly treatments she couldn't see an improvement. The doctor said the good cells were waging war with the toxins and though the good guys were winning, the toxins were putting up one heck of a fight. Everyday she prayed they had made the right decision. Prayed. How do people pray when they don't really believe in God? She prayed to herself, she guessed.

And now the dress issue. Windy insisted on looking for dresses at a local dress shop, she refused to go near the bridal shop because the prices would be higher. Windy found the dress she liked; a simple, straight satin dress, full length with narrow shoulder straps. They were now waiting for Valerie to bring the two girls in to try theirs on. Debbie shook her hand and rolled her eyes. Her daughter could be so stubborn.

"I'm wearing a soft pink dress, just like the girls." Windy restated.

"But why? And don't give me that, because white is for purity…every bride wears white now, and no one is a virgin anymore."

"Mom!"

"Oh, get real, Windy. You're not 18, for crying out loud, haven't you done any growing up in the past 5 years?"

"Mom?"

Debbie placed her hands over her face. She was so tired. So tired. "I'm sorry, baby. It's a simple dress, why are you making such a fuss?" *Why are you?* She asked herself.

"Why don't we go home, now? We don't have to be here while the girls try on their dresses, the saleslady can take care of everything. I'm sure Dad's tired of waiting for us. Stopping here after Dad's appointment wasn't a good idea."

"Maybe not." Debbie sighed. "I just want everything nice for you. You deserve it, honey, after all you've been through."

"Thank you, I appreciate that. But really, I'd be happy marrying Rick in jean shorts and tank tops."

Debbie frowned.

"Well, maybe that's going a little too far." Windy hugged her. "My life has finally come around; you're the one going through the difficult time right now."

"I wish we could do more, honey."

"Mom, stop. Dad is the priority here, not me.

"But Rick's family shouldn't have to pay for your wedding.

"Their aren't. Valerie is buying the girls dresses. Cora is buying her own. I'm buying mine. The men all bought their own clothes. Rick's buying the flowers. Connie's paying for the food, she and Valerie helped Cora cook. Mom there's really nothing for you to pay for. Besides you and Dad already paid for one wedding."

Debbie nodded, to satisfy her daughter. This is not what she planned, this was not where she wanted to be. She wanted her husband healthy, her daughter happy and her son here. And she didn't want to be 50. 50! Life sucked.

At that moment Valerie's two teenage daughters burst on the scene. They almost caught up to their chatter by the time they reached the dressing rooms.

"I'll tell Val we're leaving." Windy whispered.

"No, they're here; we can stay a few more minutes." Maybe Valerie could say something to make Windy change her mind about the dress. But did she really want this woman to have more influence over her own daughter?

All three girls went into the dressing room, their excitement heard throughout the quiet store. When they immerged, Debbie had to admit they all looked lovely; especially Windy, even in her pink dress.

Valerie stepped up and checked over each of her girls' dresses, inspecting the fit. She nodded her approval until she came to Windy. She looked for several minutes.

"Spit it out, Valerie, what's wrong?" Windy asked.

Valerie looked at Windy, her daughters and then at Debbie.

"Why," she hesitated. "Why are you wearing pink?"

Debbie wanted to jump up and hug the other woman.

Windy closed her eyes. "You know why." She said.

"Seems you're the one who talked about coming to our son, not as a divorced woman but a new creature in Christ. Don't tell me you're doubting Christ's ability to cleanse and purify."

Debbie wasn't sure she heard right. Was Rick's mother telling Windy to wear white, not because no one else was a virgin, but because she was?

Her head hurt.

Windy made a decision and although she didn't feel good about it, she did feel relief.

On Thursday she went into the Pregnancy office as usual. There were no appointments so she took the time to catch up on some paper work. In the afternoon she made a phone call.

"Jean this is Windy. I'm at the Office."

"Hi Windy, how are you?"

"I'm fine. Life is rather hectic right now, but I'm doing well."

"How are things at the office?"

"This time of year, it's pretty quiet; unlike my life at the moment."

"Oh? Is everything okay?"

"Yes, actually it is. There's just been a lot happening lately and my life has gotten quite busy. I'll be getting married in two weeks, my fiancé is recovering quite well, from an accident, my dad is going through cancer treatment, to name the main ones."

"Oh, my goodness." Windy could hear Jean's hesitation. "Does this mean you're not going to continue working at the office?"

"That's why I'm calling. I still want to volunteer and I know you were hoping I might take over the directorship, but I just can't make that commitment. I thought you might want to let the board know."

"Yes, I will. They need to start actively looking for a director. There's a meeting next week, I'll let them know?"

"My heart is still here, Jean, whether my time is or not. But I think I should take the rest of the month off, August isn't very busy, Barb and Susan can handle things just fine."

After hanging up, Windy sighed with relief. Maybe later, in the next year or so, after Dad began to mend, she would consider a more active part, if the board still needed her.

Rick had one more week of being off work and she hoped it would go by quickly. He was doing way too much and she worried about his complete recovery. He'd seen the doctor last week and everything looked great, Rick had begged to be released but the doctor stood firm. Windy thought Rick would probably be less active if he were working. At least he would be sitting in a car for 8 hours, instead of doing yard word, cleaning the barn, painting outside house trim. He wanted the place to look good for the wedding and although the guys tried to anticipate Rick's moves, they couldn't keep him from working.

The door opened and Windy looked at the clock. Rick had arrived for their visit to the flower shop.

"I hope you don't mind that I tagged along." Connie said.

"Not at all." Windy greeted them. "I have just a couple things to finish up.

Rick pulled Windy into a hug and kissed her. "I missed you."

She smiled, enjoying the pleasure of having some one to love.

"Show Connie the house if you like. At least it's not freezing today."

She busied herself putting things away and preparing for the next volunteer. When Rick and Connie returned to the office Windy could see a change in Connie's demeanor.

"Oh, Connie, I'm sorry. I should have warned you." Windy grabbed her purse and headed for the door almost pulling Rick. Once outside Connie waited for Windy to slide into the truck next to Rick.

"Connie has done some flower arranging and she'd love to help us." Rick explained.

"Well, I'm sure she can add a lot of work to our moral support." Windy looked at the pale lady sitting next to her and decided that at some later date they would talk about what Connie had seen at the office. "I can't even grow flowers, much less arrange them."

"I understand the girls' dresses are pink. So you'll probably want mostly pink flowers."

"Sweetheart roses." Rick stated.

Windy looked at him surprised. He'd mentioned going to the flower shop with her, but she didn't know he had a preference for which flowers.

"Because my bride is a sweetheart and prettier than a rose."

"Oh my!" Connie laughed, delighted. "I love it. Men don't usually care about the flowers, so I'm surprised by your input Rick."

"I would like to see everyone with one pick sweetheart rose, everyone except Windy, of course. Does that sound dumb?"

"Not to me, but what do you think Windy?"

Windy's eyes were still on her man, her love for him obvious. "It sounds wonderful. We do want to keep things simple."

"I was going to ask if you were sure you wanted fresh flowers and not silk, because you can keep silk ones forever. But, roses will freeze just fine and if you have a small amount they won't take up any room to speak of."

"Fresh." Rick decided. "Can you make those little things the guys wear?"

"Boutonnieres. Yes, those and the ladies corsages will be easy. One long stem pink rose with pink and white ribbons for the girls?"

Rick nodded.

"And for Windy…

"I'll talk to you later on that one." Rick winked at his girl. "I have something special in mind."

With that the three headed into the flower shop.

Chapter Fifty-Seven

Rick pulled into the station parking lot and locked his truck, something he hadn't done in five weeks. He wanted to get back into the activity. He missed the work and the guys. Besides, his sisters were driving him nuts. He needed the call from the Chief that morning though he wasn't sure what his commander wanted to discuss. Cold air blasted him when he entered the station, for a moment it shocked him, then it felt good.

Sergeant Montgomery nodded toward the chiefs closed door, a somber look upon his face.

Rick knew his injuries had mended, the doctor said one more week to be sure. He intended to return to work, neither chief nor doctor would stop him; but a gnawing sensation hit his stomach. He tapped lightly on the door but heard no response.

"Better go on in." Monty said, his tone reinforcing Rick's gut feeling. The Sergeant stood right behind Rick and when Rick still hesitated, Monty reached around the young man and turned the knob.

An explosion of noise hit Rick as everyone associated with the station yelled "Congratulations."

Blue uniforms and people in street clothes filled the small room. He had no idea what to say.

"This is your return to work, slash, bachelor party." the chief announced.

Someone placed a can of cherry cola in his hand, while another officer pushed him toward the chief's desk on which sat a large brown box.

"We don't go in much for fancy wrapping."

"But we can't let this opportunity get away."

One by one the men pulled a gift out of the box, never letting Rick see its entire contents. Rick just rolled his eyes at some of the gag gifts, thinking that even before he'd given his life to the Lord, he wouldn't find these things funny.

"This is to set the mood," announced one friend handing Rick a cassette of romantic music.

"Here's a gift card to Buy-mart, should be enough for a weeks worth of food." Rick looked at the amount; maybe, just maybe he and Windy could eat that much food in a week.

"Guess you might need a little gas in that truck of yours."

Rick looked at the gas card and shook his head. "This ought to get us to work and back for a month."

"Here's a map in case you get engrossed in your pretty new wife and forget where the station is." The Michigan county atlas was opened, not to Kent county, but to Osceola, some 50 miles north. Rick noticed red lines heading north then working their way east and north again.

"What is this?" he asked.

"And I think you'll need these." Joe held up a set of keys. They looked like house keys.

"What are you people up to?" Rick shook his head.

"They're the keys to your honeymoon suite, my cabin located in the middle of nowhere."

It finally registered. Food, gas, music, keys.

"We're not taking a honeymoon." He reminded the men.

"I talked to your doctor last week," the chief interjected. "I told him if he let you come back a week early, we'd keep you inside; away from speeding cars and bad guys. He agreed. You come back tomorrow, Officer Notts and you are taking a honeymoon."

"But Windy's job..."

"We made a visit to her boss," Monty stood up and puffed his chest out, the man still stood an inch shorter than Rick. "Seems the man has a healthy respect for officers of the law, and their guns." Laughs sounded around the room. Even Rick laughed at that one. Don King was not a man to be intimidated. He was probably one of the instigators.

Rick's small dining room bustled with activity. Valerie and Connie finished getting Tami and Tari ready, then moved on to Cora. She looked lovely in the soft pink dress, her white fair framing a sweet face.

Valerie dabbed at a tear running down the little ladies cheek. "Are you going to make it through this?" Valerie asked.

Cora nodded and sniffed. "I'll make it through, for Windy's sake."

Windy held still as Connie wove the tiny pick rosebuds into her hair after Mom finished arranging it in a lovely swept up style. Connie pulled the last touch out of a plastic bag and handed the bouquet to Windy.

"You're so beautiful," her mom said, kissing her cheek. "I'm so glad you changed your mind on the dress."

"So am I." Windy pulled her mom close and held her. "I'm sorry I gave you such a hard time about it." She whispered.

The three ladies moved from the dining room to the kitchen where Dad stood waiting. He kissed Mom before she, Connie and Valerie exited the back door.

Windy listened to the muffled music from the upstairs bathroom window where Rick had placed his tape player. He said he had put together a special arrangement just for their special day.

She looked out the rear kitchen window at the people gathered on her lawn, yes HER lawn, or at least it would be very soon. Chairs from the church had been set up in the back yard, facing the creek, parted for an aisle down the middle.

The first heads she saw on 'her' side were dark with tight black hair. Don, Colleen and their 4 children took up the whole back row. Just a few months ago, Don had been asking her about divorce. Now he sat holding the hand of his 'timid little girl'. Although Don kept busy with his small supermarket, where he had recently added a whole aisle of organic food, he and Colleen had started going to antique shops together and had even started restoring an old dining room table and chairs.

Wil, Missy and their children sat in the next row. Windy thought of the mittens she had knit for those children almost 3 years ago.

Mary sat in front of the Packards, little Hannah perched on her lap. Windy felt a tingle run down her spine as she thought of Mary's wedding and how Andrew couldn't take his eyes of his bride. Today, Windy would be the recipient of that look from her very own husband.

Mom sat in the front row waiting for dad to join her. Having them here meant so much and Windy prayed that God would bless her little family the way He had blessed her.

On Rick's side, Jimmie's parents sat in the back row. They wanted to be a part of this celebration, but they didn't want to interfere, Julie had told them.

Tom, Carol Anne and their 3 children sat in the next row.

Connie joined her parents in front of them. This whole unexpected family still worked on fitting in. Or maybe Rick was trying to fit in with them. Either way, it would take time.

Doug and Valerie sat in the front row. She could see the look of pride on Doug's face, matched only by the look of adoration on Valerie's. Windy smiled as she recognized Aunt Shirl's brown-gray hair. Doug had made a 'quick' trip yesterday to bring the precious lady here. They planned to keep her for a couple days.

"There's a lot of people here," Cora commented, joining Windy at the window. "Not like...before...when I was the only one."

"Yes," Windy agreed. "God has certainly blessed me with a lot of new friends."

"And family." Cora added.

"I think they're about ready." Windy turned at the sound of her dad's voice and met his gaze.

Tami and Tari stood by the back door waiting for the signal to start the procession. Windy had never heard them this quiet. Cora moved to her place beside them, holding her pink sweetheart rose in one hand and an already wet hankie in the other.

Everyone, accept Windy, had one pink sweetheart rose just as Rick had requested. Earlier Rick had handed her a beautiful bouquet of 4 of the tiny roses. "One for each year that I've loved you," he explained. She held those flowers now, marveling at all God had accomplished in 4 years and anticipating what He had in store for them in the next 40.

One more look out the window showed Windy the men had taken their places. Pastor Jason faced the house, but looked at Rick, his lips moving. Rick grinned and Windy thanked God for this brotherly relationship the two men shared.

Rick looked so handsome in his crisp gray slacks, white short sleeve shirt and pink tie. She smiled. She suggested gray ties to match their slacks but Rick insisted that pink would match the ladies dresses. One look at Joe's face when he saw the ties told the whole story.

Joe stood proud next to his young friend. Windy thought of Joe as a mentor to Rick, now she hoped God would turn the tables and use Rick as an example of a fine Christian man for Joe.

Rob and Andrew were so handsome; so solemn. Andrew turned his attention to Mary and Windy caught a glimpse of his face. She could see how the young man longed to be next to his wife.

Jason motioned to the house and all five men looked that way. Tami opened the door for Cora and held the older woman's hand as the three ladies made their way down the stairs. At the bottom Tari moved first down the aisle followed by Tami and Cora.

Windy felt her dad's hand on her elbow. She turned and found him looking at her. She saw his pride in her, but she also saw a deep sorrow. Did he know something she didn't?

She refused to give those thoughts audience today. She hugged her dad and kissed his cheek. "I love you Daddy!"

"I love you, Honey Girl." He guided her across the porch and down the steps to a couple of very familiar musical notes, upbeat notes, certainly not the wedding march. She froze, Rick wouldn't play '*Windy*' would he?

But the notes slowed down and the beautiful love song, '*Cherish*' began.

As Windy moved closer to the man who owned her heart, she caught her breath. '*Please, Lord, don't let this be a dream, don't let me wake up alone in my own bed.*'

Jason began to talk; Dad responded and placed Windy's hand in Rick's before kissing her. Windy didn't see him move toward his seat. She only saw Rick's face, his eyes pouring out his love for her. She listened to each word understanding what Jason said and how it affected her life from this point on. She savored every moment, soaking them up in her heart. She responded at the appropriate times, all the while unable to take her eyes from Rick. He in turn gazed steadily back. The two entered into their own world, where the people around them became the stars in orbit.

Young Robert Jordan helped himself to another glass of raspberry/ 7Up punch. He wished for something a little stronger.

Mom and Dad held up through the whole ceremony, with mom crying, but not too bad.

Dad just sat, watching everything as though committing it to memory. Rob didn't know what the future held for his parents, but he wanted to be a part of it. After 6 weeks of treatments, Dad's condition didn't seem to be improving, not on the outside anyway. Monday he would have tests, blood work, x-rays, maybe there would be good news.

After the ceremony, tables had been brought out of the barn and the chairs set up for the meal; an excellent meal.

"Hey, Rick, tell everyone how I introduced you two." Joe suggested.

"You didn't introduce us."

"If I hadn't stopped for that car on the side of the road, we wouldn't be celebrating today."

Rick and Windy began a humorous dialogue of their first 'meeting'.

Robbie looked at his seat between his two most ardent fans, Rick's sisters, Tami and Tari. Andrew had left the 'wedding party' as soon as permissible to join his wife and daughter, leaving Robbie to deal with the girls. They were cuties; but very young cuties. He wasn't quite old enough to be their dad, but too old to take a second look. Now, Andrew's wife on the other hand, was a real beauty; dark hair with light flawless skin and beautiful big blue eyes. Rob could understand Andrew's devotion.

He glanced around, not knowing what he looked for. Life in central Michigan just didn't compare to what he was used to. In eleven years in the Marine Corp he had seen as many countries. He'd seen military action during Desert Shield and Desert Storm. He loved his life and didn't want to leave it. Even the thought of retiring didn't intrigue him. As much as he wanted to be here with his parents while they needed him, he longed to be back in the midst of a little action.

Rob watched Joe excuse himself and moved toward the house, only to veer toward the garage when no one noticed. Maybe the best man had a little best booze hidden for this solemn occasion. He watched as Joe disappeared inside the garage. Since no one noticed Joe's exit he decided to investigate.

Once inside Rob looked around. He heard a hissing noise, but could see no one. Rick's black pick up sat in the only stall, facing out. Rob walked around to the back and found Joe kneeling beside the vehicle, letting air out of the tire. Rob grinned.

Joe noticed the movement and looked up but continued his work. When the tire held just enough air to keep it on the rim, Joe stopped, stood and dusted off his hands. He raised an eyebrow at Robbie.

"Well, a flat tire made their paths cross. Another flat tire brought them together. I figure it's a good sign and they might as well start out marriage on the right foot." Joe explained.

"Or tire." Rob interjected.

"Or tire." Joe agreed.

The two walked out of the building and headed down the driveway a short distance, entered the house from the front and exited the back door, with no one wiser.

After the meal, tables were moved out into a circle and it was time for the bride to dance with her father; the groom with his mother and then the couple to dance their first dance as husband and wife.

Even in crisp, green grass Doug and Valerie outshined everyone as they moved perfectly in time to the music.

A couple hours later guests began leaving and preparations for the next week were confirmed.

Chapter Fifty-Eight

Windy and Rick stood on the front porch of their home and waved goodbye to the last car to pull from their driveway.

Rick drew Windy to him.

"Alone at last," he whispered. "And with no restrictions."

Windy allowed herself to   be drawn into his arms, into his presence. Strains of a beautiful old love song came through the open window and he began to move her to the music.

"I love how your eyes close, whenever you kiss me," Rick sang softly against her head. He kissed her hair, her ear, her cheek. "But darlin most of all," he continued. "I love how you love me." He rubbed his cheek against hers, his nose against hers.

Windy tightened her arms around his neck. The music, the swaying, the closeness of her husband relaxed her. She sighed and nestled her head on his shoulder. They danced through several slow songs, the sounds of the birds, the leaves rustling in the trees, the quiet gurgle from the creek adding to the romance. Windy felt contentment she'd never known before; security in the arms of the man who loved her, peace from knowing that God held their lives in His very competent hands.

Rick sought her lips and she allowed his passion to touch her soul.

"Are we all packed?" he asked, his voice heavy with emotion.

"Yes," she whispered.

"Any thing else we need to do to get ready to leave tomorrow?"

"Nothing." She drew in his scent, his wonderful grassy scent.

Rick reached down and picked her up, carrying her into the house. He set her down but held her close. "Welcome to your home, Mrs. Notts."

She kissed him. "I'm very glad to be here."

He kissed her back, then turned to the door and locked it. Windy followed him into the kitchen where he repeated the procedure. She put a couple leftover items in the fridge, and grabbed a flavored water. Together they went upstairs and checked their suitcases.

"I can't believe we're actually going on a honeymoon."

"Don't get too excited," Rick answered. "Remember this is Joe's hunting cabin. We have no idea what awaits us."

"Still it was wonderful of him and the guys to make such preparations for us."

Rick laughed. "Oh, I'll pay for it when we get back. I'll be the station entertainment until something else comes along to take their mind off me."

"Hmm," she wrapped her arms around him. "I don't want to cause you any pain. Are you sure this'll be worth their harassment?"

"Every word," he assured her.

She scooped up the pink silk nightie that lay on the bed. "I'll be back." She promised, leaving the bedroom. She closed the bathroom door behind her and shivered with excitement. Rick's footsteps sounded on the stairs and she knew he would brush his teeth in the downstairs bathroom. She laughed, thinking how fun it would be to watch him brush his teeth.

Windy carefully took off her wedding dress and arranged it on the hanger, slipped into the nightie, pulled a washcloth from the closet and began cleansing the make-up from her face.

She desired meeting her husband in the next room in a few minutes, yet, the anticipation itself made her tingle. She tenderly unloosed the beautiful array of flowers from her hair. The very ones Rick had chosen; strange for a man to chose the wedding flowers. But then, Rick was a strange man.

Her strange man.

He tapped at the door. "Whachadoin?" he asked.

"Nunayerbisnis." She answered.

"I'm going outside to feed the animals." He informed her through the closed door. "Make sure everything's been put away, see if the garage is locked. Then I'll check all the downstairs doors and windows. I'll be quiet when I come in, just in case you've fallen asleep."

Windy opened the door and stood close to her husband. "Joe and Robbie fed the animals and locked up the garage." She placed one hand on the back of his neck. "Wil and Doug took the tables and chairs back to the church." She placed the other hand beside it, working her fingers into his short hair. "And you already checked all the doors and windows, I watched you." Windy pulled his head to hers looking directly into those lovely gray eyes. "And I have no intention of falling asleep."

The ticking clock woke Rick to a darkened room. He shifted his weight. Something, everything seemed out of place. The soft bed felt unfamiliar, the linens smelled new. He drew a deep breath and smiled. And the arm across his chest belonged to his wife. His wife. *'Interesting,'* Rick thought. *'This is the first time in my life I have awakened with a woman in my bed. And I like it.'*

Windy stirred and he pulled her closer. They were one now, as it should be. One in body, mind, soul and in their Lord. Her hand moved and touched his lips, caressed his cheek.

"I love you," she whispered.

"I love you more." he answered.

"How do you figure that?"

"Well, they say your heart is as big as your fist. If that's true, since my fist is bigger than your fist then my heart is bigger than your heart and I can love you more."

"Hmmmm...sounds like something a woman would say. Do you love me all the way to Texas?"

"Yes."

"Sure?"

"Yes."

"And I love you all the way to Texas. So it would seem that we love each other equally. But since my heart is littler than your heart, it has to work harder to go the same distance, so therefore I love you more."

"Sounds like something a man would say."

"Guess we're meeting each other on our own levels." She sighed. "Are we going to church before we head north?"

"I don't think it would be wise."

"Why?"

"I wouldn't want to be the entertainment committee again."

"You plan on executing hymnals?"

"No, but I'm on my honeymoon and I have no intention of minding when you tell me to behave." He lifted her soft hair in his fingers and brought it to his nose. "Smells like roses."

Windy smiled. She had no intention of telling him to behave. "We could always wait till tomorrow to leave for up north. Everyone will think we're already gone…"

Windy carried the small suitcase out to the garage and opened the walk through door. She hit the button next to the light switch and the large door opened. The truck looked funny. Lopsided, maybe.

"Rick?" She called.

"Right here." He entered the garage carrying a larger suitcase.

"What's wrong with the truck?"

"Nothing, why?"

"It looks funny."

"My truck doesn't look fun…" He set down his burden and walked to the rear discovering the almost flat tire. Windy joined him and he turned to her. "I believe it's your turn."